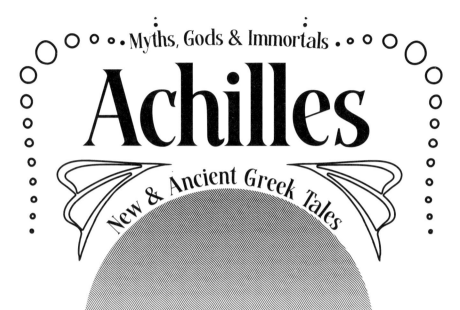

# Achilles
## Myths, Gods & Immortals
### New & Ancient Greek Tales

This is a FLAME TREE Book

Publisher & Creative Director: Nick Wells
Editorial Director: Catherine Taylor
Project Editor: Jocelyn Pontes
Editorial Board: Gillian Whitaker, Catherine Taylor, Jocelyn Pontes, Jemma North,
Simran Aulakh and Beatrix Ambery

FLAME TREE PUBLISHING
6 Melbray Mews, Fulham,
London SW6 3NS, United Kingdom
www.flametreepublishing.com

First published 2025

Copyright in each story is held by the individual authors
Introduction and Volume copyright © 2025 Flame Tree Publishing Ltd

Quotations from ancient sources in 'Ancient & Modern: Introducing
Achilles' are all translated by the author unless otherwise stated.

25 27 29 30 28 26
1 3 5 7 9 10 8 6 4 2

ISBN: 978-1-83562-262-9

All rights reserved. No part of this publication may be reproduced, stored in a retrieval system, or transmitted in any form or by any means, electronic, mechanical, photocopying, recording or otherwise, without the prior written permission of the publisher.

Publisher's Note: The stories within this book are works of fiction. Names, characters, places, and incidents are a product of the authors' imaginations. Locales and public names are sometimes used for atmospheric purposes. Any resemblance to actual people, living or dead, or to businesses, companies, events, institutions, or locales is completely coincidental.

Content Note: The stories in this book may contain descriptions of, or references to, difficult subjects such as violence, death and rape, but always contextualized within the setting of mythic narrative, archetype and metaphor. Similarly, language can sometimes be strong but is at the artistic discretion of the authors.

Cover art by Flame Tree Studio based on elements from Shutterstock.com: Anatoly Vartanov, Dmitry_Tsvetkov, FXQuadro, Panos Karas, tsuneomp

A copy of the CIP data for this book is available from the British Library.

Printed and bound in China

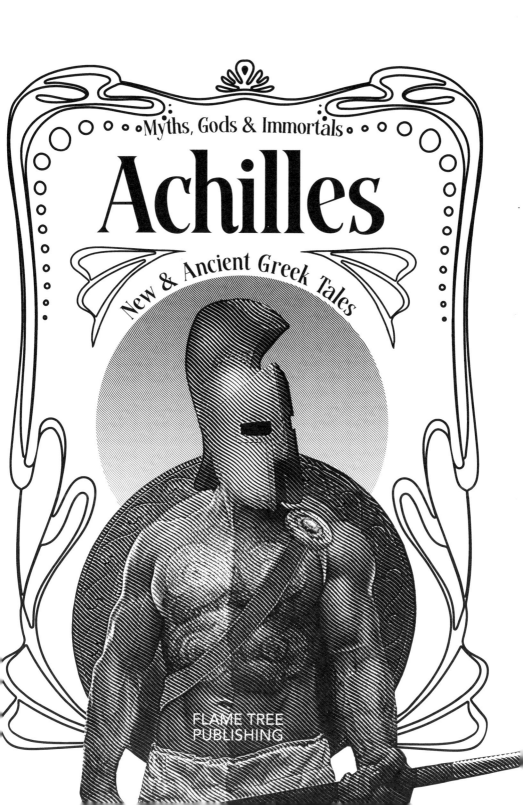

# Contents

**FOREWORD**
Prof. David D. Leitao ............................................................. 6

**ANCIENT & MODERN: INTRODUCING ACHILLES**
by Jonathan S. Burgess ........................................................ 10
1. Achilles in Antiquity ........................................................ 11
2. Achilles in Post-Antiquity ............................................. 102
3. Modern Reception of Achilles ..................................... 106
4. Themes in the Story of Achilles ................................. 116

**MODERN SHORT STORIES OF ACHILLES**
The Second Fate
Amber S. Benham ............................................................ 122
The Achilles Wheel
Hammond Diehl ............................................................... 137
The Boldest of the Greeks
Corey D. Evans ................................................................. 153
How Achilles Grew Up
Kenzie Lappin ................................................................... 169
The Last Angry Hero
Russell Hugh McConnell .................................................. 180

# CONTENTS

**The Choice of Iphigenia**
Zenobia Neil .................................................................. 193
**Waiting for Clear Waters**
Mari Ness ....................................................................... 208
**Spindle, Rod, Shears**
Parker M. O'Neill ............................................................ 218
**Achilles in City Island**
Celeste Plowden ............................................................. 234
**Veiled Stratagems**
Sultana Raza .................................................................. 249
**The Eyes of the Pentekonter**
Chey Rivera .................................................................... 265
**Tears in the Sea**
Patricia Scott .................................................................. 281
**Achilles in the Underworld**
Susan Shwartz ................................................................ 292
**Immortality in Song**
Rose Strickman ............................................................... 302
**The Healing Mountain**
Adam B. Widmer ............................................................ 317
**Last Stand**
Ernie Xu ......................................................................... 331
**A Glass Heart in an Unbreakable Ribcage**
Lily Zimmerman ............................................................. 346

**BIOGRAPHIES** ............................................................. **360**
**AUTHORS AND CORE SOURCES OF**
**ACHILLES MYTHOLOGY** ............................................. **366**
**MYTHS, GODS & IMMORTALS** .................................... **367**
**FLAME TREE FICTION** ................................................ **368**

# Foreword
## Prof. David D. Leitao

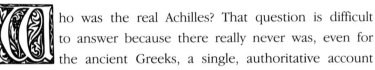ho was the real Achilles? That question is difficult to answer because there really never was, even for the ancient Greeks, a single, authoritative account of Achilles' life and exploits. There are some elements of his story that are particularly well known today. He was the most skillful warrior to fight on the Greek side at Troy, the slayer of Hector, champion of the Trojans. He was fiercely devoted to his boyhood friend and fellow soldier Patroclus. And he died at Troy at the hands of Paris (or Apollo), from a wound to his ankle, the only part of his body that was vulnerable.

But there are so many other features of the ancient Greek Achilles myth, which are less well known today, but no less beloved by ancient Greek writers and artists, not to mention those, later, from Rome, medieval Europe, and the modern West. Take, for instance, Achilles' exploits on the battlefield. Achilles killed not only Hector, but also Hector's brothers Lycaon and Troilus. He slew Sarpedon, a son of Zeus, and did battle with the river-god Scamander. He also killed two warriors who came as allies to the Trojans later in the war, the Amazon queen Penthesilea and the Aethiopian prince Memnon, son of the dawn goddess.

# FOREWORD

Achilles was endowed with healing abilities, which he learned from his teacher, the centaur Chiron. There is a famous drinking cup showing him wrapping a bandage around the wounded arm of his comrade Patroclus. He also healed a Mysian king named Telephus, whom he had wounded previously, though in some versions it is not Achilles himself, but his spear that does the healing. This story was frequently told, including in a very famous lost play by Euripides.

The flexibility of the Achilles legend can also be seen in the various accounts of his relationships with women and men. A number of female partners are attributed to him. While an adolescent on the island of Skyros, where he was hidden, wearing women's clothes, so that recruiters from the Greek army could not find him, he seduced the maiden Deidamia, who became the mother of Achilles' son Neoptolemus. In Homer's *Iliad*, he shares a bed with the captive Briseis. And when the Amazon queen Penthesilea came to Troy's aid later in the war, Achilles was teased by one of his fellow soldiers for being smitten with her; there are famous vase paintings in which Achilles locks eyes with the Amazon at the very moment he pierces her body with his spear, as though falling in love with her just as her life ebbs away. Some later authors tell the story of how Achilles fell in love with Polyxena, the sister of Hector, when he was negotiating for the ransom of Hector's body, while others suggest that Polyxena sacrificed herself on Achilles' tomb so that she could be his bride in the afterlife. Another later story has Achilles marry the sorceress Medea on the Isles of the Blessed!

There are also male objects of Achilles' love. He is, as we have noted, perhaps best known today for the intense feelings he had for his boyhood friend Patroclus, on display especially after the latter's death in battle. In Homer these feelings appear to be non-romantic: indeed, the intensity of the love between these two brothers-in-arms is perhaps all the more powerful for enduring in the absence of the obvious rewards of physical sex. But in later authors, their relationship becomes explicitly homoerotic. Aeschylus, for instance, makes Achilles the lover of Patroclus, whereas Plato, a century later, and for complex philosophical reasons, insists that Achilles was the beloved and Patroclus the lover. This later reimagining of the romantic life of the hero is perhaps also the context in which to understand the story of Achilles falling in love with the Trojan Troilus: like Penthesilea, Troilus was both an object of Achilles' desire and a victim of his spear.

Achilles was the subject of countless stories and legends, but he was also an object of worship in religious cults. There was a hero cult in his honor at Sigeum, near Troy, which Alexander the Great famously visited centuries later, and there were hero cults to him also on the Black Sea. And at Elis, to kick off the quadrennial Olympic games, the women gathered in front of his cenotaph in the local gymnasium and beat their breasts. In later times, Achilles was sometimes represented as immortal: the poet Pindar suggests that he was transferred by his divine mother Thetis to the Isles of the Blessed (whereas in Homer, he is clearly mortal), and during the Roman era he came to be worshipped as a god in Olbia, a city on the Black

Sea, with two temples in his honor. Even the later story of his invulnerability (except for his ankle) suggests ambivalence in the Greek mind about whether Achilles was man or god, and some scholars have suggested that the story of Thetis dipping him in the River Styx to immortalize him was inspired, at least in part, by the Christian rite of baptism.

Why so much diversity in the Greek stories told about Achilles? The reason is simple: different generations of Greeks had different needs of this hero, and the myth had to adapt to serve those needs. Different literary and artistic genres played a role too: the Achilles we encounter in Archaic epics looks very different from the one we see in classical tragedy or Hellenistic romance.

It is this, almost infinitely protean Achilles from Greek antiquity and beyond that justifies modern adaptations inspired by the ancient myth, such as David Malouf's *Ransom*, a retelling of the story of Achilles' ransom of Hector's body, and Madeleine Miller's *The Song of Achilles*, which explores the love between Achilles and Patroclus. The imaginative contributors to this volume are similarly justified in creating new versions of Achilles who can speak to our modern needs. Perhaps it is this protean Achilles that *is* the real Achilles.

*Prof. David D. Leitao*

# Ancient & Modern: Introducing Achilles

## by Jonathan S. Burgess

# 1.
# Achilles in Antiquity

*Sing the wrath, goddess, of Achilles son of Peleus, destructive, which caused countless griefs for the Achaeans and hurled many sturdy souls of heroes into Hades and made their bodies pickings for all the birds and dogs, and the plan of Zeus was accomplished.*
– Homer, *Iliad*, Book 1; the poet invoking the Muse

(Note: all translations are by the author unless otherwise stated)

chilles is a complex and fascinating character of ancient Greek myth who inspires storytelling to this day. In the Trojan War he was the best Greek warrior who killed the best Trojan fighter, Hector (as well as notable Trojan allies). As well as being a ruthless fighter, Achilles often feuded with allies as well as enemies. After the Greek commander Agamemnon confiscated his concubine Briseis, he refused to fight for the Greeks. Only when Hector slew Patroclus did Achilles return to battle to kill the Trojan hero, along with scores of other Trojans (some captives were also sacrificed over Patroclus's grave). However, the hero had many other sides to his personality. He was close to his mother, the divine sea nymph Thetis, as well as to Patroclus, his *therapon* (assistant and battle wingman) and Briseis, his enslaved concubine.

In the *Iliad* Homer explored Achilles' complexity. He portrayed a character who, while sometimes resentful, violent and disloyal, could also be tender, eloquent and merciful. Authors and artists of antiquity emphasized different sides of his character; they also narrated parts of his life that Homer does not cover, notably his childhood and death. Though fundamental aspects of Achilles' life and the Trojan War remained consistent in antiquity, some authors already radically modified tales about Achilles, sometimes to suit their own culture and time period, and sometimes to be creative. Many of these modifications, popular in later antiquity, endured into medieval times. Gradually these, due in part to the loss of knowledge of ancient Greek, displaced Homeric narratives.

The earliest surviving literary references to Achilles occur in the epics of Homer. In antiquity early Greek epic was composed in a metre of six 'feet' (a metrical unit) featuring dactyls (a long syllable followed by two shorter ones). Dialects used by the Greeks of Asia Minor, where the genre was developed, also feature prominently in early Greek epic. Achilles is the main character of Homer's *Iliad;* he also appears twice in Homer's *Odyssey* as a shade in the underworld. Achilles' exploits in the Trojan War before and after the *Iliad* were narrated in various epics of the Epic Cycle, while Greco-Roman literature continued to tell stories of Achilles from birth to death and into the afterlife.

Contemporary Homerists typically date Homer to around 800 BCE (though I would date the two epics about a half century later). In the Linear B script used by the Mycenaean Greeks of the second millennium BCE, *a-ki-re-u* would seem to represent the name 'Achilles'. Arguably the name, although not necessarily referring to the mythological figure, is of pre-Greek origin. Many consider the story of the Trojan War to stem from historical events. Mycenean armour is sometimes described in Homer, possibly as heirlooms, and the Homeric poems do name locations where Mycenaen ruins have been discovered. Yet the evidence for an actual Trojan War is sparse and thin. In any event, the fantastic heroic world of Homer is hardly historical; straining to make it so seems to risk not fully appreciating Homer's literary power.

## ACHILLES IN HOMER'S 'ILIAD'

The *Iliad* is a long epic of 24 'books' (a conventional term for sections) that stems from traditional oral poetry. The whole of the *Iliad* or the *Odyssey* would have taken about 24 hours to perform. The *Iliad* at its start identifies its topic as the *menis* ('rage') of Achilles against Agamemnon after the Greek commander's seizure of Achilles' slave concubine Briseis. In response to Agamemnon's threat to do so, he announces his withdrawal from battle and then asks Thetis, his goddess mother, to persuade Zeus to help the Trojans. After the Greeks suffer defeat in battle, Agamemnon sends an embassy with promises of generous compensation if he should return.

Achilles listens to the ambassadors patiently, but rejects their pleas with eloquence and passion.

After further Greek losses, Patroclus persuades Achilles to let him wear his armour and to impersonate the hero on the battlefield. Achilles reluctantly agrees and Patroclus routs the Trojans. However, the Trojan hero Hector eventually slays Patroclus, causing Achilles to return to battle to take vengeance on his killer. When Priam, king of Troy, seeks to ransom his son's body in person, Achilles relents. The epic ends with the funeral of Hector.

## The Wrath of Achilles

Many mythological heroes, notably berserkers of Norse and German tradition, display extreme rage in battle. Achilles' slaughter of Trojans after Patroclus's death represents such violent rage. His anger continues after the death of Hector, for Achilles repeatedly mistreats Hector's corpse, and at the funeral of Patroclus he sacrifices 12 captive Trojans. As a theme in the plot of the *Iliad*, however, his wrath is nuanced and changeable. The story begins with Achilles' fury being directed against Agamemnon, the Greek commander. After Agamemnon had reluctantly agreed to release his enslaved concubine Chryseis to her father, he declares that she should be replaced by the concubine of another Greek leader. Achilles, who had earlier encouraged the seer Calchas to report Apollo's anger at Agamemnon, criticizes his commander, and an argument arises. Achilles, son of Peleus, publicly insults Agamemnon:

## ANCIENT & MODERN: INTRODUCING ACHILLES

*Peleus's son again with bitter words spoke to the son of Atreus and did not let go of his anger. 'You sack of wine with the eyes of a dog and a deer's heart! You never dared in spirit to arm with your men for battle or go for an ambush with the best of the Achaeans.'*
Iliad, Book 1

After Achilles refuses to fight, the Greeks are gradually pushed back to their ships. The Greeks are critical of his stubbornness – among them Patroclus, who in fear of the Greeks being slaughtered on the beach persuades Achilles to allow him to fight in his distinctive armour. After Hector kills Patroclus, however, Achilles' wrath falls upon Hector. Now his fellow Greeks can barely restrain him from entering battle, and once the fighting resumes he single-handedly drives all the Trojans inside the walls of Troy. All, that is, except Hector, who bravely resists him.

When the two heroes engage in dialogue, Achilles taunts Hector with threats. His ferocity eventually causes Hector to run, though in time he takes a stand again and bravely attacks Achilles. However, Achilles is the better warrior, and he also has divine help from Athena. He kills Hector and, as he had threatened to do, continually abuses the prince's body. The wrath against Hector comes to an end only when King Priam, Hector's father, appears in his hut and the two men come to an understanding. Achilles releases the corpse and promises to restrain the Greeks from battle until the Trojans can give Hector a funeral. Achilles thereby again undercuts the authority of Agamemnon. Yet in reaching a shared sense of humanity with Priam, he displays a much more civilized side to his character than is often observable in the poem.

### Achilles and Briseis

Achilles' speeches in reply to the ambassadors in Book 9 are angry, philosophical and sometimes a bit rhetorical. He makes a good point when he complains about Agamemnon taking his concubine even as the Greeks are fighting to retrieve Helen, his brother's wife:

> *From me alone of the Achaeans he took and holds*
> *my soul mate. Let him enjoy sleeping beside her.*
> *Why is it necessary for the Argives to fight Trojans?*
> *Why did the son of Atreus gather and lead the army*
> *here? Indeed, wasn't it for fair-haired Helen? Do*
> *the sons of Atreus alone of mortals love their wives?*
> *Since any who is a good and thoughtful man loves his*
> *own and cares for her, as I also loved that one from*
> *my heart, though she was captured in war.*
> Iliad, Book 9

In some ways the comparison is a bit strained. Helen as a queenly woman is hardly comparable to the war captive Briseis. Apart from this, the sentiment about loving a wife seems sincere. But can there be love between a Greek warrior and a captive non-Greek who has been enslaved and forced to be a concubine – and not the only one Achilles sleeps with?

Briseis does not do or say much in the *Iliad*, but we have two passages that indicate her point of view. When Agamemnon had sent men to take Briseis away, Achilles is characteristically polite with the visitors, assuring them that he blames Agamemnon but not them. We are told that Briseis left with the ambassadors unwillingly and that Achilles immediately went to sit by the sea to weep and call upon his goddess mother. Perhaps this suggests that the two were in love.

But 'love' is defined differently in different places and times, and the single time Briseis actually speaks in the *Iliad* suggests a more complicated wartime relationship. In Book 19 when Briseis is returned to Achilles' camp and sees the body of Patroclus, she and the other slave women mourn over him. Briseis speaks not only of the kindness of Patroclus, but also of the hardship of her own life. She reports that her husband and her three brothers were killed by Achilles when he attacked their town. Patroclus is also praised for trying to cheer her up by claiming he would bring about her marriage to Achilles back in his homeland of Phthia. Such talk of marriage, whether realistic or not, imagines Briseis as a real wife, just as Achilles had claimed.

Briseis's moving speech is a tale of past tragedy and hope for a future with Achilles, even though he is her husband's killer. It is telling that Homer reports that the slave women grieved publicly for Patroclus but privately for their own sorrows. At the very least these scenes represent Homer's unflinching presentation of the messiness of human thought and emotion.

## The Plans of the Iliad

Achilles is usually careful to blame Agamemnon in particular for his refusal to fight the Trojans – and so might seem to be guilty only of disloyalty to a bad leader. In private conversation with Thetis, however, he expresses hope that the Trojans will drive his fellow Greeks to the ships and slay them:

> *Her just now heralds led off, the daughter of Briseis, whom the sons of the Achaeans gave to me. But you, if you are able, act on behalf of your son. Going to Olympus beseech Zeus…if perhaps he might be willing to aid the Trojans and drive the Achaeans to the ships and sea as they die, so that they all might suffer the consequences of their king, and the son of Atreus wide-ruling Agamemnon might realize his delusion, that he did not honour the best of the Achaeans.*
> *Iliad,* Book 1

Here Agamemnon is still blamed, but Achilles wants the Greek army to suffer losses to put pressure on their leader. Achilles assumes that the Trojans would beat the Greeks if he were not on the battlefield, and the poem supports this assumption. However, like everyone else in the Homeric world, Achilles knows that everything depends on the gods. He therefore asks Thetis to convince Zeus to help the Trojans. As it happens, Zeus is currently off feasting with the peripheral and exotic Aethiopians, so Thetis must wait until near the

## ANCIENT & MODERN: INTRODUCING ACHILLES

end of Book 1 to go and make the request on behalf of her son. When she does beseech him, Zeus is reluctant to agree because he knows that Hera favours the Greeks, along with Athena and Poseidon. Only after Thetis reminds Zeus of her past support of him does he agree. Hera then realizes what has happened and an argument arises before Hephaestus succeeds in calming the two.

Zeus's agreement to favour the Greeks while Achilles sits out of war is perhaps the 'plan of Zeus' that the proem announces at the beginning of Book 1. If so, the head god seems very reluctant to initiate his own plan. It is Achilles' plea to Thetis, and Thetis's request of Zeus, that serve to trigger the 'plan of Zeus' that is operative in the *Iliad*. We hear that in the Epic Cycle (*see* below) there was a broader 'plan of Zeus' to cause mass destruction of humans at the request of Gaia, 'earth'. Ancient evidence suggests that this 'plan of Zeus' to reduce the human population was enacted by the Theban Wars and the Trojan War, with the latter causing the deaths of both Greeks and Trojans. Achilles' wrath and the subsequent deaths of both Greeks and Trojans in the *Iliad* would be merely one aspect of such an overall plan.

Achilles' plea and Thetis's request initiate an Iliadic 'plan of Zeus', which backfires for Achilles. His refusal to fight allows the Trojans to succeed for a time, but it also leads to the death of Patroclus, an event that in turn leads to Achilles returning to battle and the deaths of countless Trojans, not Greeks. Achilles' hope that Trojan success will make Agamemnon regret dishonouring him has further consequences that the hero did not anticipate. The fighting in the *Iliad*, which covers only four major days of battle within a couple of months, causes massive deaths for both Greeks and Trojans, and for this reason serves a larger 'plan of Zeus', not the plea of Achilles.

### The Embassy to Achilles

After Agamemnon proposes that the Greeks return home at the beginning of Book 9, Diomedes publicly rebukes him and Nestor advises that ambassadors be sent to Achilles to persuade him to return to battle. Chosen as ambassadors are Odysseus, wily and rhetorically gifted, Ajax, the best warrior with the exception of Achilles, and Phoenix, a mentor of Achilles when he was a child. When the ambassadors arrive, Achilles is surprised but polite:

*Welcome. Indeed, as friends you have come, indeed there is perhaps a great need; you are the most dear of the Achaeans to me, even though angered.*
*Iliad,* Book 9

Odysseus first informs Achilles of Trojan success on the battlefield and Hector's threat to drive the Greeks into the sea and burn their ships. He then reminds Achilles of his father's advice that he control his emotions, and he lists the extensive gifts that Agamemnon offers should Achilles return: tripods, cauldrons, horses, gold and seven skilled and beautiful slave women from Lesbos, as well as the return of Briseis. If the

Greeks take Troy, Achilles can also fill his ship with gold and bronze and have 20 enslaved Trojan women. Finally, when the Greeks return home Agamemnon will give him a daughter of his choice to marry, a dowry and many cities to rule. Perhaps sensing that Achilles is not impressed, Odysseus then begs Achilles to have pity on the Greek army, who will honour him and spread his fame, especially if he kills Hector.

Achilles bluntly states that he will not be enticed by the embassy, perhaps implying that Odysseus is being typically manipulative. He complains that he has not received spoils in war commensurate with his fighting prowess, claiming that he led the sack of 11 towns near Troy and raided 12 others by ship, only to turn over the spoils to Agamemnon to distribute, though the leader did not participate in the raids. More to the point, he complains that Agamemnon took Briseis even though he and the other Greeks are fighting for the return of his brother's wife Helen from the Trojans. He then points out that Hector was not so successful when Achilles fought, and claims that he and his men will leave for home the next day. More angry words about Agamemnon follow. The hero states that he would not accept even many more gifts. Nor will he marry a daughter of Agamemnon; instead he will marry a woman of his choice in his homeland. Finally Achilles turns philosophical, noting that life is worth more than treasure; he reveals that Thetis had told him he is fated either to die at Troy, and thereby earn fame, or to return home and live long without glory.

The ambassadors are stunned into silence. Then Phoenix speaks up, reminding Achilles that he helped to raise him in his infancy and at Peleus's request teaches him how to speak and behave. Then he tells the tale of how he left his homeland after he took his mother's side in a dispute with his father, who prayed that he might never have a son. Tempted to kill his father, Phoenix instead fled and ended up being taken in by Peleus. He states that Agamemnon has dropped his anger and is offering a generous number of gifts.

Perhaps perceiving that Achilles is not moved, Phoenix relates the tale of Meleager of Calydon, who, when angered by his mother, refused to defend his city from attack until his wife persuaded him. Meleager was a traditional hero, but it appears that Phoenix modifies the story here to reflect the current crisis. Arguably Homer has Phoenix tell this story to foreshadow Patroclus's later intervention in Achilles' wrath (the name that Phoenix gives to Meleager's wife, Cleopatra, has been suspected of being an inversion of the name of Patroclus).

In response Achilles asks Phoenix to stop telling sad tales in service to Agamemnon; instead, he should join him on his return home to Phthia. Then Ajax suddenly speaks up. He tells Odysseus that they should return because Achilles is stubborn and disregards their friendship. Noting that even a murderer can be forgiven after providing recompense, he cannot believe that Achilles is refusing the generous gifts of Agamemnon. Turning to Achilles, he asks the great hero to respect his guests and friends. Though Ajax is a better warrior than speaker, and though this is the shortest of the speeches made to Achilles, it is the most effective. Achilles acknowledges that Ajax has argued effectively, but affirms that he cannot drop his wrath against Agamemnon. However, he now modifies his position and states that he will return to battle if Hector starts to burn the ships of the Achaeans.

Homeric epic contains a lot of character speech, but Book 9 almost completely consists of the narration of the voices of different characters. Achilles and Agamemnon exchange fierce speeches in Book 1, Hector and Andromache make heartfelt speeches to one another in Book 6, and Achilles and Priam respectively employ words to reach a surprising understanding in Book 24. Yet I consider Book 9 the most impressive collection of rich and varied character speeches.

## Achilles Impersonated

Though the proem speaks of the 'plan of Zeus' and in Book 1 Achilles asks Thetis to persuade Zeus to help the Trojans and not the Greeks, which she does, for most of the poem the battles of Greeks and Trojans go back and forth. Not until Book 8 do the Trojans get the upper hand, which inspires the Greeks to seek Achilles' help. Though he refuses, the Greeks nonetheless have some success for a few more books until the Trojans reach the ships and set fire to one. It is only in Book 15 that Zeus first announces what exactly will happen: Hector will drive the Greeks to the ships, Achilles will send Patroclus into battle, and Hector will kill Patroclus after he drives back the Trojans. Then in anger Achilles will kill Hector and eventually Troy will be sacked. The last part, the sack of Troy, is fated to happen, though this occurs after the events of the *Iliad*.

Though Zeus is correct that Patroclus will drive the Greeks back, his claim that Achilles will rouse Patroclus to fight is somewhat misleading. It is Patroclus who urges Achilles to let him fight in his armour:

> *What so declines thee? If thy mind shuns any augury,*
> *Related by thy mother-queen from heav'n's*
>   *foreseeing eye,*
> *And therefore thou forsak'st thy friends, let me go ease*
>   *their moans*
> *With those brave relics of our host, thy*
>   *mighty Myrmidons,*
> *That I may bring to field more light to conquest than*
>   *hath been.*
> *To which end grace me with thine arms, since, any*
>   *shadow seen*
> *Of thy resemblance, all the pow'r of perjur'd Troy*
>   *will fly.*
> Iliad, Book 9, translation by George Chapman, 1611

Achilles denies that he is afraid of any prophecy, but he reluctantly agrees to lend his armour to Patroclus so that he can lead his men into battle. Though Achilles had promised the embassy that he would then drive the Trojans back when their ships are in danger of being burnt, Patroclus is the one who saves the day after the first ship is set on fire. Though Achilles accedes to Patroclus's plan, he hardly rouses him to join the battle. In a sense it is Patroclus who eventually rouses

Achilles to fight, not by words, but by his death. It is this that finally inspires Achilles to pursue his wrath – not against Agamemnon, but against Hector, the killer of Patroclus. At this point there is some delay, as often happens in this long and majestic poem. Hector took Achilles' armour that Patroclus had borrowed for himself, so Thetis must go to Hephaestus and request new, divine armour for her son.

It is an indication of Achilles' mixed feelings about staying out of battle that he has been watching the action from his camp. When in Book 11 Achilles observes a wounded Greek carried off the battlefield, he sends Patroclus to find out who it is. This is certainly not rousing Patroclus to battle, as Zeus says Achilles will do in Book 15, but it starts a chain of events that leads to Achilles allowing Patroclus to fight against the Trojans. After finding out it is Machaon the healer who was injured, Patroclus heads back to Achilles but on the way meets the wounded Eurypylos. Despite his eagerness to report to Achilles, he stops and tends the man's wound (one of many indications of his good character). Finally, he returns to Achilles in Book 16, weeping over the Greeks' losses.

Patroclus reports the bad news and reproaches Achilles for his anger, even suggesting that Achilles refrained from fighting because of the prophecy that he would die at Troy. Achilles denies this, but grudgingly agrees to renounce his wrath against Agamemnon. Patroclus proposes a new plan that will drastically change the plot. He asks Achilles to lend him armour so that he can impersonate the hero and drive back the Trojans (Homer comments that Patroclus was asking for his own death).

Take my armour and save the ships from being burnt, Achilles tells Patroclus. He then insists that Patroclus return immediately once the Trojans retreat from the ships, and not attack Troy. At this point in time the Trojans set the first Greek ship aflame. Though Achilles had told the embassy that he would return when this happened, he remains committed to Patroclus's new plan. Now very worried about the Greeks he once refused to help, he urges haste. Addressing his men, he interestingly displays some self-awareness by suggesting that they had criticized him among themselves for not fighting. Then in prayer to Zeus, he asks that Patroclus fight successfully and return safely. The charge of Patroclus, wearing Achilles' armour and leading the Myrmidons, sends the Trojans into panicked retreat. Patroclus goes on to kill many Trojans and their ally Sarpedon, much to Zeus's regret, since Sarpedon was his son. But Apollo, joining the battle in defense of the Trojans, stuns Patroclus, who is then wounded by Euphorbus and killed by Hector.

## Grief over Patroclus

Achilles was too far away from the battlefield to observe the death of Patroclus. Menelaus tells Antilochus of the death of Patroclus, an event that makes Antilochus speechless with tears, and orders him to run to Achilles and to report the sad news to him. Antilochus, still weeping, arrives to confirm what Achilles had already feared:

## ANCIENT & MODERN: INTRODUCING ACHILLES

*Thus while he thinks, Antilochus appears,*
*And tells the melancholy tale with tears.*
*'Sad tidings, son of Peleus! thou must hear;*
*And wretched I, the unwilling messenger!*
*Dead is Patroclus! For his corse they fight;*
*His naked corse: his arms are Hector's right.'*

*A sudden horror shot through all the chief,*
*And wrapp'd his senses in the cloud of grief;*
*Cast on the ground, with furious hands he spread*
*The scorching ashes o'er his graceful head;*
*His purple garments, and his golden hairs.*
Iliad, Book 18, translation by Alexander Pope, 1715–20

Achilles collapses on the ground as if he wants the very earth to swallow him. Female slaves, whom the poet here points out were captured by Achilles and Patroclus, scream and beat their chests by Achilles, falling to the ground themselves. They will mourn Patroclus again in Book 19 when Briseis is returned to Achilles' camp and sees the body of Patroclus (she recalls Patroclus comforting her with talk of marriage to Achilles, as we saw above). At the end of this scene Homer adds one of his small but devastating observations: 'Thus she spoke, lamenting, and the women grieved about her, apparently for Patroclus, but each for their own sorrows.' The comment reflects the natural behaviour of those grieving, but it also speaks to the irony of non-Greek slaves mourning the death of a Greek warrior who had assisted Achilles in attacking their communities, enslaving them and forcing them to be concubines. Patroclus is universally regarded in the *Iliad* as a decent person but, as with Briseis's complex reaction to the death of Patroclus, the slave women understandably find it hard to forget their own tragic experiences as they mourn the death of a kind man who also had controlled their lives.

After Achilles falls to the ground in Book 18, he yells so loudly that Thetis and her fellow Nereids hear it in the bottom of the sea. Thetis begins to wail herself and the Nereids, like the slave women about Briseis in Book 19, beat their breasts and provide a chorus of grief. Thetis leads them with a touching speech:

> *Listen, sister Nereids, so you all may well know by hearing how many sorrows are in my heart. O my, I am wretched, O, I the unfortunate bearer of the noblest son, I who after giving birth to a son blameless and strong, excelling among heroes. And he rose up like a shoot. That one, having nurtured him like a plant on the slope of a garden, I sent away with the curved ships to Troy to fight the Trojans. And now I will never receive him returned home again in the home of Peleus. Yet it seems that while he lives and looks upon the light of the sun he grieves, and when I go to him I am not able to help him at all. Yet I will go, to look on my dear son and hear what grief has come to him even staying back from the battle.*
> Iliad, Book 18

This mourning by a divine woman and her divine companions is comparable to the complicated grief of Briseis and her fellow slaves. Whereas the slaves sincerely mourn over Patroclus yet cannot help but recognize how servitude separates them from their owners, Thetis and the Nereids mourn Achilles' death as divinities separated from human mortality. Here as elsewhere in the *Iliad*, Thetis expresses both her love for her son and her discomfort with his mortality. As we will see below, in non-Homeric stories Thetis did not wish to marry Peleus. She had mixed feelings about having children and, though proud of Achilles, was worried about his mortality. Despite being willing to comfort him and speak for him to Zeus, she never seems to comprehend what seem to her to be the petty problems of humans. In many ways her mourning over Achilles prostrate in grief on the ground seems to anticipate her later mourning over the corpse of Achilles – something mentioned in the *Odyssey* and told in the *Aethiopis* of the Epic Cycle.

Achilles' deep friendship with Patroclus and his intense mourning over his death has inspired many over the years to wonder about their relationship. We will see below that retellers of his tale, both from antiquity and from post-antiquity, explore this issue, which is certainly valid in 'reception' (creative retelling of a previous work). In this section, however, I must report that the *Iliad* only describes Achilles and Patroclus as heterosexual in their sexual behaviour. Homer never describes sexual activity in detail, but Achilles and Patroclus routinely spend their nights with slave concubines. After Achilles fiercely complains at length to the embassy about the loss of his 'wife' Briseis, he spends the night with another enslaved woman, Diomede, whom he had captured at Lesbos. Patroclus lies down with Iphis, whom Achilles had given to him after sacking Skyros. Though Achilles had publicly told Agamemnon in Book 19 that he wished Briseis had died before they quarrelled, in Book 24 she is once more his bedmate. Clearly Achilles loved Patroclus as a good friend, even if Patroclus is his underling in socioeconomic terms. Something similar (non-sexual but intense friendship) is seen among other warriors in the *Iliad*, especially major warriors with their wingman (the term in Homer is *therapon*). As early as Aeschylus, however, the two are described as lovers, and narratives afterwards sometimes chose to portray them as such.

## The Death of Hector

Once Achilles has new armour made by Hephaestus (decorated with images of the cosmos and seasonal activities of the human world), he kills many Trojans and they retreat within the city walls. But Hector remains outside the walls. His father King Priam and his mother Hecuba beg him to come inside the walls, but Hector blames himself for the Trojan losses; he is determined to kill Achilles or die at his hands. Yet at the approach of the speedy Achilles, he cannot resist running away in fear. As the Greek hero chases the Trojan hero four times around the city, Homer employs bird and animal predator/prey similes to portray the chase, as well as the haunting comparison of their running to a dream in which one cannot catch up to another and the other cannot escape. Yet the poet also pauses for a digressive description of the springs where Trojan women had washed clothes 'in a previous time of peace, before the arrival of the sons of Achaeans', a note of pathos that underscores the brutality of wartime life.

Hector seems doomed, especially when Zeus symbolically weighs their fates and Hector's sinks down to signify his impending death. It seems unfair that Athena then comes down from Olympus, telling Achilles to stop so that she can trick Hector; she then approaches Hector disguised as his brother, pretending to assist him. Confident once again, Hector suggests that they agree to not abuse the corpse of the loser, but Achilles flatly refuses to accept:

*Talk not of oaths (the dreadful chief replies,*
*While anger flash'd from his disdainful eyes),*
*Detested as thou art, and ought to be,*
*Nor oath nor pact Achilles plights with thee:*
*Such pacts as lambs and rabid wolves combine,*
*Such leagues as men and furious lions join,*
*To such I call the gods! one constant state*
*Of lasting rancour and eternal hate:*
*No thought but rage, and never-ceasing strife,*
*Till death extinguish rage, and thought, and life.*
Iliad, Book 22, translation by Alexander Pope, 1715–20

Hector's spear throw is foiled by Achilles' shield. Hector then shouts to 'Deiphobus' for another spear and discovers he is not there. Knowing he is fated to die, he chooses to do a 'big thing,' charge and earn glory. Now Homer compares Hector's rushing attack to an eagle swooping down on prey, but Achilles is no lamb or rabbit. His spear finds a vulnerable opening in Hector's armour. Achilles taunts Hector by predicting dogs and vultures will eat his corpse, but the dying Hector begs him to allow his father to recover his corpse in exchange for ransom. Achilles shockingly denies the request by saying he'd like to eat him raw, but Hector gets the last word: he predicts that Paris with the help of Apollo will kill him at the gates of the city.

We remember that Achilles is very aware that he is fated to die at Troy, a motif repeated through the poem. In Book 19 even Achilles' horse Xanthus, temporarily able to speak, had foretold his death 'by a god and a mortal'. Achilles informs the dead Hector that he will accept his fate and then tells his men that 'We have won great fame; we have killed godlike Hector, whom the Trojans prayed to as if he were a god'. He then ties Hector's corpse to his chariot and drags him back to camp. Achilles goes on to abuse the corpse repeatedly by dragging it behind his chariot in the dirt. Even after Patroclus is buried in Book 23, Achilles continues to drag Hector's body around his friend's burial mound. The hero does not stop this desecration until Priam makes a surprise visit to Achilles in Book 24.

## Priam and Achilles

At the beginning of Book 24, the gods debate Achilles' behaviour towards Hector's corpse, with Zeus finally pronouncing that Hector's corpse will be returned to the Trojans, though openly, not secretly. That means Achilles will need to be persuaded to release the corpse. Zeus summons Thetis and assigns her the task of relaying the gods' will to Achilles (Zeus's request of Thetis to convince Achilles of something is a reversal of the Achilles-Thetis-Zeus chain of communication that initiated the plot in Book 1).

The divine messenger Iris finds Thetis under the sea, still mourning her son's approaching fate. She goes to Zeus without complaint and readily accedes to his command. Speeding down to Achilles' hut, she finds him still mourning Patroclus. Thetis, besides advising Achilles to eat, sleep and have sex with a woman, and reminding him that he will soon be dead, reports Zeus's anger at this treatment of the corpse. He must accept a ransom for it. Achilles readily accepts the gods' wishes: 'So may it be.'

Now Zeus asks Iris to tell Priam to ransom the corpse with gifts, going alone with a muleteer and wagon. Zeus also indicates that Hermes will intervene to guide Priam to Achilles' tent, and that Priam should not worry that Achilles will kill him. Having received this message, Priam immediately sets about getting a mule cart ready. He also seeks out his wife Hecuba to tell her the news. He affirms that he wants to go, but he asks her what she thinks. Hecuba is not impressed. She thinks he has lost his mind to believe such a ruthless and untrustworthy man would pity him (adding that she wishes she could eat his liver). But it turns out that Priam is not interested in her opinion; he affirms that he will follow the advice of the gods.

After Priam abusively orders some of his sons to pack up the gifts on the mule wagon, Hecuba arrives and suggests that Priam seek confirmation from Zeus that he should go to the Achaean camp. Priam agrees to do so, after which he makes a libation and prays to Zeus, asking for a bird of omen. An eagle immediately appears over Troy, so Priam and the muleteer start on their way. As night falls Zeus tells Hermes to guide Priam into the camp of Achilles.

Hermes' intervention is both spooky and humourous. Disguised as a young man, he approaches Priam and his muleteer on foot. The muleteer alerts the king that someone is coming, but Priam in his fright cannot move. Hermes addresses him sympathetically and promises to protect him. Priam is grateful, but he is alarmed when the stranger wonders whether the old man is leaving Troy now that his son has died. Startled, Priam asks who he is, noting that he spoke well of his unfortunate son. Hermes teasingly suggests that Priam is testing whether he knows the son is Hector. The stranger affirms that he does, offering praise for Hector, even though he identifies himself as one of Achilles' men. Priam takes the opportunity to ask about Hector's corpse, and the stranger assures him that the gods have preserved it despite its abuse. Priam offers a cup if the 'Myrmidon' guides him to the camp, but Hermes refuses, pretending that Achilles would be angry if he received goods meant for him. However, he is happy to lead Priam and the cart to the camp, magically put the guards to sleep and then tell Priam that he is a god sent by Zeus to help him. He advises the Trojan king to go in and plead with Achilles on his knees.

Priam does exactly that, and he also 'kissed the terrible man-slaughtering hands that had killed so many of his sons'. The Greek hero's attendants are amazed as Priam makes a plea, employing a theme hinted at by Hermes. He tells Achilles to think of his father, of the same age as he is and as defenseless as he is now. The Trojan king also enumerates his many sons who have been killed in the war, notably Hector, killed recently by the Greek hero. Achilles' reaction is to push the king back from his knees and to mourn for his own father as well as Patroclus as Priam weeps for Hector:

> *Thus spake he, and stirred within Achilles desire to make lament for his father. And he touched the old man's hand and gently moved him back. And as they both bethought them of their dead, so Priam for man-slaying Hector wept sore as he was fallen before Achilles' feet, and Achilles wept for his own father, and now again for Patroklos, and their moan went up throughout the house.*
> *Iliad*, Book 24, translation by Andrew Lang, Walter Leaf and Ernest Myers, 1883

When he stops, he lifts Priam up and addresses him politely, marvelling at his bravery in coming alone to the killer of his sons. Sitting him down, he philosophizes about the fate of men and speaks of his father Peleus, a king with a divine wife whose sole son is doomed to an early death. Priam similarly was fortunate in his rule and wealth and children, Achilles adds, but the war has made him grieve for the loss of sons killed by Achilles himself, now including Hector. Achilles counsels the old man to endure and stop weeping, perhaps appreciating that this is also good advice for himself. Priam urges action, not talk: release the corpse and take the ransom. Achilles is annoyed, pointing out that he certainly will, given the command of Zeus delivered by Thetis. He also guesses that some god must have guided the king to his camp. Finally, he warns the old king to not agitate him, for he did not want to lose his temper and fail to follow Zeus's orders.

Priam is afraid, but Achilles and his attendants quickly go out to attend to the mules, lead in the muleteer and unload the ransom, leaving cloaks to wrap about Hector's corpse. Servant women are ordered to wash the corpse away from Priam's sight, fearing that Priam's reaction might cause Achilles to kill the king. Putting the washed corpse in the wagon, Achilles prays for forgiveness from Patroclus. Once back inside, Achilles tells Priam to spend the night in his camp before taking the corpse home. He urges the king to eat, telling the story of Niobe losing her children to provide a mythological paradigm for remembering food after grief. They share a meal and Priam asks for ten days of peace to give Hector a burial. Achilles readily agrees. In the morning he returns to Troy with the corpse, and the *Iliad* ends with the funeral of Hector.

The scene is stunning in its complex portrayal of two enemies, both mourning and exhausted by years of war, reaching an understanding with mutual respect and sympathy. The character of Achilles is seen in all its complications in this scene. His fierceness and hot-tempered nature are apparent, as well as excessive inclination to grieve, but he carefully controls his emotions and proves to be a model host. Other Trojans also comment on the respectful qualities of this most dangerous of enemies, as when Andromache recalls to Hector in Book 6 that Achilles had released her mother for ransom after killing her seven brothers.

## ACHILLES IN HOMER'S 'ODYSSEY'

If Achilles is the dominant character of the *Iliad*, Odysseus is the dominant character of the *Odyssey*. The Homeric poem tells the story of Odysseus much delayed in his dangerous return home from the war. Often his journey enters the supernatural realm; he meets monstrous humans (for example the Cyclops Polyphemus) and fantastic natural dangers (such as Charybdis, the whirlpool across from the monstrous Scylla). Circe tells Odysseus that to return home safely he must seek advice from the seer Teiresias in Hades. Travelling to the underworld by boat, he not only receives advice from the seer, but also relishes the opportunity to encounter the shades of deceased mythological characters, including those that died in the Trojan War. One of them is Achilles.

## The Shade of Achilles

After the shade of Achilles expresses amazement to see Odysseus in the underworld, Odysseus flatters Achilles as being honoured in death as much as he was when alive. Achilles is a contrarian, especially when Odysseus is around, and he will have none of Odysseus's smooth talk. In reply he firmly rejects the quality of existence in Hades, before returning to the concern for his father and son that he displayed in *Iliad* Book 24. First he asks for news of Neoptolemus, and then Peleus:

> *'Say not a word,' he answered, 'in death's favour; I would rather be a paid servant in a poor man's house and be above ground than king of kings among the dead. But give me news about my son; is he gone to the wars and will he be a great warrior, or is this not so? Tell me also if you have heard anything about my father Peleus – does he still rule among the Myrmidons, or do they show him no respect throughout Hellas and Phthia now that he is old and his limbs fail him?'*
> 
> *Iliad*, Book 11, translation by Samuel Butler, 1898

Some are surprised that the hero who valued fame in the *Iliad* would rather be a hired hand above the earth than a king below it, but here Achilles is being his typical contrary self. In the *Iliad*, Book 9, embassy scene, he had responded to Odysseus's ingratiating praise by saying, 'Hateful as the gates of Hades is that one who hides one thing in his thoughts and speaks something else', a rejection of dissimulation that seems to be directed at Odysseus. The remark is certainly consistent with Achilles' hatred of the underworld when he ends up there.

But Achilles quickly pivots to a major theme in his colloquy with Priam in *Iliad* Book 24: his concern for family, especially fathers and sons. He asks about Peleus, worried, as he was at Troy, that he is unable to protect him. His characteristic fierceness shines through as he wishes he could visit Peleus to defend him from his antagonists. Odysseus replies that he has no news of Peleus, having been lost at sea for years, but he is happy to provide news about the actions of Achilles' son Neoptolemus in the Trojan War. He first reports that he brought Neoptolemus to Troy from the island of Skyros (where Achilles fathered Neoptolemus with the local princess, according to variant myths discussed below). Odysseus is eager to report that Neoptolemus was a good public speaker and a brave fighter. To illustrate the latter point, he tells the story of the wooden horse. While most of the Greeks sat unnerved in the darkness, Neoptolemus was begging to leave the horse and attack Trojans (he goes on to kill Priam and Hector's young son Astyanax in myths of the Trojan War). Apparently Achilles is pleased by the story, for his shade walks off proudly through the underworld.

## The Shades of Agamemnon and Achilles

If the appearance of the shade of Achilles in *Odyssey* Book 11 is fascinating, so is the second appearance of this shade in *Odyssey* Book 24. After Homer describes the shades of the slain suitors arriving at Hades, he narrates a scene between the shades of Agamemnon and Achilles. Death has removed their mutual antagonism. Achilles listens sympathetically to Agamemnon's complaints about being murdered by his wife and her lover Aegisthus, while the hero who once angrily berated his leader now expresses the wish that Agamemnon had died at Troy, where he could have been honoured by a tomb. Agamemnon picks up on the theme by telling Achilles the details of the rescue of Achilles' corpse and his burial. Trojans and Greeks had fought over his corpse (as they fought over the corpse of Patroclus in the *Iliad*). When the body was recovered, the Greeks in mourning were joined by Thetis and her fellow Nereids, grieving about his body as they had about the prostate Achilles in *Iliad* Book 18, as discussed above.

The Nereids lament over the corpse of Achilles and clothe it; even the nine Muses arrive to sing a dirge as the Greeks wept. After 17 days of mourning, Achilles was cremated, accompanied by much sacrificial livestock, honey and oil. Soldiers in full armour went around the pyre. Finally the bones were gathered and put in a jar provided by Thetis, along with the bones of Patroclus. As Achilles had planned when burying Patroclus in Book 23 of the *Iliad*, the two heroes are then buried under the same tomb by the Hellespont near Troy:

> *Your mother brought us a golden vase to hold them
> – gift of Bacchus, and work of Vulcan himself; in
> this we mingled your bleached bones with those of
> Patroclus who had gone before you, and separate
> we enclosed also those of Antilochus, who had been
> closer to you than any other of your comrades now
> that Patroclus was no more. Over these the host of
> the Argives built a noble tomb, on a point jutting out
> over the open Hellespont, that it might be seen from
> far out upon the sea by those now living and by them
> that shall be born hereafter.*
> Odyssey, Book 24, translation by Samuel Butler, 1898

Funeral games followed, as they did for the burial of Patroclus in *Iliad* Book 23. 'Even in death, your name did not die,' Agamemnon concludes. We will see that the funeral of Achilles was also narrated in an epic of the Epic Cycle, discussed in the following section. The Cycle and later literature provide further stories from the life of Achilles, and we will find that they emphasize the same traits of the hero that we find in Homer. He is obviously a skilled, dangerously powerful fighter, but he is also quick to anger and often feuds. In persisting to indulge in his wrath towards Agamemnon, he disregards the safety of his fellow soldiers in his request that the gods help the Trojans. Though slow to give up his anger, Achilles can also be inconsistent about what he wants to happen. Nonetheless, in some situations he can behave quite civilly towards enemies and antagonists, as he does with Priam in the *Iliad* 24 and as he does with Agamemnon in the underworld.

## ACHILLES IN THE EPIC CYCLE

*'Zeus plans with Themis concerning the Trojan War. Strife, present among the gods feasting at the wedding of Peleus, instigates a quarrel over beauty among Athena, Hera, and Aphrodite, who are brought by Hermes at the command of Zeus to Alexander at Ida for judgement; Alexander chooses Aphrodite, excited by marriage to Helen.'*
Proclus, summary of the *Cypria*

The Epic Cycle was a collection of early Greek epics about the origins of the world and gods (cf. Hesiod's *Theogony*), the Theban Wars and the Trojan War. The Trojan War section is what concerns us here, since it involves the early years as well as the post-*Iliad* career of Achilles at Troy and his death there. There is no reason to think that such poems were written in a co-operative manner, as in 'OK, Stasinus, you cover what happens immediately after the *Iliad* and I, Lesches, will finish your beginning of the "contest of arms" and continue as far as the wooden horse'. It is an indication that select sections of these poems were artificially joined together that Stasinus's *Aethiopis* starts but does not finish the contest over Achilles' arms and that Lesches' *Little Iliad* finishes that story but stops after the wooden horse episode.

All of the Epic Cycle poems are lost, but a summary of the Trojan War section survives, along with brief information about their authors, by a certain Proclus (usually dated from the fifth century CE). Apollodorus (possibly dating from the first or second century CE) is another ancient mythographer whose *Library* summarized ancient myth sequentially, including the Trojan War. Unfortunately, his account of the war is lost, though an epitome (called, well, the *Epitome*) that summarizes it survives. Whereas Proclus concentrated on specific poems of the Trojan cycle, including basic information about the authors and their dates, Apollodorus employs sources other than the Epic Cycle. However, one is often tempted to view some details about the war as material in the Cycle poems that Proclus left out.

It would be a mistake to assume that the authors of the Epic Cycle invented the content of their poems, though of course poets were free to modify or extend traditional myth. The Cycle poems were early Greek epics, perhaps orally composed at first, that narrated traditional material. When the Cyclic poets and Homer report the same story, it is best to conclude that Homer and the Cycle independently employed traditional myths rather than assuming that the Cycle filled out minor details invented by Homer.

We have a few fragments of verse from the Trojan Cycle poems, as well the summary of them by Proclus and ancient commentary about the poems. The fragments, though few in number, suggest that the poems were not as skilled as the Homeric ones and covered a larger amount of material at a faster pace than the *Iliad* and *Odyssey*. Apollodorus is more informative than Proclus about Cyclic stories, though he seems to have employed later material to fill them out as well. The poems themselves apparently fell into disuse by the Hellenistic period, when their contextualization of Homer became more valued than the poems themselves. Summaries such as the type that Proclus produced served a desire for Homeric contextualization more efficiently than the actual poems. There are also visual representations of the Trojan Cyclic narratives with text, for example the so-called Megarian cups (often focusing on Homeric poems) and Iliac Tables (small tablets visualizing with much tiny text the Cyclic epics on the Trojan War), that also served to present Cyclic myth to contextualize the Homeric poems.

We will first employ the Cycle (and supporting evidence by Apollodorus) to survey non-Homeric stories about Achilles' life. These include his childhood, his early exploits in the Trojan War and his battles and death after the *Iliad*. Technically, the summaries and fragments of the Epic Cycle do not directly refer to Achilles' childhood. Nonetheless, I believe that later stories about Achilles as infant and child already existed in some form in early mythological traditions. Homer and the Epic Cycle do not narrate such material directly, but why should they? Their job was to narrate the collective group effort of the Greeks to retrieve Helen from Troy. As it happens, we have already seen that Homer provides hints about the hero's childhood, while early tales of Achilles' youth seem to underlie the very succinct summary of the *Cypria* by Proclus. At the very least, eventual tales of Thetis with the baby Achilles and Chiron with the young Achilles are thematically consistent with how Achilles, Thetis and Chiron are characterized from our earliest evidence.

## Achilles' Heel

What about 'Achilles' heel', arguably the most famous thing in all of the Achilles myth?

Thetis is usually portrayed as being fully aware of Achilles' fate – perhaps simply because as a divinity she knows the future. Achilles has learned of his fate from her, as his frequent reference to a fated death at Troy in the *Iliad* documents. For a time in the epic he supposes that he could avoid this outcome if he returned home from the war, but he drops this conceit soon enough. As for 'Achilles' heel', the ancient story focused on the ankle of Achilles, not his heel (cf. the medical name 'Achilles' tendon' in the modern world). The canonical version has Thetis dip the baby Achilles in the River Styx in the underworld. This has the effect of making the child immortal – except for the spot behind one ankle, where Thetis held the baby.

Versions of Achilles' death that follow this motif have Paris shoot Achilles near the ankle with an arrow, with the help of Apollo. But there is no suggestion of Thetis having made her son semi-invulnerable in Homer or the Epic Cycle. The

*Iliad* emphasizes that Achilles needs a new set of armour for protection after Hector confiscates the armour that Patroclus borrowed.

The earliest explicit reference to the motif of Achilles' heel is in the *Achilleid* by Statius in the first century CE (discussed below). The event is not directly narrated; Thetis only later recalls it ('Often I myself – horror! – imagine I bear my son down to the emptiness of Tartarus and submerge him a second time in the waters of Styx'). By the time of Statius, artistic scenes of the hero's childhood, notably his training by Chiron and his stay at Skyros disguised as a girl, often included the Styx dipping scene. Images of Achilles' early life were arranged on circular or rectangular artefacts in order to provide a visual cycle of his life. The similarity of these iconographical cycles suggests that they were inspired by mythographical summaries of the type of Proclus and Apollodorus (Apollodorus as well as Hyginus, a Roman mythographer, later describe Thetis dipping the baby Achilles in the River Styx). In the third century CE a certain Philostratus (which one is disputed) describes such a cycle in the *Imagines*:

*Cheiron flatters him by saying that he catches hares like a lion and vies with fawns in running; at any rate, he has just caught a fawn and comes to Cheiron to claim his reward, and Cheiron, delighting to be asked, stands with fore-legs bent so as to be on a level with the boy and offers him apples fair and fragrant from the fold of his garment... This is the scene at the*

> *entrance of the cave; and the boy out on the plain, the one who is sporting on the back of the centaur as if it were a horse, is still the same boy; for Cheiron is teaching Achilles to ride horseback and to use him exactly as a horse, and he measures his gait to what the boy can endure, and turning around he smiles at the boy when he laughs aloud with enjoyment.*
> Imagines 2.2.2, translation by A. Fairbanks, 1931

Such images, based on mythological summaries, reach back centuries earlier than Statius. The summaries must be based on even earlier literature. The concept of what we might call 'Achilles' ankle' existed at an early date. If it was as early as Homer, the poet ignores the motif, for Achilles is wounded in the arm and another character remarks on his vulnerability as a mortal. However, the motif could have been an organic consequence of Thetis's obsessive concern with her son's mortality. Thetis is typically characterized as uncomprehendingly appalled at the mortality of her son, hence her desperate efforts to prevent it.

Nonetheless, early evidence for 'Achilles' heel' is hard to find. A vase painting from the sixth century shows Ajax defending the corpse of Achilles, which has a prominent arrow stuck through his leg by his ankle – but another arrow is also shown in his torso, from which blood flows. No invulnerable hero is therefore implied. Other early images show Apollo clearly holding out an arrow towards Achilles, sometimes with a downward tilt that arguably threatens a future lower wound.

This, along with other scenes of Trojans aiming at Achilles' lower body, are certainly suggestive but they may indicate a desire to slow down the famously fast hero. By the Hellenistic period, at least, Etruscan and Roman gems show a warrior kneeling with an arrow stuck in his heel, foot or ankle. Though Achilles is not identified, they may be meant to suggest the Achilles' heel motif.

Another approach is to suppose that a multiform (a version similar if in some ways different) of the 'Achilles' heel' motif existed at an early date. An arrow hitting a lower spot not protected by armour might reflect the folklore conceit of one's life spirit concentrated in a particular location. Poison has also been suggested as a plausible explanation of such a lethal wound. More suggestive, however, are stories about Thetis desiring to put the baby Achilles into flames or boiling water. In such narratives Thetis is either testing the mortality of her baby or children (in some stories there are many) or attempting to make Achilles immortal. In the testing version, which reportedly existed in an early epic poem, many children die before Peleus arrives in time to save Achilles.

In the immortalizing version, an alarmed Peleus ruins the magic of the immortalization. Apollonius of Rhodes in the *Argonautica* and Apollodorus in the *Library* portray Thetis employing fire and ambrosia on Achilles, which would have immortalized him had Peleus not interrupted her. A well-known scene in the *Homeric Hymn to Demeter* of the Archaic Age portrays Demeter, goddess of agriculture and the harvest, disguised as a maid, trying the same experiment on a baby before she is interrupted.

It is possible to conclude that experiments on human babies by divinities was an early motif that existed in multiform. In one type, the experiment is made with the intention of testing a child's mortality, with death being proof of mortality; in another type, the experiment is meant to make a child invulnerable or immortal, though the magic is interrupted. One can readily imagine that the application of fire and ambrosia magic on a mortal baby was a free-floating motif also employed in the early Achilles myth. Such a tale could then have been transformed into the 'Achilles' heel' motif, which may have been in existence before the Hellenistic period.

## The Youth of Achilles

Phoenix in Book 9 claims that as a suppliant of Peleus he took care of the baby Achilles. He paints a loving image of giving much meat and wine to the heroic infant. In one of the most charming passages in the epic, Phoenix claims that baby Achilles spurted up the wine on to his chest.

> *I dwelt in th' utmost region rich Phthia doth extend,*
> *And govern'd the Dolopians, and made thee what thou art,*
> *O thou that like the Gods art fram'd. Since, dearest to my heart,*
> *I us'd thee so, thou lov'dst none else; nor anywhere wouldst eat,*

> *Till I had crown'd my knee with thee, and carv'd thee*
> *tend'rest meat*
> *And giv'n thee wine so much, for love, that, in*
> *thy infancy*
> *(Which still discretion must protect, and a*
> *continual eye)*
> *My bosom lovingly sustain'd the wine thine could*
> *not bear.*
> Iliad, Book 9, translation by Alexander Pope, 1715–20

The memory rhetorically serves Phoenix's plea that Achilles give up his wrath. However, we do not hear much of Phoenix's role in Achilles' childhood in myth. Though there is much variation in the tales, we usually hear of Thetis leaving Peleus and Achilles out of frustration with a mortal husband and despair over a mortal son (themes deeply embedded in the *Iliad*). The figure usually credited with nurturing and training the younger Achilles is Chiron the centaur, but early evidence about Achilles' youth remains thin and inconsistent. Achilles' youth is not covered in the first poem of the Trojan Cycle, the *Cypria*. That is no surprise, since the poem narrates the gathering of Greek forces as a group for the Trojan War, rather than the biographies of individual warriors. Nonetheless, we will have occasion below to wonder whether some events in the *Cypria* are predicated upon stories of Achilles' youth; we will also occasionally suspect Homer of knowing some episodes in Achilles' youth. As we trace stories of Achilles down through the ages, we will find that enduring fascination with the hero's youth throughout antiquity provides fascinating stories of Achilles.

## Pre-Iliad Achilles in the Epic Cycle

By 'pre-*Iliad*' and 'post-*Iliad*' I mean narrative that precedes or follows the story of the *Iliad*, not any implication of the date of Cycle poems. Achilles is first mentioned in Proclus's summary of the *Cypria* for wounding Telephus, a son of Heracles who ruled Mysia in Asia Minor. This event occurred following the first of two gatherings of the Greek fleet at Aulis in Boeotia, in central Greece. Achilles is a grown man by the time of the Trojan War, of course, but an incident after his battle with Telephus is relevant to stories of his early life. After the Greek fleet was dispersed by a sea storm, Proclus reports that Achilles ends up at Skyros, where he marries the princess Deidameia. This simple and flat statement is of interest for two major reasons: Deidameia was apparently Achilles' first love, and ancient myth and literature report that she was the mother of Achilles' son Neoptolemus. Homer's references to Neoptolemus are brief but numerous (Achilles worries about him in *Iliad* Book 19 and, as we have seen, Odysseus tells Achilles about him in the underworld in *Odyssey* Book 11).

Skyros is the location of a popular myth in which Thetis or Peleus conceal the young Achilles, disguised as a girl. The story would thus be predicated, like the 'Achilles' heel' motif, on the recurring theme of Thetis trying to prevent Achilles' death. Disguised as a girl, Achilles was able to have covert sexual relations with Deiadameia, the princess of Skyros. An ancient commentator on the *Iliad* summarizes this story and attributes it to 'Cyclic' authors, by which he may simply mean 'non-Homeric'. If the story was in the Epic Cycle, it would have to be in the *Cypria*. Proclus does not report it, however.

Arguably Achilles impregnated Deidameia at Skyros in the *Cypria*, from where he was recruited for the war. He later returned to sack the island and marry the princess. More likely is the possibility that Stasinus's *Cypria* assumed knowledge of some such episode, which, as with the personal biographies of other heroes, could not be fitted into a narrative about a group expedition of Greeks to Troy.

The birth of a son by Achilles and Deidameia (who are always said to be his parents) must have at least been mentioned in the *Cypria*. Neoptolemus features prominently in later parts of the Trojan cycle; the *Little Iliad* includes Odysseus bringing him to Troy from Skyros (Proclus). In surviving narratives of the Skyros episode, Odysseus tricks Achilles, disguised as a girl, into revealing his true identity. Once at Troy, Neoptolemus turns out to be even more ferocious than his father. In the *Little Iliad* (as reported by Pausanias describing a Classical-period mural) Neoptolemus kills Priam and his grandson Astyanax; in the *Sack of Troy*, Neoptolemus kills Priam and Odysseus kills Astyanax (Proclus). Poets and artists down through antiquity emphasized the ruthless and savage violence of Neoptolemus, who apparently did not inherit the empathetic and humane side of his father's temperament.

After the dispersal of the Greek fleet in its first gathering, Telephus's festering wound is healed by the rust of Achilles' spear. Telephus repays the favour by promising to guide the Greeks to Troy after their second gathering at Aulis. Here the romantic life of Achilles arises once again, if falsely. After the goddess Artemis, angry with Agamemnon, prevented the Greeks from leaving Aulis by means of bad winds, the seer Calchas reports that the goddess would be appeased by sacrifice of Agamemnon's daughter Iphigeneia. The young woman is deceitfully lured to Aulis by a misleading promise that Achilles will marry her (*Cypria*). In the Cycle poem, Iphigeneia is saved from sacrifice when Artemis whisks her away to the northern Black Sea and makes her immortal.

When the Greeks pause their journey at the island of Tenedos, Achilles quarrels with Agamemnon 'because he was invited too late' (according to Proclus; probably to a feast). Tension between Achilles and Agamemnon is thus in evidence long before the tenth year of the Trojan War. In the first battle at Troy, Achilles pushes back the attacking Trojans and kills Kyknos, the son of Poseidon. The *Cypria* then features an episode in which Achilles wants to look at Helen, an encounter arranged by Aphrodite and Thetis. The meeting is intriguing, since such a meeting does not occur in Homer, nor anywhere else in antiquity. Some suppose that Achilles and Helen had sex. The fact that Aphrodite as well as Thetis brought them together may indicate this. Occasional reference to Helen being with Achilles in the afterlife is less pertinent, however, as several other women were also randomly linked to Achilles in the underworld (*see* the section 'Cult' below).

Even if the encounter was not sexual in the *Cypria*, however, there may well have been an erotic charge between the two. Perhaps Achilles as a young man who readily gets entangled in relationships with women simply wanted to look upon the woman celebrated as being the most beautiful in the world. Let us also remember how Achilles had complained in Book 9 that Agamemnon had seized his 'wife' Briseis when he himself was fighting for the wife of Menelaus. It may be that Achilles wanted to see whether Helen was a worthy cause of war. The succeeding episode in Proclus's summary of the *Cypria*, in which Achilles restrains the Greeks from returning home, suggests that he was certainly impressed by her. Their meeting is also fitting because both the alluring Helen and the destructive Achilles were central to Zeus's plan to reduce the number of humans on earth by means of the Trojan War.

When a Greek embassy to Troy fails to get Helen back, Proclus indicates that Achilles sacks nearby cities:

> *And then he rustles the cattle of Aeneas, sacks Lyrnessos, Pedasos, and many of the surrounding cities, and slays Troilus. Patroclus takes Lykaon to Lemnos and sells him, and Achilles chooses Briseis as his prize from the loot, Agamemnon Chryseis. Then there is the death of Palamedes, and the plan of Zeus to aid the Trojans by removing Achilles from the Greek alliance.*
> **Proclus, summary of the *Cypria***

Many different events are listed in my quotation of this section of Proclus's summary of the *Cypria*. As we have seen, the *Iliad* alludes to raiding led by Achilles in the early stages of the war. Troilus is only mentioned once in the *Iliad*: in Book 24, when Priam refers to him as already dead, but the story of Achilles killing him was a favourite episode in antiquity. A radically transformed story of Troilus in late antiquity became extremely popular in the medieval period, as we will see below. Achilles recalls the selling of the captured Trojan Lycaon when he later encounters him again on the battlefield and kills him (Book 21). The raiding of Aeneas's cattle by Achilles is an event that the hero recalls when Aeneas challenges him in battle in Book 20. Palamedes was a very clever man who tricked Odysseus when the Greeks recruited him at Ithaca; later in the *Cypria* he was murdered by the similarly wily Odysseus.

More consequential for the story of the *Iliad* is Proclus's report of the capture of Chryseis and Briseis. These two enslaved women are instrumental to the discord that arises between Achilles and Agamemnon at the beginning of the *Iliad*. When Agamemnon agrees to return Chryseis to her father Chryses (of the town Chrysa; the personal names simply mean 'Mr Crysa' and 'daughter of Mr Chrysa'), Agamemnon demands someone else's concubine in her place; this turns out to be Briseis.

The *Cypria* thus looks as if it was designed to be a prequel to the Homeric epic. Yet Proclus's claim that the *Cypria* also ended with Zeus's plan to remove Achilles from battle and a catalogue of the Greek forces is evidence against this conclusion. Why would a prequel narrate material already in the subsequent poem? It seems the two poems narrated these two episodes independently. It would also be odd for the Cyclic poem to end with a catalogue. The remainder of the poem, which may have covered all the Trojan War, seems to have been curtailed when the Trojan cycle began to be summarized.

## Post-Iliad Achilles in the Epic Cycle

The *Aethiopis* followed the story of the *Iliad* (at least in Proclus's summary) and featured new allies coming to help the Trojans. Proclus's summary begins with the arrival of Penthesileia, the Amazon queen. She and her fellow Amazons are fierce warriors, but Achilles nevertheless slays her. Thersites then mockingly taunts Achilles for falling in love with her. Thersites had been portrayed in Book 2 of the *Iliad* as a scrawny yet rhetorically gifted soldier who rebelliously criticizes both Achilles and Agamemnon. Odysseus heads off the incipient revolt by beating Thersites.

In the *Aethiopis* Thersites misbehaves for the last time, for Achilles kills him. This is murder, a very different matter from killing an enemy in battle. As a consequence, Achilles must purify himself. He therefore travels to Lesbos to sacrifice to Apollo, Artemis and Leto. Below we will have occasion to explore whether Achilles did fall in love with Penthesileia, but by his accusation Thersites evokes the theme of Achilles' romantic relationships once again.

Proclus then summarizes two of the most important and popular episodes in the life of Achilles: his defeat of Memnon and his death by Paris:

> *Memnon the son of Eos arrives, with armour made by Hephaestus, to defend the Trojans. And Thetis foretells to her son events concerning Memnon. And when battle occurs Antilochus is slain by Memnon. Then Achilles slays Memnon, and Eos gives him immortality, having asked for it from Zeus. When routing the Trojans into the city, Achilles is killed by Paris and Apollo.*
> **Proclus, summary of the** *Aethiopis*

The Trojans had welcomed another foreign and exotic ally, Memnon, king of the Aethiopians and a son of Eos ('dawn'). The reference to the goddess of dawn reflects the vaguely eastern location of the mythological Aethiopians. Memnon arrives with an army to assist the Trojans. Just as Achilles takes vengeance on Hector for killing Patroclus, in the *Aethiopis* Achilles slays Memnon for killing Antilochus. Achilles is then killed by Paris by an arrow at the gates of Troy with the help of Apollo – a fate often predicted in the *Iliad*, most specifically by the dying Hector. Just as a fierce battle occurred over the corpse of Patroclus in the *Iliad*, an extended struggle takes place over the corpse of Achilles, a famous event in ancient myth of the Trojan War. While Odysseus defends him, the famous warrior Ajax carries Achilles' huge corpse back to the ships (the relative value of these different types of valour is subsequently debated in the contest by the two over Achilles' arms).

Funerals for Antilochus and Achilles follow. Proclus refers to the attendance of the Muses, as the shade of Agamemnon reports to the shade of Achilles in the underworld (*see* the section 'The Shades of Agamemnon and Achilles' above). The visitation of the Nereids is not mentioned, but the cremation is interrupted by Thetis when she removes the corpse of Achilles from his pyre and takes him to the island of Leuke, a central location in the cult of the hero (*see* the section titled 'Cult of Achilles' below). The Achaeans heap up a burial mound and hold funeral games, as Agamemnon reports to Achilles in the underworld. Finally, as noted above, a quarrel arises between Odysseus and Ajax over who should receive the armour of Achilles.

Proclus's summary of the *Aethiopis* ends without a decision about the armour, which must have been in the original poem. For some reason Proclus begins to summarize the *Little Iliad* with the abrupt introduction of the awarding of the arms, without reference to the preceding quarrel. The abrupt ending of the *Aethiopis* and the abrupt beginning of the *Little Iliad* is proof that Proclus is not seeking to summarize the complete scope of the Cycle poems. The poems may have concentrated on different sections of the war, but the originals apparently overlapped; arguably many of them told the story of the whole war in different ways. In any event, we are told that in the *Little Iliad* Athena aids Odysseus, who wins the armour. Ajax loses his sanity and slays sheep under the impression that they are fellow Greeks. In shame, he kills himself.

However, the story of Achilles in the Epic Cycle does not end here. He continues to play a role from beyond the grave (*see* his underworld appearances in the *Odyssey* described above). After Odysseus fetches Neoptolemus from Skyros, his father's shade appears to him at Troy, probably by his tomb. Later, after the sack of Troy, Princess Polyxena, daughter of Priam, is sacrificed at his tomb (a romantic intrigue between the two is claimed in later myth). And in the *Nosti*, Proclus reports, the shade of Achilles appears to Greeks leaving Troy with warnings of future dangers. Though Achilles dies before the sack of Troy, he is clearly the most memorable character in the war. He arguably also seems to be central to the larger plan of Zeus to reduce the human population. One ancient commentator, in reporting on this larger 'plan of Zeus', has the head god effecting it by the births of Helen (cause of the war) and Achilles (responsible for the deaths of both Greeks and Trojans).

We have seen that Achilles in the early epic genre of Homer and the Epic Cycle is a vivid, dramatic and memorable character. His character is complex, with a mixture of fierce and civilized behaviour. He is loyal to those close to him, such as his parents Thetis and Peleus and his friends Patroclus and Antilochus (there is even a certain *simpatico* between him and the very different Ajax, noticeable in the embassy scene of Book 9 of the *Iliad*; this probably explains why Ajax hangs out with Achilles in the underworld). Certainly he is fierce with antagonists, most notably Agamemnon and Hector. Yet he is also capable of modulating his anger, especially when cultural and religious norms are observed.

In *Iliad* Book 19 he formally makes peace with Agamemnon, and in *Iliad* Book 24 he accedes to Priam's request to release the corpse of Hector, promising that the Greeks will not fight again until the funeral is over. His intelligence is not in doubt, as demonstrated by his eloquent and long speeches that question the rationale for the war and challenge the fairness of distribution of booty by leaders in Book 9 of the *Iliad*. Much more than a brutish killer, Achilles often turns philosophical, as in Book 21 when he muses about the human condition to the suppliant Lycaon (and then kills him).

There are many other stories about Achilles, both ancient and modern, in many genres and media. It can be difficult to ascertain whether Homer hints at tales about Achilles that he does not explicitly relate or whether later poets and artists expanded upon inventive contextual details provided by Homer. There is no doubt that the story of Achilles was traditional, but it was certainly modified and expanded. In the next section we will survey stories of the childhood of Achilles and of his actions before and after the *Iliad*. Later sections will demonstrate the popularity of such myths in art, as well as explain how Achilles' story continued into the afterlife.

## ACHILLES IN OTHER ANCIENT LITERATURE

*I am said even in those tender and yet crawling years, when the Thessalian elder received me on a steep mountain, to have gorged on unusual food, not satisfying my hunger at a nourishing breast, but gulping down the rough innards of lions and the marrow of a half-dead wolf. These*

## ANCIENT & MODERN: INTRODUCING ACHILLES

*were my first bread and gifts of gladdening Bachus, for thus that father gave to me...already then weapons were in my hand, already then quivers were at my shoulder.*
Statius, *Achilleid*

In this section I will discuss Achilles in Greek and Roman literature of the Greek classical and Hellenistic periods and in the Republican and Imperial periods of Rome (the last including much Greek literature). I will organize the material discussed under the categories of poetry, drama, epic and prose. Though we will discover that there are many variations and extension of myth about Achilles in the time periods of this section, we will find a relative lack of material to discuss. Achilles remained famous through antiquity as a warrior and a lover, but much ancient work has not survived. In addition, though Achilles may have been the dominant character in the *Iliad*, he was not the central character of the Trojan War as a whole.

We will also note that some literature stressed his negative characteristics of anger and violence, especially in the Roman culture that claimed descent from Trojans. Achilles is often mentioned, but we have few works that focus on Achilles alone. The *Achilleid* by the Roman Statius is the only major work that focuses on Achilles, but this unfinished epic consists of only a book and a half of poetry. The surviving epics *Argonautica* by Apollonius of Rhodes (Hellenistic period) and the *Aeneid* by Virgil (Imperial period) also contain some material relevant to Achilles; the epic of Quintus of Smyrna (fourth century CE) entitled *Posthomerica* survives as an epic narration of Cyclic material that follows the events of the *Iliad*. Furthermore, the *Epitome* by Apollodorus, dating from the Imperial period, provides a summary of the Trojan War that is somewhat more generous in detail than Proclus's summary. Below I seek to provide examples of literature about Achilles in various genres. Sometimes fragments or second-hand information will be required to fill out the evidence.

## Poetry

By 'poetry' I refer to relatively short non-epic and non-drama poems. The early exemplars of lyric poetry in its strict sense were Sappho and Alcaeus of Lesbos, of the later seventh and early sixth centuries BCE. Both poets were well respected in antiquity, especially Sappho as the most prominent ancient female author. Their lyric poetry has not survived well, but it contains a few mentions of Achilles in largely non-Homeric ways. A fragment of Sappho compliments a bridegroom by comparing him to Achilles (the bride is compared to an unpicked apple at the top of a tree). One fragment of Alcaeus celebrated the wedding of Thetis and Peleus. Chiron assisted in their union and the wedding was attended by the gods. More ominously, the subsequent birth of Achilles to Peleus and Thetis is associated with future disaster for the Trojans, although Alcaeus blames Helen for the war. A second fragment of Alcaeus identifies him as a ruler of Scythia, referring to the hero cult of Achilles popular in the northern Black Sea (*see* the section titled 'Cult' below).

Pindar and Bacchylides, active in the early fifth century BCE, speak of Achilles more extensively in odes celebrating athletic victors. Pindar refers to Achilles as a model of excellence, notably in odes praising athletic victors from Aegina, the home of Achilles' grandfather. In some rather brief tangents in the relatively long odes, Pindar refers to the prophecy of Thetis's son becoming greater than the father and to Chiron's role in the marriage of Peleus, as well as his training of Achilles at a tender age. Brief sections also speak of Achilles' encounters with antagonists in the Trojan War (the wounding of Telephus and the killing of Cycnus, Hector and Memnon).

A few lines in one ode describe the Muses singing at the funeral of Achilles, while another ode mentions Thetis taking Achilles' corpse to the Isles of the Blessed (an alternative utopia to the island of Leuke, the usual location for Achilles' cultic afterlife). Another fragment depicts Achilles praying to Thetis, similar to the prayer he makes to his mother in *Iliad* Book 1. Bacchylides, in a rather longer section of an ode, covers much Iliadic material, including Achilles' wrath over the seizure of Briseis, Ajax's attempts to prevent Hector from setting the Greek ships on fire in the hero's absence, and Achilles' return to battle and subsequent slaughter of the Trojans. If more of their work had survived and been less fragmented, it is probable that there would be even more references to Achilles.

The *Alexandra* by Lycophron is a long poem of about 1,500 lines. It dates from the Hellenistic period, reportedly the late fourth century BCE, though its references to the power of Rome suggest a later date. The title refers to a byname of Cassandra, the Trojan princess with the ability to see into the future. The poem represents her long prophecy of myriad events, mythological and historical. As is typical of the language of prophecy, her extensive lament over the Trojan War and its aftermath is opaque, with the poetic style of Lycophron amplifying this obscurity. As the sister of Troilus and Hector, both killed by Achilles, as well as of Polyxena, slain over Achilles' grave at his request, Cassandra has many negative things to say about Achilles' childhood (including allusions to a variant of the 'Achilles' heel' motif), his Trojan War exploits (both Homeric and Cyclic) and his afterlife (focusing on his otherworld romances). She portrays Achilles negatively in paradoxical ways, for example, lustful yet effeminate.

In the Hellenistic period Achilles' relationship with Deidameia at Skyros, which produces Neoptolemus, was told in the first century BCE in the *Epithalamium of Achilles and Deidameia,* attributed to Bion. We saw that in the Epic Cycle Achilles sacks Skyros and marries Deidameia, and that Neoptolemus is later brought to Troy from Skyros. It seems justifiable to assume that the hiding of Achilles at Skyros, resulting in sex with Deidameia and the baby Neoptolemus, was deemed the logical prelude to these events. Some scholars rather stubbornly resist this conclusion, perhaps fooled by Homer into thinking that early Greek epic was averse to the hiding of a hero dressed as a girl. Of course, traditional myth does change and it was often expanded. However, we will see below that Achilles' Skyros experience was already well established in classical-age drama.

In the brief bucolic *epithalamium* (the Greek word refers to a wedding song), one shepherd sings to another a song of Achilles' adolescent love for Deidameia at Skyros. Achilles has been disguised as a girl and brought to Skyros to avoid recruitment for the coming Trojan War. After indicating that Achilles and Deidameia had sex (which produced Neoptolemus), the poem takes note of Helen eloping with Paris before returning to Achilles' flirtatious wooing of the beautiful Deidameia on Skyros. The song inherits the motif of Achilles hidden at Skyros from the Classical Age (*see below*), and arguably earlier in epic traditions, as I have discussed above.

Romans may not have been as respectful of Achilles as earlier Greeks, given their claimed lineage from Trojans. However, the strong influence of Greek culture on that of the Romans led to much literary attention being given to Achilles. The childhood of Achilles was a popular theme in Roman literature and art. A relatively long epyllion ('short epic') by Catullus includes a section of the Fates predicting the birth of Achilles; this in turn leads to the death of many Trojans and the sacrifice of Polyxena at his tomb. The imagery is rather gruesome:

*Often will mothers attest over funeral-rites of their*
*sons his glorious acts and illustrious deeds, when the*
*white locks from their heads are unloosed amid ashes,*

*and they bruise their discoloured breasts with feeble fists...For as the reaper, plucking off the dense wheat-ears before their time, mows the harvest yellowed beneath ardent sun, so will he cast prostrate the corpses of Troy's sons with grim swords...His great valour will be attested by Scamander's wave, which ever pours itself into the swift Hellespont, narrowing its course with slaughtered heaps of corpses he shall make tepid its deep stream by mingling warm blood with the water. And finally she will be a witness: the captive-maid handed to death, when the heaped-up tomb of earth built in lofty mound receives the snowy limbs of the stricken virgin.*
**Catullus, *Carmina*, translation by L.C. Smithers, 1894**

Unfortunately, nothing as long as this passage occurs in shorter Latin poems, but frequent mentions of Achilles reflect his enduring fame. Horace in one of his *Satires* briefly speaks of the anger of Priam and Hecuba at Achilles, the killer of their son. In one of his *Odes* he describes a powerful, brutal and short-lived Achilles, with comparative praise of Aeneas, the eventual ancestor of the Romans. The passage is representative of the Roman attitude towards Achilles.

Propertius in an elegy complains of being scorned by a girl, despite his previous support of her. He claims that after losing Briseis Achilles was overcome with emotion, to the point that he complacently looked upon the deaths of fellow Greeks and the Trojan torching of their ships. More tragically for Achilles, he blamed the death of Patroclus on his loss of Briseis. Even after she was returned, he continued to rage by dragging the corpse of Hector in the dust (here the logic is loose, since the loss of Patroclus, not Briseis, is the impetus for this). With a finishing flourish, Propertius emotes: 'Such great grief rages, when love is snatched away...Is it any wonder if love triumphs over me, I who am much lesser in mother and fight?'

In one passage of his long *Ars Amatoria*, Ovid more interestingly describes the training of Achilles in both hunting and culture by Chiron. Roman fascination with the childhood of Achilles seemed to expand the range of education provided to Achilles by Chiron. We have seen above an emphasis on hunting skills (also useful in war), and Homer lets it be known in *Iliad* Book 11 that Patroclus had learned of plants with medicinal qualities from Achilles, who in turn had been taught about such skills by Chiron.

Rather more inventive is one of the poems of Ovid's *Heroides*, a collection of letters by mythological women. The third of these is written by Briseis to Achilles, in a time shortly after the embassy scene described in *Iliad* Book 9. She has complaints: Achilles should not have allowed Agamemnon to take her, and he refused Agamemnon's offer of her with many gifts ('What have I done that I am held thus cheap by you, Achilles? Whither has fled your light love so quickly from me?' [translation by G. Showerman, 1914]). She recounts her tragic past, as she did in *Iliad* Book 19, reflecting upon Achilles' sack of her town and the killing of her husband and family. Nonetheless, she was fond of Achilles and is horrified to learn that he told the embassy of plans to sail home. The thought of being left behind stirs her emotions, to the point of wishing for death. She pleads that she leave with him, even as a working slave, not a wife – he can marry a woman of his homeland.

Briseis urges him to take her back from Agamemnon and join the battle against the Trojans, comparing him to Meleager destructively refusing to fight, just as Phoenix does in his Book 9 speech. Vowing upon the memory of her dead husband and brothers, she swears that she has not had sexual relations with Agamemnon and suspects Achilles has not refrained from sex with other slaves (very true, as we saw above). Briseis suggests that Achilles has lost his spirit for fighting and desire for glory. Finally, she proposes that he kill her, before requesting that he take her back, whether he stays at Troy or not. As with the other letters, the poem wonderfully provides the perspective of a hero's lover, not just that of the hero himself. With a sophistication that anticipates modern creative reception of ancient myth, the voice of Briseis, only heard momentarily in *Iliad* Book 19, emotionally pleads with Achilles and effectively criticizes his reason and ethics.

### Drama (or, Psychostasia, Qu'est-ce Que C'est?)

Many plays in Greek drama demonstrate interest in Achilles, but plays exclusively about Achilles have not survived. Nonetheless, a lost trilogy by Aeschylus (recreated by the Roman playwright Accius, also lost) retold the second half of the *Iliad* (although Homeric material is usually avoided on the Greek stage). The first drama in the trilogy is thought to be the *Myrmidons* (the ethnic name of Achilles' army), which features the death of Patroclus as a consequence of the hero's wrath against Agamemnon. The second play in the trilogy was the *Nereids*, whose title refers to the chorus of Thetis's sisters. One surmises that Thetis's consolation of Achilles in his grief and her acquisition of a new armour were the principal content, followed perhaps by the killing of Hector. A final play, the *Phrygians*, featured the ransom of Hector by Priam (with 'Phrygians' serving as a byname for Trojans who provided the chorus).

In the *Phrygians*, the encounter between Priam and Achilles is rather less philosophical in tone compared to their emotional meeting in the *Iliad*. Scales are employed, for example, to match Priam's gold to the weight of Hector's corpse. A passage in Homer's *Iliad* seems to be the inspiration of the weighing scene. Achilles adamantly tells Hector that he would refuse to return Hector's body even if he were offered its weight in gold. Some fragments of the trilogy have survived, a couple of which seem to indicate a sexual relationship between Achilles and Patroclus. This would reflect the aristocratic culture of the early Classical period, in which older men whose women were secluded child-bearers found social as well as erotic pleasure in the company of younger men admired for their looks. Aristocratic ideology may also inform our impression that Aeschylus's Achilles is estranged from soldiers of common rank in the army. Euripides will employ such a divide to make the hero look foolish.

In another (unfortunately) lost play by Aeschylus, the *Psychostasia* ('souls-weighing'), scales were employed to weigh the *psychai* ('souls', or in this context 'fates') of Achilles and Memnon, to signal who would die in their duel. The play thus retells the story of the Cyclic *Aethiopis*, in which Achilles killed the Aethiopian king Memnon, who had travelled to Troy with an army to assist the besieged Trojans. Pisistratus in the *Odyssey* (Book 4) weeps at the memory of the death of his brother Antilochus at the hands of Memnon. The death of Antilochus, second only to Patroclus as a friend of Achilles, presumably inspired Achilles to take vengeance on Memnon in the *Aethiopis*. Early vase imagery, some possibly inspired by Aeschylus, depict the *psychai* of Achilles and Memnon being weighed, watched by their anxious mothers Thetis and Eos. Their intense concern over the fate of their sons is suggested by the detail given in Proclus's summary of the *Aethiopis*, Eos's plea for the immortality of her dead son Memnon, which was granted.

In a lighter tone, in his comedy *Frogs* Euripides has Aeschylus's shade in the underworld propose that scales be employed to prove that his verse was weightier than that of Euripides. The weighing of souls in drama stems from its employment in the *Iliad*, whether for two antagonists or for the Greeks and Trojans as a whole. The scale that is lowered the farthest signals the loss or death of one side (although in *Frogs*, as noted, it signals the greater profundity of Aeschylus's poetry).

No play by Sophocles directly focuses on Achilles, though *Philoctetes* features the increasing unease of Neoptolemus as he assists the wily Odysseus in persuading Philoctetes to join the Trojan War. From the Classical period onward it has been common to describe Sophocles as the most Homeric playwright of antiquity because of his exploration of heroic character. Achilles, even when not a character in a play, lurks in the background of contested heroic values in the plays *Ajax* and *Philoctetes*. We also know of a lost play by Sophocles entitled *Skyrioi*, which apparently featured the fetching of Neoptolemus from Skyros.

Though Euripides can praise Achilles (for example, in choral ode in *Electra*, although the praise is shadowed by foreboding), Euripides typically shows the hero in a bad light. *Iphigenia at Aulis* describes Agamemnon's willingness to sacrifice his daughter in order to appease Artemis, who had been offended by his actions. The plot involves fetching the maiden under the ruse of her marriage to Achilles. When Achilles finds this out through a chance encounter with Clytemnestra, he vows to save the girl.

Euripides being Euripides, however, Achilles' heroic intentions gradually appear less than noble. Achilles seems more concerned with his reputation than the maiden's life, and when his Myrmidons vociferously object to his plan to prevent the sacrifice of Iphigenia to Artemis, he quickly abandons it. This is not the way in which the Homeric Achilles or his Myrmidons would behave. In general, the work of Euripides challenges the nobility of epic heroism. Iphigenia, on the other hand, is characterized positively as a brave woman willing to die for the greater good of the Greek cause.

In Euripides' play *Hecuba* the eponymous Trojan queen, already thoroughly demoralized by the deaths of both her son Hector and her husband Priam, is driven to frenzied grief at the sacrifice of her daughter Polyxena on the grave of Achilles (and later by the death of her son Polymestor). She is angered by reports that the shade of Achilles had cruelly demanded this human sacrifice (maybe a self-serving rumour generated by the Greeks). In later antiquity and beyond the hero will be said to be in love with Polyxena.

Unfortunately, many other relevant ancient dramas have been lost. Some plays of the Classical period featured Achilles but have not survived, among them Sophocles' work intriguingly entitled *The Lovers of Achilles*. Nor has much of relevance survived in Roman drama. In the late third or early second century BCE the Roman author Ennius is known to have composed a now-lost play entitled *Achilles*. As noted above, another lost play by Accius was based on Aeschylus's trilogy about Achilles. However, *Hecuba* by Seneca the Elder, written in the first century CE, has survived; it reworked the play by Euripides from a Roman perspective (the Greeks seeming even more despicable).

## Epic

Though, in my opinion, all ancient epics pale in comparison to the *Iliad* and *Odyssey*, they are nevertheless valuable for narrating material outside of the Homeric poems, whose scope is limited (a few weeks in the Trojan War; one out of many heroic returns). We will examine several other ancient epics, including the Greek Hellenistic epic *Argonautica* by Apollonius of Rhodes and the Roman epic *Aeneid* by Virgil. The former only glancingly refers to Achilles, while the latter mostly employs the figure of Achilles in a meta-poetic way. However, in Book 2 Aeneas views Trojan War images on the temple of Juno in Carthage. These include Achilles chasing Trojans, the killing of Troilus, the dragging of Hector's corpse and its ransom by Priam in exchange for gold. In his rich and varied *Metamorphoses*, Ovid recounts several episodes concerning Achilles. We are also lucky to have one epic focused on Achilles, the Latin epic *Achilleid* by Statius, though unfortunately only its first book and half of the second were completed.

The *Argonautica* by Apollonius of Rhodes primarily narrates the journey of Jason and the Argonauts, but it also refers on occasion to Achilles' youth. When Chiron sees the Argonauts off, his wife holds the young hero in her arms (Book 1), and a later passage describes the interruption of Thetis in her attempt to burn off the baby Achilles' mortality, as noted above (Book 4). The greatest Roman epic is that of Virgil, written in the late first century BCE. Though it features the story of the Trojan Aeneas after the fall of Troy, the epic's hero wanders on the sea like Odysseus, engaging in battles reminiscent of the Trojan War.

Virgil's work reveals complex layers of Homeric and Cyclic intertextuality as his Trojan hero travels circuitously to the Italian world to establish a new home for the Trojans. In Book 6 the Sibyl explicitly describes his future battle there as a new Trojan War that will feature an 'alius Achilles' ('another Achilles'). Aeneas's opponent Turnus considers himself Achilles in Book 9, but the Trojan Pandarus seems for a time to play the part of the Greek hero. It is Aeneas, however, who is most comparable to Achilles. However one explicates the Homeric doubling, the shadow of Achilles persists in the *Aeneid* long after the hero's death.

Ovid composed his magnificent *Metamorphoses* in the early first century CE. Centred on the theme of metamorphosis, a common occurrence in ancient myth, the poem covers a lot of material, ranging from the beginning of the world to the deification of Julius Caesar. Amidst the myriad tales of metamorphosis, often involving romance and sex, some extended narratives emerge, among them major parts of the Trojan War. The birth of Achilles is featured in Book 11. After Jupiter avoids Thetis because of a prophecy of her son being stronger than his father, the rape of Thetis by Peleus follows. Her ability to change shape provides much material for Ovid. Peleus's first attack is not successful, but with divine help the future father of Achilles overcomes the sea nymph.

Later, in Book 12, we find the story of how Achilles killed Cycnus (whose name is similar to *cygnus*, 'swan', which inspires a metamorphosis story). Cycnus was a ferocious warrior who, according to Ovid, killed over one thousand invading Greeks. Achilles first strikes his enemy with a spear throw, but is surprised when it fails to wound the invulnerable Cycnus. A little slow in perceiving the situation, the Greek hero tries again and again in frustration to pierce Cycnus's skin. Finally, he pushes Cycnus back and on to the ground. There Achilles succeeds in strangling his opponent. His father Neptune then transforms him into a swan.

At the end of Book 12 Ovid narrates the death of Achilles. Neptune, still angry over the death of his son Cycnus, reminds Apollo of how they had once built the walls of Troy, now threatened by Achilles, and suggests that Apollo kill him by bow and arrow. Revealing himself to Paris, Apollo advises him to shoot at Achilles and then guides the arrow to its target. Ovid comments on the irony of the great Achilles being subdued by 'a coward who seduced a Grecian wife' (translation by Brookes More, 1922).

In Book 13, Ajax and Ulysses contest over the arms of Achilles. Ajax confesses that he is poor at speaking, but in fact provides a long rhetorical argument that the Homeric Ajax could never manage. Ulysses is also eloquent in stating his case, as one would expect. Among his remarks is an account of Thetis concealing her son at Skyros in women's clothes; Odysseus reminds his audience that it was he who revealed Achilles and convinced him to join the Greek forces. He thereby claims some credit for Achilles' various success at Troy, as well as claiming to have carried the corpse of Achilles out of battle (usually Ajax is said to have done this, but Odysseus was sometimes credited). Again in Book 13, the ghost of Achilles demands the death of Polyxena, which is done over his tomb. The story proceeds as in Euripides and in Seneca, though it adds an old legend that Hecuba in her grief is transformed into a dog (another metamorphosis).

We do not have a sustained literary treatment of Achilles' youth until Statius's Latin epic *Achilleid* of the second half of the first century CE. Unfortunately, the work was never completed, with only a book and a half surviving. Statius's unfinished work focuses on Achilles' adolescent experience of love at Skyros and describes the hero's training by Chiron. The Skyros episode is inspired by Thetis's constant fear of the potential death of Achilles. Worried that her son will be recruited for the Trojan War, she asks Neptune to sink the Greek fleet. When he refuses, she seeks out Chiron and his pupil Achilles in Thessaly. Thetis takes Achilles from there to Skyros disguised as a girl, something that the hero at first refuses. Upon viewing the beautiful princess Deidameia, however, he changes his mind. Thetis then persuades the king to accept the 'girl' at the royal court, and soon the disguised Achilles falls in love with Deidameia, who realizes Achilles is male:

> *For as rough Achilles stood in the group of girls, free of awkward shyness with his mother departed, he at once befriends her though the whole group gathers round. He applies new and charming wiles on her guileless nature. He follows her about and wilfully hovers by her, renewing his attentions again and again with his eyes...with skill he shows her the sweet strings of the lyre and the gentle modes and songs of Chiron, and he guides her hand and places her fingers on a resonant harp. He strokes her mouth as*

> she sings and hugs her tightly and praises her with
> a thousand kisses. She happily learns of steep Pelion
> and Peleus and is riveted when hearing of his name
> and deeds. She even sings of Achilles in his presence.
> Statius, *Achilleid*

Meanwhile the Greek forces gathered at Aulis decide to send Ulysses and Diomedes to find the missing Achilles. Before they reach Skyros, the tender lover Achilles turns forceful and rapes Deidameia, who becomes pregnant. When Ulysses arrives with Diomedes, Achilles is still in disguise, but he is soon revealed by Ulysses' famous trickery. He and Diomedes set out military gear amidst more feminine implements, and Achilles is revealed as a boy by his attraction to a shield:

> Now the other girls, following their relaxed
> gender and nature, handle the shiny wands or the
> resounding tambourines, and fasten bejewelled
> bands to their head. They see the weapons but think
> they are gifts for the prominent father. But rough
> Achilles sees the glowing shield nearby, engraved with
> battles – it also was ruddy with the violent blows of
> battles – resting on a spear. He groaned, rolled his
> eyes, and his hair rose above his brow. No more his
> mother's advice, no more his secret love: Troy fills his
> whole chest.
> Statius, *Achilleid*

Achilles is readily persuaded to join the Greek troops, but he must first explain to the king that he has made his daughter pregnant. King Lycomedes allows the couple to marry (cf. the marriage after the sack of Skyros by Achilles in the *Cypria*). Though it saddens both Achilles and Deidameia, the young man then leaves with Ulysses and Diomedes. Ulysses tells Achilles about how the war started (i.e., Helen's elopement) and Achilles tells him of his training by Chiron. That is as far as the epic was composed.

Quintus of Smyrna, of the third or fourth century CE, composed in Greek an epic in 12 books based on the Epic Cycle. It is possible that he had recourse to the Cycle poems, if they survived to his time; he may also have founded the work on summaries of the poems (for example that by Proclus) and other retellings (such as the *Epitome* of Apollodorus). Beginning at the end of the *Iliad* (hence the title *Posthomerica*), it tells the events of the final year of the war, including the sacking of Troy. In other words, the narrative includes the deaths of Penthesileia, Memnon, the contest between Ajax and Odysseus over Achilles' arms, and finally the destruction of Troy itself. It has been demonstrated that, despite the Cyclic content, there is intertextual employment of the *Iliad*. There is consequently much of interest in this epic retelling of the later stages of the Cycle in Greek hexameter verse, especially since the Cycle poems are themselves now lost. The poem, besides being concerned with the *Iliad*, also reflects the interests of Greek culture in the Imperial period.

## Prose

The number of references to Achilles in ancient prose is enormous, though relatively few works concentrate on Achilles in particular. We will thus need to be selective. I will begin with Plato of the Classical period, whose accounts of the dialogues of Socrates often featured Achilles. Following is Dio Chrysotom of the first century CE, a Greek of Asia Minor whose *11$^{th}$ Discourse* argued that the Trojans won the war. The argument may seem absurd, but it is founded on the literary, philosophical and rhetorical studies of his day. Next I will provide a short piece from *Dialogues of the Dead* by Lucian, a Syrian of the second century CE. Despite his enormous learning and sophistication, Lucian was often humourous, with his dialogues satirizing those of Plato. Finally, I will add some relevant sections of mythographical summaries by Apollodorus of the Imperial period and the Roman Hyginus of the late first century BCE and early first century CE. These summaries regarding the myth of Achilles will serve as examples of mythography in later antiquity; they also provide a useful overview of Achilles material, discussed above and below.

This selection of prose writers thus provides a sample of various educated responses to early Greek myth about Achilles. Their revisiting of stories sometimes preserves lost ones, sometimes interprets them, and sometimes challenges their status as canonical. Such dedicated yet probing treatments will prepare us for fictional expansions on ancient Achilles myths in the medieval period, as well as the creative 'reception' of such stories in the modern world.

Plato's dialogues typically feature Socrates engaged in intense if casual long conversations with interlocutors. Plato was a student of Socrates, but these compositions are essentially fictional, with Socrates appearing as a character, even though they are based on thorough experience with the elder philosopher. The *Apology* is an account of the speech Plato made at his trial on the charge of corrupting the youth. The title of the *Apology* refers not to our meaning of 'apology' as a confession of mistakes. It is the technical term for the defense speech of an accused person, often featuring much autobiographical and discursive material.

Our interest is in the frequent discussion of Achilles by Plato's Socrates. In the *Apology* we see that Socrates does not just refer to Achilles as a famous Homeric character; he engages with his words and actions as if he were a real person whom we might variously praise or censure. In the *Apology* Socrates compares Achilles to himself. He sees parallels in Achilles' steadfast commitment to his ideals, even when death is the recognized consequence, to Socrates' stubborn defense of his own philosophical activities when confronted by the threat of death by prosecution. Achilles died for his commitment to what he felt was right; Socrates is willing to do the same.

In the *Crito* Socrates again compares himself to Achilles, this time in a rather mystical and poetic manner. Crito warns him that he will be executed when a ship from Delos arrives at Athens. Socrates states that the ship is not imminent, for he had a dream in which a beautiful woman in white said,

'On the third day you will come to fertile Phthia.' Socrates – or rather the woman in his dream – alludes to something Achilles says to the embassy in Book 9. Rejecting requests to return to battle, he threatens to leave Troy and reach home by ship in three days. Socrates' re-employment of Achilles' words may seem arrogant, but their exact relevance is not clear. He primarily praises Achilles for fighting to help his fellow Greeks and to avenge Patroclus, but this threat to return home is the antithesis of those subsequent decisions. There is room here to wonder what the quotation says about Socrates as well as Achilles.

In the *Hippias Major* Socrates brings up Achilles again. Countering conventional measures of a good life (beauty, wealth, health), Socrates refers to Achilles as a positive model for fighting on despite knowledge of an early death after the death of Patroclus. Socrates praises Achilles in a selective manner; Achilles often did not act in a manner that the philosopher could approve. In the later *Republic* Socrates quibbles with Achilles' fatalistic comments about the human condition in his meeting with Priam. More generally, he recognizes that the hero's passionate emotions are antithetical to calm philosophical reasoning. He also objects to the excessive grief of Achilles after the death of Patroclus, going so far as to blame Homer for such faults, not the hero himself.

The wide-ranging *Symposium* is relevant to our discussion about the relationship between Achilles and Patroclus. Like Aeschylus, Plato as an aristocrat in the Classical period is comfortable with sexual activity (albeit rather limited, from the perspective of the modern world) between two males. But aristocratic practice conventionally paired an older man with a younger and still beardless partner. Socrates claims that Aeschylus has portrayed Achilles wrongly. The hero was not the older lover as opposed to the younger beloved. Achilles was the more beautiful man, he claims, with no beard. Once again I am surprised that Socrates distinguishes between Achilles as a character in narrative with Achilles as a historical person. For me, there is no evidence of a Trojan War nor of an ancient hero named Achilles; he is instead a rather supernatural mythological character. Plato's Socrates may serve to reveal how seriously the ancient Greeks took their myths. As we move forward in time, however, we will see that the old Greek myths increasingly develop the status of material for fictional and inventive narratives.

Dio Chrysotom's *Discourse 11* turns the Trojan War upside down. With the current residents of Roman Ilium at the site of ancient Troy in mind, and with evidence supposedly obtained from an Egyptian priest (a trope typical of the ancient novel of the Imperial period, with roots in early epic and Herodotus), he challenges Homer's account of the war. In the perverse world of this speech, Helen was legitimately married to Paris, Hector killed Achilles and Troy won the war. The result is a type of fiction, to be sure, but with a willingness to contemplate the paradoxical and to pursue a thesis, no matter how unlikely, with rhetorical skill (modern academics are comparable). Dio finds fault with Homer for presenting implausible scenarios, such as Achilles' fight with the River Scamander (and the involvement of the gods in general), and omitting major aspects of the war (for example the deaths of Memnon and Penthsileia). He opines that 'Homer was either unintelligent and a bad judge of the facts, and thus chose lesser and poorer material, leaving to others the greatest and most serious topics, or he was not able, as I said, to support his lies...'

In particular Dio criticizes Homer for concentrating on Achilles alone, when in fact he was not central to the story of the sack of Troy. Having reviewed the Cyclic context, we must concede that he has a point. Dio admits that Homer's initial narration of Hector defeating Greeks is truthful, but he accuses the poet of falsely having Achilles kill Hector (instead of the reverse) and wrongly having the Greeks defeat the Trojans (instead of the reverse). Yet knowing the truth, Homer hints or temporarily accedes to Trojan success. Achilles' death at the hands of Hector is omitted and replaced by the prediction of Achilles' death by the weakest Trojan. Should we think that Dio really doubted Homer or that he believed in a conspiracy theory about the Trojan War? No. What we should appreciate is the strict logic and persistent rhetorical skills with which Dio makes his case. I suspect even the residents of Ilium perceived the humour of this recalibration of the Trojan War, no matter how much it favoured their homeland.

Lucian, as noted above, was a second-century CE Syrian, highly educated in Greek culture. He wrote a variety of prose works. *True Story* tells an autobiographical tale of travel that includes a trip to the moon, time spent inside a whale and a visit to the Isles of the Blessed, where Achilles and other heroes reside. The humour of that story is also present in *Dialogues of Dead*, which interestingly brings together shades of different people, something we have observed above in the colloquy of the shades of Achilles and Agamemnon from *Odyssey* Book 24. In one of Lucian's dialogues, Achilles and Antilochus (second only to Patroclus as a friend of Achilles) have a conversation. Antilochus begins by criticizing Achilles for telling Odysseus that he would rather be a servant on earth than king of the dead (referencing the passage in the *Odyssey*'s underworld scene discussed above). Antilochus finds this sentiment unworthy of a hero who should embrace a glorious death. He also alludes to Achilles' inclination to return home in the embassy scene: 'It gives the lie to all your life; you might have had a long inglorious reign in Phthia, and your own choice was death and glory.' Achilles replies that he considered fame better than life, but now he thinks it is of no value. He adds, 'Let folk up there make what verse of it they will.' (Translations by H.W. and F.G. Fowler, 1905)

Antilochus replies by speaking of the necessity of death. He points out how many of their contemporaries are below earth, with Odysseus surely soon to follow. He's sure that great heroes such as Heracles would not choose to return to earth as poor men. Achilles is uncharacteristically agreeable, but insists that Antilochus as well as other shades below must have fond memories of their past lives, as he does himself. He claims that it is worse to hide one's pain at death, but Antilochus denies this: 'Be silent, bear, endure – this is our resolve, lest such longings bring mockery on us, as on you.' (H.W. and F.G. Fowler)

Apollodorus's *Library* is a functional summary of myth, of a type common in later antiquity. Even bowls and plaques in antiquity were employed to provide verbal/visual summaries of the Epic Cycle. The apparent lack of texts of the Cycle demonstrate Homer's stranglehold on Greek culture and education, but the popularity of Cyclic summaries underscore the need to contextualize the *Iliad* and *Odyssey* within the broad story of the Trojan War. Cyclic narratives remained popular through other poetic genres (as we have seen above), and also through artwork (as we will see below), in what I call a 'Homero-Cyclic' type of reception of early epic. The *Library*'s Trojan War portion, the so-called *Epitome*, is more informative than Proclus's summary of the Epic Cycle, possibly because it has recourse to Homero-Cyclic reception. Apollodorus and Proclus often employ similar phraseology, however, which must reflect a long and wide tradition of such Cyclic summary.

Apollodorus therefore represents a popular trend in later antiquity. Below I provide selections that feature Achilles. The *Epitome* does not have the poetry of Homer or the narrative skills of Plato or Dio. However, it provides a coherent and linear reminder of all the episodes that we have covered, and will often meet below as we survey the images and narratives of Achilles:

**3.16** *So Agamemnon in person was in command of the whole army, and Achilles was admiral, being fifteen years old.*

**3.17** *But not knowing the course to steer for Troy, they put in to Mysia and ravaged it, supposing it to be Troy. Now Telephus son of Hercules, was king of the Mysians, and seeing the country pillaged, he armed the Mysians, chased the Greeks in a crowd to the ships, and killed many, among them Thersander, son of Polynices, who had made a stand. But when Achilles rushed at him, Telephus did not abide the onset and was pursued, and in the pursuit he was entangled in a vine-branch and wounded with a spear in the thigh.*

**3.20** *But Telephus, because his wound was unhealed, and Apollo had told him that he would be cured when the one who wounded him should turn physician, came from Mysia to Argos, clad in rags, and begged the help of Achilles, promising to show the course to steer for Troy. So Achilles healed him by scraping off the rust of his Pelian spear. Accordingly, on being healed, Telephus showed the course to steer, and the accuracy of his information was confirmed by Calchas by means of his own art of divination.*

**3.26** *So when the Greeks were standing in for Tenedos, Tenes saw them and tried to keep them off by throwing stones, but was killed by Achilles with a sword-cut in the breast, though Thetis had*

forewarned Achilles not to kill Tenes, because
he himself would die by the hand of Apollo if he
slew Tenes.

**3.29** These were, however, saved by Antenor;
but the Greeks, exasperated at the insolence of the
barbarians, stood to arms and made sail against
them. Now Thetis charged Achilles not to be the
first to land from the ships, because the first to land
would be the first to die. Being apprized of the hostile
approach of the fleet, the barbarians marched in
arms to the sea, and endeavored by throwing stones
to prevent the landing.

**3.31** On the death of Protesilaus, Achilles landed
with the Myrmidons, and throwing a stone at the
head of Cycnus, killed him. When the barbarians
saw him dead, they fled to the city, and the Greeks,
leaping from their ships, filled the plain with bodies,
and having shut up the Trojans, they besieged them;
and they drew up the ships.

**3.32** The barbarians showing no courage, Achilles
waylaid Troilus and slaughtered him in the
sanctuary of Thymbraean Apollo, and coming by
night to the city he captured Lycaon. Moreover,
taking some of the chiefs with him, Achilles laid waste
the country, and made his way to Ida to lift the kine

of Aeneas. But Aeneas fled, and Achilles killed the neatherds and Nestor, son of Priam, and drove away the kine.

**4.1** Achilles did not go forth to the war, because he was angry on account of Briseis,...the daughter of Chryses the priest. Therefore the barbarians took heart of grace and sallied out of the city. And Alexander fought a single combat with Menelaus; and when Alexander got the worst of it, Aphrodite carried him off. And Pandarus, by shooting an arrow at Menelaus, broke the truce.

**4.3** The Greeks made a wall and a ditch to protect the roadstead, and a battle taking place in the plain, the Trojans chased the Greeks within the wall. But the Greeks sent Ulysses, Phoenix, and Ajax as ambassadors to Achilles, begging him to fight for them, and promising Briseis and other gifts.

**4.6** But when Achilles saw the ship of Protesilaus burning, he sent out Patroclus with the Myrmidons, after arming him with his own arms and giving him the horses. Seeing him the Trojans thought that he was Achilles and turned to flee. And having chased them within the wall, he killed many, amongst them Sarpedon, son of Zeus, and was himself killed by Hector, after being first wounded by Euphorbus.

**4.7** *And a fierce fight taking place for the corpse, Ajax with difficulty, by performing feats of valour, rescued the body. And Achilles laid aside his anger and recovered Briseis. And a suit of armour having been brought him from Hephaestus, he donned the armour and went forth to the war, and chased the Trojans in a crowd to the Scamander, and there killed many, and amongst them Asteropaeus, son of Pelegon, son of the River Axius; and the river rushed at him in fury. But Hephaestus dried up the streams of the river, after chasing them with a mighty flame. And Achilles slew Hector in single combat, and fastening his ankles to his chariot dragged him to the ships. And having buried Patroclus, he celebrated games in his honour, at which Diomedes was victorious in the chariot race, Epeus in boxing, and Ajax and Ulysses in wrestling. And after the games Priam came to Achilles and ransomed the body of Hector, and buried it.*

**5.1** *Penthesilia, daughter of Otrere and Ares, accidentally killed Hippolyte and was purified by Priam. In battle she slew many, and amongst them Machaon, and was afterwards herself killed by Achilles, who fell in love with the Amazon after her death and slew Thersites for jeering at him.*

**5.3** *Memnon, the son of Tithonus and the Dawn, came with a great force of Ethiopians to Troy* against the Greeks, and having slain many of the Greeks, including Antilochus, he was himself slain by Achilles. Having chased the Trojans also, Achilles was shot with an arrow in the ankle by Alexander and Apollo at the Scaean gate.

**5.4** A fight taking place for the corpse, Ajax killed Glaucus, and gave the arms to be conveyed to the ships, but the body he carried, in a shower of darts, through the midst of the enemy, while Ulysses fought his assailants.

**5.5** The death of Achilles filled the army with dismay, and they buried him with Patroclus in the White Isle, mixing the bones of the two together. It is said that after death Achilles consorts with Medea in the Isles of the Blest. And they held games in his honour...

**5.23** And having slain the Trojans, they set fire to the city and divided the spoil among them. And having sacrificed to all the gods, they threw Astyanax from the battlements and slaughtered Polyxena on the grave of Achilles...
Apollodorus, from the *Epitome* section of the *Library*, translation by J.G. Frazer, 1921

It will also be interesting to compare Apollodorus on Achilles with the more detailed accounts that the Roman mythographer Hyginus, writing in the first century CE, provides about Achilles in his *Fabulae*:

**96** *Thetis the Nereid, when she knew that Achilles, the son she had with Peleus, would die if he went to fight Troy, commited him to King Lycomedes on the island of Skyros. He protected him among his maiden daughters in women's clothes with a false name, for the girls called him Pyrrha, since his hair was light, and in Greek reddishness is said to be flame-coloured [pyrros]. When the Achaeans discovered that he was hidden there, they sent spokesmen to King Lycomedes to beg that he be sent to help the Danaans. The King denied that he was there, but gave them permission to search the palace. When they couldn't discover which one he was, Ulysses put women's trinkets in the fore-court of the palace, and among them a shield and a spear. He asked the trumpeter to blow the trumpet all of a sudden, and called for clash of arms and shouting. Achilles, thinking the enemy was at hand, stripped off his women's garb and seized shield and spear. In this way he was recognized and promised to the Argives his aid and his soldiers, the Myrmidons.*

**101** *Telephus, son of Hercules and Auge, is said to have been wounded by Achilles in battle with the spear of Chiron. When for days he suffered* *cruel torture from the wound, he sought oracular advice from Apollo for a remedy. The answer came that no one could heal him except the very spear that wounded him. When Telephus heard this, he went to King Agamemnon, and by Clytemnestra's advice snatched the infant Orestes from his cradle, threatening to kill him if the Achaeans did not heal him. Then since the Achaeans had been given an oracle too, that Troy could not be taken without the leadership of Telephus, they readily made peace with him, and begged Achilles to heal him. Achilles replied that he didn't know the art of healing. Then Ulysses said: 'Apollo does not mean you, but calls the spear the inflictor of the wound.' When they scraped it, he was healed. When they begged him to go with them to attack Troy, they did not obtain their request, because he had as wife Laodice, daughter of Priam. But in return for their kindness in healing him, he led them there, pointing out places and paths. From there he departed to Moesia.*

**107** *After Hector's burial, when Achilles was wandering along the ramparts of the Trojans and saying that he alone had reduced Troy, Apollo in anger, taking the form of Alexander Paris, struck him with an arrow on the ankle which was said to be vulnerable and killed him. When Achilles was killed and given burial, Telamonian Ajax demanded from*

*the Danaans the arms of Achilles, on the grounds that he was cousin on his father's side. Through the anger of Minerva they were denied him by Agamemnon and Menelaus, and given to Ulysses. Ajax, harbouring rage, in madness slaughtered his flocks, and killed himself with that sword he had received from Hector as a gift when the two met in battle line.*
Hyginus, Fabulae

## Ancient Art

Ancient images of Achilles presented the broader range of the hero's biography, not just episodes of the *Iliad*. Though early artists might have been inspired by performances of Homer and the Cycle, later ones would over time have been influenced by other literary genres. Nevertheless, they often continued conventional topics and followed the arrangement as established by earlier artists. Images of warriors were common by the Archaic Age, but more realistic iconography that clearly visualized Trojan War material first developed in the seventh century BCE. Such images often included inscriptions that indicated characters or topic. I will highlight some common topics relevant to Achilles in the story of the Trojan War.

The extraordinary Francois Vase of the early sixth century BCE serves as a type of encyclopedia of myth, with Achilles one major theme. Rectangular scenes of this large vase provided wide and detailed imagery. A prominent band features the wedding of Peleus and Thetis, attended by gods. Peleus stands and Thetis sits as their high-profile guests arrive. Chiron, instrumental in helping Peleus capture Thetis, and later to be a mentor of their child Achilles, leads the divinities. Another frieze shows the ambush of Troilus. The wide screen of the image allows us to perceive the sequence of events. Achilles ambushes Troilus by a fountain outside Troy, abetted by Athena and Hermes. In the middle we see Achilles (or at least his leg) on what remains of the vase; he is chasing Troilus on a horse. Troilus's sister Polyxena is seen running ahead of Troilus. On the far right we see Hector and other Trojans, leaving Troy to help. The alarmed Priam is shown sitting on a chair.

A band below shows a chariot race during the funeral games for Patroclus. Greek spectators excitedly observe the finish of the race. Achilles stands by a tripod, apparently one of the prizes. Both Diomedes and Odysseus are named among the racers. The race does not exactly match the *Iliad*'s account, reminding us that though Homer provided inspiration, artists could – and did – employ other sources, including earlier artwork. Finally, both handles show Ajax impressively carrying the corpse of Achilles. The work as a whole seems like a range of snapshots from Achilles' life. There are also scenes of other myths, one featuring Theseus and another a battle with centaurs (Chiron was unique as a 'good' centaur). The frieze depicting the Calydonian boar hunt is of interest to readers of the *Iliad*, as Phoenix narrates it to Achilles in the embassy episode.

Artists were fond of many other scenes in the life of Achilles. I will survey these motifs in the chronology of their narrative order, with an emphasis on early vase images. One motif was the story of Thetis (or Peleus) hiding Achilles, disguised as a girl, in Skyros. Above I argued that Skyros at least was intertwined with the stories of Achilles and Neoptolemus as early as Homer and the Epic Cycle. However, surviving images of the disguise motif are only known in the fifth and fourth centuries BCE, as reported by later accounts. The scene would become very popular throughout the Imperial Age, especially in visual cycles of Achilles' biography. Some early classical-period images depict Achilles departing for the war as Peleus and Thetis watch. Scenes depicting the popular topic of Thetis and her fellow Nereids delivering divine armour to Achilles are probably set at his home in Thessaly, rather than Troy; after all, the hero required a set of armour at the start of the war. The Homeric description of the shield of Achilles is a tour de force, but it may have been invented by Homer to include the episode within the limited temporal scope of the *Iliad*.

One singular scene depicts Achilles bandaging a wounded Patroclus, apparently in the early years of the war. This seems to confirm the *Iliad*'s hints that Achilles received medical training from Chiron. The taking of Briseis from Achilles' camp is not common in ancient art, but such images typically depict Achilles seated sadly alone. One classical-period vase depicts Agamemnon personally taking Briseis in the presence of Ajax, Odysseus and Phoenix. This is conflation of the embassy scene with the earlier seizure of

Briseis, an interpretation that should be considered brilliant artistic narratology, not a mistake. Other images from the Classical Age do portray the embassy scene with a traditional mourning Achilles.

There are also artistic renderings of Homeric battles. An early vase depicts Menelaus and Paris in their duel in Book 3 on one side, with Ajax and Hector duelling in Book 7 (a popular image) on the other side. Aphrodite is depicted in the first scene (she rescues the failing Paris in Homer) and Athena is pictured on the other. Thetis and Eos, the mothers of Achilles and Memnon, were commonly depicted in scenes of their duel and its aftermath.

The duel between Diomedes and Aeneas was also a very popular feature of early Greek art. In the middle of the *Iliad* there is a unique episode of Odysseus and Diomedes on a night mission into Trojan territory (Book 10). They come across a Trojan spy, Dolon, who offers information in exchange for his life, though Odysseus eventually kills him. The scene appears on late Archaic and classical-period vases, though Dolon's death first appears on vases of the fourth century BCE from Greek colonial areas of Italy.

The *Iliad*'s plot comes to the fore in depictions of Patroclus vanquishing Sarpedon (a famous vase painting by Euphronios magnificently depicts divine Sleep and Death lifting his huge corpse as Hermes looks on). Another Homeric vase from the Archaic Age depicts Menelaos and Hector duelling over the corpse of Euphorbos, who according to Homer tried to remove Achilles' armour from Patroclus before being slain himself.

The battle over Patroclus remained popular throughout the Archaic Age.

Other Homeric scenes continue in the Archaic Age: a grieving Achilles, often with Thetis, who often is with Nereids carrying his new armour. Some classical-period scenes show Thetis with Hephaestus, who makes the divine armour in Book 18. Images of Hector are, of course, found often in ancient art. A few show him leaving for battle, and more show his duel with Achilles in the later Archaic Age and early Classical period. The terrible dragging of Hector by Achilles was also a popular feature of late Archaic Age vases, sometimes with the tomb of Patroclus also visible. This scene leads naturally to images of Priam and Achilles. Their encounter is displayed on bronze reliefs on shield bands dating from the sixth century BCE, as well on late Archaic and early classical vases, though these depict a reclining Achilles with the corpse of Hector below him as Priam approaches. A later relief from the Classical period, perhaps based on the *Phrygians* by Aeschylus, depicts Priam filling scales with gold to match the weight of Hector's corpse.

Cyclic material follows. Amazonomachies ('Amazon battles') were popular in early Greek art. Inscriptions indicate that some show the encounter between Penthsileia and Achilles, on vases and shield bands, in the Archaic and Classical periods. A famous sixth-century BCE vase by Exekias has Achilles seemingly locking eyes with Penthsileia as he kills her, a scene sometimes interpreted as erotic (recall Thersites mockingly claiming Achilles loved the Amazon in the Cyclic *Aethiopis*). The erotic element is certainly indicated more strongly in later vases from south Italy. The duel between Achilles and Memnon was also popular on vases, some of which depict Hermes weighing their souls (cf. the lost *Psychostasia* by Aeschylus mentioned above). Thetis and Eos are often present in such scenes, popular in the Archaic and Classical periods and often appearing on media such as public architecture. An image from the early fifth century BCE by Douris famously shows the winged Eos lifting the body of her son off the ground.

The death of Achilles is not as common. However, I discussed above a now-lost vase that features an arrow wound near Achilles' ankle. Other vases with archers and fighters may or may not be relevant; without inscriptions it is impossible to tell. However, images of a warrior carrying another warrior on his shoulders are popular from the eighth century BCE up to the end of the Archaic Age. Even without inscriptions, it is tempting to see them as Ajax with the corpse of Achilles, as on the Francois Vase. Vases from the sixth century BCE also depict the ensuing quarrel over the inheritance of Achilles' arms by Ajax and Odysseus. Polyxena was present in many depictions of the scene of the hero ambushing and killing her brother Troilus. There was certainly some indication of Achilles' attraction to Polyxena by the Roman Imperial period, and the concept increased in popularity during the medieval period. However, I do not think this theme explains her presence in the Troilus scenes (which sometimes suggest Achilles' pederastic interest in Troilus). I prefer to think that the Troilus and Achilles images sometimes include Polyxena as an allusion to his later demand for her sacrifice.

Certainly ancient artists would be aware of the full scope of Achilles' Cyclic biography and would not focus on single episodes in isolation. Perhaps the anger the hero directed towards Troilus was also turned to Polyxena. We know, again from Proclus, that in another of the lost epics of the Trojan cycle, the *Sack of Troy*, Polyxena was sacrificed at the tomb of Achilles after the fall of Troy. A particularly brutal depiction of the event appears on an Attic vase of the mid-sixth century BCE; it shows the moment when Neoptolemus, the son of Achilles, cuts her throat. Later painters chose to show her being led to the tomb, and Pausanias tells us that it was the subject of a wall-painting in Athens.

One artistic motif for which we have no narrative is a scene where Achilles and Ajax play a board game; Athena is shown moving towards the pair in alarm, perhaps to tell them about a Trojan attack. Though we do not know the context, such images serve to suggest the collegial relationship between the two. It is Ajax in the embassy who most effectively asks Achilles to return, and it is he who is credited (usually) with rescuing the hero's corpse from the battlefield. Ajax is devastated when Odysseus wins the arms of Achilles, which apparently sink to the bottom of the sea, along with Odysseus's ship, on his return (Book 12 of the *Odyssey*). The *Cypria*, however, claims Odysseus gave Neoptolemus his father's arms. But in a pleasing late story told by Pausanias and others, Achilles' armour eventually washed ashore by Ajax's tomb near Troy. The shade of Ajax also is present alongside Achilles' friends Patroclus and Antilochus in the *Odyssey*'s underworld – an indication that his compatibility with Achilles extended to the realm of the dead.

## Cult of Achilles

Greeks from the Archaic Age on engaged in the cult worship of heroes. Tombs and places associated with heroes were visited and offerings were provided. Achilles was the recipient of cult worship at his tomb in Troy and especially in the Black Sea area. Achilles' Trojan tomb (believed by some to be located at the Sigeion Cape) was reportedly visited by Alexander the Great and many Roman emperors. In myth, however, Thetis brought Achilles to the island of Leuke, an alternative to a heroic afterlife at the Isles of the Blessed or Elysium. Leuke became localized in the Black Sea at Zmiinyi Island ('Snake Island'), recently prominent again in the Russian war against Ukraine. Material culture and inscriptions attest to cult activity at Leuke and in the vicinity of the Milesian colony Olbia in the sixth century BCE. As noted above, Alcaeus calls Achilles 'Lord of Scythia', and the hero was addressed as 'Pontarches' ('Lord of the Black Sea') in Olbia during the Roman Imperial period. Worship of Achilles was also practised at other locations in the Greek Mediterranean world. The theme of the hero in love was applied even to his life after death: he was variously said to be joined by Helen, Medea, Polyxena and Iphigenia.

Cult of heroes of the Trojan War such as Achilles are present in the third-century CE *Heroicus* by Philostratus. This long prose account features conversation between a Phoenician traveller and a man who tends the tomb of Protesilaus in Thrace near

Troy. Provided information by the shade of Protesilaus, the local regales his visitor with tales of the conflict. As with other Imperial narratives, the stories often counter Homer. A major section focuses on Achilles, describing his appearance, nature and cultic life on Leuke. Included is an account of Achilles' death at a sanctuary outside of Troy, where the hero came to negotiate marriage to Polyxena – a story that became popular in later antiquity and beyond.

# 2.
# Achilles in Post-Antiquity

*When the anniversary of Hector's burial came, Priam, Hecuba, Polyxena, and other Trojans went to his tomb. Coming across them, Achilles noticed Polyxena, was transfixed, and began to love her intensely. Driven by his ardor, he began to spend all his time miserably in love.*
– Dares the Phrygian, History of the Fall of Troy

In this section I trace cultural representations of Achilles after antiquity. At first we discuss two prose works of later antiquity that purported to be autobiographical versions of the Trojan War (possibly dating from the fifth century CE, but founded on earlier Greek versions that are now lost). The authors identified themselves as a Trojan Dares and a Greek Dictys. Both works are patently fake to our modern eyes, but they were taken seriously in the medieval period – perhaps in continuation of the perverse and paradoxical trend to counter Homer in later antiquity. Dares in particular became influential on medieval poetry, notably for the story of Troilus and Cressida. In the Renaissance, when Homer began to be read in Greek once again, there was a revival in the study of Homer and the *Iliad* and *Odyssey*. The romance of Troilus and Cressida continued its hold on literature, however, as shown below in an exploration of Shakespeare's *Troilus and Cressida*, composed long after medieval times.

## MEDIEVAL ACHILLES

In post-antiquity Achilles rarely becomes the central figure of any work. Where he does feature it is usually as a student of Chiron or a lover, rather than as a warrior. The allegorist Fulgentius of late antiquity employed the 'Achilles' heel' motif to link the hero with the theme of lust. He claims that the heel is connected to sex organs, and he describes Achilles being sent to Skyros 'as if to the kingdom of lust.' Furthermore, Achilles dies from his love for Polyxena, which is his real 'Achilles' heel'. Boccaccio's section on Achilles in his *Genealogy of the Pagan Gods* refers to Fulgentius's interpretation, while in the late medieval period Dante places Achilles in the second circle of Hell in the *Divine Comedy*, in which he is perceived as a victim of lust, along with Helen and Paris.

When knowledge of Greek in Western Europe became lost, the account of the Trojan War by Dares was employed in an influential French version of the Trojan War by Benoît de Sainte-Maure. Dating from the twelfth century CE, this work claimed that Dares was more accurate about the war than Homer. Benoît's version was the basis of a Latin version by Guido delle Collonne, which in turn inspired other similar accounts in modern languages. Under Dares's influence, a number of Trojan War themes became popular in the medieval period. These include the promotion of Troilus to a prominent warrior and a romance between Polyxena and Achilles.

Troilus is mentioned only briefly in Homer as a son of Priam, though Achilles' ambush of Troilus (which may have had erotic implications) became a popular theme in art and literature, as discussed above. Although not a Homeric character, Polyxena is often present in images of the ambush of her brother Troilus by Achilles. We have also seen above that the shade of Achilles later demanded her sacrifice over his tomb in non-Homeric literature and art. Achilles' request was eventually explained as a result of his anger at being ambushed by Paris after he arranged to meet Polyxena. This story already featured in the mythographical work by the Latin author Hyginus in the first century CE, and the prose *Heroicus* by Philostratus, written in the third century CE.

Benoît himself is responsible for a further story about Troilus: his romance with Briseis, whose name became conflated with that of Chryseis, the concubine of Agamemnon. As 'Cressida' she also has a romance with Troilus, but then becomes enamoured of Diomedes after arriving in the Greek camp with her defecting father. In the medieval period and into the Renaissance the revised story of Troilus and Cressida remained popular. The tale was told by Boccaccio, Chaucer, Caxton and, most famously, by Shakespeare. Employing essentially the same plotline used by Chaucer, Shakespeare situates the story within the Homeric story of Achilles' withdrawal from battle and subsequent return after the death of Patroclus. Shakespeare may have known the *Iliad*'s story through George Chapman's translation. Troilus and Cressida begin a sexual relationship with the help of Cressida's uncle Pandarus, but she is then sent to the Greek camp, to which her father had previously defected.

Troilus sneaks out of Troy to find her, but in the meantime Cressida has become enamoured of Diomedes, leaving the devastated Troilus to return alone to Troy. Achilles then defeats Hector, but only after being bested by him and having to resort to trickery. It is Achilles' men, not the hero, who actually kill Hector, though Achilles takes the credit. Troilus wants to take revenge, but the play ends with no reversal of its dominant tone, that of unheroic behaviour and unfaithful love. Achilles contributes to the tone by having a sexual relationship with Patroclus while engaged with an affair with a Trojan woman, probably Polyxena. Outside of Troilus's story, however, Achilles is not featured in any major work in the medieval period. The theme of love not war seems to be associated with the hero in the Renaissance as well.

# 3.
# Modern Reception of Achilles

*For I, united with my friend Patroclus, will be honoured
by an impressive mound raised on the heights by the sea, a
monument for people of future ages.*
– Johann Wolfgang von Goethe, *Achilleis*

n classical studies the term 'reception' refers to creative retelling of ancient literature. In this section I will highlight notable modern portrayals of the Homeric and Cyclic Achilles. Achilles is the dominant character in the *Iliad*, but he is featured in just a few episodes in the long Trojan War. He is thus just one of many famous heroes in the ancient world and the medieval period. It is my impression that he is more central to modern conceptions of the Trojan War, perhaps because of the renewal of interest in the *Iliad*. As in antiquity, however, Achilles in the modern world receives a mixed reception. Those influenced by Homer's complex characterization of the hero might emphasize either the violent or thoughtful sides of his personality.

Much also depends on historical contexts; the American Civil War and the two World Wars seem to have inspired negative takes on the hero, while the Vietnam War seems to have fostered admiration of his resistance to authority and questioning of the war's purpose. The Cyclic episodes of Achilles also present a wider range of images, from the child trained by Chiron and Achilles' youthful love affair with Deidameia to the warrior involved in the sacking of towns, the enslaving of their women and the killing of many opponents. As occurred in the Hellenistic and Roman eras, many modern works focus rather upon the hero's various and intense personal relationships – with Deidameia, Helen, Briseis, Patroclus, Troilus, Polyxena and Penthsileia, among others. Below I discuss some responses to the ancient Achilles in the modern world, organized into three categories: poetry, prose and visual.

## POETRY

The dearth of modern epics compared to ancient ones makes it convenient to include epic in the category of 'poetry'. Johann Wolfgang von Goethe started an epic in the late eighteenth century, but he did not finish it. The plan was to focus on Achilles' love of Polyxena in eight cantos. The poem began with the funeral of Hector at the end of the *Iliad* and Achilles' thoughts of his own death. The gods are then portrayed discussing Achilles and his fate. Informed by contemporary travellers' reports of the heroic tumuli at Troy, Goethe also gives much attention to preparing Patroclus's tomb to receive his ashes as well. Athena approaches Achilles disguised as Antilochus; she joins him at the tomb and urges him think of his eternal fame. The plot intended to turn the hero's thoughts to Polyxena, encountered when she is a hostage among the Greeks.

The modern Greek poet C.P. Cavafy composed much memorable verse on Homeric themes. His 'The Horse of Achilles' evokes the Homeric scene of Achilles' horses mourning the end of Patroclus: 'The horses of Achilles began to weep; / their mortal nature was upset deeply / by this work of death they had to look at' (translation by E. Keeley and P. Sherrard). Michael Longley, who often employs Homeric themes, evokes the same scene in the poem 'The Horses': 'Immovable as a tombstone, their heads drooping / In front of the streamlined motionless chariot, / Hot tears spilling from their eyelids onto the ground...' In Homer, one of these horses later predicts the death of Achilles, much to the hero's annoyance.

Achilles readily serves verse about war. In 1915 the classically trained Patrick Shaw-Stewart wrote a famous poem about Achilles before the battle of Gallipoli. Entitled 'Stand in the Trench, Achilles', the poem is all the more haunting because Shaw-Stewart was later killed in the war. The ending is justly famous: 'Stand in the trench, Achilles, Flame-capped, and shout for me.' W.H. Auden's 'The Shield of Achilles' (1952) provides a grim contemplation of the bleak world of war and totalitarianism following the Second World War. Whereas Homer's description of the divine shield of Achilles portrays both martial and peaceful scenes, Auden describes a bleak and downtrodden world ('That girls are raped, that two boys knife a third...').

The poet Louise Gluck, recently deceased, masterfully provided modern verse on Homeric themes. 'The Triumph of Achilles' also provides a bleak meditation on death and friendship ('... Achilles / grieved with his whole being / and the gods saw / he was a man already dead...'). The magnificent book-length poem by Alice Oswald, *Memorial*, ignores the basic plot of the *Iliad* and instead remodels scenes of death in the epic, notably Homer's touching mini-obituaries of minor characters, their names capitalized as if on a gravestone, juxtaposed to Homeric-based similes. Achilles is rarely mentioned, but the scene of his slaughter of fleeing Trojans by the River Scamander is evoked thusly: 'But Achilles killed so many men / Standing downstream with his rude sword / Hacking off heads until the water / Burst out in anger lifting up a ridge of waves / That now this whole river is a grave.' The focus on death reminds one of Simone Weil's classic meditation of the effect of violence in the Homeric poem in her *The Iliad or the Poem of Force* (1939).

The epic poem *Omeros* by Derek Walcott is a masterpiece. Lyrical in metre and tone yet postmodern in plot, the poem features a protagonist much like Walcott who travels from his Caribbean home of St Lucia to America and Europe. Yet at its heart is a narrative of local fishermen on the island: Achille, Hector and Helen. The names are familiar, but the story is not Homeric. The lovers Achille and Helen break up, Helen moves in with Hector, Hector leaves fishing to become a cab driver, Helen attempts to find work and Achille continues to suffer over the loss of Helen. Eventually, we learn of Hector's death in a crash, Helen's pregnancy and her return to Achille. Besides being modernized, the plot is very different from the *Iliad*. There are also Cyclic elements, for instance a repeated theme of Achilles' heel.

# PROSE

Many creative retellings of the *Iliad* have appeared in recent decades. *Troy* by Adele Geras conveys the *Iliad*'s narrative with all the sophistication of a novel, though pitched to young adults. Elizabeth Cook's *Achilles* was composed for performance. However, it can be read as a profound and poetic novel about Achilles, with a fascinating tangent to the surprisingly relevant life of John Keats. Chiron, Helen and even Keats contribute their perspectives. A Cyclic overview of the hero's life is provided, including Peleus's rape of Thetis, Achilles' life as a girl at Skyros, the killing of Hector and the release of his corpse, the killing of Penthsileia and the Trojan ambush version of the hero's death. We also find the shade of Achilles questioning Odysseus in Hades.

Alessandro Baricco's *An Iliad*, composed for a public reading, is narrated in a series of different character voices. This overlooked work is composed of long and calm monologues addressed to us in the audience; it wonderfully allows characters to reveal themselves and their perspectives in their own words. *The Song of Achilles* by Madeline Miller tenderly tells the story of young love between Patroclus and Achilles. The hero is his usual impressive self, but Miller's uncanny ability to express the feelings of sensitive characters allows the sympathetic Patroclus to steal the show. Cyclic myth informs scenes of the two growing up under the tutelage of a nurturing Chiron before the story of the *Iliad* is summarized.

David Malouf's *Ransom* employs a common device in reception, the perspective of a minor character. Here the muleteer who drives Priam and his ransom to Achilles' hut is the narrator. The encounter between king and warrior is as moving as the Homeric passage, with the muleteer providing a commoner's perspective usually absent in the *Iliad*. In Pat Barker's *The Silence of the Girls* Briseis not only provides an effective portrayal of her lover Achilles, but also reveals her life among other concubines of Greek heroes, set against the gritty reality of the Greek camp.

*The Death of Achilles* by Boris Akunin – not to be confused with my own academic book *The Death and Afterlife of Achilles* (2009) – was given to me as a lark by my father. I found it an excellent mystery novel with a colourful detective. Though a character who is assassinated is nicknamed 'Achilles' for his fierceness, I at first saw no major parallels to ancient myth. However, the book's second half narrates the story from the perspective of the villain Achimas. This and other seemingly significant names captured my curiosity. When Achimas as a child arrives at an orphanage disguised as a girl, I realized that this gripping story was suffused with Achilles motifs.

Achilles has also received attention in psychological studies. In *Achilles in Vietnam*, Jonathan Shay sees Achilles as a mythological exemplar of post-traumatic stress disorder among war veterans. The anger of Achilles, not only directed at Agamemnon and Hector but also experienced on the battlefield in berserker mode, is described as a common reaction to war conditions. W. Thomas MacCary's *Childlike Achilles* (1982) portrays Achilles as immaturely narcissistic, while Richard Holway's *Becoming Achilles* (2012) employs attachment theory to explore Achilles' dysfunctional infancy and upbringing.

## VISUAL

Renaissance art in a time of lingering ignorance of the *Iliad* featured standard scenes of Achilles with Chiron and at Skyros, apparently interpreted as exemplifying aristocratic cultural values. Rubens, for example, produced a cycle of the life of Achilles in wall tapestries, with titles identifying the stories shown: the dipping of the infant in the Styx, his education by Chiron, the recognition of Achilles at Skyros and other Homeric scenes. Neoclassical art employed Achilles as a topic in such works as Jacques-Louis David's 'The Anger of Achilles' (in which Achilles' hand is on the hilt of his sword as Agamemnon leads Iphigenia away to be sacrificed), Giovanni Battista Cipriani's 'The Education of Achilles' (Chiron training Achilles in throwing a spear) and Gavin Hamilton's 'Achilles Lamenting the Death of Patroclus'. The large-scale statue of the dying Achilles in Corfu at the Achilleion, built by the Empress Elisabeth of Austria in the late nineteenth century, is impressive in both size and drama.

Neoclassical painting provided images with greater clarity, for example in the image of the funeral of Patroclus by David and the embassy received by Achilles by Ingres. The late eighteenth-century illustrations for the *Iliad* by John Flaxman sensitively portray characters' emotions in clean and simple lines. Examples from nineteenth-century art include Delacroix's ceiling painting of Achilles wildly riding Chiron in a hunt. Honore Daumier satirically challenged the heroic world with images of Thetis 'baptizing' a squalling baby Achilles in an unimpressive Styx, the sickly Chiron showing the ABCs to a weak-looking Achilles, and Agamemnon angrily pointing at Achilles withdrawn from the battle and now casually fishing. As in literature, art takes a darker turn in the war-riven twentieth century, in which Achilles is often portrayed as wounded or battered.

The story of Troy has a long history in cinema. As explained in the research of Pantelis Michelakis, the story of Troy was the subject of silent film as early as 1902 (*Le jugement de Paris* [*the Judgment of Paris*]). In 1924 another film, three hours in length, thoroughly covered the story of Helen. Also memorable is *Helen of Troy*, directed by Robert Wise in 1956. The poem narrates the Trojan War with some non-traditional aspects. Paris meets Helen when she rescues him after a shipwreck, after which the pair fall in love. Menelaus plans to kill Paris, so he flees with Helen. Realistic aspects such as the unhappy marriage of Menelaus and Helen, her cool reception at Troy and the greed that motivates the Greek attack are effectively surrounded by big-screen effects, among them the Trojan Horse.

The most famous film featuring Achilles is the blockbuster *Troy*, directed by Wolfgang Petersen and featuring Brad Pitt. *Troy* claims to be inspired by the *Iliad*, but it has the scope of the hero's Cyclic biography. Pre-war scenes not only explain the elopement of Paris and Helen, but also portray Achilles as a spectacular warrior (he may be short, but he can jump high!) in Agamemnon's mainland army. Five days of the war follow (the quarrel between Agamemnon and Achilles; duels between Menelaus and Paris, Hector and Ajax; the embassy to Achilles and the death of Patroclus; and the death of Hector and the subsequent ransom of his body). Several days of truce follow before the sack of Troy follows. Besides key episodes of the *Iliad*, such as the meeting between Priam and Achilles, well-known Cyclic episodes are included. The motif of Achilles' heel is suggested by a bird's-eye view of the dying Achilles pulling out arrows from his body, except for one by his ankle. Many details are non-Homeric (Achilles is alive to help in the sack, for example) and the film avoids depicting his mother Thetis as a supernatural deity.

Graphic novels and comics can also represent the story of Achilles and the Trojan War in a sophisticated manner. Arguably Homer constructs a visual image of Achilles' shield when in the *Iliad* 18 he employs words that allow us to imagine a sequence of scenes. We are told that the River Oceanus surrounds the rim of the shield, as it does the earth in Greek myth. In the very centre are stars, the moon and the sun. A central polarity imagines a city in peace and a city at war. The seasons are then suggested by description of ploughing, reaping and the gathering of ripe grapes. Finally, a circular dance surrounds the various word-pictures of human life.

The edited volume *Classics and Comics* provides different perspectives on the influence of classics on popular visual comics. Notably epic is the continuing series on the Trojan War by cartoonist Eric Shanower, a project entitled *Age of Bronze: The Story of the Trojan War*. Shanower wittily contributes to *Classics and Comics* with a comic in which his self-portrait explains the project. *Classics Illustrated* is an American comic book series dating from the mid-twentieth century. It retells classic literary works in comic form, seeking to attract young people towards serious literature. The Homeric poems were featured in two issues, something that I find charmingly old-fashioned. Marvel Comics have produced more colourful and sophisticated versions of both the *Iliad* and the *Odyssey*. In some ways these are rather over the top, however, featuring a range of buxom, scantily clad women and monsters in a sci-fi style.

# 4.
# Themes in the Story of Achilles

*Hecuba, sad because her two very brave sons Hector and Troilus had been killed by Achilles, devised a reckless plan in a feminine manner to avenge her grief. She summoned her son Alexander and urgently asked him, in order to avenge himself and his two brothers, to ambush Achilles unawares.*
– Dares the Phrygian, *The Fall of Troy: A History*

e have covered a lot of ground exploring the rich and varied myths that surround Achilles. The character dominates Homer's *Iliad*, appears in the underworld in the *Odyssey* and is a major character in the Epic Cycle, though he dies before the fall of Troy itself. His birth, the result of a union between a mortal and a goddess, not only explains Achilles' extraordinary skills, especially in war, but also suggests his complex character. The most subtle and thorough character study of the hero is by Homer.

On the one hand, in the *Iliad* Achilles betrays his fellow soldiers in a dispute over a slave concubine; many Greeks die as a result, notably his closest friend Patroclus. He is not just vengeful in killing Hector, but he outrageously disrespects his corpse, violating all heroic norms. On the other hand, Homer often shows a more positive side of Achilles. Though furious with Agamemnon in Book 1, he articulates his complaints about the leader's bad behaviour effectively. Politely hearing out Odysseus, Phoenix and Ajax in the embassy scene, he replies with speeches that are magnificently emotional yet also philosophical. He also gives good evidence of his fondness for his mentor Phoenix and his respect for Ajax. When he is later upbraided for his stubbornness by Patroclus, his closest friend, he listens and readily agrees to end his wrath. By allowing Patroclus to fight in his stead, however, he tragically sets in motion a chain of fatal events.

Achilles' grief and guilt over his friend's death consumes the hero. He has trouble eating and sleeping, but nonetheless becomes a killing machine on the battlefield. Yet in the final major scene of the epic Achilles receives Priam, the father of Hector and the king of the Greeks' enemy, with politeness and respect. Their conversation is profound and sincere, and the hero is able to come to an understanding with his enemy despite his raw grief and lingering anger towards Hector. On this occasion he does respect the cultural conventions of the Homeric world, by returning the corpse and ensuring that there will be peace long enough for the funeral of his arch enemy to take place.

Portrayals of Achilles in other poetry and in other media are not as subtle, with Achilles sometimes portrayed as a hothead or a misfit. The lost Epic Cycle, which was based on traditional myth and served as a template for Achilles stories down through time, characterized Achilles as a powerful warrior.

Even before the Greeks arrive in Troy, he wounds Telephus and kills Cycnus in the *Cypria* (see Proclus); other sources report additional killings. Once at Troy he sacks many towns in the Troad, slaying untold numbers (including the husband of Briseis) if no famous heroes. Besides Hector, he mows down scores of Trojans after returning to battle. His post-*Iliad* career includes killing the powerful Memnon, another son of a goddess, and Penthesileia, the exotic queen of the Amazons. Nonetheless, he is himself slain by an arrow from a bow wielded by Paris, a far inferior warrior who is aided by Apollo. Sometimes Achilles is portrayed dying at the gates of Troy, on the verge of breaking into the city. It would certainly be logical for the Greeks' most powerful fighter to bring about the fall of Troy, but Greek myth loved perversity. Just as the weakest Trojan warrior kills the mighty Achilles, it is the most wily Greek, Odysseus, who brings about the sack of Troy by means of a trick: the Trojan Horse itself.

In myth about Achilles, his death is not just bad luck; it is specifically fated. This explains Thetis's pathological fear about his mortality. The theme produces alternative 'Achilles' heel' stories in which she tests the mortality of her children with boiling water or seeks to burn their mortality off. This theme of fated mortality also leads to the tale of Achilles being disguised as a girl at Skyros. Such strategies are bound to fail – a spot by the ankle is not invulnerable; the trickster Odysseus uncovers the deceit. Thetis remains confused by the mortal realm into which she has been forced by Peleus, with the help of Chiron and the connivance of Zeus. Homer explores

Thetis's bewilderment and discomfort with the mortality of her son. The poet does this using his most effective method: showing us the nature of characters by their words and actions, rather than telling us as an omniscient narrator what makes them tick. Achilles knows well that he is destined to die – yet, despite a half-hearted threat to return home, he pushes forward towards death, clearly attracted to the consolation prize of *kleos*, or 'fame'.

Finally, there is the enduring theme of love. It is difficult to compile a full list, and individual sources provide different stories. However, above we have identified Deidameia, Iphigenia, Helen, Briseis, Patroclus, Penthesileia, and Troilus as objects of his sexual interest. We do not know that Homer, or even the Cycle, knew of the hiding of Achilles at Skyros, but early epics clearly indicated that Neoptolemus at Skyros was the child of Achilles and Deidameia. The story of the sacrifice of Iphigenia is not Homeric; later versions narrated her marriage to Achilles as a ruse to entice her to be sacrificed. Nonetheless, we have seen portrayals of Achilles pleased with the idea of marriage to her. There is also the unexplained request of Achilles to see Helen when he arrives at Troy, which some perceive as a sexual encounter.

In the *Iliad*, Briseis is his love interest. Or is it simply a sexual relationship, of the type that Achilles has with other slave women? Achilles speaks of her to the embassy as being equal to a wife, and Briseis reports that Patroclus spoke of their wedding, but Achilles' strong emotions often peter out. In Homer, Achilles has an intense relationship with Patroclus but not a sexual one. Yet there should be no problem with labelling this as love, and later tellers of the Troy tale did portray the two as lovers (for example Aeschylus, Shakespeare, and Madeline Miller). As for Polyxena, I rather doubt that this character, who does not appear in Homer, was a love interest at any early point in time; her brother Troilus is a better candidate, at least on the evidence of iconography. Though Thersites mocked Achilles for being in love with Penthesileia in the *Aethiopis*, this libellous chatterer is not a good authority on the matter. Nonetheless, some vase paintings suggest the idea occurred to some. As my arguments have stressed, we can argue about what's exactly in the Homeric poems, but much is left to interpretation. We also need to allow different authors, writers and generations to portray the mythology of Achilles as they wish.

What is clear is that along with the themes of Achilles' mortality, his mother's attempts to forestall his fate, his extensive training by Chiron, his lethal skill in battle, his fated early death and his resultant *kleos*, a persistent theme of love and sex was attached to Achilles. It is so strong that the shade of Achilles at Leuke (or in alternative otherworld utopias) was variously paired with Helen, Medea, Polyxena and Iphigeneia.

# Modern Short Stories

# of Achilles

# The Second Fate
## Amber S. Benham

The stone towers glisten in my mind's eye, dust swirling around my ankles as the sun scorches my skin and the heavy armour weighs me down.

"Ultimately, it is your choice," my mother says passively, her eyes suggesting it isn't really up to me.

I am brought back to my actual environment, the waves lapping at my feet, the sun setting behind the horizon and lazily streaming across my view.

"It is hardly a choice, it's his fate," Patroclus says next to me, the tension between the two of them suffocating me as I weigh up the prophecy. His copper skin stretches over his lean figure as his hand finds my arm and rests possessively there. My mother's eyes flash at the overt display of affection, the almost black colour of her eyes temporarily turning a dark blue.

"Enough," I announce as I step away from them both. "I won't be going. If the Greeks have truly raised the greatest army then they won't need me, and I can stay here with you." I turn to face Patroclus. "And we can stay as happy as we are now." I turn back to face my mother, Thetis, whose shoulders sag in relief, her hair, which can only be described as a mess of seaweed straggling down her back, floating slightly as she jumps to hug me. I hear a grunt of disbelief and release my mother to once again face Patroclus who is staring at me indignantly.

"You have made the right choice, my dear Achilles, I shall relay this," my mother whispers in my ear and I hear the sound of a wave crashing and before I can say goodbye she has gone, leaving Patroclus and me alone.

"How could you decide to not go? You are the greatest warrior of our generation, and you want to waste your life, our life, in this remote kingdom? Die a nobody? Be forgotten and turned to dust? You could live on for eternity! You could be the greatest hero of all time!" His voice rises with each sentence as he starts to pace. I grab his shoulders to halt him and turn his body, so he is facing me, and we are mere inches apart.

"I don't want fame, I don't want to be remembered for killing and slaughtering men, for ruining countless lives. I don't want to be remembered at all, if it means I can't spend a lifetime with you. I want to stay here, laughing with you and loving you for as long as life allows me. Why would I want to waste my life surrounded by men who seek nothing but *kleos* and have no real honour when I could spend it alone with you; far away from the prying eyes of others," I say softly, and, slowly, his eyes soften. I pull him close to me and he muffles something against my chest. "What was that?"

"I love you. If this is what you want then it is what we shall do." He places a kiss on my lips. The sun's final rays dip beneath the ocean as Helios retires for the day and Patroclus and I stumble back to our palace and lose ourselves within one another as Selene's moon shines thinly through the windows. Somehow it feels final; while every setting sun is, this one feels personal and intimate as I share it gleefully with my love, but I keep seeing the flashes of the stone towers whenever I close my eyes.

I fall asleep pressed to the warm skin of Patroclus, my hair falling in waves on his chest. But as soon as I drop off I am bombarded with dreams so realistic I feel sick to my core. I see a thousand ships, the largest fleet ever congregated, lying idle in a windless bay. I see a young maiden, pretty and clearly just blossoming from childhood. I watch as if a part of the crowd as she processes amongst the gathered soldiers with her mother watching, happy tears streaming down her pinched face. I see a dark, massive figure almost eclipse the sun as she reaches a makeshift altar. I witness the flash of steel, the spurt of red, the scream of anguish, the smell of iron, as the maiden collapses in a bloody mess on the altar. I run through the crowd to help her, to understand what madness I am watching, but I can't move, I am frozen in place as the scene unfolds and I wake up screaming and dripping sweat.

"Achilles, my love, please, there is no girl, there is no blood. You are fine." I finally register Patroclus straining and screaming as his face swims into my vision.

"She's dead," I whisper. "He killed her. He killed her for a wind. She thought she was getting married. She thought she was marrying me. No one had told her I wasn't joining the war."

"Who's dead? Who killed her? Achilles, please, you are frightening me. Please tell me what you are talking about." I glance up and through tears I see Patroclus's eyebrows creased in concern and his lower lip wobbling as he tries not to cry. I explain the dream, how lifelike it was, how horrible it was. Eventually he soothes me back to sleep and I sleep in darkness, no longer bombarded by cruel dreams. Just dreams, that's all. One nightmare.

The next morning a servant runs into the atrium and, after being fed and washed, he delivers his message.

"Agamemnon, King of Men, has successfully created a wind at Aulis. The fleet is to sail tonight, and Troy will fall within the year."

My blood slows in my veins as I feel a chill creep up through my spine as if there is a shadow engulfing me.

"How?" I mean to sound calm, but it comes out forced and staccato.

"King of Phthia, I do not understand. What do you mean, 'How?'" the messenger asks, avoiding eye contact with me, but glancing up at Patroclus, standing just behind my throne with a poker face stuck firmly on.

"I mean, 'How?' How did he create a wind? He may be King of Men as you say but he is no God. How does a man create a wind? What did he do to create a wind? Make an offering to the gods?" I ask and pray my suspicions are wrong. It was just a dream. A nightmare.

"Agamemnon, King of Men, had angered the mighty goddess Artemis with his hubris, so in order to appeal to her for forgiveness he committed a sacrifice. She forgave him and the winds soared once more," he says looking strictly at a point just past my head but not at me directly. I can see the beads of sweat developing and rolling down his face, see as his hands start to shake and his gulps become deeper in between breaths. The shadow creeping up my spine moves to engulf me and I sit forward in my seat, urging my mind to still.

"And what did he sacrifice?" I ask, repressing the tremor in my voice. I feel a hand on my shoulder and almost collapse out of pure fear, thinking the shadow has become real and is here to take me away. I turn to see Patroclus's eyes looking at me, gleaming with concern as he nods his head in question to me. I nod back and regain my posture as he steps back.

"Agamemnon, King of Men, sacrificed what Artemis wanted, as told by the seers and augurs," the messenger says, his composure slipping slowly but surely from him.

"I will not ask you again. And if you fail to answer me this time you will not live to see the outcome of this war. What. Did. He. Sacrifice?" I say, anger bubbling from my chest to my head as I temporarily forget my fear out of pure frustration at the messenger's incompetence and ignorance.

Silence reigns with oppressing force in the hall. Even the cicadas outside still. The very wind itself stills to hear what the messenger says next. Just when I am about to strike the messenger with deadly force, he mutters something incoherent. "Repeat yourself with clarity," I demand, ice turning each syllable into a dagger of fear for the messenger. Instead of pulling himself up straight, he slumps so far down that he seems to be trying to compress himself into the ground.

"He sacrificed Iphigenia, his eldest daughter, under the pretence of marrying her…" he stalls slightly "of marrying her to you, your Highness." All at once the shadow engulfs me and darkness ebbs at the edge of my vision and the nightmare flashes in double speed behind my eyes and I can't hear the yelling happening and I feel myself sliding off the floor just as I hear "Agamemnon, King of Men—"

"DON'T YOU DARE CALL THAT MAN A KING!" As my vision returns, and I come back to the room it takes me a minute to realize it was me who yelled. The messenger is quaking, shaking so hard he seems ready to fall over and never rise again. The rest of the interaction goes by in a blur, and it isn't until I am alone in the hall with Patroclus that my heart rate returns to normal, and I can think coherently again.

"It isn't your fault; in fact you have nothing to do with the whole affair," Patroclus whispers behind me, his hands tight on my shoulders.

"I told you last night it would happen. And now it has. I have never had any seer abilities before, how was I to know it wasn't just a nightmare?" I mumble, unable to turn and look at him. I didn't know it was real, I didn't know anything.

That night I don't want to sleep. I sit in the atrium, alone, drinking and eating in the silence, running laps in the gymnasium, anything to keep my eyes from closing. The moon shines fully in between wisps of clouds. After the wine has warmed my cheeks and slowed my thoughts I lie on the sandy floor of the gymnasium and admire the stars. They wink in and out of existence, always coming back, as if reassuring me that all will be well. For the first time today, my thoughts aren't centred around the dream, or the reality I suppose I should say. The stars radiate a calmness which slowly makes its way down to me all the way from the heavens. Finally at peace, I stumble to bed and a foolish smile splits my face as I admire Patroclus asleep. His limbs are thrown in a careless circle around him as his chest slowly rises and falls. I climb into bed beside him, and he shifts to encompass me. I quickly fall asleep feeling protected by both the stars and my love.

Not even the stars can save me it seems. I see thousands of Greek men, some I know and some I don't, reduced to shells of themselves. Convulsing, dying and decaying all over the camp, because of some divine illness. I also see bloodshed on a mammoth scale. Both Trojan and Greek men being cut down all day, as well as civilians in neighbouring villages. The death toll steadily increases daily, as weeks and months flash by in one dream. Once again, I wake up in a cold sweat screaming and explain everything to Patroclus. This keeps happening for days, weeks and months, and slowly each messenger comes and confirms that they are not dreams, but the truth. Constant envoys come and go begging me to join the fray, with countless gifts of tripods, gold, women, blades. I refuse them all and finally stop allowing them into the atrium. I hide away and force Patroclus to sit on the throne as an interim King of sorts, as I spend all my time in the gymnasium, closing it off to anyone else.

After months of this strife, Patroclus convinces me to visit the Oracle of Delphi in order to seek her help. I travel alone, not wishing to burden him with my struggles. I make the two-day journey and find her in her adyton.

She sits upon her tripod, her eyes closed as she sways from side to side, muttering nonsense under her breath. The vapours oppress my throat and make it hard to breathe, but she seems at peace, the vapours swirling around her, making her appear obscure. I open my mouth to address her, the priests of Apollo behind me to assist in perceiving whatever she says, if she says anything at all.

Before I can announce myself she screams, a blood-curdling noise that shocks me to my core. I almost scream myself in pure terror and confusion, but she abruptly stops just as she had started. "Achilles, the King of Phthia or the Great Warrior. The saviour of the war or the reason they fail. The one who can see what happens but does nothing to stop it. What will he do what will he do what will he do what will he do what will he do what will he do…" She continues this rambling for what feels like an eternity, the words swirling around in my mind.

"Pythia, most revered Oracle, please, I have come here to ask why the dreams are happening, and how I can get them to stop. I wished for no part in this war," I say, and the words sound meek despite my usual strong presence. I curse myself for sounding so childish and desperate in front of her.

"What will he do what will he do what will he do what will he do…" she continues, her voice crescendoing until she is screaming. I glance behind to the priests for assistance, but they stare blankly ahead, barely moving. Suddenly she stops and I turn back to face her, righting my posture and looking at her as directly as I can within the vapours. I see that her auburn hair is a matted mess across her shoulders, visible beneath her red scarf draped across her head and shoulders, contrasting brightly with the golden peplos she dons. "What will he do indeed?" She pauses, stilling her body entirely.

"Son of the mighty Peleus, King of Phthia's lands, you are destined, bound to the fateful war, though your heart turns away from its conflict. Choosing to shun the fight does not sever the threads of your fortune. Still, you remain at the heart, though your spear shall not taste of the battle. Now, you are cursed to foresee all the turns of the war that approaches, helpless to change their course, like Cassandra, the voice of the future."

I feel the hopelessness I have been keeping at bay creep up, threatening to suffocate me. "But what do I do?" I ask, falling to my knees as the wind is knocked out of me as the vapours move from swirling around her to stifling my every breath.

"Nothing can halt the dreams; they are woven too deep in your slumber. Should you turn to the dense fray, then perhaps they might come to their ending. Yet is it worth to exchange your life for a moment of silence? Peace, at the cost of your breath, would you bargain your fate for that stillness?"

"No, that can't be it. Tell me more. Please, I need to make it stop," I scream, the noise barely scraping out of my throat.

"What will he do what will he do what will he do..." She returns to her swaying and muttering as I feel hands on my shoulders heaving me back; the priests. She is done with her prophecy. There is no fix. There is nothing. Nothing at all.

The two-day journey takes me four days to complete to return home, as I feel like a shell of myself, too powerless to even try. When I finally return I relay all the events of Delphi to Patroclus.

"Well maybe that's what you have to do," he says plainly. This angers me, there is nothing simple about this situation.

"What?" I say, not wishing to lash out at him.

"You join the war. We both do. We go to Troy as soon as possible and turn the tides of the war and you fulfil your fate. We shouldn't have tried to cheat it by staying here, and the dreams are your punishment." He says this softly, as if it is a simple decision. Life or death. Peace or Pain.

"You think it is that simple? We go, fight, win, return home? You know what the prophecy is! If I go, I don't return! My body dies there on that foreign soil! If I go, I become famous, famous for killing, for brutality, for exchanging my life for *kleos*. That isn't who I am! That isn't who I want to be. I have told you this countless times. I can't believe you would even suggest such a thing so innocently. And you. We do not know if you survive. You think I could bare myself even in the afterlife if you died because of me and my fate?" I yell at him.

"But it seems to be the only option!" he yells back.

"Well maybe you are just too naïve. Maybe you don't know me at all if you think I would choose that over my life here," I say coldly, turning from him and leaving the room. I regret it immediately, knowing that he is right. I must join the war. I just don't want to. I run to the sea and scream my mother's name. Like clockwork, she appears shimmering from the waves, her blue-tinted skin dripping with water and salt.

"I assume you know of Delphi, and what I must do," I say to her, tears building behind my eyes.

"My son, you do not have to do anything you do not wish to do. I told you that before and I am telling you again now. You know I wish you to not join the war, you know I don't want to witness you die young when you could live to old age in happiness," she says smoothly, reaching out to touch me but I turn from her.

"You know I can't ignore this any longer. How much pressure are you under? From Zeus? To convince me to go? Patroclus will lose his respect for me if I don't go. I might lose myself, but I can't lose you both," I whisper, the tears streaming freely down my cheeks.

"Achilles, please, I'm begging you." I turn to see her on her knees, a sight which makes me cry even more. "Don't go. You didn't ask for this, so why should you be subjected to it?" she begs.

"My mind is made up. It is time to face the facts. What must be done will happen," I say, composing myself as I leave her there on the shore to return to the palace.

I give all the orders, we are to leave tomorrow, and then I hide away in my room, but I bolt the door, so when Patroclus comes later that night, he cannot get in, despite how much he knocks and shouts. If I am to end my life, I wish to spend one final night by myself, in peace, without the burden of other people's expectations. I drift off to sleep only to be attacked with the worst dream yet.

I see myself on the battlefield, magnificent armour gilding my godlike body, the Trojan armies running in fear just from the sight of me. I charge and cut them all down, leaving a stream of blood and death in my wake. I enjoy it, I can sense it in the dream. This destruction and pain I am causing, I thrive on it. I see Patroclus, looking as handsome as Adonis in his armour, and I think that perhaps it is the right decision to join the war. I will die, but I will live on forever, and as long as I guarantee Patroclus lives on to see the end of the war, then it will all be worth it. The dream fast-forwards years, and I see myself being slighted over a slave girl, withdrawing all the Myrmidons from the war, the Trojans thriving in my absence, many of my own side suffering. I see multiple fights I have with generals, Odysseus, Diomedes, Menelaus, Agamemnon more than any other. The sense of achievement first held at the beginning of the dream slips from me as I watch myself purposefully sit out on fighting over a matter of pride. Why would it matter so much to me? If I join will I truly become so obsessive over matters of pride, honour, *kleos*? How can I change so much? I see Patroclus, his face slightly aged but no less beautiful, as he appeals to me to rejoin. I deny him. He looks so hurt. I would never hurt him. Do I come to care for him less? Impossible. It is odd, watching myself from within my own dream, my own future. I seem like a different person. I look at him; swift-footed Achilles they will call me, and I hate him.

I see the disinterest cross my face as I allow Patroclus to wear my armour just in order to scare the Trojans and give the Greeks a boost. I tell him firmly to not enter the fray. The dream fast forwards again, and I am at a loss for words. I wake up, not screaming, not sweating, but perfectly still.

I calmly move to where the servants and Myrmidons are prepping, and I tell them that we are not going. Despite everyone's disputes I tell them that anyone who disobeys and travels to Troy will be killed. The matter-of-fact nature with which I deliver this silences any objections. I find Patroclus asleep in a guest room, and I climb into his bed. He sleepily rises and looks at me, lost in his confusion.

"We aren't going. I have cancelled all preparations. I will not have any objections from you, and I will not have anyone else, mortal or divine, even so much as suggest that I am to go to Troy. You are to stay here with me, where we will live happily until we are old, and this is quite simply the last I want to hear of it," I say to him. He looks so shocked I am unsure if I have broken him. I sigh, knowing he will never let this go without further information. "You die. I become a horrible, twisted version of myself. We lose sense of who we really are. After multiple hubristic acts on my behalf, you enter the war costumed as me and are killed by Hector. I saw it all. I saw your body—" I choke on the word and finally, after keeping it all in, break down. I tell him everything, the whole dream, barely getting words out in between sobs. Once I am done, he says nothing, just holds me. Eventually he says, "OK." And that is the end of it. We never discuss joining the war again.

## EPILOGUE

I sense a thrill enter the shades around me, and I wander towards the epicentre of excitement, pushing my way past through the other dead. Finally, I see a strong pale light emitting from a shade in the midst of the crowd, only to realize upon closer inspection that it is not a shade, but a living mortal. Furthermore, it is not any old mortal, but one I know, one who spots me in the crowd and calls to me, allowing all the other shades to dissipate around me and leave me standing before him, all alone.

"Achilles, King of Phthia, it was Phthia, correct? I am cursed it would seem, as I have yet to touch the land of my home, instead I have been journeying across the world, and I am here to seek help from Teiresias, the blind seer. I am unlucky, while you are the luckiest man who ever lived! You deflected from fighting in the war, and although we all suffered because of it you thrived in your remote existence. I fear maybe my life would have been more enjoyable if my display of madness had been believed and I too could have avoided joining the war." His words are laced with venom, and while on the surface they seem complimentary, it is clear that he resents me, hates me even, for not joining the war. Maybe born from jealousy, maybe from contempt, his pathetic display of his own sufferings in an attempt to belittle me infuriates me.

"Resourceful Odysseus, do not attempt to reconcile me with my choices, perhaps you should focus more on your own. How much blood is on your hands? What is it like to know you missed your only child growing up, are you even aware of the state of your *oikos*? Perhaps you think I regret my decisions, and that I wish I had joined the battle, saved you all, gone down in eternal history in exchange for my life. Maybe you have even convinced yourself through that twisted kaleidoscope of a mind you have that you did the right thing by going to Troy, sacrificing your life in order to save your reputation. Allow me to tell you something one only learns after their death, which I promise you will learn soon, but too late all the same. Once you die, you are gone. Perhaps you will be immortalized by the bards, but do you think immortality and life are the same? Who is to know whether or not in a million years people will hear of your story and focus on your longevity, your successes, rather than your sliminess, your infidelity, your fickle nature and selfishness? I may be forgotten, or perhaps even remembered as a coward, but I am glad that I lived, and what do I care for people's opinions I have never and will never meet? I died with the knowledge that those I loved, loved me in return. Can you honestly say the same? Now go back to the living, I wish to enjoy this eternity in peace until you come here in death, and when you do, do not seek me out as I have nothing left to say to you." I spit the last words at him and watch as his mortal flesh burns red and blotchy with rage, and I see the flash in his eyes and the twitch in his neck as he pushes it down to laugh heartily. If nothing else, he will perform. He starts to respond but I simply walk away, back to the shades, I seek out Patroclus, whom I lost in the business. He smiles at me, a proud look. It is hard to emote sometimes or read emotions on shades, but with him, everything is easy to me, it always has been and always will be. We stroll back to our eternity, our souls intertwined forever, surrounded by our love even after death. Why would I swap this for anything else?

# The Achilles Wheel
## Hammond Diehl

Sing, o muses, as old Achilles, bunions screaming under his sandals, takes the wheel of his moldering tour bus. See him send up a prayer to any god who still bothers to listen to him; he can't afford for this old thing to break down again.

The engine sputters. The chassis lets out a shriek that spooks half the passengers, if not Persephone herself, wherever she is.

And he's off and away. He speaks into his PA system, telling stories that will, gods and saints willing, earn him some tips. The good stories, you understand, at least half of them true. He does this as he steers his tour bus up and down the caldera, on roads narrower than a naiad's pretty white ankles. Sometimes the roads are so packed with traffic that he has to drive the bus sideways to get around it. You may think that's because he's Achilles, Lion-Hearted, Glorious, but it's because he is a Greek bus driver. All Greek bus drivers can do this. They see the face of Hades every day and laugh.

Achilles pauses for dramatic effect. Did you know, he announces, that the grill of this very bus is reinforced with the shield of the hero Achilles?

"What a fraud that bloke was."

It's a British lady, wearing a purple fisherman hat she bought in the next town over.

"Shakespeare had the right of him," she's saying. This kind of offense would usually send Achilles straight back to his tent to sulk, but he doesn't argue. He's spotted something out the bus window. New homes, nearly ready for their million-Euro price tags.

The roofs are all flat.

Deep down in Achilles' brain – *very* deep, I'm saying – something shifts. Don't get all excited just yet. That would be a mistake.

"Maybe I should do something," Achilles says. He doesn't mean to say it into the microphone, but he does.

"Do what?" Purple Fisherman Hat says.

"Save some lives," Achilles says. He doesn't say "again."

He raises a gnarled finger, points to some older homes higher up, away from the road. "See those roofs there, with the domes. That's not just because domes are pretty. All the time, we get the earthquakes. Domes offer better protection against those farts from Poseidon, but, they're not sexy right now, I guess."

"The flat roofs are a right bit sexier," the British lady allows.

"They're also deadlier," Achilles says. "Three men were trapped in such a house, just last year. Flattened to death, all three of them."

"Just sacrifice a bull to Zeus next time!"

A man who's very likely Purple Fisherman Hat's husband, face florid with ouzo or raki or both.

"Zeus does the lightning," Achilles says. He adds to himself, but maybe I sacrifice you to Poseidon, the Earth-Shaker, if only in my dreams.

Purple Fisherman Hat's husband laughs at his own perceived wit. Old men can be very good at saying things they think are funny. Achilles doesn't laugh. It may cost him in tips. He doesn't care. That strange new sensation is still buzzing in his brain. As soon as his tour ends, Achilles seeks out the mayor in the town square.

You know these squares: a fountain in the middle, dedicated to this or that anti-Ottoman rebel. At the top, a little statue of the owl of Athena glaring with outrage at man's perpetual lack of wisdom. All surrounded by cafes selling coffee, gelato and keychains to ward off the evil eye.

Achilles buys his coffee and looks for a bench, but they're all taken. St Nikiphoros the Leper sits next to Poseidon the Earthshaker, who sits next to St. Epaphroditus, who sits across from a gaggle of naiads, who are fawning over Dimitrios the mayor. Dimitrios is wearing his sash of office.

Achilles also thinks he's spotted the Blessed Virgin on the other side of the fountain; if so, she's eating gelato and casting her pristine glow upon Dimitrios the mayor.

When he's not sitting, Dimitrios the mayor stands six feet and seven inches. He has a chest like a gorilla's and legs like the pillars that hold up the Acropolis and a beard like an Argonaut's after three years at sea. He laughs and waves to old Achilles, who, what can he do? He comes over.

"Why are you all in a fawning array like this?" Achilles says.

"I hear you oppose my support of the sexy flat houses," Dimitrios says. "Well, here are all who support *me*! Well, not all. My greatest patron, he isn't here, but he exists, this I swear."

"So, you would sleep soundly with deaths of your countrymen on your conscience?"

A heavy, telling silence fills the square.

"Don't make me say the obvious," Dimitrios the mayor says.

Achilles glowers.

"Meet me on the beach," he says.

Everybody else cracks up.

"Watch out, Dimitrios," Poseidon says. "The mighty Achilles comes to" – and at this he makes air quotes – "slay you!"

The sea god guffaws so hard that chunks of sea salt rain down from his beard.

Curse that Shakespeare. How that noodle-necked little man with the flower for a collar learned the truth about Homer's *Iliad*, Achilles has never discerned. Likely one of those cursed muses sang her treachery right into the bard's ear. No matter. Ever since that pointy-chinned little man wrote *Troilus and Cressida* for his pasty-faced queen, the world has known who really killed Hector.

An unarmed Hector, by the way.

And it wasn't Achilles.

It was his Myrmidons.

Achilles sent *his* men to do *his* job. He hadn't meant for things to turn out that way, but Achilles was in a foul mood that day, and Ajax had wanted to play some petteia, and it had seemed like a good idea at the time.

Sometimes Achilles wishes he were mortal.

"And the rest of you?" Achilles says to the crowd. "You would allow the mayor to permit those houses?"

## THE ACHILLES WHEEL

St. Epaphroditus goes in for the kill.

"You crawl into a tent like a toddler whenever someone displeases you," he says. "Since when do you care about how grownups live?"

Achilles, being Achilles, is now officially offended. He considers stomping back to his tent, but he doesn't want to give St. Epaphroditus the satisfaction. Achilles approaches the fountain instead. The bubbly water, you understand. Sometimes it can soothe him.

The statue of the owl of Athena sees him. It speaks.

"Go to her," Athena's voice says. "Find my wisdom there."

"Please gods no," Achilles says, but Athena says nothing more.

Briseis is four feet tall, a ya-ya many times over, and not once by Achilles. She hikes for six miles every morning, up and down the caldera that tourists pay so much to see from their rental homes and yachts.

The only other sentient being in her home is a dog. He's very old, very small and very fat. His name is Elephant.

At the sight of Achilles through the peephole, Briseis opens the door, leaves it open and walks back into her kitchen. Her home is in a cave, as are so many on this island. Inside is cool but not damp or chilly. The slow cooker emits a rich smell of garlic and oregano.

Elephant stops Achilles just inside the front door.

"I have something to say," the dog says.

This has never happened before. But also the Blessed Virgin has never appeared in the town square eating gelato, so.

"I'm ready for your wisdom, Athena," Achilles says.

Elephant gazes up at him with big silver eyes that should be a dead giveaway, but we're dealing with Achilles here, so the goddess in disguise decides to have some fun.

"Who said anything about Athena? It's Elephant. What, you think because I'm an old dog I have nothing to offer? Feh on you."

"All right, all right," Achilles says. He eases into the kitchen and watches as Briseis opens a cookie jar sitting against the backsplash. Dog kibble, you understand. She feeds Elephant from the cookie jar, and then herself from the slow cooker. She offers neither to Achilles. Achilles knows better than to ask. This is the house of Briseis, not the beaches of Pylos.

Elephant says, "Achilles, you're a twerp."

Achilles looks very far down at the tiny old dog.

"As are you. What of it?"

"I'm only a twerp in size."

"Elephant has you there," Briseis says.

"If this is about the Hector thing," Achilles starts to say.

"Oh, it goes way beyond that," Elephant says.

"I was one of the mightiest warriors of my day," Achilles says.

"On account of how you killed Troilus by *accident*?" Elephant says.

"On account of how you prayed for the Trojan enemy to grow stronger, just so you could gain some glory later?" Briseis says. "Do you know how many Acheans died because of that?"

"I killed a ton of Trojans," Achilles says.

# THE ACHILLES WHEEL

"Only after Patroclus died," Elephant says, "and only because you felt bad about it. Patroclus, who died in your stead, I might add."

This beastly affront would normally send Achilles back into his tent for at least one whole tourist season, if not two.

But the dog. It just confuses him so much.

"Are you sure you're not Athena today?" Achilles says.

"Of course I'm Athena today, you sentient slab of bull fat. Listen to me. I would impart wisdom on you."

Achilles gestures to a little kitchen nook where Briseis is eating.

"May I sit first?" he says.

"No," Briseis says. "You once told your men…"

Achilles cradles his head.

"… that you wished I were dead," Briseis says, "so guilty did you feel about withholding your sword from battle. You blamed me. *Me*, Achilles, for your own ram-headed tantrums. Sit on the floor."

Achilles lowers himself to the kitchen floor and props himself against a trash can.

"You have a lot of nerve coming here," Briseis says.

"Athena told me to come," he says.

"Don't you want to know why?" says Elephant who's Athena today.

"*I* sure do," Briseis says.

"Because, Achilles, I think you're finally worthy of me. The last time I helped you, I regretted it. Do you remember?"

Achilles winces.

"We were playing petteia," Achilles says.

"On. The. Battlefield," says Elephant who's Athena today. "You and Ajax, right there in the middle of the carnage, so absorbed in your board game that neither of you saw the Trojans a-sneaking up on you. I warned you, saved you. Until today, I wasn't quite sure why I did that. Only that I should."

"I'm still not sure why you did that," Briseis says.

"Because," Elephant says, "I'm far of sight. That's not just an epithet, you know. Sometimes I'm so far of sight that I don't know what the hell I'm seeing, only that I'm seeing it."

"I don't follow," Achilles said.

"That's because you're not wise," Elephant who is Athena today says. "But now I understand. I saved you because one day you would *want* to be wise. To be brave. To be worthy of your own name. Not just in the eyes of Homer. Not just in the eyes of all those cultists who worshipped you for generations. No. In the eyes of Clio. Of the truth. I think that day has finally come."

"You're kidding me," Briseis says. "What could possibly make him change?"

Two very astute sets of eyes bore into Achilles'. He tells them.

"I didn't know you followed the lives and deaths of my boyfriends," Briseis says.

"I've often wished the latter on said boyfriends," Achilles says. "But that's the thing, isn't it? When I saw those new houses going up, I remembered the earthquake deaths of three of your boyfriends last year – the crushings, you understand – and I felt – I don't know the word. But it wasn't happiness. It was – weird."

"It's called a desire for justice," Athena says. "It's how normal people feel when their countrymen die needlessly."

"I don't like it," Achilles says.

"So he's finally ready to change," Briseis says, "and we're going to help him?"

"Yes!" Athena the dog says.

"Those sexy flat houses are horrible," Briseis allows. "But what can Achilles do?"

"He can face Dimitrios at the polls," Elephant who is Athena today says. "Or he can convince the gods and saints of his superiority the old way, and run unopposed. That means a classic challenge."

"Slaughtering Dimitrios on the beach?" Achilles says.

"The other challenge," Athena says. "A race. Once around the caldera. First to return to the square wins it all."

Briseis perks up at this. Her eyes dance like sunlight on the Aegean. Achilles thinks, why has she never taken me up on my 76 offers of marriage?

"This is your chance to be the man worthy of all that worship," Briseis says. "Not the man of Shakespeare."

Achilles very much wants to stomp his feet. He wants to say, "Woman, I've always been that man," but by now, he knows. He knows that a gospel has landed on him. Hard.

"You're quiet," Athena who's a dog says.

"What if," Achilles says, "it's too late for me to change?"

A long silence.

"What, you want us to tell you?" Briseis says. "That's for you to tell us."

"Patience, Briseis," Athena the dog says. "A very old man is trying to evolve. Go to the square tomorrow. If Achilles is there with his bus, then, well, he's told us who he wants to be."

The next day, Briseis goes to the town square. All the same people and gods and saints are there. I won't waste your time.

Helios drives his golden chariot across the sky; he drives and drives until he begins to dip. Venus appears just above the horizon to see if any intrigue is going on. Nyx steps into her wine-dark chemise and prepares for her nightly walk across the earth.

The bus of Achilles pulls into the square. It reeks of new paint, and because Nyx is running late today, the whole square can see it's bronze. He has pasted decals depicting the owl of Athena on the front and back windshields.

Achilles also has reinforced the side flaps, rear flaps and bumper rails with pieces of his ancient bronze and silver armor, and because they all came from the forge of Hephaestus, the whole bus gleams as if it were new.

And yes, fastened to the prow, that really is the silver shield of Achilles.

Briseis walks up to the bus.

"Not bad," she says. "But your back left wheel is still exposed."

"I ran out of armor."

Meanwhile the owl statue on top of the fountain is speaking.

"Give up now, Dimitrios the mayor," it cries, "for my champion competes today for the rule of this island."

Dimitrios the mayor stomps a boat-like foot. The earth shudders so hard that even Poseidon seems caught off guard. A jagged maw opens in the earth between the paving stones in front of the gelato shop.

And here emerges Hades, the greatest of the mayor's sponsors in this matter, because of course. He's wearing his usual scowl and carrying a woman in his arms. The woman is wearing winged sandals and looks furious. Hades looks around for a place to dump her and settles on the fountain. He jumps back into the hole, the hole crashes shut, and the woman in the fountain sits up, drenched.

"I give you," the mayor says, "Atalanta, the fastest runner our country has ever seen."

The naiads gawp.

"I guess I'm running a race then," Atalanta says. "Not that anyone tells the dead anything."

"She can outrun a bus?" Briseis hisses to Achilles through his driver's side window.

"I can hear you," Atalanta says. "I don't know what a bus is, but yes. Now are we racing, or what?"

Achilles leans out of the bus and says, "Once around the island, ending back here in the square."

Someone asks, "Do they race over the caldera or around it?"

"I race wherever the hell I want," Atalanta says.

"Well, I'm a Greek bus driver, so, so do I," Achilles says.

Achilles expects Atalanta to say something like, "Well so do *I*," but instead she takes off.

Achilles guns the engine, Briseis hops into the shotgun seat, and they follow.

It takes longer to catch up to Atalanta than one might think; she really is that fast. The two racers are neck and neck as they reach the first curve of the caldera.

The only thing Hades loves more than death is opening doors to his kingdom. Sometimes he hides these doors under bushes – Persephone can confirm – but more often, Hades prefers his gateways to oblivion to be massive and unmissable.

Such a gateway yawns open, just ahead of Achilles, on the left of his path.

And – well. Paris doesn't exactly *emerge* from the maw; he's Paris. He levitates out of the fissure, because of course. Paris is as beautiful as he was the day he died, many generations ago, and even though there's nobody here to swoon at his beauty, he's still just so thrilled to be here.

He's carrying a bow and arrow.

"Not again," Achilles says. And just as he says it, the bus passes Paris, who slings an arrow into the back left tire.

The bus lurches.

Atalanta pulls ahead.

"We can't go on," Briseis says. "We're dead in the water."

"The bus is dead," Achilles says. "But didn't I make you memorize my epithets when you were my prize? One of them was Fleet of Foot. I'm pulling over. Get out and get on my back."

She almost says, "But your bunions," but knows better.

They catch up to Atalanta just as she's hugging the second curve of the caldera. They're once again neck and neck.

But Hades isn't done.

The second crack he opens in the Earth is so daunting that at first Achilles thinks he can see the whole of hell in its depths. It cuts straight across his path this time, and it's the width of five Argos and the length of Scylla's tail twice over.

Atalanta says nothing at this new wrinkle. She simply makes a hard right and starts to climb the caldera. The caldera is so steep as to be almost vertical. She runs faster.

"If only I still had my bus," Achilles almost says.

But then, there it is.

In his head.

The wisdom of Athena. And more than that: the humility of Hestia. And the forgiveness – of himself – courtesy of a very little-known, but very handy, goddess named Eleos.

Achilles walks away, back in the direction of his bus, disappearing briefly over the horizon.

Briseis says nothing. She knows she has to be patient when an old man is evolving.

He returns with his shield. Even from her perch high in the night sky, Venus, or Aphrodite if we're being proper, can see it. Can see the dozens and dozens of small people lovingly etched by the hands of Hephaestus, faces upturned in joy at an unseen hero, all rendered in a silver pure enough to rival the color of Athena's eyes.

"Christos the boyfriend of Briseis!" Achilles cries. "Giannis the other boyfriend! Costas the third boyfriend, if I recall correctly! Hear me! In life you were better men than I, and your death denied you glory! I race in your honor!"

Achilles swears he hears a sound like "Huh?" from inside the crack in the Earth.

"Peleus," Achilles continues, "son of Aeacus, father of my own self, pillager of Iolcus! Telamon, who was my uncle, confidante of kings, slaughterer of sea beasts, the first to break the walls of Troy!"

A hitch rises up in the old man's throat. Achilles shouts, "Patroclus, leader of soldiers, glory of his father, beloved of Poseidon, the most beautiful of all men!

"Myrmidons all! Rise up! Rise up and hear my prayer of thanks! Come and take not my shield, but yours, rightfully won on the blood-black beaches of Troy!"

Peleus sticks his head out of the breach. He looks pretty good, considering.

"You would surrender your glory freely?"

"It was never my glory," Achilles says. "I've found a new renown. This has always belonged to you."

Another head pops out of the fissure in the earth. It's Patroclus.

The heart of Achilles leaps inside of his chest. For a moment he thinks that he'll join these men in their pit, right now. But then his heart steadies.

Patroclus climbs out of the pit and sits on the edge. It's been a long time, but Achilles knows that Patroclus would have him sit too. The race, feh. Who cares? Well, Achilles does, but Athena and Clio and Eleos have entered the contest too, haven't they? Winning suddenly means something different.

Briseis gives them space and takes a mini-hike up the caldera.

"What's this new honor you speak of?" Patroclus says.

His voice. As ambrosial and golden as the sun shining through honey.

"I'm a Greek bus driver," Achilles says.

"I don't know what that is, but if it's allowed you to earn your glory at last, I'm glad of it."

"I face Hades every day," Achilles says, "and laugh."

They sit in cozy silence. All thoughts of Atalanta have gone from Achilles. But Patroclus has followed the exploits of Hades with great interest.

"I don't like what I hear of these deadly new flat sexy houses," Patroclus says.

"Can you help me?" Achilles says.

Patroclus shrugs.

"My spear-throwing arm is still the terror of my enemies."

They look at each other.

"Do you think," Achilles says, "you could throw me all the way to the square?"

Patroclus looks irked.

"Of course I can. The question is, do you need it to hurt?"

Achilles thinks about it.

"I think I do," he says.

And before he knows it, he's hurtling through the air, high enough to kiss the very feet of Venus.

The square is still packed when Achilles lands – in the fountain, for what it's worth. Athena has demanded that Poseidon fill it extra high, to cushion some of the impact, but Achilles' old ass is likely going to sting for another generation or two.

Atalanta arrives exactly four minutes later. She's furious all over again.

The rest of the people and saints and gods in the square are too, but what can they do? Achilles is mayor now. Dimitrios hands over the sash of office, which, in a cute coincidence, is bronze.

Briseis arrives. Venus dips low on the horizon, but she doesn't set. Not yet.

Achilles looks up at the goddess of love and has a new thought.

"Just no," Briseis says.

He had to try.

He eases out of the fountain, holding his new sash, and looks up at the owl statue of Athena.

"So this," he says, "is what honor feels like."

A month later, after his tour bus is repaired and he's taken on a fresh load of Brits, Achilles will impart to his passengers the story of his race around the caldera, his landing in the fountain, and his final prayer to Athena.

The statue was silent this time, he'll tell the tourists. But he could swear he saw it wink.

# The Boldest of the Greeks
## Corey D. Evans

ARGUMENT: *Thersites' Final Goads*
In the ninth year of the war of Troy, Thersites, the hunchbacked critic of the Greek generals and most beloved by the common soldier, witnesses the death of Hector at the hands of Achilles and the subsequent mistreatment of the corpse. He first complains about the defilement to Dictys, the scribe, and then directly to Achilles. The defilement continues for twelve days until King Priam ransoms his son's body from the Greeks, after which a truce is called for the funeral of Hector. Following the truce, Amazon warriors attack the Greek armies. After the battle, Thersites criticizes Achilles for the final time.

\* \* \*

Thersites watched Achilles chase after Troy's champion. The two great warriors circled the city a second time without exchanging a single blow of either sword or spear. Running the distance in full armor and with weapons was no small feat, but a mighty foot race was not what the Greek soldiers had gathered to see.

"Swift-footed Achilles spent too many days inside his tent," Thersites said to the man beside him. He slushed his words;

his tongue struggled to form consonants with too few teeth in his mouth.

"Aye," agreed the other, "Hector is getting away." They stifled their chuckles, but not before Dictys, the Cretan scribe, heard the outburst and turned his noble attention towards the irreverent onlookers.

"Be glad Achilles fights for us," Dictys said with a haughtiness that exceeded his station. "We would all be fleeing before Hector had he not roused Achilles back to battle."

"I will not be glad until this long war is over," Thersites said and spat in the sand between him and the scribe. Dictys' nostrils flared, and Thersites sneered at the small man's rage. Though he was nearly bent in half by many wounds received in the war against Troy, Thersites stood a head taller than the scribe. His bronze armor was green and dented from nine years of hard battle testing, while Dictys' chest plate shone bright and brilliant in the afternoon sun. Thersites' face was sullied with scars, his head bald from the rub of his helmet. Dictys had long hair as thick as a horse's tail and a youthful face. Unlike Thersites' mangled and broken fingers, his hands were manicured and smooth. He was clean-shaven, too, which made the man look even smaller than he was, like a young boy playing soldier in his father's kit. The scribe came to Troy to record his king's deeds in battle, whereas Thersites was a foot soldier compelled to do the fighting attributed to others.

Dictys glared on as Hector led the vengeful Achilles around Troy for a third time. Thersites pointed as the two heroes disappeared beyond the high walls.

"How will you record this day, scribe? Will you write that Athena bore Hector away from the battle on her chariot and that Achilles rode Hermes' golden backside in pursuit?" The same man beside Thersites gave a hearty laugh, but Dictys was not amused by the other's wicked tongue.

"Scribes do not embellish as the poets and bards," Dictys said, "though I will be sure to record each of your many blemishes accurately." Thersites spat again, this time closer to the feet of the Cretan, forcing the man to step away or else have a mess on his toes.

"Would you write that my deformities were from birth? I would hate it if future generations thought I earned any honor from this farce of a war."

"Truly, your disrespect knows no bounds," said the scribe, who turned from the conversation to have the final word, and a pregnant silence fell over the Greeks while Thersites bit his tongue. He had more words to say to the scribe, but he was not standing in the hot sand to argue with stylus pullers. Like all the others gathered outside the fortified camp – home for almost a decade – Thersites came to witness the great Achilles and noble Hector do battle, and Hector rounded the far corner of Troy again with the vengeful Achilles hot on his heels.

The breaker of horses, unable to break mighty Achilles, finally stopped running and turned to face his doom. A murmur rose up from the Greek warriors gathered to watch. What they came to see formed before their eyes like water pooling in the sky to make soft clouds. Swift-footed Achilles and Hector, Prince of Troy, locked spears for the final time.

Despite coming out to watch, Thersites focused his eyes upon the back of Dictys' head rather than the combat. He was certainly no stranger to death by the spear, but at the moment, he felt little urge to add another man's bloody end to his mind's library of pain and suffering.

The men around him held their breath as the two warriors threw spears. Achilles' flew first. His aim was wide and missed Hector by a great margin. Thersites was right that Achilles spent too many days away from battle. His spear arm was out of shape. Hector threw his spear more accurately, and it embedded into the Greek champion's shield. But the damage caused no harm to mighty Achilles. Disarmed of ranged weapons, the fight turned to swords. The Trojan drew his in a flash of fiery bronze and closed the distance, but Achilles somehow produced another spear, and the men around Thersites gasped at the unexpected deceit.

"More cunning than Odysseus," whispered the scribe. Thersites rolled his eyes.

Hector still approached Achilles and crouched to make himself a small target. Achilles whirled his spear, and Hector backed away. He brandished his short sword, but the blade was useless unless he could come close to the flesh of his enemy. Hector threatened a charge, and again, Achilles chased him back with the tip of his spear.

"How long will the cat play with the mouse?" Thersites asked, but he did not wait long for the answer. Hector charged once more, and Achilles found an opening in his defenses. He thrust the spear with deadly accuracy. Bronze and ash wood penetrated the cleft of Hector's armor beneath the throat, and blood spilled upon the Trojan sand. Hector stumbled back and stood for a moment, suspended like a pitted boar with Achilles' spear protruding from under his chin.

Those watching from the Greek camp cheered while Hector choked and gasped. He helplessly groped at the shaft sticking out of his neck and fell to his knees. Achilles watched the dying man with pitiless eyes. Thersites could see Achilles' hate for the enemy even from his vantage point across the field. Any other Greek would have finished their foe with the sword, but not Achilles. He was content to deny Hector a clean death. Lions do not let lambs suffer long, but Achilles was no lion, and Hector was no lamb. They were men, and Thersites was disgusted that the Greek sword remained mercilessly sheathed.

At last, Hector died, but the day's capacity for cruelty was not met. A tumult arose from the walls of Troy as the Greek hero stripped their favorite son of his clothes and armor. Achilles lashed Hector's body to his chariot and dragged the naked corpse around the city while he roared in triumph. The walls of Troy wailed and bemoaned its fallen hero. In response, Achilles lofted Hector's helm in the air with one hand and whipped his horses to run faster with the other.

Silence fell over the Greeks. They expected Achilles' victory and longed for it, but the defilement of Hector went too far for even the most hardened veterans gathered to watch.

"My disrespect just met its boundary," Thersites said to Dictys, the scribe, "you can embellish my scars and exaggerate my crooked spine, but you will find nothing in all the world that is uglier than this black day."

\* \* \*

One black day turned into another and then another. Each morning, Achilles awoke to find the body of Hector – still lashed to the chariot – deserving of more punishment. He whipped the horses into a frenzied gallop before dawn could stretch its rosy fingers across the wine-dark sea. He dragged the body of Hector and awoke the city of Troy with his howls of war, like some horrible cockerel loose from the depths of Tartarus.

On the seventh morning, Thersites walked about the Greek camp at the end of his watch. Fires from the night before smoldered nearby, and men snored from within their tents. The sea crashed in the distance like a giant waking from a long and deep slumber. Thersites left odd tracks in the sand as he shuffled; one of his knees was broken in the first years of the war and fused back oddly. He limped to the camp of the Myrmidons, Achilles' famous fighters, and stopped outside their leader's tent. It was too early even for the wrath of Achilles, and Thersites spied the chariot with its rancid cargo tied about one of the rails. Despite being seven days dead, the body looked no different than that of a sleeping Greek nearby. Its only blemish was the grievous wound from which Hector's life fled.

"Impossible," Thersites heard the cool air say. He would have mistaken the words as his own thoughts had they not been spoken by a woman. He stepped back as Briseis emerged from the other side of the chariot. Achilles' Trojan slave girl did not notice him and she gazed upon Hector instead.

"Even in death, you continue to thwart the mighty Achilles," Briseis continued. She knelt beside the body to wipe away errant dust from its brow and to shake the mud from its hair. Thersites watched her curiously as she handled the dead. She was careful, as though Hector might wake up if her touches were too rough; she anointed the head with a sweet-smelling perfume and held one of Hector's hands. The scene was tender, and Thersites looked away in her final moments of grief. Once she finished, she left without acknowledging the presence of another mortal soul.

Achilles emerged from his tent with a flourish of flaps and cloth. He was wearing his armor, and Thersites imagined that the hero slept in bronze. Unlike Briseis, Achilles noticed Thersites' presence at once.

"Who goes there? What are you doing?" he demanded, and Thersites turned towards the man of rage.

"I'm admiring your craft," Thersites said, ever quick-witted.

"Thersites?" Achilles asked. "It is you. I should have known. Who else has a spine as crooked as their tongue?"

"How could I bow to the mighty Achilles if this war had not made me so lame?" Thersites said with a gap-toothed smile. "The gods know I would never humble myself before you willingly."

"If only you were a Trojan. I'd drag you behind my chariot next to Hector this morning."

"Alas, I was born across the sea," Thersites said, miming a sorrowful gesture with his hands. "The gods saw it fit for me to fight alongside you, Ajax, Odysseus, and all the rest of the mighty Achaeans."

"Only a fool would list you among those born of the gods."

"Oh yes," Thersites grinned, "I forgot only the god's supposed bastards get to be heroes. Forgive me for knowing both my mortal parents' names."

This last remark went too far, and Thersites felt Achilles' grasp around his neck before he saw him step close enough to grab. They were rough, thick hands with enough power to throttle men like fattened geese.

"They are right to call you swift," Thersites choked out with what might have been his final breath had Briseis not reappeared from the dark.

She did not speak or touch Achilles to put him at peace. She merely watched with her sad, bright eyes. Achilles caught a glimpse of her disapproval through his anger and released Thersites, who wasted no time shuffling away. He came out of the Myrmidon's side of the camp when he heard Achilles whip the horses and begin his morning cries.

*  *  *

A few days later, Achilles returned Hector's body to Priam, the old king of Troy. He offered a twelve-day truce for the funeral rites, and the Greek camp relaxed while the Trojans mourned. Thersites kept his protests to himself during the truce and avoided the noble Greeks he often rebuked. He sat around the fires with men like him, the lowborn foot soldiers who rowed a thousand ships to Troy and fought the battles that won their kings glory, gold, and prizes.

Evening fell on the last day of the truce, and word spread around the camp of an offensive planned for the following day. The grating of bronze against stone sang through the night as men sharpened their swords and spears.

Thersites sat with some of the Ithacan sailors, men who fought for Odysseus, and polished his dented breastplate by firelight. Spirits were high, though anxious thoughts of battle and death kept the men subdued.

"We will take the gates of Troy tomorrow with Achilles," said Eurylochus, pilot of Odysseus's ship. "We will sail for home before the new moon."

"The Trojans will waver without Hector to lead them," said another, "they will cower before us like women."

"Pass the whetstone," Thersites interrupted, "I have beaten my wits dull against many fools in this war. My edge needs honing."

"Here," Eurylochus said, tossing him a stone, "grind your wits into dust. They have only brought you shame in this war."

"I am the least ashamed of all the Greeks," Thersites said.

"I agree," said the other Ithacan, "but your goads have become tiresome to bear."

"If our kings were wiser, braver, and less loathsome, I would gladly seal my lips and follow them blindly to Hades' gates."

"You should pledge your allegiance to Ithaca," Eurylochus said, "who is braver, wiser, and less loathsome than Odysseus."

"Ally myself with my most violent critic?" Thersites exclaimed, "I'd rather not."

"He approves of your words."

"He has a strange way of showing his approval. My back still aches from his blows."

"He beat you for speaking out of turn in the council but not for speaking untrue words. He despises this war as much as you."

"It is his oath that brought him here."

"All the more reason for him to feel guilt. Have you not heard how King Agamemnon found Odysseus when he called him to war?"

"I'm sure he was honing his knives and anxious for battle."

"No," Eurylochus shook his head. "Odysseus played a fool. He put an ox and an ass to the plow and sowed salt into the fields of Ithaca in front of all the kings of Achaea. And he did so as naked as the day he was born."

"Really?" Thersites asked, genuinely intrigued by Odysseus's scheme.

"Truly, and his ploy almost worked, had the lords not put Telemachus, Odysseus's infant son, in the path of the deranged plow. He all but tossed the animals aside to protect his boy and gave in to the summons to war."

"Then why does Odysseus assent to Aggamemnon's foolhardy rule?"

"Because to resist would only prolong this war. We would all be home and fat from eight years of harvest if the other kings obeyed as Odysseus."

"Achilles, too, would rather not fight in this war for another man's bride," said the other Ithacan.

"Bullocks," Thersites said. He rubbed at his throat where the bruises left by the demigod's hands had been and spoke a curse.

"It's true," Eurylochus said rapidly before Thersites' vitriol could gain momentum. "I was with Odysseus when he fetched Achilles. We found him in a harem disguised as a woman."

"Odysseus might as well have brought the other women along, too." Thersites said. "Few among our mighty kings and generals are better warriors than the women they force to take their beds."

"Hear, hear," agreed some other warriors around the fire.

"I'd rather a woman take my place in the coming days," another said, adding his voice to the conversation for the first time. His wide-eyed gaze was long, though everyone sat nearby. A soldier with nine years of the ways of war under his helm, and still, the eve of battle filled him with dread. "Though this war's end draws near, I fear I may never see my home again."

Some warriors nodded, while others shook their heads as if attempting to rid the same sentiment from their minds. Thersites, who was as quick to comfort his comrades as he was to criticize his kings, stood and walked to the scared man. He placed a hand on the warrior's shoulder.

"Take heart," Thersites said, his all but permanent tone of mockery gone from his voice. "There are worse places to die than on the beaches of Troy, but better places to live than

Ithaca." The other men groaned, but Thersites' meaning was not lost on the man he consoled. He chuckled and nodded.

"How do you do it?" the man asked. "How do you find courage? You face the Trojans and our lords so boldly."

Thersites shrugged his hunched shoulders. "It is not courage I possess," he said. "The men of Troy are no different than you or me, but if one of us must die, then I choose that it be the other. That is not courage. It might be more courageous not to fight at all. And the men we follow who claim to be born of gods – men like Achilles or Odysseus – need us more than them. They need us to fight their wars and tell their legends. Without men like you and me, Achilles is nothing. In a way, I think my mockery of our heroes is just as important as another's admiration. Just as a man needs a woman to produce an heir, Achilles needs Thersites."

\* \* \*

Women killed many of the Greek men that following day. Unbeknownst to them, Amazons joined the Trojans' cause and attacked at dawn. These mysterious women of war were the fiercest foes faced yet. If one fell, they were sure to take ten men to Hades with them. Worst of all, the Amazons stirred up the women of Troy. They no longer fled, hid, or surrendered but fought like their husbands, brothers, and sons. Even the war brides, the women held captive in the Achaean camp like Briseis, turned against the men they were made to serve.

The battle against the Amazons grew long. In the confusion, Thersites found himself fighting among Achilles and the Myrmidons, but this was no safe haven. The greatest division of the Greeks pitched itself against the most capable of the enemy, Penthesilea, queen of the Amazons, and twelve of her personal guards.

The Myrmidons outnumbered the thirteen Amazons but suffered heavy losses in their efforts to overwhelm the queen. Penthesilea hewed down eight warriors herself with a two-bit ax that she swung more deftly than any woodcutter alive. But the tide of battle was against her, and soon she was alone, surrounded by Myrmidons and their leader, the mightiest of all the Greeks.

Achilles approached Queen Penthesilea with cunning steps. She growled at him like a mother bear cornered by dogs and spun her ax with impressive skill. The men formed a perimeter about the two champions as the greater battle swirled around them. Thersites watched, too, safe for the moment.

A hot sun blistered overhead as if Helios himself brought his fiery chariot down for a closer view of the duel. Penthesilea cursed at Achilles, who made sure, deliberate steps closer and closer to his enemy. He took shelter behind his great shield and leveled his spear against the queen. It would be easy for him to throw the weapon at her – Penthesilea did not carry a shield, but he intended to give her close combat. He stepped within reach, then, quite unexpectedly, exchanged his spear for the sword and charged the final distance. Penthesilea cleaved Achilles' shield with a heavy blow of her ax, but she had no time to parry the thrust of the sword. Achilles stabbed her through the heart, and the last Amazon smiled as her soul fled to the ferryman.

The battle shifted swiftly after the queen's fall. The women of Troy lost heart and fled back behind high walls. Those who had turned against their captors were subdued. The battle came to a close. In the waning hours of the day, under a sun as red as the sand, Achilles gathered his men about the thirteen bodies of Penthesilea and her guards.

"Help me carry them to the Trojan gates so that they may be given proper rites," he said. "Warriors such as these deserve our respect." Before another Greek could answer, an incensed Thersites stepped forward.

"Achilles, are you mad?" he yelled. "Why do you honor these thirteen, who killed many of your men, when you disgraced Hector, who only sinned against you once?"

"Bite your tongue, Thersites," Achilles shouted, but Thersites went on.

"You are cruel to ask your men to carry the bodies with you." He came near the enraged Achilles, who stood over the slain Penthesilea. He shouted face to face with the legend.

"Do you hate your comrades to ask them to do this while the blood of their brothers is still wet in the sand? Do you hate them like you hated Hector? Or do you love this Amazon more than the men who have bled for you?"

Achilles, swift and powerful, hit his accuser in the jaw. Blood and teeth erupted from his mouth like fire belched out of a furnace. The force of the blow broke the hunchback's crooked spine, and Thersites ridiculed no more. He fell on top of a dead Greek, one of the nameless many never spoken of by the poets.

The Greeks that bore witness to the murder stood still. More than fifty pairs of eyes glared at their commander as though he had become their enemy. Then, one by one, they turned to carry their own dead, but no hands helped Achilles honor the fallen Amazons.

Finally, when all but Thersites remained, Odysseus and Phoenix – one of Achilles' generals – came to retrieve the body.

"This sin lays heavy upon the men," Phoenix said.

"I do not care," Achilles murmured.

"You should," Odysseus boomed. The wily commander was rarely forceful in his speech, so the outburst surprised Achilles. "Thersites' death by your hands is the worst thing to happen for our cause. A lord has struck a commoner dead with rage, and you were in the wrong."

"I did not intend to kill. Even you have stricken Thersites before."

"I struck Thersites with a scepter wrought of wood and gold. Your hands are like swords. Their only purpose is to kill. A father does not correct a child with a spear. A mother does not call her babes to suck with slings and arrows."

"I will not be bothered by your riddles anymore." Achilles turned aside to carry Queen Penthesilea away.

"The men refuse to fight until you repent," Phoenix said. "Just as you withdrew when Briseis was taken away, they will not fight until you make this right."

"Let them retreat. My men have done their fair share of fighting in this war."

"It's not just the Myrmidons, but all the Achaeans," Odysseus said.

"Impossible."

"It's true," Phoenix asserted. "Thersites was the boldest of them all. He was their heart and soul, and you have broken both." He knelt to lift Thersites by the ankles, and Odysseus joined him with the head and shoulders.

"What would you have me do?" Achilles asked, but the two lords solemnly carried Thersites away. "What am I to do?" he cried, but there was no one left on the battlefield except the dead.

# How Achilles Grew Up
## Kenzie Lappin

Achilles was born.

No one thinks of that, of the great hero as a crying child, of a mother sweating and screaming. Of chubby cheeks and child-innocence.

But he was born, to his mother, Thetis.

Thetis was a sea-nymph, powerful and beautiful. She was raped. That *is* a story everyone's heard before, but it's just been with a hundred different women, and swans, and young girls.

Thetis was supposed to have a powerful and important baby. The baby was supposed to be greater than its father. So it followed the father had to be a man who was, to begin with, not that great. The gods chose him for her.

Let's go for the charitable way of looking at things.

Thetis and the man who would become her husband met. The man, the great mortal warrior, held her. She, the great shape-changer, switched between every form she knew how: gas, fire, screaming beasts. She tried to escape his grasp. But he held fast. At the last, she exhausted herself, and looked into his eyes, and fell in love. And they married.

Certainly, it must have been love.

Achilles was born, and grew up, but not all the way.

The little boy, with his ringlet-curls, was a boy before he was a warrior.

His mother worried about him all the time.

Achilles was a bright boy, shining in the sun, greater than his father. There were still folds of fat on his wrists, his heels and feet, the curve of his cheeks. When he walked, it was to his mother.

She took him one day when his father was off doing his heroic deeds. She took him to the Underworld. She carried him to the side of the river.

"Mama," he told her, taking his thumb from his mouth. "Mama, I'm scared of the water."

"It is all right," said Thetis. "It will only be for a moment."

"Mama," he told her, "I'm scared I will be carried away."

"Never," said Thetis. "I will never let harm come to you, so long as I have a choice in the matter."

And she dipped him in the waters of the River Styx. Achilles there learned what it was to be borne up by something greater than you – a river's currents, the whims of the gods, the love of a mother.

There he was pulled and grabbed by the water. It went into his eyes and burned his nose. Where he swallowed the water, it hurt, icy-cold, thick in his chest. Air became desperate. He thought, for a moment, he was going to die.

And then his mother pulled him out and hugged him tight.

"I'm sorry," she said, rocking him back and forth, wiping the child-tears from his eyes. "I'm sorry, my baby. But now you will never be hurt. You will never hurt. They will never hurt you."

Achilles was learning what kind of man the baby would become. He nodded, brave and heroic. "Thank you, mother. I'm glad I now know what it's like to be invincible."

His mother's face was wet from the spray of the magical water. She looked sad. "Almost. Almost."

\* \* \*

Achilles went to the great forge of his honorary uncle, Hephaestus.

He liked the forges. They were filled with fire, with ash, with *noise*. Achilles could go and touch the boiling pools of iron all he liked, could amuse himself by swinging mystical weapons and watching his uncle play with stars as heat sources.

Achilles was a man now. Or at least he was if you asked him. He was a teenager.

"Wow!" Achilles said, playing with a bow and arrow; he could pull it back now to his ear without having to strain the burgeoning great muscles of his biceps. "You are impressive, Uncle. Imagine the great battles that will be fought with these!"

Hephaestus chuckled. When he laughed, it was like the booming of anvils. "Imagine how great the worlds would be if we no longer needed to fight battles."

Achilles hesitated, confused.

"Ah, don't listen to an old man," Hephaestus said. He used his two hands to prop his leg up on a stool.

"Oh," Achilles said. "You spoke to my mother."

"You *are* still mortal, Achilles."

"There are so many great hunts in this world!" Achilles beamed. "So many monsters to kill, so many quests to fulfill! How am I supposed to sit at home and watch a life of obscurity go by! It is not like I will be hurt."

Hephaestus breathed a great gusty sigh. "Not in most ways."

"Oh," Achilles said. "You're talking about my heel. You know, Mother frets so much about it." He pulled up the skirt of his tunic, revealing pale marks on his left foot. There were five white stripes on his otherwise lovely golden-brown heel. "I hate it too."

"It's not so terrible as you imagine, Achilles."

"It's the thing that can kill me," Achilles scowled. "My one weakness. It's hideous."

Hephaestus, the old and tired god, said, "The marks on your heel are from your mother. When she dipped you in the pool that would make you invulnerable to all the physical hurts of the world, she left her hand on your heel."

"Yes," said Achilles, who, like everyone else, knew the story.

"She did not let you go. She held onto you, Achilles. She knew you were a frightened little boy, and she was not willing to leave you to be afraid alone, not even for a moment."

"Oh," said Achilles.

"How wonderful it is, to let love make us ugly," said Hephaestus. "And to let it mark us."

So the man, or the boy, or whatever he was, learned much that day. Every armor must have its soft parts, so it may be

## HOW ACHILLES GREW UP

worn without killing its wearer. Every wall must have a hole in it, so you can enter. Every thing must not be perfect, or it will be destroyed. Or it will not serve its purpose, and will become something other than it was made to be.

* * *

Achilles grew still.
　He grew, and grew, like a willow.
　His mother, fearing his destiny, hid him away.
　There he lived a simple life for a while. His bones ached and his joints pulled each night as he got taller and stronger. He would be strong and powerful. He was being built for a life which he did not yet have.
　Cunning Odysseus came to find him one day. Once he had tricked Achilles into revealing himself from hiding, they sat together as friends.
　"I will not go," said Achilles.
　"The war will only be won with you," said Odysseus.
　Achilles hesitated. "I promised my mother."
　"Lots of men have a mother," Odysseus said, amused. "For now."
　"I really shouldn't leave the safety here to go and fight," said Achilles, although perhaps his heart wished otherwise.
　"Don't you love your country? Don't you love your people?"
　Achilles' eyes flashed with anger. "Of course I do! You don't know how much I love."

"A love for a country carves into your soul," Odysseus said, softening. "It hurts, but it's worth it. It's worth pain to have a home."

"The war *will* be painful," Achilles said. "And some of us won't make it home."

"Come on, what kind of attitude is that for a soldier!" said Odysseus, clever Odysseus. And Achilles knew. But he left his life of solitude and peace anyway.

\* \* \*

Achilles fought. He became the greatest warrior of the war of Troy.

Achilles grew tired of fighting, though he was very good at it. Perhaps because he was very good at it.

He went to the riverside, sneaking away from camp, to speak to his mother.

Thetis met him there.

"How goes the battle?" she asked.

"I'm in love," said Achilles.

He knew his mother well enough to see her hesitate a little, to freeze minutely. She was afraid. But she didn't show it. "Oh?"

"His name is Patroclus," Achilles said, almost shyly.

His mother said, "Achilles, you know that you are only invulnerable in your body…?"

"Yes," Achilles said. "It's very strange, to purposely let something happen that makes you weak. I'm not used to it."

"It's very dangerous."

"Yes."

"Well. I knew this feeling, when you came around," said Thetis. "But I must say it is not something I had wished for you."

"Oh, but it's quite wonderful."

"For now."

\* \* \*

In the bowels of a giant wooden horse, Achilles dozed.

He was older now. War makes you older.

He was still in love.

The mass of soldiers, of young fighting men, sweated and jostled, pressed together in the horse's hot scaffolding. Some were scared, and some were bored.

"Achilles," said one of the young soldiers. "Why will Troy take us into their city? Why will this plan of Odysseus work?"

"They can't help it," said Achilles. "Every wall has a gate. And every gate will eventually be opened."

"But why?" asked another.

"You can live a life, safe, always. You can keep your city safe if you never open the gates. You will stay protected. But is that a life worth living? A life without fresh fruits, without new faces, without discovery of the world outside? A gate is made to be opened. That is how you find good things."

"But it's dangerous."

"Yes. But watch them open it and let us inside."

And the Trojans did, and they hopped out from the horse in the night-time, and the battle renewed.

\* \* \*

Achilles grew even more weary of being the greatest Greek hero.

And he lay listening to Patroclus playing the lyre and dreamed about open fields and rivers and his childhood.

"I don't want to fight anymore," Achilles said.

"You're good at it," Patroclus said.

"Yes."

"Okay," Patroclus said. Because he had one weakness in his invulnerability, too. It was Achilles. "Okay, don't fight anymore. But the fighting still has to be done. So I will fight for you."

He took up Achilles' armor and went out into the battle.

He fought bravely.

He was killed by the enemy of Achilles, Hector. Hector thought he was Achilles.

\* \* \*

Achilles cried into his mother's arms.

"I'm sorry, my baby," Thetis told him. "This pain you feel is dangerous."

"No," Achilles said. "It's not the pain. It's what I'm going to do with it."

## HOW ACHILLES GREW UP

They knelt together on the ground by the river. She wrapped her hand around the five pale marks on his heel, matching perfectly.

She said, tightly, "There are prophecies about you. That you will be a great warrior. That you will be greater than your father."

"Yes."

"That if you fight Hector, you will die."

"Yes."

His mother sighed. "Then don't. Then don't, my son the great hero. You have not yet given anything away which you might not get back. Patroclus had taken your armor. Your uncle has made you more. You have given your heart, but that might yet go back inside. You have walked away from that which might hurt you. You don't have to go back."

Achilles was no longer a child. Perhaps he never was one. Perhaps he still was.

"No, Mother," he said. "I'm going. I have to avenge him, and I have to win this battle. I loved him too much for anything else."

"*Love*," she said derisively. "It hurts."

Achilles smiled bright.

"Yes, it does."

\* \* \*

Achilles died.

You know that story, too. The arrow pierced his vulnerable naked heel.

That was inevitable, maybe, from the day he was born, with him screaming and his mother screaming too.

They say his ashes were mixed with those of Patroclus and put together in a golden urn that Thetis made.

His mother found him in the Underworld and came to visit, passing the River Styx. She took up her skirts so they did not brush the water.

She looked out across the golden fields of wheat and saw her son there, and his love. They walked together in the sun. They were peaceful.

When Achilles saw her, he beamed.

He said something to Patroclus and broke away from him, going to his mother.

Thetis did not try to embrace him. She didn't want to feel how death had made him a shade.

"Aren't you going to ask if we won the war?" asked Thetis.

"No," Achilles said.

Thetis smiled. "You look happy, son."

"I am happy."

"It was hard to know that you would end up here," said Thetis, studying him closely. "I always wondered if you knew it would end happily, after all the blood. Or if you just recklessly chose to keep your vulnerable parts exposed, without the gift of knowing the future."

"That is what love is," said Achilles.

They looked together at Patroclus, who was not wearing armor as he walked the fields, running one gentle hand over the wheat stalks.

His mother looked at Achilles' heel. "Was it worth it?"

Achilles said, "Yes."

Achilles said, "Every person I chose to love, every mark that they gave me – they're worth it. Yes. I wouldn't have it any other way."

# The Last Angry Hero
## Russell Hugh McConnell

I'm fucking furious.

They're remodeling Tartarus. Apparently, they're not even calling it "Tartarus" anymore.

I know I shouldn't care. I've always hated it here, and what difference does it make what it's called? But it still makes me angry, because everything makes me angry, because my anger is the only thing stopping me from becoming like all the others: the losers who don't care about anything.

I died on my feet, roaring in my wrath, and I kept roaring all the way down. I didn't even bother with Charon and his boat: when I reached the Styx I plunged right in. (Second time for me.) My rage was so red hot that I sent clouds of steam billowing for miles around. The others looked like shadows in the humid gloom, which is to say they looked like what they had all become: has-beens, nobodies, losers.

Ajax arrived not long after I did, and at first he gave me hope because he still had a bit of spirit left – stomping around and yelling about Odysseus getting my armor instead of him. Of course, I knew Odysseus would show up sooner or later – nobody lives forever, right? – and I thought the two of them might fight. But it turns out that wily bastard made it to old age. By the time he showed up,

Ajax wasn't angry anymore. He was resigned. A shadow. A loser, like everyone else.

This place is like that. It gets to people, saps their passions, hollows them out. When I found Patroclus it was as if he barely even remembered who I was. People keep arriving – all kinds of people, some of them from parts of the world I've never heard of. But they all end up the same.

Not me though. I hang onto my anger for all I'm worth, because now it *is* all I'm worth. Sing of the wrath of Achilles, O motherfuckers. I'm the one person in this chthonic dump who hasn't given up.

Anyway, now there's a team down here remodeling the place. Big guys. Huge, actually. Twice as tall as a normal man. But they're beardless like women, and they've got big fruity multicolored wings. I identify the one who seems to be in charge and I roar at him until he notices me and swoops down to talk.

"Peace, pagan," he says. "God loves you."

"Which god?" I growl.

"God," he replies imbecilically.

"Fine, have it your way. What are you assholes doing here?"

"Your pagan underworld requires reconstruction," he says, with that placid, beatific expression that makes me want to punch his teeth down his throat, if only I could reach that high. "This area is being converted to Limbo, where the virtuous pagans shall reside."

He shows me some complicated plans on a sheet of weird-looking papyrus that he calls a "blueprint". Although I won't admit it to this guy, I can't make much sense of them. In fact,

I can only tell which way up they go because the bottom right corner is signed "D. Alighieri". Whatever. I don't care who did the designs, or what the new place will be like: I just want to hit somebody.

I don't have my spear and shield anymore. There aren't even any rocks here. So even though it's unfair as fuck, I attack the big winged guy with my bare hands. Why? Because why not? Because I'm angry, that's why.

The fact that I'm not able to hit him isn't the worst part. It's certainly bad enough – him flitting up and out of the way like a cowardly butterfly. No, the worst part is the way he looks at me with pity. He won't even show me the respect of getting mad. *Nobody* around here ever gets mad, even the staff.

"Peace, pagan," he says. "God loves you."

"Never heard of him," I snarl, and launch myself at his feet. If I could just get him around the ankles, I might be able to drag him down to the ground, and then I'll show this androgynous fuck how the Myrmidons get it done. But he just flies away, looking down at me with a sad, wise expression that would make me puke my guts out if I still ate food.

"Peace, pagan," he says again.

"Come down here and fight me, you tubby bitch!" I shout, but he's already gone, floating off to do his oh-so-important work.

Odysseus says that this God guy has replaced Zeus as ruler of the universe, and is reordering the cosmos to suit him. I tell him I don't care. And the prick doesn't even get mad at me. Loser.

We don't have days and nights here, so it's hard to say how long it takes these winged guys to finish the remodeling. Every time I see one of them I try to attack him – every single damn time, even if it's impossible, because *somebody* has to make an effort. And every single damn time they just fly up where I can't reach them. I'm pretty sure I'm not even slowing down their work. Soon they're gone.

Now that Tartarus is Limbo, I have to admit that the lighting is better. A lot better, actually. And it's not so featureless anymore. There's a nice castle in what Odysseus says is the modern style (like he even knows), and a river, and a fresh green meadow.

I hate it.

And the whole place is a nonstop party now. Not a *good* party, mind you. It's the sort of crappy party that someone like Nestor might throw – no booze and lots of boring conversation.

It makes me mad. Abraham keeps telling his one story over and over, which starts out okay because it seems like there's going to be some action, but then always ends up having a dumb ending. Socrates goes around asking people stupid questions. And don't even get me started on Avicenna. These losers have spent a thousand years or more wandering around like ghosts, and now they're all reveling like fools just because some jackass with wings told them to.

"What are you celebrating anyway?" I roar at them. "What battles did you win? What cities did you found? What do you have to dance and sing about? What do you even have to *talk* about?" Nobody gives a sensible answer.

Odysseus says that we get to be here because of the honor that we accumulated in life, and that our great names echo up to somewhere called Paradiso and God likes that or something. I ask him how the hell he knows, and he says that one of the angels told him, and I tell him to go fuck himself, and again he *doesn't even get mad*.

The only one who's allowed to leave is Virgil, Aeneas's flunky, who somehow got a job giving tours of the whole complex. He talks about it a lot. (Actually, he talks about nothing else.) He says there are nine layers of the Inferno – burning lakes and bleeding trees and people being tortured and some giant douchebag stuck in a hole at the bottom. Then on the other side of the world, there's the mountain of Purgatorio with angels flitting around, and some poor bastards who've had their eyes sewn shut because God loves them so much. When I hear that, I figure the gods haven't changed as much as everyone says.

If you ask Virgil what comes next, he gets a bit cagey. "Paradiso, of course," he says, and then clams up. It takes a lot of prodding (and of course I'm the only one willing to do it) but eventually it emerges out even Virgil, aka Mr. Fancytoga, isn't allowed up there.

Oh, and he also had a story about a snake telling people to eat an apple, which was apparently a big fucking deal. I don't get it, and I'm too angry to listen to his explanation.

"Look," I say to him, "why not make a run for it? Just ditch this whole stupid place when they give you a day-pass?" But he just gives me this funny look and it's like he can't even understand the question.

And that's how it goes, for another thousand years or so.

I don't quite notice the change happening. I'm too angry to pay attention, and I can't stand conversation with the others very often. Everything they say is just so listless and uncommitted, so totally without anger. So I spend most of my time alone, stomping around the landscape and yelling. But after a long time I suddenly realize that I haven't seen anyone in a while, and I start looking for the castle. It takes me a while, but I do find it, although I don't recognize it right away because it's mostly fallen down. Just crumbled into bits. What a shitbox. The green field is all brown and dead, and the river has run dry.

Eventually I find two people, and fuck me if it isn't Odysseus and Virgil. It figures: everyone vanishes and the only two people left are these dorks.

"Where is everyone?" I growl.

They look at me like I'm the last guy to know, which I guess I am. But they're also eager to explain, because when you're that kind of person, the only pleasure you can get out of life (or death) is lecturing people, and it's rare they get to tell anyone anything that they don't already know because almost nothing ever happens.

"Things fall apart, the center cannot hold," says Odysseus. "It's like what happened before, only worse: the structure of mass conviction has decayed. That was the only thing underwriting the metaphysical superstructure of this cosmos."

"What?" I say.

Virgil pipes up: "Nobody believes in this place anymore. Or not enough people, at least."

Odysseus adds, "When people stopped infusing Zeus with belief, he became ontologically weak, and was supplanted by the new deity. This time there's no new deity, and therefore no usurpation, but this reality is no longer holding together properly. The paradigm is collapsing with nothing to replace it. Virgil says the prisoners below aren't being tortured anymore. The torturers and prisoners alike have either disappeared or wandered off."

"Well I'm not going to be the only chump left behind," I say. "I've been hanging around for over three thousand years and *someone's* getting an ass-kicking."

"I can show you the way through," says Virgil. "I can make the trip, one last time."

And so he does, leading me down through the Inferno, or what used to be the Inferno. From what he says it used to be pretty badass, but now it's just layer after layer of huge empty caverns. At one point we pass some dead, fallen trees that Virgil says used to be a forest of self-murderers. I don't ask him to explain. There's also a dry lake bed that he says used to be filled with hot blood. Stuff like that.

Sometimes in the distance I catch sight of movement – distant shambling forms that never come near. Former denizens that haven't quite disappeared yet, I guess.

Down and down we go, until we hit the bottom, and there's nothing here but a gigantic skeleton. I thought those winged guys were big, but whoever used to live here was like a titan.

Now he's a titan of dry bones, wedged legs-first in a big hole in the ground. And damn if the skull doesn't have three faces. Freaky. Virgil never mentioned that detail.

When we get down to the edge of the pit, I poke one of the giant ribs and my finger goes right through it.

"Hollow," says Virgil, and I can't tell if he's happy or sad about it. "Just shells, really. Soon they'll disappear entirely."

We climb down the big leg bones, and they're practically falling apart under our weight. When we get down past the giant feet, I feel incredibly disoriented, and I have to ask Virgil which way is up.

"We're in the center of the world," says Virgil. "Every way is up."

Everything this guy says still pisses me off.

But I still follow him, because he's been here before, and we climb and climb up through an endless tunnel. It feels like days, and it's boring as all fuck, but I've got nothing better to do.

We come out at the foot of a mountain of Purgatorio that rises into the sky. All around is the wine-dark sea, glittering under the stars. Virgil starts to make a speech, but I tell him to shut up and stop dawdling. Up the spiral path we go, right now. I just want to *get* somewhere.

Eventually we come to an empty field, dead and brown, and I guess Virgil still likes the whole tour guide role, because he stops and points at it like an asshole. I want to tell him that I'm already looking at the field, because there's nowhere else to look, idiot.

"This used to be where they did the daily reenactment," says Virgil. I must look confused because he adds, "It's a kind of allegorical play, demonstrating the defeat of evil. It's the foundational story of this whole mythology, so it hasn't crumbled as completely as everything else yet."

"What's a play?"

Virgil blinks at me and for once actually looks slightly annoyed. "You really don't know that? I mean you must have met Aeschylus hundreds of times."

"I've been too mad to pay attention."

"A play is a performance. People act out roles to tell a story."

"Sounds stupid. Why not just do something real?"

Virgil sighs. "It doesn't matter now. They used to do a reenactment of the snake being driven out of Paradise by two angels."

"I thought the snake got those two people to eat the apple and they got in trouble."

Virgil nods. "That is the central narrative in this now-crumbling paradigm."

"So the angels *didn't* drive the snake away. Not in time, at least. So it's not a reenactment at all, it's just a load of bullshit."

"Well, uh..." says Virgil and he looks so stupid I want to pull his head off. "There's no snake anymore anyway," he says, "and one of the angels disappeared decades ago." He looks up. "But *that* one still comes."

I look and see one of those big angel guys come flying around the side of the mountain. He looks like the ones who rebuilt Tartarus, except that he's got a big flaming sword in his hand. I've got to admit that it does make him look kind of cool, even though he still has no beard, but as he gets closer he starts to look less impressive. The flame of his sword is guttering, and he seems tired. He swoops down low over the dead field, holding his sword up like it's some sort of trophy.

Of course I've *got* to make a try for him. I'm too angry not to. It's been a thousand years since I had a chance to grab an angel out of the air.

I run as fast and hard as I can and launch myself at him. And it must have been a long time since there was anyone here because he's got lazy and isn't looking properly. He doesn't even see me until the last second, and tries to pull up.

My fingers close tight around his left ankle.

I can tell his nerves aren't so good, because the moment I grip his ankle he jerks with surprise and I feel about eighty percent of his confidence go, and you can't give someone like me an edge like that. I allow myself a brief, fierce grin before I sink my teeth into his Achilles tendon. (Is that irony? I was never very clear on irony.)

He screams, and we crash to the ground. He lands on top of me, but I don't care. I don't even feel it. For the first time in three thousand years, I'm in a fucking fight. And I can tell in less than a second that this clown has never been in a fight in his life. He's just been flying around waving that sword around and thinking he's a badass. See where putting on plays gets you? Well I'm going to show this angelic fuck what badass really looks like.

He's twice my height and at least four times my weight, and he's got strength and speed, plus those wings and that sword. But I've got thirty centuries of anger, and a reputation that sits on top of a mountain of dead Trojans. This guy never had a chance.

Now it's pure, glorious violence, just like the old days. He makes a half-hearted swing with the guttering sword, and I can tell he's afraid of hitting himself with it. I duck the blade, then drive my elbow hard into his wrist and the weapon falls to the ground, its flames winking out like a snuffled candle.

Through all that time in Tartarus and Limbo I never forgot the joy of combat. Limbs grinding together, muscle against muscle. As soon as I get on top it's all over, and I don't stop pounding his stupid angelic face until I can actually feel my fist hitting the dead, brown grass through the gritty paste that used to be his head.

I roll off him then, and pick up the fallen sword. In my hand it flares white hot. There's nothing wrong with the blade, then. It just needs a real man to wield it. Someone who means it.

I find Virgil cowering a short distance away. When I approach he flinches back from the heat of the weapon. "Come on, poetaster," I say. "I want to go all the way. I want to meet the boss."

I'm expecting him to protest, but he doesn't dare. He just nods, gets to his feet, and continues leading me up the mountain, round and round the spiral path. We pass a few ghostly figures on the way, a few crumbling structures, but I don't pay them any attention.

At the top of the mountain is a garden, or at least something that used to be a garden. It's not overgrown. Faded, more like. The leaves and grass are brown, the bushes look withered. Although it's night and I can see the starry sky above, it's somehow still bright enough that I can see everything.

"This is it," says Virgil. "The end of the road."

"Where is he?" I demand.

"P-Paradiso," stammers Virgil, pointing upwards.

"Up there? How the fuck do I get up there?"

Virgil just shrugs helplessly.

I was already mad, but now I'm *really* fucked off. I start screaming at the sky. I'm not even using words; I'm just roaring. Because I have never, ever, ever, ever stopped feeling angry. And now that I was finally getting somewhere, my enemy is up in the firmament, hiding like a bitch.

"You can't fight God, you maniac!" cries Virgil.

I turn to him. "I've fought a god before. Scamander."

"That was *a* god. This is *God*."

"What's the difference?"

"You can't fight Him!"

"Let's find out. Doesn't seem like he's doing so well these days." I turn my gaze back up towards the stars. I talk to this God guy again, but this time I don't shout. And I use words and everything. "Come on," I hiss. "Come on, come on, come on, come on, come on. Don't pussy out on me now. Don't you dare. You know me. My honorable name echoes up to Paradiso. I'm Achilles, the last real hero, and I demand a shot at the king."

Then there's a clap of thunder that shakes the garden all around me. Virgil hurls himself on his face and cowers. Like a loser.

"That's more like it," I say. "Go on, shout. Get mad. Grow a pair."

Then comes the great thundering voice from out of the sky. "Who is this that darkeneth counsel by words without knowledge?"

I brandish the sword. "I got all the knowledge I need right here."

The voice thunders again. "Where wast thou when I laid the foundations of the earth? Declare, if thou hast understanding. Who hath laid the measures thereof—"

"Big talk, big man," I say. "You want me to bow? Too bad." I wave the sword again. "I say you're nothing but talk. I say your shit is all falling apart. So stop being weak and come get some."

The voice is silent for a long moment. The grass under my feet is smoking and curling in the heat of my wrath.

Then a gate appears – just pops out of nowhere right in front of me on the dead grass. A big white gate. Looks like ivory. Very fancy.

"I will tell your story," quavers Virgil. I had forgotten he was still here.

"Whatever," I say. And, head held high, with flaming sword in hand, I stride boldly through the ivory gate.

# The Choice of Iphigenia
## Zenobia Neil

"Your father has summoned us," my mother said. Larissa and I looked up from our weaving.

"Does he lack soldiers?" I asked. It was a bad joke, but ever since Father had left, taking most of his men, we had allowed ourselves to speak freely. The cloud of shame that began when my aunt Helen ran off with some Trojan prince had lifted. The men were away at war. Mycenae was full of women. It was like a dream.

My mother eyed me gravely. Larissa bit her lip.

"Forgive me, Mother. It hasn't been that long since he left." I pushed away the other questions that rushed through my mind. Does he miss us so? Can he not leave without seeing us one last time? Why call us now?

Mother smoothed down her black hair. I sometimes forgot how beautiful she was, as stunning as her sister Helen, only dark instead of fair.

"Iphigenia, darling girl." She touched my cheek. Dread pitted my stomach. "Your father has found a husband for you."

Ice flooded my veins. The very thought of a man owning me, of touching me, made me ill. I had hoped this war would keep me from being wed. *Great Artemis, save me from this.*

I prayed to the great goddess every night to let me be like her, free of men, free of marriage. She must not have heard my prayers.

"Iphigenia, the groom is not a bad choice. And if you are wed while he is at war, no other man will bother you."

I wiped away my tears. I was no longer a child, and despite my dreams of becoming a priestess of Artemis, there was no reasonable hope of escaping marriage, especially if Father had already decided.

"Your father chose well for you. You are to be wed to Achilles, son of Peleus and Thetis."

I let out a breath. "The one who dressed as a girl to avoid the war?"

My mother laughed, a sound I did not hear often. "Yes, Achilles who was caught by Odysseus hidden with the daughters of King Lycomedes. Achilles who is needed to win Troy. They say he is the most divine warrior."

At least he was not an old man. I exchanged a glance with Larissa who appeared intrigued.

"It is odd timing, but a sound plan for us," Mother said. "If Achilles dies at war, all that is his will become yours. His father is old. His mother is a goddess. She has no need of mortal goods. Of all the matches that could have been made, this is not a bad one." She smiled weakly.

"What else did Father say?"

"Not much. His note was very short. I suppose he'll explain tomorrow. Now choose your best dress. We'll leave for Aulis in the morning."

## THE CHOICE OF IPHIGENIA

"Tell me about Achilles," I said to Larissa as we folded my dresses into my small cedar travel chest. Like many handmaidens, she knew all the gossip. Unlike me, she remembered details about famed warriors.

"He's young but has great renown. They say when he runs, he's as fast and light as the wind. He and his sworn companion Patroclus were raised by the centaur Chiron who taught them all kinds of skills."

"Companion?" I smiled. Perhaps Achilles and I could be a good match after all.

"Yes, his sworn companion since youth. They say his mother dipped him in the River Styx to protect him. He is destined for greatness, but from all I've heard he doesn't care for fame. In fact, he was hidden away with King Lycomedes' daughters pretending to be a girl."

"Yes, this is the story I recall." Images floated through my mind, a handsome youth, dressed in skirts, learning to weave badly, whispering among the maidens, not wanting to touch them like a boy, but gently like a girl.

"It is said that the war in Troy cannot be won without him, but that he has no interest in going or in being a hero."

That was rather romantic. All my father and his brother had ever wanted was fame. Even my little brother Orestes thought the goal of life was to do something great, to be remembered for all time.

"They call it the choice of Achilles," Larissa said, "to die young gloriously or live a long comfortable life and be forgotten."

"Will he die in Troy? Is that foretold?"

"Iphigenia, what I'm telling you is idle gossip from the market, not a prophecy from Delphi."

I chuckled. "And even if it were from Delphi, nothing would be certain." I stood and closed the cedar chest. "What would you choose?"

"Hmm?" Larissa's brow furrowed in confusion.

"If you had the choice of Achilles, what would you choose?"

"Me? No one would give me such a choice. I'm nobody. No one will remember me."

"But, what if—"

"No this is not a choice for me. But you, beautiful girl, princess of Mycenae, bride of Achilles – you can ask that question of yourself."

I pondered the question as I went to the sacred grove. I prayed to Artemis as I did every evening as the moon rose. Her statue had always been here, but I was the one who insisted it be cleaned and enrobed with a new garment every year. I purchased the silver bows and paid for the sacrifices held on her feast days.

"Mistress of the Silver Bow, She of the Wild Things, I come to you as I do every night. I've begged you many times, great lady, to remain a maiden as you are, but now Father demands I marry. Tomorrow. Please give me guidance, great Artemis."

I kissed her sandaled foot and her calf, wishing as I did every night that the goddess were there in her mortal form for me to worship properly.

In the sky, a crescent moon hung low on the horizon. Was it an omen of my new life, just beginning, or a symbol of darkness to come?

"Please send me a dream," I said to the moon.

Artemis had sent me many dreams over the years. The first ones were simple, the moon shone down on me, and I glimpsed the goddess above.

As the years went on, she sent me dreams that let me know she saw me and appreciated my worship. After I demanded her statue be cleaned and clothed the first year, I dreamed of her upon the full moon. I floated on a cloud with her, warmth and comfort all around.

*You have done well, brave one*, she whispered in my ear. *I was all but forgotten in Mycenae, save for young girls and pregnant women afraid of dying. That will not do. And then you renewed my statue.* She caressed my neck, moved her hand to my waist. *Even kings like your father need remember me. For like my brother Apollo, I too can spread pestilence and death.*

I shuddered in her arms. I had wanted her attention, and now I had it. Even in my dream, I feared being in the presence of an immortal, but excitement eclipsed the fear. The goddess had come to me!

She came to me many times over the years. Some dreams I remembered clearly, in some I only recalled the sensation of being with her. And always I prayed that she would allow me a way to be with her. I begged her to free me from marriage. I told the goddess I would rather die for her than be forced into such an arrangement.

Now perhaps she had granted me a kind of reprieve. I would only need meet Achilles, marry him, bed him, and he would be off. Some said the war would be over quickly, that Helen would change her mind and come home or that our men would easily overtake Troy, but others said the war could last a long time, maybe three years, maybe even five.

Marrying Achilles didn't seem that bad after all. I would drink wine tomorrow night, and I would picture him in his dresses with the other girls. Perhaps I might even like my new husband. Anything was possible.

The next day, as we approached Aulis, I stared in surprise at the harbor. So many ships all in one place.

"All of this because of Aunt Helen?" I asked Mother.

She pressed her lips together. "That is what they say."

The sailors needed to row us in. I was busy with my mirror, trying to make myself look like an excited bride instead of a seasick girl who had no interest in men.

When we docked, it was the stillness and heat I noticed first and the strange silence. The lack of wind was strange. It pricked a feeling I had when my mother had told me I was to marry before the war started. Why had I been called to this place by Father?

Unmarried men without children were not meant to go to war, lest their line die with them. Perhaps my father had tried to promise Achilles an heir.

The noises men make as they train for war met us: lockstep marching, chanting, banging on shields, the clang of swords – noises I had heard my whole life. This was another reason it had become so peaceful once the men were gone, and here we were in the center of it.

Was Achilles practicing with his men? Did he need to beat his sword against his shield to be heard? I hoped not. I hoped he was stealthy and quick, like a sleek cat that is rarely seen but whose leap takes your breath away.

My uncle Menelaus greeted us. He nodded at my mother and me. He did not appear happy for me, but relieved. "You came, brother's wife. How good. This way."

Our escorts circled around us tightly. Fear prickled my skin as we followed.

Where was Father? Why had he not met our boat? And what of my groom and his men? Of course this was a camp of men, I did not expect a festive wedding arrangement, but the dust that coated every tent and the sun baking the land made everything appear bleak.

"What has happened here?" Mother asked Uncle Menelaus.

"We have had no wind for three days, Clytemnestra." I had never heard him address my mother by her name. There was a strange resolve in his tone I had never heard before. Losing Aunt Helen to that Trojan prince had changed him. Practically the whole world knew that she had thrown him over for a young, attractive foreigner. Though the Spartans did their best to circulate the story that she had been abducted, anyone who had met Helen knew that she did only as she wished.

"We're almost there. It will be cooler soon," Uncle Menelaus said.

At Father's tent, I nodded to the familiar guards outside. Though I had known them for years, they gazed past me as if I weren't there.

Inside the tent, the air was stifling. Breathing became a conscious effort. My father stood, enrobed in black, his back to the tent flap. When he turned toward us, his eyes were red, and he seemed to have aged in the short time since we had last seen him.

"Agamemnon?" Mother said, "What is amiss?"

"Nothing. Nothing dear wife. It is only war. Come, let us get ready. The priest awaits."

As we were escorted out of the tent, all my fears from the previous day tightened into a knot in my belly. *Artemis, give me strength.* I touched the pouch I wore around my neck that held a small image of my goddess.

Before us stood a path lined with men from all over Hellas: from Sparta, Ithica, Elis, Achaea, Argos and other lands I did not recognize.

"Where is Achilles?" Mother asked Father. Ahead of us stood a priest dressed in black and a sacrificial altar. I glanced back at Mother. The guards followed her closely. I wanted to run, to flee from this place. But where could I go? Into a crowd of soldiers?

*Am I to die? Great goddess, am I to die here instead of be married?* No. Father wouldn't do that to me. But I glanced at the men in the crowd. They did not look at me. They hid their eyes from my mother. This was no wedding.

"Where is Achilles?" Mother asked again loudly. Without the wind, her words seemed to echo.

I began to tremble as I approached the altar. The priest grinned slightly to see me.

# THE CHOICE OF IPHIGENIA

"Where is Achilles? Agamemnon, what is this?" Mother said. My father turned to us, sliding a knife from his belt.

"My dearest daughter, I committed a crime against a goddess. She has stopped the wind from blowing and demanded that I sacrifice you. That is the only way we can go to Troy."

"Coward!" Mother screamed. The guards closed in on her and gripped her wrists. "You would kill your own child! Agamemnon, for what? For your brother to have my sister back? No. No! It's gold you all want and fame. You don't care one bit for Helen. You just want an excuse to sack Troy. You're all so bored in your little lives with your petty fortresses." Her feet began to slip in the dust as the guards tried to pull her away. She cast around desperately.

"What if you don't go to Troy? What if Iphigenia lives? What if all the people you plan to kill just go on living?

"Menelaus, get a new wife. She may not be as pretty as my sister, but she'll love you. Agamemnon, don't give away your daughter's life. Don't give away the love I have for you. Don't make it turn to hate."

The guards held her tight, but she pulled away in her fury. She turned and addressed the men who would not meet her gaze.

"How many of you will die in Troy? How many of you will return home? Some of you may have riches. You – you think it will be you. But it won't. You'll die from a Trojan arrow or of blood poison, of pestilence. Stay here. Stop this foolish war. Live. Live!"

"Take her away," Father said softly.

"No!" Mother screamed. "Achilles! Where is Achilles? Achilles, do you know what they do in your name?"

And through the crowd, a man sprinted, quick as lightning, just as Larissa had described.

Clearly a demigod, an essence shone over him. Even in this hot, dry place and after running he seemed composed. He must have been practicing for he wore only a short brown leather skirt.

"What is this now?"

He looked at me, noting my bridal dress, Mother held back by guards, Father's sacrificial blade.

"Agamemnon? Who is this and what is happening?"

Father firmed his mouth into a thin line. Mother answered.

"We were told to come here, Achilles, that Iphigenia was going to marry you. Instead, my murderous husband plans to kill her. Do you allow this in your name?"

"What?" The rage that descended upon Achilles was almost magical. His body didn't change as much as seem to lighten, as if any movement could be possible within seconds. I would not have been surprised if he could fly.

"Agamemnon, how dare you use me in your scheme? You dishonor me and all the men here with this ruse. I will not allow it." He went from standing before my father to holding my shoulders and before I even knew what had occurred, we were walking. He smelled of honey and leather.

His men surrounded us, shielding us from the crowd of shocked soldiers. I followed silently, through the camp and to the seaside.

"I had heard the rumors that your father angered the goddess and that's why the winds stopped. And other rumors that the goddess demanded a human sacrifice, but this..." He stopped and stared at me fully. Head on, his beauty was too much to bear, but I made myself hold his gaze. It seemed likely I would not have much to look at in the future.

"Here, sit with me." He gestured to a grassy patch on the shore. His men remained a distance away, but close enough to fight if needed.

"Agamemnon never should have involved me in this. I already hate this war, and it hasn't even begun."

"Yes, I heard how you hid with King Lycomedes' daughters." Given my predicament it was an odd thing to say, but it was all I could think of.

He grinned. "Those were good days. I wish they could have lasted."

We gazed at the sea, at the sky. This would be the last sea I saw, the last time sweat trickled down the back of my neck. I had not even said a proper goodbye to Larissa, to little Orestes. He would forget me. He would grow up without me. Achilles sat with me in silence and a part of me loved him then. He wanted to save me, but how could he?

Just then a youth stepped through the wall of men who watched from a distance. He had a casual air about him – no chest thrust out and preening like so many of the other soldiers. He was not loud or full of himself. This was the form of someone who knew his worth, who knew he was loved. This must be Patroclus.

"Achilles," he bowed to me, "Princess, I come with solemn news. There is fighting in the camp. All the men know of the sacrifice now. They've heard Achilles is protecting you, but they do not care. They say that if you are not sacrificed by the time the moon rises tonight, they will kill us – me, Achilles, your mother and father."

"I am to die," I said, trying to convince myself.

Achilles grasped my hand, an odd familiar gesture that would have been surprising under different circumstances, but here all sense of propriety was gone.

I stared out at the sea, the waves muffled and far away. What strange goddess demanded my life? I pictured a vicious sea goddess demanding my blood be poured in the sea, turning it dark red. A wife of one of the main winds, angry over some slight.

I looked at Achilles and Patroclus, ignoring my tears. "I am to die for this war. For the victory of all those men." I thought about what Mother had said and added, "for the victory of a few of the kings."

We sat in silence listening to the waves, to the plaintive sound of seabirds. My own mortality made me brave. "I heard you had a choice, Achilles, to live a long happy life or a short glorious one. How did you decide?"

Achilles smiled crookedly. "I have not yet decided."

"But you are here."

"I was caught by that wily bastard Odysseus and brought here after getting my men. I will go to Troy, but if I do not fight there, I will not die. So, for now the Choice of Achilles has not been decided by Achilles. And what is the choice of Iphigenia?"

"What choice do I have? I am to die."

"But you can choose how to die, willingly, like a princess who saves her family or dragged to the altar. Or if you choose, I will fight for you. I could die here instead of at Troy, and we will lose the war that never was."

I squeezed his hand. How many would die by this hand? How many would be slaughtered by this stranger who had been so kind to me, who now offered to lay down his life for me? But what difference did it make? We were outnumbered. In the end I would die here on Aulis. I might as well return to the altar and give my neck to the blade willingly.

An image of my father's knife flashed through my mind. I envisioned women screaming as their villages were sacked; all the warriors I had seen today, bloodied and full of rage, their purses full of gold.

"Perhaps it is best that I leave this life before all the bloodshed and cruelty that will occur in Troy. All those deaths that my death will allow to happen."

Achilles stood, clenching his fist. "Your father should not have killed a sacred deer of Artemis, but why would she demand your sacrifice?"

His words shot into me like a bolt.

"The goddess who requires my sacrifice is Artemis?" How many times had I told her I would rather die than be married? My father had said a goddess – not my goddess. Artemis had stopped the winds for me? For this?

I laughed, a jagged sound like rocks hitting each other. "Perhaps my death is a choice I've already made." I stood. "Let us go. I will yield to the blade. I am the only one who needs to die today."

When we returned to the camp, the tension among the men was palpable. I had seen men fight, but never before had I felt such rage. The stillness of the place. The lack of wind, it was maddening. Unnatural for a place like this to be so still.

I did not see Mother. I wished I could say goodbye. She had been so brave to try and save me. I would be brave too.

"I will go willingly," I said. "I will be a sacrifice to the great goddess Artemis. If she wants my life, I will give it gladly."

Father had been arguing with Uncle Menelaus and the priest. They fell silent at my words.

"Thank you," I said to Achilles. I smiled weakly at Patroclus. "Take care of each other in Troy."

*Great goddess, I am yours.* I walked toward Father and the blade. The men parted for me. Staring at me now, some in awe, some in fear. *I will die now, but you will die too, battling for foolishness. At least I will die to save those I love and to go to my goddess.*

Tears streaked Father's face. "I do not want this, daughter, but I have no choice."

I looked at my father, King Agamemnon of Mycenae, at once so powerful and so pathetic. I wanted to sit and talk with him of fate, of choices and destiny. I wanted to tell him that we all have choices even within the confines of fate. I wished I could sit with Achilles and hear of his days with the daughters of King Lycomedes. I wished all these men, so eager to go to Troy, to kill, and rape, and murder, could stay home and remember civility. But none of that would happen.

I stood up straight, lifted my head and offered my father my throat. "Artemis, I give myself to your will."

And the blade came down.

A brief moment of pain and then, up and up and up, I soared away from the hot, dry dust of Aulis, away from the men eager for war, away from Achilles who had turned away from the altar and run into the sea, swimming out away from the men. From above, I saw Patroclus sitting on the shore, scanning the water for his love. I could not see Mother and I did not look at Father.

Below me, bloodied on the altar, was a slain deer.

"Iphigenia, at last you are mine." The goddess held me in her arms, not in dream form but solid, her silver eyes shining in delight.

I put my arms around her neck and kissed her.

# Waiting for Clear Waters
## Mari Ness

So look, there I was, quietly burbling away, minding my own business, when this group of so-called *heroes* shows up. Not just a few of them, either: a whole *army* of them, about half claiming to be descended from some god or other.

Yeah, I was less than thrilled.

Oh, I'm not against heroes, exactly. Especially in the singular. Some of them – not all, not even most, but some – seem decent enough. The rest though – even I'd heard about that poor snake-girl, just trying to live a decent life out in the rocks, and that poor three-headed dog. Still not the same, from everything I've heard. And all about those girls guarding those golden apples. Not to mention what we all went through that day that one *hero* decided to try to drive the chariot of the sun. Me, I still haven't recovered. I can show you the scars.

And we all knew the stories about what had happened with that ship of heroes. You ask me, their leader got off easy. Can't believe it took that long for his ship to kill him.

So you can imagine my concern. Our concern. Every tree shook, and I know for a fact that most of the water nymphs swam away in minutes. Oh, sure, a couple of them squeaked about needing a break, and maybe they did, but a bit coincidental that they just happened to need to go away for ten years, don't you think?

Me, though, I'm bound to this water. I *am* this water.

So I stayed.

And at first it didn't seem too bad. They were interested in the city, not me. Or so they said. Specifically, some woman or other *inside* the city. Ridiculous, and I wasn't the only one to say so. Not saying breakups aren't hard and all that, but recruiting an army to sail across the sea to harass an entire city because you've been dumped for a prince? It's just not really something people *do*, you know? Stalk the woman, sure. Drink to excess, sure. Maybe even follow her down to the underworld. I don't know. But a war? No. Not even for a daughter of a god.

No, me, I've always thought they were after the gold. Not that the city had a lot of gold, you understand, but they did have some, from Egypt, no less. Highest quality craftsmanship – gold plates with pictures on them, gold goblets, gold other things. And silver and copper and turquoise and other jewels. Some real gems in there, they said. That's what I thought they were after.

Or the land.

Or the glory and the fame.

Well, they got some of that, I suppose. The fame, that is, though to tell you the truth, I don't see that lasting all that long – it'll all be forgotten in a thousand years or so, and we'll be singing about other things.

Trust me. I've seen that happen again, and again, and again. You think you'll never forget – that no one can ever forget

– and then, people forget. We forget, and we're rivers. And trees. And oceans.

Anyway.

At first, as I said, it wasn't that bad. They kept most of the big boats out in the ocean – at least then – so the beach wasn't that crowded – and just set up a few tents and dug some shallow trenches here and there. Never really got the point of that, if I'm being honest, unless they were hoping to collect water – which they clearly weren't. They started taking water from me almost immediately, over my protests.

"Go dig a well," I told them. "Several wells."

"We're not going to be here that long," they said.

I slapped them, and pulled them beneath the water. The ones who couldn't swim drowned, but after that, they mostly stayed on the shore, or sent those who could swim to collect water. Bucket after bucket and bucket. I did what I could. They started building things just up off the beach – not just tents, real huts, made with wood and mud – and singing. A lot. And clanging weapons. A lot. The city ignored them. I tried to do the same. Tried to think of happier things. Trees. Stars. The way I could – slowly – shift my banks if I really tried.

I really tried.

Because they didn't leave.

And what they did to my water – well. I don't really want to think about it. Or repeat it. But before they arrived, I tell you, my water was clear and sparkling. You could see right through it, right down to the grasses I nurtured under the water, and the tiny baby fish that thrived there. Even some of the ocean beasts dared to enter my fresh water, just to see the marvels – and, yes, nibble on those baby fish.

That ended as blood and mud kept draining into my water.

I cried, of course, but when you're a river – well. No one notices a few extra drops of water.

And then their ongoing assumption that I would be *happy* to carry the bodies of their dead down into the ocean, as if I had nothing else to do. I mean. Honestly.

And the noise. The endless noise. Not that the city had ever been quiet, but it had never been like this: endless clanging and talking and singing and clanging, right next to my banks.

I wanted to flood. I *needed* to flood.

I never had enough water. Not unless I wanted to try to suck it from the ocean – and I didn't have the strength for that.

I just had the strength to cry.

Years of this.

Years.

And then came that plague.

I had nothing to do with that. Not exactly, that is. I don't think all the filth in my water *helped,* but they had the choice to start digging wells, and they never did – and it was *their* filth, not mine. But I won't deny whispering here and there that it might not be a bad thing to have some of them, you know, get too sick to keep making all that noise. Maybe that got back to whoever sent that plague. Maybe it didn't. I never had the opportunity to find out. Because I kept having to deal with *them*. And sometimes hopeful heroes from the city, too. But mostly *them*.

And him.

You know the one. The one with all the wrath. He was pretty much always angry, but the plague made him even angrier. Something about some girl, and his best friend – I don't know. I wasn't really paying attention. I was too busy trying to get my waters clean, to try to get all of that mud and blood either up to my banks, or down to the ocean. Most of it came back, either sliding down from the banks or pushed back by the ocean – who didn't want any of it either. But I had to be clean again. I had to.

And then he threw a dead body right into me, screaming something about fish and blood and bones and letting me – ME – deliver the body to the ocean.

I roared. First all that blood and mud, and now this? I roared again – and smashed his legs with a wave of water.

He snarled.

I sent another wave.

"You'll regret this," he said.

And another.

He stalked off.

I didn't follow. I had that dead body to deal with – a body that I didn't want, and that I was pretty sure the ocean wouldn't want, either. I was right about that. We argued and pushed back and forth and finally tossed the body up on the shore, not far enough away from either of us for our liking, but at least not *in* either of us, either, and called out that the gods needed to take care of this. They didn't answer; they were too busy taking care of everything else.

And then I retreated back to my banks, to try to deal with this latest pouring out of blood, not to mention the branches of nearby trees that I'd distinctly heard *snap*.

Only I couldn't, not immediately, since floating right next to the banks? Two more bodies, one still bleeding.

I roared again, and sent my waters – my muddied, bloodied waters – flooding over the banks.

A few hours later, they brought more bodies. Far more. More than I could handle; more, I knew, than the ocean could handle. I threw walls of water against them, but this did no good; they simply dropped the bodies where they stood, and rushed away. I thought about following and flooding their camps then and there – but someone had to deal with those bodies, and that someone apparently was me. And all of this had caused still more mud to churn in my waters, weighing me down. No. Bodies first, and then—

I heard shouts from their camp.

Maybe – maybe – they would take care of the problem for me.

They did not.

By the next morning I felt less heavy, when *he* came – holding a flaming torch in one hand, and a copper sword in the other hand, a rope tied to his wrist. A rope, I realized, that was dragging along another man by the neck. A gravely wounded man.

I hadn't even been able to get rid of the *last* set of bodies. I hissed.

He stopped right at the edge of my banks.

I hissed again.

Anyone *else* would have gotten the hint, but no, not him. He just knelt, and moved the torch down, letting the flames hover just over my waters. I could feel the heat. His mouth widened.

I roared up with everything I had, and smashed him to the ground. But not for long. The torch dropped, and went out, but he was up again, running – as best he could with the wounded man still tied to him. I followed, roaring. I should have been able to take him down, easily, but he cried out, and after that, *something* protected him.

That just increased my wrath. I cried out, too, and sent out a tendril of water – strong enough to drag him back towards me, towards my banks. He struggled, as did the man attached to him – I wanted to detach them, but I also didn't want to lose control. I pulled with all of my strength, and then he was over the banks, under my waters, slashing with that sword that shouldn't have stung, but did, kicking to get himself back up to the top. I sunk my teeth into his heel, to hold him under the waters. He kicked and slashed with his sword and kicked again. It *stung*, and I felt something tugging at him.

At us.

I looked up, to see a score of *them* tugging at his head, his hands, his shoulders, to drag him away from me. They were all covered in blood and mud, letting more filth sink into my waters. I pulled. They pulled back.

I was ready to drown him and every single one of *them*.

Until every tree around me burst into flame.

A god, undoubtedly. That's the other problem with heroes – they're always bringing gods with them, and those gods never hesitate to destroy everything around the heroes. Heroes first, apparently; trees – living, breathing, *healing* trees – decidedly second.

I had to save them. I had to save *myself* – the smoke from the fires rushed across my waters, and flaming branches were already falling into me. I could quench those quickly enough, but I could feel the heat; could feel the steam rising. I was terrified. I threw myself over the trees, over and over again. It *hurt*. I could hear myself roaring and screaming and roaring again. And then I threw myself against those flames, again and again.

Once they died down, leaving smoke and ash, I saw him, limping away, clutching his side.

Blood dripped from his ankle.

Did it make a difference? I don't know. I'll never know. He certainly didn't seem to have any problems killing that prince afterwards. Or any number of other people. Of course, anger seemed to give him extra strength and speed, so perhaps not. But I had harmed him. I knew it. And not just on the ankle.

And he did die.

Eventually.

I didn't.

I listened to the wailing and the grieving – seventeen straight days of that, if you can believe it. I honestly couldn't.

Five days, I thought, was more than enough. Three days would have been enough. But no. Seventeen days of wailing.

That should have been that. But it wasn't. I nursed my wounds and tried to think of trees and stars while they stayed, banging and clanging and throwing things into my waters, until they finally thought of that trick with the horse. Why they couldn't have thought of that right from the start, I don't know, but no one's ever accused most of the heroes of having all that much intelligence.

The flames danced in the sky.

I thought about bringing them some water when the screams started. I really did. But, I told myself, my waters were already thick with blood. And soon they would be thick with ash.

We all have our regrets.

And many of them came anyway, still screaming, to plunge their burned skin into my waters.

My churning, filthy waters.

I still have their bones.

But not the bones I wanted. Not the bones that once held the wrath of a self-named hero with a weak ankle. Not those.

All I have of him is some grey ashes, held fast in my hands.

The right thing to do, I know, is to release those ashes to the ocean, to let his mother collect them in her grief.

But I remember the bodies he threw into my waters. The way he stung me with his sword. The way he held that torch just above me, to heat my waters and make me scream.

I remember all of those trees, bursting into flames.

## WAITING FOR CLEAR WATERS

I remember those horses, dragging that body around and around the city walls, as dust flew upwards before falling into me.

So I hold those ashes tightly. She can wait a little longer, to have something to hold in her grief. As I have to wait, for my waters to clear.

# Spindle, Rod, Shears
## Parker M. O'Neill

### THE SPINDLE

It always ends the same: the arrow, the heel, the sudden spasm of their joining.

In the house of Peleus, husband to the nereid Thetis and father to a newborn prince, I twirl my spindle and wind the flax around the shaft. My practiced fingers tease out the fibers, twisting them into the shape of a man's life, wrapping the thread around my distaff. The sound of my humming is incongruous in the hot, dim birthing chamber, but I have to keep up appearances. My sisters must sense nothing out of the ordinary.

Spindle, rod, and shears: with these tools, we Moirai mark the fates of mortals.

I take no responsibility. My lot is to spin the thread, not to dictate what comes, or even to see it. Lachesis reads the lifethread and measures it; Atropos cuts. Part of me even believes this, believes that my culpability extends no further than my spindle. That a hundred million mortal lives have passed between my hands and I should content myself with never knowing what becomes of them.

Today I will reject this lie. If I must determine the fates of mortals, I want to see the course of their lives, to feel what they feel, to at least try to understand.

## SPINDLE, ROD, SHEARS

Lachesis and Atropos suspect nothing. My sisters could pass for statues, shadows dancing across their faces as they loom over Thetis in the birthing bed. Lachesis has the languid calm of a lion about her, clever eyes fixed on the midwife who stands nervously by the door. Atropos, gray and bent, is as quiet as the grave.

Achilles, demigod prince of Phthia, peers up towards them from his mother's arms, ignorant, beautiful, unaware that all his future pains can be traced to this moment. The pressure building in my chest means that I'm nearing the end of this lifethread, and I give my spindle one last twirl. My lot is to spin the thread and no more. But I have to know. As I wrap the last handspan onto the distaff, I run my fingers over the thread and read the newborn's fate.

\* \* \*

There is a sense of richness, of biting into a pomegranate, of rivers rushing out to sea. Piquant and deep and savory. Are all mortal lives so vivid? Or have I chosen my demigod well?

Visions of his glories and sorrows unfurl before me like peony petals, red-drenched and dripping. This prince's life will be short, radiant, full of rage. How many mortals, I wonder, devote their lives entirely to violence? How often do those lives end in brutality? My fingers trace the thread and I swim between a thousand of the moments that make up his life. I see his childhood, his training, his anger, his battles, and the way it will end: the heel, the arrow.

\* \* \*

Here is a myth: time is a river running downhill. It's the nature of mortals, I think, to see things in terms of moments, of linearity, a series of scenes filtered and understood through limited perception. For my sisters and me, time is an ocean of currents, tides, and waves. In this moment, Achilles has just been born, in another, he is fighting his enemies, in another, he is a distant memory. All at once I spin his thread, Lachesis measures it, Atropos cuts. All at once Achilles lives, Achilles struggles, Achilles dies.

And here is a fact: I cannot mark the course of a person's entire life – their failures, their victories, their grief, their joy – without loving them. Could anyone?

\* \* \*

"What did you see?"

The visions evaporate; the dim birthing chamber rushes back. But that voice is neither the even murmur of Lachesis or the throaty gasping of Atropos. Thetis, clutching her child, stares at me with the desperation and hope that only a new mother can conjure. I curse myself – I should have known she would be watching closely, hoping for some sign, and now my sisters will know what I have done.

"You read his lifethread," she says, her eyes piercing me, damning me. "So tell me, Clotho. What will be the course of my son's life?"

"Impossible," Lachesis whispers. She crosses her arms, her measuring rod held tight in one hand. "Clotho's lot is to draw out the thread, and nothing more. Don't insult us, sea nymph."

"Ask her yourself," Thetis says. "I watched her do it. Can you change his fate, Clotho? Avert whatever you saw?"

She is as bold as her son will be. Again I see the arrow and the lifeblood of a demigod spilling out on the sand. Could I save him?

Before I can react, Atropos speaks. "The nereid has sharp eyes," she says. Her voice is hoarse and dry as a sepulcher. She sounds weary, like all this was decided long ago, like my rebellion is entirely expected and entirely exhausting. "Clotho, tell us what you've done."

There's a chill in the room. The midwife murmurs an excuse and rushes out. Thetis clutches her son to her breast as though she can protect him from us, armor him against the world. Achilles begins to cry, and in my mind I see him at Troy, weeping over a pyre.

There is nothing – no reasoning, no defense that I might summon – which could withstand my sisters. Lachesis is as calculating as the measuring rod; Atropos as inevitable as her shears. Our roles are graven into us, indelible, immutable. I am the spinner, never the measurer. To read Achilles' fate is to reject my nature, and my sisters will never accept that, they will never grant a shred of leniency.

So I don't try. "I needed to know," I say. "I needed to see the course of his life and decide how it ends."

"Witch," Lachesis spits. "You'll be punished for this." And only now do I realize the matter is settled; she will never forgive me.

Turning on one another is unfamiliar territory for us. My stomach twists in shame and denial. But I hold the life of Achilles in my mind now, that peony bloom of unutterable violence and anger. I let his battle-memories seep into me and guide my limbs. All that anger burns the regret out of me, clears my mind, keeps me focused as I step towards Lachesis.

She has measured the lifethreads of countless warriors, but never the greatest. Never Achilles.

I'm across the room in an instant, telling myself I just need time to think, time alone, time away from my sisters. But there's something else I need. Lachesis, her eyes wide, swings the measuring rod at me like a club. I parry with my spindle and grab her by the wrist. From the other side of the bed, Atropos cries out, "Clotho, enough!" and I wrench the rod out from Lachesis's grasp and drive my shoulder into her chest. As Lachesis stumbles back, Thetis and I lock eyes.

"Tell me," she says again. She, who has seen only the first moment of her son's life. She, who has a hundred thousand hopes for what he might accomplish. She, who could never bear to hear the truth of the heel and the arrow, and I, who could never bear to tell her.

I turn, measuring rod in hand, and step away, abandoning myself to the ocean of time, stepping out of the birthing chamber, stepping into the thin infinite space between moments.

# THE ROD

It always ends the same: the arrow, the heel, the death of Achilles. Why do I feel as though his thread is incomplete?

Lachesis calls mortal life an expression that must eventually equal zero. She sees us as the ultimate Pythagoreans: enforcers of a natural law set down before the rise of the Titans. How many rules am I breaking to change the fate of Achilles?

Sometimes a thing is only noticed in its absence. Here on the mountainside, it's only in the deep winter silence that I realize how keenly I feel the hole where my sisters should be. My abandonment of them is an inversion of the natural order, an upending of the way of things. But why must the way of things be so hard? I see Achilles, the only mortal I've ever truly known, face-down in the dry earth, and my heart aches. I see Thetis in the birthing bed, the look on her face as she realizes that her son's fate is so awful as to be unspeakable. There must be something I can do.

Lachesis has always made it look so easy. So mechanical in her movements: she measures, she marks, she hands the string off to Atropos. I try to feel the tool, to somehow intuit its usage. Pressure builds behind my eyes. And nothing comes; no matter what I do, Achilles goes to Troy.

The pressure sharpens to a headache so suddenly that I drop the tool in the snow and have to fumble around for it, squinting against the sun's brightness.

That's when he finds me. It's rare for a mortal to surprise me, even a demigod, but the boy stepping out from behind a fir tree has a quicker, quieter step than most.

I know him immediately, of course. I have seen out of those eyes.

He levels his homemade spear at me with casual grace. "An intruder on the mountain? Attack me, then. I could use practice."

When I don't move, he cocks his head. "If you won't attack, then tell me your name. There's little company to be had up here."

I give him these things: a false name, a reasonable excuse for my presence, a smattering of news from the rest of the world.

I withhold these things: his fate, any whispers of the conflict brewing with the Trojans, the truth.

We sit by his fire and talk. We eat. But I'm overtaken again by that keen sense of absence. He is here, yes, learning the ways of war from the centaur Chiron. But there is a sense of wrongness about the place, about him. A coldness, almost a casual cruelty. The boy in front of me is no older than twelve – he hasn't yet seen the horrors of war. What has he suffered, to make him like this?

I could review the lifethread, go through the moments of his childhood until I find the source. But it feels kinder to ask him, to only augur whatever fate he is willing to share.

It doesn't take long. I see the way his hands clench when I ask after his mother. The tightness around his eyes. And suddenly I have it, and I'm filled with a rage that is entirely my own.

\* \* \*

## SPINDLE, ROD, SHEARS

All mortals come to this place eventually. From my clifftop vantage point, I can see both sides of the river: sweeping hills on one side, a yawning cave where Hades begins on the other. The black water in between, cold and unyielding and as solemn as the gravest oath. Even now, Charon and his ferry are making their slow and ceaseless transit across the broad current. A hundred mortals with vacant eyes huddle together on the deck, dimly aware of where they're headed. Dimly aware, perhaps, that Atropos has done her work, that their lifethreads have been cut.

Once, long ago, I came here to think. To hide from my sisters and wonder as to the shape of this universe that has damned the three of us to our roles. Perhaps all immortals, we Moirai and the Olympians and the Titans are all subject to the whims of some higher order. Perhaps even a nereid acts only as her fate dictates. The idea brings me no comfort.

I've uncovered one use for the measuring rod, at least: this moment was pinpointed with greater specificity than I thought possible. And right on time, she arrives.

Thetis has chosen her place well, tucked behind a mound of earth on the grassy side of the river. The infant Achilles squalls from his place on her back as if sensing what's to come.

I curse the nereid as I curse myself. Which of us has done more to protect him? To harm him? The mother, or the witch?

I heft the rod like a spear. I can keep him safe in this moment, at least. Stop his mother from doing something out of love that will hurt him more than anything else could.

Just as I take my first step down the hill, a pair of arms wrap around me and pull me to the ground.

We grapple silently, rolling in the tall grass, unwilling to alert Thetis, trading blows in the dirt like feuding rams. But my opponent has the advantage of surprise. In the end she pins me facing the river on my belly.

"Don't struggle," Lachesis says. "We can talk once Thetis is finished. Just remember she's only doing this because of you. What's happening to Achilles is your fault."

\* \* \*

I am watching Achilles drown.

I remember it now. Blurred and hazy, a flash of terror in his childhood. Black water in the lungs, coughing up tarry mucus for hours after. A kindness, his mother told him. A protection against the world.

Watching Achilles from the hill, Lachesis on my back, I can feel it: Styx's freezing water on my teeth, the cold burn of it on my skin, the fear that Thetis is not saving me but killing me, disposing of me like an unwanted animal. A single ankle, exposed and unfrozen, which will grow over time to be a point of resentment, of shame. Calcify into nothing more than a reminder to Greece's greatest warrior of how weak he is.

The moment his mother plunges him into the icy waters of the Styx, he begins to drown. I think in some sense he will be drowning for the rest of his life. Even now I can feel his rage simmering, billowing, waiting to blossom into blood-drenched peony petals.

## SPINDLE, ROD, SHEARS

\* \* \*

"I'm sorry, Clotho," Lachesis says once the nereid has carried her insensate son away. "But fate is fate. Look at what your meddling brought him."

"I could've stopped her."

"What then? What are you trying to save the boy from?"

A glimmer of hope. If Lachesis and Atropos haven't read his lifethread, then I have something to trade. "Get off my back and I'll tell you," I say.

Lachesis just snorts. "Atropos will have to teach you about seniority," she says, and shifts her weight to reach for the lifethread tied to my waist.

I can almost hear Achilles telling me when to push upwards with all my might; when to twist to the side to buck her off. We tumble, breaking apart, rolling down the hill towards the Styx. I scramble to my feet and hold the rod over the riverbank.

"I can't alter his fate, but you can," I say. "Give him a chance, Lachesis. Or I'm sending your measuring rod to the bottom of the river."

"It can't be changed," she whispers. "It's as fixed as the course of the sun."

"Lachesis. He's the only mortal I've ever known. Please."

Her eyes soften. "You're naive, sister. How many warriors have I watched die? How many priestesses that I could've saved from their destinies? This is the way of things, Clotho. We bear the burden."

I hesitate. Then I toss her the lifethread. "See for yourself."

She succumbs to muscle memory; her fingers are reading the story of Achilles before her mind can catch up. And I keep talking. "I'm not asking you to change the way of things," I say, and I can't tell if I mean it or if I just want her to agree to help Achilles. "Just make an exception. If you want me to keep bearing this burden, one exception is my price."

Lachesis finishes reading the thread. When she speaks, the words come slowly, as though each has been weighed with exacting precision. "There is one thing I can do," she says. "But you will meet with Atropos. She'll decide what to do with you."

I nod. "How do I know you'll keep up your end of the deal?"

She gives me a look of disdain. "Give me that." I can't help but wince as she takes the rod. But her honesty shames me. When she's done, she keeps the rod and hands back the lifethread.

"I gave him a choice," she says.

"Tell me."

"Atropos will tell you," she says. "Good luck, sister." And with a step, she vanishes between the moments.

## THE SHEARS

It always ends the same: the arrow, the heel, the death of another demigod in a war that will claim hundreds of their number.

Mortals take after the gods: they're violent, petty, they make war. But the gods can war forever; they can spend an eternity feuding and making up and fighting once again. A hundred old grudges wait in the depths of Tartarus, hoping to be unleashed, embers begging to come alight again.

Atropos calls death a gift. Mortals are free of the eternal struggle, she says; there's always an end in sight. No matter how miserable they are, how wretched, their suffering can only last so long. I imagine she takes comfort in that.

I let the currents pull me to her. When I step out from between the moments, my eldest sister and I are alone on a hilly field, a gentle wind blowing the tall grass around us in waves. I'm disoriented, adrift in space and time, but a fishhook sense behind my navel tells me I've been here before.

"The thread, please," Atropos says.

"What is this place?"

"Don't you recognize Troy?"

I whirl around. The great gates are nowhere to be seen; the city sounds and battle-din have been replaced by the chirping of birds and the soughing of the wind.

But she's right. There is the gentle rise where Briseis will one day be taken. There, the place where Hector will fall and where Achilles will desecrate his corpse.

"Why here? Why so far in the past?"

Atropos laughs, guttural and rasping. I picture the old Titans down in Tartarus chuckling along with her.

"Not the past, Clotho. We're far beyond Troy, in the other direction. Achilles is long dead. His bones have been dust for hundreds of years."

I feel sick. Dizzy. Mortal. "Tell me how he lived."

"Clotho, Clotho. You're holding the thread. You tell me."
I take a breath. I close my eyes.

* * *

It always ends the same.

Can I blame him?

There are Fates, and there are fates, and he was ensnared by both. His birthright was war and ambition. Styx-plunged, centaur-trained. Achilles was born a weapon and sharpened his whole life.

Ask a knife if it wants to cut. Ask a spear if it wants to be thrown.

A choice from the gods is no choice at all.

* * *

Atropos's face is a grinning, monstrous mask.

"He chose," she says. "Lachesis told his mother, who shared it with him in due time. He didn't want to stay in Greece and live a long and uneventful life. He knew what going to Troy meant."

"But he only made that choice—"

"You're going to think yourself in circles, sister."

"Why bother with any of this? If his story still ends here?"

Atropos points at the ground. "We're just in time," she says, still smiling. "Look."

I follow her gnarled finger. A blooming of late spring flowers. Peonies. A field of them, red beneath our feet.

"The beauty of these flowers is in the bloom, the rot," she says. "Mortals are quick in their living and long in their storytelling. The shadow of Achilles is many times greater than the man Achilles."

We sit there and watch the flowers bloom. We sit there for a long time.

\* \* \*

"You aren't satisfied," Atropos says.

"Was this his fate all along? To be dragged along by the Moirai without ever knowing? To die a bitter young man who never knew peace?" For the first time I notice the flowers wilting.

"Would it bring you comfort to think otherwise?"

"Something was missing," I say, gaining confidence. "Even after Lachesis gave him his false choice, something came unraveled." I run my fingers over it again, feeling the length of it. I am a spinner, and a spinner knows her thread. "There is a flaw."

"Hand it over," she says. "We can't change fate. But in the case of a flaw – it would need to be remedied."

I hold the lifethread out for Atropos to examine, all my hopes pinned to it. I think of Thetis so long ago, her entire world contained in one swaddled bundle.

My sister holds the thread up close to one yellow eye. Her smile fades for a moment. Then it comes burning back.

"You have sharp eyes, sister. Don't go yet," she says. "I need to lend you something."

\* \* \*

I cast my eyes around the house, waiting politely for the old man to finish coughing. It's something in his lungs, something wretched and rotten that makes me think of the black water of the Styx. As pitiable as he is, his eyes are still vivid: blue, sharp, sad. I could almost imagine that he knows, somehow, that this isn't the way it was supposed to be.

"It was when I was very young," he says. "I was supposed to be sent to Phthia, but something happened."

"Your parents heard a rumor from a midwife," I say gently, as though speaking to a child.

"That's right," he says. "Strange omens in the house of Peleus. Rampant, deranged goddesses. So I stayed here."

"And you lived out your days."

He nods, setting off another coughing fit. There is an abiding sorrow about him, the feeling of a life wasted. I run my fingers over the lifethread in my hand, feeling out its unfamiliar contours, sensing the unfamiliar memories. Partway up the thread, a telltale flaw: a collection of split fibers where something went awry. A match to the flaw in Achilles' thread.

I could just do it. I could fix this man without even letting him know. A part of me sees this as a kindness. But the greater part of me sees through the lie.

"Would you like to go to the house of Peleus?"

He looks at me, confused and weary. "I'm too old for making long journeys."

I smile at him. "I can explain it all, Patroclus, but I want you to choose."

Later, as the shears part the thread, he lets out a sigh of relief. And then I'm stepping back between the moments.

I can already see how the threads will weave together. And I'm not fool enough to think this will give Achilles the life I wanted him to have. Achilles will still be plunged into the Styx by his mother. Achilles will still choose to go to Troy, knowing that he'll never come home. Achilles will live, Achilles will struggle, Achilles will die. But up until his last days, he won't be alone.

And when the arrow meets his heel, he'll breathe a sigh of anticipation. Soon, he'll be with Patroclus.

# Achilles in City Island
## Celeste Plowden

Crossing the green steelwork bridge to City Island was like entering another world. *Welcome to City Island, Seaport of the Bronx,* the sign overhead read as the car passed under the nostalgic green-blue steel archway, and the lady within imagined the ornamental finials atop were heralding the entrance to a classical fortress of dreams. There were numerous pleasure boats in the water on either side of the bridge as she looked out from the back seat of her white Rolls as it glided over the turquoise expanse of waters in Eastchester Bay. A variety of seafood restaurants lined the main street of the island, with showy signs of giant lobsters, and red rooftops over quaint brick or white-painted buildings, giving the island an illusion of a New England fishing village. A calming zephyr under the late day summer sun carried smells of concrete and blacktop infused with the odor of freshly caught fish in only the hint of damp, salt air. But then, it was attached to New York City, and not Cape Cod or Nantucket. "I'd like to take a walk around," the lady suggested as her driver, a lanky man with a head of grizzled, unkempt hair, pulled into a parking place in front of one of the eateries.

"Have a look, Madam?" He bowed again as she pranced ahead of him into the shop.

Inside the darkened, narrow walls the dank air smelled as if sunlight and time had altogether abandoned the old building and its contents, and a faint smell of tobacco and musty rope lingered about the place. The oak floorboards creaked in agony at the weight of feet trampling over them – trespassers from the living world who meant to invade the secret dreams of bygone days and the spirits that inhabited the neglected articles within, once prized and wrought by hands that had since departed the earth. The shop contained two large glass cases that occupied nearly the whole room, and were neatly laden with antique objects, including small sculptures, jewelry, and carved conch shells.

There appeared to be nothing else in the room except a lamp with a bottle-green glass shade that sat atop one of the cabinets which startled the visitors when it clicked on and offered a dim light to the murky atmosphere. A statuesque young man in fitted bib overalls and no shirt surfaced behind the cases, the greenish cast of the lamp highlighting his muscular physique, and the outline of his scant black beard and mustache enhanced his impressive cheekbones and prominent nose. His round, sepia eyes darted over the customers.

"Nice afternoon," he greeted them, surveying this athletically built, middle-aged woman wearing a sleeveless shift of golden silk, a strand of long pearls that swayed as she walked, and a rhinestone headband with several tall peacock feathers. She stared boldly at him with her glittering aquamarine eyes, but he looked away.

"Indeed," replied the lady as she perused the display of gewgaws on the glass shelves. "I'm Juno, by the way," she added with a simper.

"Hello, Juno. Is that kind of like *Hera?*"

She lifted her head regally and told him, "One and the same, but I prefer Juno."

"Do you like scrimshaw, Miss Juno?" the man asked, noticing her eying a section in the cabinet that had several such artifacts. "Antiques," he informed her. He took out several larger pieces and laid them gently on the countertop. "Look at this one, a row of carved mermaids."

"Antiques, really?" she chuckled, as she leaned over and surveyed the piece and the fine scrollwork of the mermaids' hair, and the intricate scales of their spritely fishtails. "It's beautiful." She lightly fingered the long whale bone, but her eyes wandered to another section of the display case which contained jewelry pieces, mostly dingy cameos set in tarnished silver, or French jet pins in fanciful shapes of whales and starfish, and strands of coral necklaces.

The shopkeeper was quick to notice her interest. "Here's one, although it needs a bit of polishing." He fidgeted with several of the pieces, realigning them on the shelf, and pointed to an oval cameo in a silver filigree mounting, depicting a mermaid on the edge of a shore, and a tiny schooner in the distant waters under a crescent moon. It dangled on a tarnished silver chain, just long enough to fit as a choker on the lady's long neck.

"How different," she remarked, eying it under the eerie lamp light. He felt her eyes on him and was careful to continue looking down at his wares. "And what is your name, young man?" she asked.

"Chris," he said, glancing up at the woman only long enough to answer her question.

She tilted her head and smiled, asking in a tuneful lilt of her voice, "May I see the piece, *Achilles*?"

He did not respond to her getting his name wrong, but quickly withdrew the requested item, which she took with her long fingers, absorbed with its fanciful beauty. "A new good luck charm for me." She looked up and beamed as her driver took his wallet out and paid for the item.

"It's a fine piece for a real siren," Chris said, his fingers skimming the novel carving as she held it in her palm.

Her Cupid's bow lips curled upwards towards her cheekbones. "Please clasp it for me," she said turning around and holding the chain around her neck, her thick, golden-blond hair gathered in a low chignon at the nape of her neck. "And now, I would be pleased to have an early bite of supper with you and you might tell me how you came to be here on this faraway island."

A corner of his mouth twitched and his eyes narrowed, as he silently pondered how to answer her. After the necklace was affixed, she glanced at herself in a small standing mirror on one edge of the counter, turning with sparkling eyes and looked directly into his drifting, shadowy ones. The shopkeeper was overtaken with an intense awareness of her commanding demeanor. "Surely," he answered, unable to quite form a smile, his palms becoming sweaty as he simply pulled his lips into a straight line and nodded.

"Lead the way, Achilles," she said, motioning to her driver to follow as they walked out, the feathers in her headpiece waving rhythmically as she turned her head to scrutinize the various restaurants. "Let's sample some of the fresh seafood of this island."

\* \* \*

An arrangement of clams on the half shell and a large pile of steamed mussels were brought to the table on a silver platter in the shape of a whale that had an edging of engraved phrases. Juno turned the dish around several times until she had read all of the words. *'Now the dancing sunbeams play o'er the green and glassy sea, come and I will lead the way where the pearly treasures be. Follow, follow, follow me.'*

"How charming, Achilles," she smiled, looking up at him.

"Excuse me, Miss Juno, but why do you keep calling me Achilles?" Chris asked, frowning at her error. "I guess I've been called worse."

She smiled radiantly and in a lyrical voice said, "Because that's who you are, my dear. Why, I was at your parents' wedding many years ago."

Chris, now anointed Achilles, blinked and looked down at his twitching fingers as they picked up a menu.

"This place is a gem," Juno continued while looking around at the seafaring artifacts affixed to the walls, and her lunch date, who had never been to this particular eatery, also took an interest in the display of the bygone relics. There were antique diving helmets, a pair of battered white oars, weathered lanterns, and several timeworn mastheads of sea nymphs who looked out over the tables full of diners, with silent, barren eyes and sun-bleached lips, most of the paint having worn off decades earlier. They served as sublime reminders of mortality for all, even half-goddesses of the ocean depths. One of the pale, bare-breasted ladies stood out in particular. Achilles glanced at the carved beauty, noting her sculpted, yellow hair falling in great waves over her shoulders, and the smooth, narrow lips barely curving up at the corners, as if to say, "Spend your youth wisely, for it is but a flash."

Quietly, Achilles reflected on his choices in life, which strangely now seemed to be on the brink of opportunity, unlike his boyhood, so lonely and bereft of hope in the small, northern town where he had spent his youth. His father was an angry man who drank to excess, and his mother, a disappointed beauty who bore it with self-loathing and aloofness. He had recognized their feelings of hatred for a world that had tossed them into their pit of misery, and he watched as they daily blamed the Gods of Fate for their imagined misfortune, accepting it as a prisoner accepts his sentence.

They lunched on swordfish steaks and cottage fries, topping it off with glasses of Prosecco, the young man still careful not to look too long or speak out of turn to this unusual lady who seemed to want something from him. Juno fingered the mermaid cameo around her neck, holding up her wine glass and saying, "Here's to our wonderful repast on this mystical island. May it be the beginning of your new destiny," as if she read his thoughts. The air in front of him was heavy with a stream of words that wanted to flow freely like the cyan-blue ocean waters under the little viridescent bridge, which he viewed from the restaurant window, but Achilles held back. Juno held her hand up to the waiter and then pointed to the wine bottle. "Might we have another, please?" She took the two bottles and her glass, motioning to Achilles to follow her out on the boardwalk, and walked toward a bench facing the water.

Faint sunbeams were in the process of setting in a lavender sky, and the ghost of a waxing moon barely peaked out from under the shadowy hills on the other side of the bay. Boats drifted back to shore just below the boardwalk where they sat. The only remnants of the sunny afternoon were whispers of footsteps made by seafarers as they stepped out of their boats onto the wooden docking area, and trails of hushed laughter as they dispersed and headed for a meal in one of the restaurants. Was it only the drink that made him feel a moment of solitary peace binding him to the secrets of these ocean waters, a serene understanding that required no words? Surely the pale orb of night was rising for him alone, heralding in a surprise to his predictable life.

Juno sipped her drink and looked out over the bay, Achilles quietly awaiting her next words. A large fish in the distance flew through the air, spraying salty dew through the late afternoon sky, sparking a distant memory of a horse, or was it a man, running over gushing waves at the edge of a beach. "Do you remember your teaching master, Chiron?" Juno asked.

He ran his fingers through his thick, wavy hair and shook his head. "I don't know any man named Chiron," he said. The image seemed to flash over the late afternoon sky, only this time it was clearly the upper body of a man affixed to the lower body of a chestnut horse. Achilles started, nearly choking on his drink.

"He was a fine teacher, a very noteworthy centaur, admired greatly by the gods," she said.

"I can't imagine what you mean," he answered, trying to keep his voice calm, avoiding her eyes. Yet the image kept recurring before him as it dashed over the sunlit hills, like a scene on a drive-in theater screen.

"I know you see him, Achilles. Try to remember who you are."

He rested his chin on his clenched fist. "Madam, what do you want from me?" he muttered between his teeth. "And what have you put in my drink?"

"You must return to your world and take your place in battle," Juno said.

"*Battle?* What are you talking about?"

She ignored his question and went on. "You were brought to this distant land by your mother, a sea nymph, envy of the gods Zeus and Poseidon who both consented to her marriage with your father, Peleus, because they knew that their son, you, Achilles, would be the greatest warrior of the ancient world. Go back and claim your fate or be forever lost to history."

"I'm happy here, although I don't remember much about my childhood." He heaved a deep breath, his magnificent chest rippling beneath his shabby overalls. "It's nice on the island, and it's my shop, so I can do as I please."

Juno glared and leaned into him, her full, perfect lips spewing out a whisper of providence. "*Really?* Achilles, famous warrior that will be remembered in glory for many centuries, or a forgotten shopkeeper named Chris?" Juno waved her arm over the view in front of them. "Watch," she said steering a confident glance at him.

Achilles sat back and lifted his glass to his lips as if to avoid thinking about the issue.

A great roar from beneath rattled the boardwalk, spewing shards of glassy sea water as a giant head pushed upward out of the bay. A set of monumental shoulders, arms, and legs followed, and stood upon a giant half-shell laden with lustrous pearls. The colossus gripped a fisherman's spear in one hand, and with the other he stroked the head of an enormous dolphin that sprang up to greet him. Achilles gasped and covered his eyes with his empty hand. "Am I mad?" he stuttered, refusing to look at the giant sea god. "Why is nobody else reacting to this creature?"

Juno placed one hand on his shoulder. "Take heart, young man. Poseidon has arrived with a message for you alone. Do look."

One hand slid down to his lap, the other hand shook as he raised his glass to his lips for another swallow of Prosecco. He closed his eyes, hearing the waters rush over the half shell and felt the breath of the god on his face, awaiting his attention. Achilles said, "I can't look."

"You will hear me!" bellowed Poseidon. "Fate is upon you and you must decide, else be forgotten as though you never existed."

Achilles, though shaking so much that it caused the wooden bench to shudder in fear, held out his glass to Juno. "More, please," he whispered, finally opening his eyes to the scene before him.

"We, the gods, cannot force your destiny, but we urge you to understand your place in a great war of classical times. You are invincible because your mother, Thetis, took you by your heel when you were but an infant, and dipped you in the waters of the river that lies between the living and the dead, to protect you from the battles you were foreordained to fight."

"Oh, so I can't be harmed?" Achilles blurted out, turning to look at Juno for assurance.

The sea god roared and thrashed his spear into the waves. "No! Only one part of you is at risk, the heel that your mother held you by because it was not anointed by the River Styx."

"Which heel, Your Majesty? Right or left?"

Poseidon shook his head, his wet hair showering a blast of droplets over the boardwalk. "I do not know," he called angrily. "You must take care of your own fate as it has been given. What is your answer, Achilles?"

Something welled up inside Achilles, his chest heaving in indignation, the alcohol he consumed firing his usually mild temperament. He pondered the loss of his pleasant, quiet life on this tiny island, and the shop he had furnished with the finest of seafaring treasures of the venerable past, where he sat leisurely waiting for passersby while he perused a book or listened to an oldies' radio program. *And now he would choose to go to war wearing sandals and a crested helmet, carrying nothing but a spear and shield?* Just as he was about to speak, a group of bikini-clad young ladies walked by, waving and smiling. "Don't forget the poker game tomorrow night, Chris," a chestnut-haired beauty said. With a wide grin he nodded and waved back.

Turning to the sea king he shouted, "My answer is no. *No!*" He took another swig of his drink and pounded his fist on the bench. "Get some other sucker to fight your wars."

He looked at Juno and yelled, "Madam, you shouldn't have come." He expected a menacing retort from her and was armed with more words of refusal for any comments she might throw at him.

Juno only smiled, waved her hand at Poseidon, saying, "Your work is done here, brother." And with that, the god of the sea dove into the water with a great splash, his pet dolphin following, leaving the pearls and half shell to sink into the deep. "At last," she laughed, pouring more Prosecco in each glass. "I see spirit in you, Achilles. You will need it in your warring endeavors."

"Begging your pardon, Juno, whoever you really are, *I'm not going!*"

Lifting one finger Juno summoned her servant who was sitting just inside at a large window, having witnessed the entire scenario with Poseidon. "Another bottle, please," she said and he retreated with alacrity to get the requested drink. With the fanfare of a French waiter, he returned with a white bar towel over his arm, bowing before he issued the calming beverage to the seated pair, his tousled hair flying over his cheeks as he poured.

"Watch," Juno said to Achilles, who downed half his drink in one swallow. She waved her arm again across the twilit sky.

"Another movie?" Achilles pushed his damp hair back from his forehead. "I hope this one's not another interactive feature." He slammed his heels down on the pavement, heaving with annoyance, and downed the rest of his drink. "You know, I'd rather go back in and have some dessert," he said.

The last ray of sun was going down over the distant hills, appearing as a narrow magenta band below the darkening cerulean sky. The rising moon, imperfect in its increasing form, shed its white glow over the lapping waters of Eastchester Bay and the three went inside. Juno made sure they were seated with a perfect view of the looming heavens over the bay.

"Let's have some spumoni and a plate of biscotti," Achilles suggested. "Ok with you, Miss Juno?" he added brightly.

"Sounds delightful."

He felt a pair of eyes upon him, perhaps Juno's servant, but looking back he saw only the masthead mermaid staring out at him from her place on the wall. Her expression had changed. Her deadened eyes now had an air of vivacity, her straight lips were parted as though she were about to speak.

Blinking, he found himself unable to take his eyes from the painted figure.

He bit into a piece of chocolate biscotti as Juno began to speak. "There's time for quite a long military career; you're young, Achilles."

He continued to look at the seaworthy fixture. Time was swirling past him, urging him to make a stand for his fortune before his youth faded. The wooden sea nymph stared out blankly at him, acknowledging his vitality and undiscovered skill, reckoning her judgement. "I'll think about it," he said between mouthfuls.

Presently the chauffer walked up, his hands clasped behind his back, his lips pursed, as if gathering his thoughts. "Young man, I urge you not to delay this decision. The time is come to determine your fate, and the outcome of the battles you will fight."

Achilles washed down his food with another sip of the bubbly drink, wiped his mouth with his napkin and said, "And who are you, may I ask?" He leaned back in his chair, one elbow resting on the arm as he surveyed Juno's servant.

"This is Odysseus," said Juno, holding her hand out to the man. "He was kind enough to take me on his quest to find you, and though it has been an adventure for me, I believe our time is running out." She smiled and awaited his answer.

"Oh, really? As in the *Odyssey?* Well this is getting stranger and stranger," Achilles retorted. "Will you excuse me for a moment?" He stood up and walked towards the mermaid.

A hush followed as he stepped towards her. There were now vast oceans in her eyes, glimmering and inviting, and turning one ear to her lips, he heard the rush of waves draw back, moaning like distant cries from an ancient sea, a sound he had never heard, calling with steady cadence of what waits beyond the shoreline: *Immortality.* The sound grew louder with each undulation, *"immortality, immortality,"* the waves spoke. Looking back at Juno and Odysseus, they seemed but lifeless shadows wavering under the dim electric light of the restaurant, caught in time like the wooden sea nymph, who was now singing tunefully into his ear, *"follow, follow, follow me..."*

From out of the large window he viewed the boardwalk that he had so often strolled along, where he had basked in the salt air during all the seasons of the year, watching the boats go in and out, the fish jumping in the shallow currents of the bay, and imagining his life would carry on with acquiring and selling more antique ocean-going relics, smoothly and placidly for many years. There had been nothing to think about other than his daily occupation there in the refuge of City Island, until now. And this here and now was taking prominence over his otherwise contented existence. *"Follow, follow, follow me,"* the weatherworn carving whispered. A new feeling, the passion of adventure, swept in and spellbound him. Achilles walked to the table, his jaw firmly set and his dark eyes wide with resolution. "I'll go," he announced, standing firmly, his fingers gripping the back of his chair, causing the muscles in his arms to flex. "Take me now."

Juno rose to her feet, elegantly lifting her head and holding out her hand for Achilles to take. Odysseus bowed and said, "My mission is fulfilled, Achilles."

* * *

They walked to Juno's Rolls, Achilles taking a seat in front with Odysseus, who asked, "Shall we, Madam?" The goddess nodded, her peacock feathers billowing in the breeze as they drove towards the steel bridge that had welcomed them.

As they crossed the water, Juno tapped Achilles' shoulder and said, "It's been a delightful evening. I'm very pleased with you, Achilles…" Her voice trailed off in a whisper as the car passed under the arch with the fortress finials, and Achilles found himself standing alone on an infinite coastline in the sweet night air. The waters sparkled under the fair moon, and in the distance he listened to the growing roar of armies as they surged towards him, shouting his name in tribute, "Achilles!"

# Veiled Stratagems
## Sultana Raza

The nobles gathered on the ramparts had to shield their eyes from the light emanating from Achilles' golden armour. Though the demigod had been shouting at the top of his voice for a few hours, he showed no signs of slowing down. Apparently going round and round in his war chariot hadn't made him dizzy either. At a respectful distance behind him, his Myrmidons and most of the Achaean army had gathered to watch these unprecedented events unfold. No mortal had willingly taken on the son of Thetis in single combat before.

\* \* \*

"I'm proud of you, scion of my throne!" Priam raised a trembling hand in blessing, as Hector bowed to pay his dear pater his last respects. They were gathered before the Main Gate of Troy.

"You're the most skilled strategist in war's art," Phareegius said encouragingly, handing his brother the Royal Sword, made of bronzed iron, studded with emerald and ochre crystals.

"With Ancient Nymphean blood, are strong your bones!" Priam shouted after his son's departing back. "Though how can I let go a piece of my heart?" He clutched his head despairingly.

"I can't bear to let my precious son depart." As Hecuba collapsed, some of her handmaidens rushed to support her.

\* \* \*

As soon as the Gates of Troy opened and Hector emerged alone from it, the Achaean army cheered his bravery. But an angry roar from the demigod soon silenced them.

"Come now, Myrmidon, be reasonable," the Trojan prince said in a soothing tone, as Achilles jumped down from his war chariot.

"You're a coward who killed a defenceless lad; but now you'll see I'm infallible!" Achilles growled.

"I was tricked! Like you, I'm just as sad!" Hector continued to argue his case, but Achilles launched into an attack without any warning, lunging at him with his sword. Every time he struck out, he recited some lines:

*"We're unique grains on the cosmic shore,*
*From the sea of hope, can we gulp or drink?*
*Molten is becoming our galaxy's core.*
*Is immortality waiting on time's brink?"*

Dodging Achilles' blows, the Trojan looked at the livid man quizzically. Had he really gone mad?

*"As cresting waves, seahorses laugh,*
*Gleeful urchins spit out salty draughts.*

## VEILED STRATAGEMS

*I wish I had a crab's hard shell,*
*So I wouldn't hear my looming death's knell!"*

Achilles managed to strike the prince as the last line ended.
"He was a poet, and a gentle soul. You killed my cousin, my fair kin!" the furious man shouted. At last Hector understood why Achilles had been spouting poetry. Most probably these lines had been written by his dear cousin Patroclus.
"On my spirit, his death's taken its toll. But I was deceived; I've committed no sin!" The Trojan's words infuriated the golden-haired warrior so much that he started lunging at him in earnest with his golden sword.

\* \* \*

"Can you whisper to Achilles, using demigod speech? No sense of fairness could his mother teach?" Cassandra took a surprised Helen to a corner of the ramparts, away from the noble families watching the unmatched, unjust fight in the dry arena. Her own green eyes were impassive as she watched Helen's icy grey ones calculating her own advantages for doing this favour for the Trojan priestess.
"You say any man you can persuade, not very fair is this duel, so bizarre. Grief-crazed Achilles, try to dissuade. Our Hector's body, he shouldn't mar." At Cassandra's query, a doubtful-looking Helen slowly shook her head.
"Do you promise I'll wed our Hectorius? You won't put obstacles in our way, if he emerges victorious? In our favour, King Priam you'll sway?" the golden woman bargained.

"Soothe him, whisper in this Nymphean Conch. His mater's from the sea, his pater's reached the sky. Calming ideas in his mind launch." Even as Cassandra nodded her head reluctantly, she took out a big white shiny Conch from a pouch hidden in her priestess's robes and handed it to Helen, who looked at it curiously.

"Will he hear me from so far, so high?" For the first time, Cassandra heard doubt threading the tones of this haughty woman.

"Neither honour nor glory will you gain. If you really care for your reputation, you'd realize you're a pawn if you were sane. Stop now, or be cursed. You'll get no cremation." As Helen started whispering in the Nymphean Conch, repeating Cassandra's words, they saw Achilles pause and look up at the ramparts in their direction.

"There's still time for you to refrain. Retreat with honour, for you have an excuse. There's glory for you if you can restrain your deadly anger. You can still choose." Seeing an opportunity, Hector tried to persuade the heartless warrior sheathed in golden armour. For a moment the son of Peleus hesitated. Then trying to stop the streams of thought entering his head in Helen's seductive voice, he roared and struck the prince down. There were a few cheers from the Myrmidons. But as the swift-footed soldier started playing a cat-and-mouse game with the mortal hero, these cheers dwindled to hushed whispers.

\* \* \*

"Can't you try harder to melt his icy heart?" Cassandra said frustratedly when the fight had been going on for four hours. She could still feel Achilles' noxious turmoil palpably, emanating in waves from the arena.

"Nothing can get through the fire of his rage. I can't do any more on my part," Helen shrugged resignedly.

"Around his head, Athena's built a cage." Closing her eyes, Cassandra could just about see how the gods were fuelling the demigod's delirium, and now they were trying to stop Helen's thoughts from reaching him.

"For the first time, there's a man I can't persuade." The proud woman sounded despondent.

"He's only half mortal, protected by the gods. Don't let their stratagems dissuade you. He's slowed down. You've beaten great odds." In a corner of her mind, Cassandra found it strange that she was consoling the conceited woman for not being able to charm or cajole a man. What else would this never-ending war make her do?

"Don't hack at helpless Hector in Hyperion's light, if you really care for your immortality.

"Glory you won't get for this unequal fight. Use your head; rein in your brutality." Grabbing the Nymphean Conch, the priestess tried to send coils of her thoughts inside the incensed man's head, but could only slow him down a little.

Her tall brother should've fallen down by now. Had she given him the correct dose? Or was he really so hardy? On the one hand, Cassandra was proud of her brother for being so tough. On the other, she was worried that if things didn't go according to her plan, then she'd fail miserably. She longed to confide in someone. But could she really trust this imperious woman by her side? What if this self-centred Spartan woman communicated her secret stratagem to the demigod through the Nymphean Conch in order to get him on her side? No, it was too risky.

Her brother was bleeding from small cuts, and was slower in his responses. It was obvious to both sides that the Commander of the Myrmidon battalion was just playing with the mortal man, stretching out his pain and humiliation. The Achaean army had stopped cheering the Phthian leader a long time ago. Now even the Myrmidons had fallen silent under the blazing sun.

\* \* \*

Since both of them had worn cloaks to disguise themselves, the guards tried to stop them. But Cassandra used her hypnotic ability to freeze the outer guards. Helen employed her honeyed voice to persuade the remaining four to open the massive side gate.

Everyone gasped as a black-robed figure entered the arena. Achilles looked up as he heard the murmurs of surprise running through the Myrmidons and the Achaean army. The livid man raised his right arm as if to throw his spear at this intruder.

So she took off her black cloak; her long flaming hair, along with her white priestess's robe, made it unmistakably clear that a woman had entered the arena.

## VEILED STRATAGEMS

"Didn't Thetis, your mother, try to warn you of the price you'll pay for immortality? Perhaps just as keenly will she mourn when you face justice for this insanity?" The green-eyed priestess used her most commanding tone, but Achilles made a twisted grimace, which would've been a smile when Patroclus was still alive. In response, he stabbed the Trojan prince through the stomach, who gave a last gasp before losing consciousness. Wailing in despair, the seeress rushed to put her black robe over her brother's stomach, and tightened his belt over it, to stem the flow of his ichor. Though the demigod was surprised to see faint glimmers of gold in the prince's blood, he grabbed Cassandra's long scarf from around her neck, and tied her brother's feet to the lowest bar of his war chariot. She collapsed on the ground, as keening wails rose from the Trojan ramparts. Grinning wildly at her, he started dragging the princely body around the arena.

Composing herself, she took a grip on her consciousness. If she couldn't get through to this madman via the strong stream of her thoughts, perhaps she could try another tack. It was imperative that Hector's body should suffer as little damage as possible.

"Oh, noble horses of a divine race! With the Great Pegasus keep your pact! Why don't you slow down your pace? Don't take part in this lowly act." The prophetess got up and whispered to the golden equines through her Nymphean Conch.

As the horse on the right veered off, the war chariot became unbalanced and fell to the side. Seeing her chance, Cassandra tried to tear off her scarf from the chariot's bar. But the fabric was stronger than it looked.

Furious, the swift-footed warrior got up and tried to hold onto the horse on the left-hand side of the chariot. But the horse on the right-hand side was trying to get away. While this tussle was going on, three arrows struck the fabric that was keeping Hector's body attached to the chariot in quick succession. By this time, Cassandra had found one of her brother's small knives in the dust, and could easily cut through the fabric. Thanking both Phareegius for his unmistakable aim and the Great Mother for not letting his arrows pierce his brother's body, she stood up to face the twisted contortion that was the Phthian leader's face. How could anyone call him attractive?

Meanwhile, his golden horses ran away towards the sea, not heeding his angry whistles, with the golden chariot dragging willy-nilly behind them. While some Myrmidons took off in their pursuit, others ran to line up behind their leader.

It looked for a moment as if Achilles would strike down Cassandra, but something in her green, fearless eyes, glittering with hatred, stopped him.

The Myrmidon Commander gave guttural instructions to his battalion in an unknown tongue before mounting another chariot made of the carapaces of giant deep-sea crabs, pulled by two black horses. He sped off towards his camp through the silent Achaean army. Though he could feel waves of their fear and disgust at his actions, he had no mind to stop and punish any of them for their unvoiced disrespect. All he wanted to do was to dive deep into the sea, to forget that Trojan's cowardly act, and to wash off his grief about Patroclus if he could.

* * *

"Very few mortals could fight for four hours our chief with fiery ichor in his veins." The massive Head Myrmidon blocked Cassandra's way to her brother, though he spoke respectfully enough.

"Don't let anyone the prince's body mar!" Cassandra's order came out as a hoarse whisper. The dust from their fighting hadn't settled down yet in the arena, but its bitter taste was like nothing before her regret at not being able to stop the madman from doing so much harm to her dear sibling.

"On his honour this death is not a stain." As the Head Myrmidon inclined his head towards the Trojan leader's body in respect, the others followed suit. They soon produced a makeshift stretcher from their ranks. Ignoring Cassandra's orders, pleas, and curses, they placed her sibling on it. While the remaining ones saluted the fallen prince, four of them picked up the pallet and made off for their camp at a trot.

* * *

As Cassandra, Charmain and other priestesses slunk along in dark cloaks through the sleeping enemy camps, they could hear a faint singing. That gave them an idea of where the madman's tent was located.

*"With Nymphean dew shines their sweat,
Jewel-like beads, exude my sons.
Like Indian pearls, their teeth are set.
Quicker than antelope, their feet can run."*

Recognizing her father's frail voice floating over the damp air, Cassandra tried to hurry, but she'd forgotten how hard it was to walk in the sand.

*"Marble-smooth their glistening skin,
Pools of hope light limpid eyes,
Beauteous hair have all my kin.
With blood of nymphs, we have deep ties."*

Priam's voice sounded closer. Fear, anger and desperation lent her feet wings. Her plan of sneaking in, hypnotizing the guards and rescuing her brother had been foiled by her own pater now. Someone was chuckling next to Priam.

*"How can I let my precious son's body
Lie and rot in a brutish tent,
Unembalmed on rough sand shoddy
On a cold beach, as my heart rents?"*

Beating his chest, as Priam almost shouted out the last words in his grief, Achilles gave a hollow laugh in response.

Both of them looked up in surprise, as a woman in dark robes stepped out of the inky night. As she threw off her hood, her hair took up the sparks of the small fire burning outside the big tent. Her sibling's body lay in front of it towards the barely audible sea.

Before anyone could move, Cassandra quickly pulled up her father, who was kneeling in front of the so-called *demigod*. There were faint flecks of foam around the king's mouth, and his head was moving from side to side. She was both angered and saddened to see her pater driven to the brink of madness. Was that why he was chanting that old nursery rhyme sung to all royal children, much to this brute's amusement? Though his Myrmidons weren't in sight, she could sense their presence nearby.

"No Minotaur or Gorgon have you slain. With no skin of Nemean lion been arrayed.

"Erymanthian Boar? Were you his bane? With Stymphalian Birds have you ever played?" Turning on Achilles, Cassandra launched a barrage of insults at his honour, but he just shrugged her off with a wave of his arm.

"Can you even control your unfair rage and grief? Though you say you can command sharks in shoals? Did the Colchian Dragon ever call you thief? As strong as your sword and arm is your soul?" As her verbal assault continued, ignoring her, the Phthian warrior began to stroll towards the sea. Four of his Myrmidons slid out from the surrounding darkness to form a barrier between her and the prince's immobile body.

"If your armour's so superior from that of mortal folk, don't use semi-divinity as your cloak!" Cassandra couldn't help shouting after his retreating back.

"We've preserved his body, as you bade us do. Leave now, my lady, while his anger cools," the Head Myrmidon said respectfully enough.

"Before his lips turn completely blue, we'll take him home now. We are no fools." The priestess spoke more to herself than to the men. Closing her eyes, she began to chant in the Ancient Nymphean tongue, "O, mother of Achilles, heed our cries. All too soon as your son dies, blame not Troy for the griefs he caused. If only spears of rage he'd paused. If only not as an automaton; with strings pushed and pulled by gods above, his infamous murders he hadn't done. If only he'd shown humanity love."

Before Cassandra had opened her eyes, her nose informed her that someone wearing an unusual perfume was approaching them from the sea. As faint glimmers of seashells and pearls solidified into a tall and regal form, they guessed it was Thetis herself, materializing through the gloom from the sea. Even Priam came out of his fit of madness to stare wide-eyed at the beautiful apparition before him, dressed in seaweed skirts and a mother of pearl blouse with red, purple and orange coral necklaces and bracelets. Cerulean shells of unusual shapes adorned her long hair, rippling in all shades of the sea from azure to indigo, light green to dark, beaded with pink and grey pearls. As the goddess chanted, her voice was both deep yet light, soft yet strong:

*"Royal and godly, my son is proud,*
*High his head, to threats won't yield!*

*He stands far above the lowly crowd,
He's by far the best in the field!"*

But Cassandra soon recovered from the awe she'd felt at first sight. Her pater was gripping on tightly to her shoulder, as if he'd fall if he didn't do so.

"Not all his celestial bronze or gold, carved in greaves or scabbards bold, can help to alleviate the crushing cold that will grip him in its eternal hold." The seeress began to tell his future with her eyes closed.

Thetis took a startled step back, but soon moved forward, pointing a finned finger at the priestess:

"Why should he withdraw from glory or fame? You won't understand, for you aren't the same."

"No need to hammer, or shape, or cut. No need to measure, or fit, or strut about his glistening glory. There aren't any buts. For soon his cruel eyes will shut," Cassandra chanted back to the goddess.

"He does the biddings of his great gods. He's bound to beat all great odds!" Thetis boasted. From the corner of her eyes, the priestess noticed a gleam of golden hair. Achilles had come back silently from the sea. Half-hidden by his dark grey tent, he wasn't looking quite as arrogant now that he thought no one was looking at him. Since he was there to listen to her, perhaps she could shame or frighten him into yielding up her brother's body.

"No need to fasten his godly armour's hooks. It can't protect him from nefarious feats. His deeds aren't better than those of crooks. Does any kind of heart in his chest beat?" the Trojan priestess said in a slightly louder voice, for she didn't want to wake up the Achaeans if she could help it.

Thetis uttered a spell in her own tongue to freeze the priestess, but was astonished to see that it didn't have much effect on her.

"His godly armour is just a waste. Of his own medicine, bitter and sour, he's bound to get the same tart taste, as closer slides his death's arrowed hour. Isn't it ironic? Shame, o shame!" Both mother and son gave an involuntary shudder at these words.

"My son can't be killed! He doesn't have a peer!" Thetis declared confidently.

"Yet a warrior who doesn't have any great fame shall make you shed a great many tears," Cassandra threw back at her.

"You know not how I've protected my son!" the goddess said in a mocking tone.

"But the Muses, our cousins, know your full tale," the seeress intoned calmly.

"From no mortal warrior will I ever run. From no battle will I ever bail." Achilles stepped out from the shadows to make this declaration in steely tones. More Myrmidons came forward and saluted him as one man. Thetis held out an arm and gave her son a half-embrace.

"Of this Trojan prince why are you so afraid that you can't release his body to his family?" Cassandra asked quietly.

"In all corners of your mind why can't I wade? I can glimpse your thoughts but sparingly." Thetis was puzzled.

"To take his body home, what's the urgency? What wily schemes do you now hide?" the tall warrior enquired suspiciously.

"My mother's very sick, it's an emergency." Cassandra let her pent-up tears well in her luminous eyes, hoping this excuse would suffice. After a quick, unintelligible exchange with her son, Thetis muttered something to the guards in their language.

"We don't hold him here because of any pride," she said to the Trojans before dismissing them from her sight. Cassandra hoped her vast relief didn't show in her eyes, as she didn't want her enemies to become even more suspicious about her real intentions. The Myrmidon guards placed the immobile prince on a stretcher, which was put on a longish van. Then they helped Priam and Cassandra get on another chariot, put his chest of gold at the Trojan king's sandy feet and drove them all away towards Troy. Cassandra's priestesses followed in another chariot, with Myrmidons running behind, to escort them back to the safety of Troy's impregnable walls.

\* \* \*

"What did that seeress mean by my 'arrowed hour'? Isn't avenging one's kin an act of honour?" the lion-maned warrior mused as he paced up and down his tent.

"She doesn't really have any great power. Though perhaps you could've fought when you were calmer," Thetis said gently, patting the cushion beside her. Sitting next to her, he put his head on her shoulder.

"But the gods were applauding. I could hear their claps," he said in a puzzled voice.

"As you know, they tend to keep their plans under wraps. Did they egg you on, to set the trap for fate's slaps? Yet without my hero, their plans would collapse." Thetis's sea-green eyes blazed with pinpoints of blue light as she considered different possibilities, peering through time's veils into her son's future.

"To choose immortality, did I do any wrong?" He sounded like the little boy she knew and loved.

"At least through the ages, they'll sing your song." As his mother began to croon the same lullaby she'd hummed when he was a child, the warrior slowly slid into a restless sleep.

# The Eyes of the Pentekonter
Chey Rivera

The smoke-charged winds swelled the single square sail of the pentekonter, assisting the fifty oarsmen as they rowed away from the burning towers of Troy.

Leaning against the railings of the forecastle, with his back to the destruction he caused, Odysseus smiled bitterly. As the waves took him away from the place that had made and unmade him, he found himself tortured by the memory of a single man – Achilles.

During the stagnant years of the Trojan War, when the Trojans hid behind their walls and the Greeks could do nothing but wait, Achilles had been more a pirate and plunderer than a warrior. The temporary stockade the Greeks had constructed had evolved into a sort of town, and towns needed supplies to survive. For nine long years, Odysseus and Achilles led countless raids across the cities and coastal towns around Troy, leaving destruction and death behind them, as well as mortal and immortal enemies.

Apollo, in particular, was not fond of them.

Now the war was over, and the crew of the pentekonter worked hard and fast as they sailed away from the Trojan coast, but Odysseus closed his eyes to the sea, lost in memories. For nearly a decade, Achilles and Odysseus had walked side by side as the same dark shadows clouded their minds and corrupted their actions. While Odysseus was a skilled and deadly schemer, Achilles had a particular talent for violence, and with each dark deed he seemed to accumulate a brand new offense to the archer god.

All through the war, Odysseus had spent many sleepless nights going over these offenses in his mind, worrying about Achilles and bracing for Apollo's revenge.

First, during a raid in the island of Tenedos, before they had even reached Troy, Achilles speared Tenes, ruler of the island and son of Apollo. "Kill no sons of Apollo," Achilles' immortal mother had warned. A hot-tempered Achilles had ignored her. Odysseus himself passed him the spear.

Second, Achilles' brutal murder of Troilus inside Apollo's temple, which shocked even Odysseus himself. A prophecy foretold that Troy would never fall to the Greeks if Troilus – the King of Troy's oldest son – lived to the age of twenty. With Athena's help, Achilles ambushed Troilus as the boy sought protection inside a temple of Apollo. Without any regard to sanctuary, Achilles cut off Troilus's head and butchered the body, blood running thick over Apollo's sacred altar.

The third and last offense was the kidnapping of Chryseis, a daughter of one of Apollo's priests, captured by Achilles after he razed the city of Chryse, and whom Agamemnon, leader of the Greek army, had taken for himself as a prize. She was one of the many captives pulled along by Achilles' and Odysseus's men as they looted and burned their way around Asia Minor.

This last offense – the kidnapping of Chryseis – had consequences for the whole camp. Apollo sent a plague that not only brought death to the Greek soldiers, but discord and dissent among the lead generals.

"You have offended the gods and yet it is I who must suffer! Once again, a sacrifice is expected of me!" roared Agamemnon. "If Chryseis, my rightful prize as lead commander, must be taken from me, then I want your prize, Achilles. Bring me Briseis, and only then I shall give up the priest's daughter. Only then will this plague end!"

But it was not Briseis whom Agamemnon truly wanted. The girl was as meaningless to him as she was to Achilles. He only sought to hurt Achilles' pride in front of the men. To take away from him the spoils of his latest raid. Because Achilles and Odysseus were to blame for Agamemnon's greatest regret: the loss of his eldest, favorite daughter, Iphigenia.

Back in Aulis, when Apollo's twin, Artemis, had demanded Iphigenia's sacrifice to end the dead calm that prevented them from sailing to Troy, Odysseus had been the first to clamor for her death, with Achilles' voice right behind him. Their men had been restless. Hungry for war yet stranded by the whims of the Huntress.

Rallying the other generals behind them, Achilles and Odysseus had given Agamemnon no choice. They made it clear that if he did not surrender Iphigenia, the whole army would turn against him and the rest of his family. And so Agamemnon had finally relented, and Iphigenia had been sacrificed to appease the goddess, with Agamemnon's own seer doing the honors.

Year after year, King Priam of Troy made Agamemnon many generous offers of peace in exchange for treasure and land – offers Odysseus thought were foolish to reject, when the alternative was to continue spilling blood in the name of a woman who did not wish to be rescued. But Agamemnon would never choose peace, not while he grieved.

"As you wish. Take Briseis," Achilles said, his golden mane shining red under the morning sun. "But from now on, I won't lift my sword in defense of your army. My Myrmidons and I withdraw from this war, and let's see how you do without us."

"Leave! We have no need for proud, arrogant boys! This war will be fought by men!" Agamemnon yelled after the retreating Achilles while the rest of his generals groaned behind him. All of them knew Achilles was their most powerful weapon.

Odysseus was not only burdened by the sacrifice of Iphigenia, he also felt the weight of Achilles' corruption heavy on his shoulders. Achilles had been barely out of boyhood when, on Agamemnon's orders, Odysseus had dragged him away from Skyros and into this war. Even then, Achilles had been a prodigy. A bright boy who excelled at everything he did. But years of war under Odysseus's tutelage had turned Achilles into a cruel, brutal soldier.

Soon enough, as the dead started to pile up, and the Trojans pressed near their camps and ships, Agamemnon regretted pushing Achilles away. And once again, he made it Odysseus's job to bring the golden boy back into the ranks.

But this time, Odysseus did not make the same mistake.

\* \* \*

Achilles' beauty was as great as his skills in the arts of war, and it struck Odysseus fully upon entering his private tent. His lean and graceful limbs, the delicate lines of his lips and nose, all contrasted heavily with Odysseus's broad chest and scarred face. Without intending it, Odysseus had intruded into an intimate moment, and was enchanted by a side of Achilles saved only for his friend and lover, Patroclus.

With Patroclus lying beside him, an armorless Achilles played the lyre and sang about long-ago heroes – Heracles, Theseus, Bellophoron, and one who almost equaled him in speed, the great Atalanta. Movement made Patroclus look up to Odysseus, which drew Achilles' notice, and the spell was broken.

Looking away from the pair, Odysseus cleared his throat, and uncomfortably stated the reason for his intrusion.

"Stay," Achilles whispered to Patroclus before addressing Odysseus.

"The old man is finally ready to beg?" Achilles smirked. "It pleases me he admits he cannot win the war without me, but my decision remains the same. Tell Agamemnon I forgive him, but that I am tired of the bloodshed, the years of futile fights and endless death. I do not like this road you have put me on, Odysseus. I no longer recognize myself. Not after Palamides." Achilles glanced desperately at his dear Patroclus, his better half. Odysseus's thoughts turned to their most recent atrocity: how they had framed Palamides, one of the most resourceful generals under Agamemnon, and orchestrated his stoning on a false charge of treason. All to satisfy an old grudge of Odysseus.

"The world has heard my mother's prophecy," Achilles continued. "I will live a long and obscure life if I were to walk away from this war. Perhaps that might be the best thing for me to do."

"But if you fight, if you bring down Troy's best warrior, the prophecy says you will be greater than any hero who has ever lived. Greater even than Heracles. And you want to renounce such a future?" Odysseus asked.

"My legacy means everything to me," Achilles said, then hesitated. "But if turning into a cruel monster is what will bring me glory, then I do not want it."

But it was plain to Odysseus how much this decision hurt Achilles. It was a lot for a young man of his talents to give up.

"Maybe those are not your only options," Patroclus said. "Why should you be confined between the two prongs of the prophecy? There is always another way."

"A third option?" Odysseus said, intrigued.

"I have an idea. It will sound outrageous at first, but bear with me," Patroclus said, looking from Odysseus to Achilles. "I don't believe Iphigenia is dead."

The matter of Iphigenia's sacrifice had been an odd one. Once Achilles and Odysseus had managed to wrench her out from her father's tent, and once Agamemnon's own seer had lowered his blade upon her, she had disappeared. In her place on the ceremonial altar was a blood-soaked deer, with a knife stuck deep in its heart. At the time, they believed that Artemis, for her own godly reasons, had turned Iphigenia into a deer before she claimed her. But Patroclus thought differently.

"I believe she still lives. If we could only rescue her, and bring her to Agamemnon—"

"We may end this war without more bloodshed," Odysseus finished for him.

Patroclus beamed. Achilles sat, lost in thought.

"We would put an end to his grief," Achilles conceded after a moment. "It may be what he needs to finally accept King Priam's offer."

Odysseus's mind whirred with possibilities, wild thoughts turning like the bloody wheels of Achilles' chariot. Yes, they could end the war, and more importantly, Achilles could take an active part in ending it, a part outside the bounds of the prophecy. An honorable deed that would allow him to redeem himself, and relieve some of the guilt on Odysseus's shoulders. Patroclus, sweet, dear Patroclus, had provided them with the means to pull themselves out of the dark.

A clever way to challenge destiny, to turn Iphigenia into a symbol of triumph rather than a harbinger of death. Odysseus had to believe that high up on Olympus, Athena was smiling upon them.

\* \* \*

Patroclus stayed behind to assure the King of Men that Odysseus and Achilles were not deserting him. Odysseus was not sure how Agamemnon would take the news, but if anyone could convince him of the plan's merit, it was Patroclus. Before departing, Achilles made Patroclus promise to stay out of the fight.

Their first stop had been Aulis, of course. Where Iphigenia's sacrifice had taken place. A series of clues led them to the island of Seriphos, then back up again through the Hellespont straits towards the Black Sea.

Months later, against all odds, they discovered that Artemis had taken Iphigenia to Tauris, in Crimea, to live as one of her priestesses. Odysseus and Achilles found Iphigenia eager to see her family, but Artemis was not disposed to let her go. Her twin, and Achilles' greatest enemy, Apollo, strictly forbade it.

Odysseus heard a divine whisper: Apollo was a vain creature.

"Your skill in archery is unmatched, my lord. Surely, you would not mind a healthy competition?" Odysseus taunted him. "Let me measure my mortal skills against yours. We shall take Iphigenia with us only if I can shoot an arrow as true as the archer god himself."

Achilles stared daggers at Odysseus, who did his best to ignore him.

Apollo cocked his head and nocked an arrow. "Very well, insolent one." A bright bull's eye burned in the center of an oak tree on the other side of the temple. With a thunderous twang of his golden bow, Apollo's arrow shot perfectly through its center. "But if you cannot match my aim, not only will Iphigenia be truly sacrificed for my sister, but I will require a sacrifice as well."

Odysseus knew who Apollo wanted before he uttered the famous name.

"Achilles."

The suggestion of an archery contest had come from Athena. Odysseus had followed the goddess's lead, although he did not understand her intentions. In Odysseus's opinion, Apollo's challenge was better suited to Achilles. It required a great demonstration of raw, God-given talent.

For Achilles, Artemis had another challenge: hunt the largest hare in her sacred forest. Odysseus groaned. It would take Achilles months, maybe even years. To hunt those wily animals trained by the great Huntress herself, a great amount of wit and intelligence was required. Odysseus was not sure Achilles had either the patience or the cleverness needed.

As ever the descendant of the trickster god Hermes, Odysseus was desperate for a way to fool the Twins, but Athena knew no trickery was needed.

"Have no fear," Athena whispered to Odysseus. In his mind's eye, Odysseus saw what the wise goddess saw: Achilles thinking like Odysseus, and Odysseus performing like Achilles.

For Odysseus had underestimated how much Achilles had learned from him, and how much he had learned from Achilles. Their bond had become so strong, they were able to channel each other's talents. When needed, Achilles could be wily and cunning like Odysseus, and Odysseus could put his full faith in the gods and excel like Achilles, like he had been destined for greatness.

Before they knew it, they had completed the Challenge of the Twins, and the bitter gods had no choice but to honor their word.

Hours later, when Iphigenia was safely inside Odysseus's ship on their way back to Troy, Achilles marveled aloud at what they had done.

"I still struggle to believe it," he said. "We bested two gods and lived to tell the tale."

Odysseus remained silent, consumed by his thoughts. He had never intended to get so close to Achilles. This intimacy had caught him by surprise.

They were alone inside Odysseus's quarters. Achilles hung on Odysseus's hammock, and for a few moments there was only the sound of the oars beating ceaselessly against the waves.

"Isn't it curious the way we paint eyes on the bows of our ships?" Achilles said suddenly.

"I beg your pardon?" Odysseus replied, startled out of his thoughts.

"The eyes of the ships. They are supposed to guard against dangers. Foresee threats. That is exactly how I have felt all my life," Achilles sighed. "Like I am preparing for some unknown danger, something I must protect my loved ones from. Maybe this worry is something passed down to me by my mother, who in her desperate wish to protect all the children she had before me, she sent them to their deaths. A kind of protective instinct that becomes a self-fulfilled prophecy. A curse."

"Nothing will happen to Patroclus," Odysseus promised. "We have Iphigenia, we will end this war, and you will escape your prophecy with both your life and your fame. In the name of Athena, you will."

Achilles tilted his head at Odysseus. "You never cared about fame, did you? I heard you feigned madness to try to get out of your oath."

Odysseus laughed. "Yes, I never wanted this. But I am glad I came, after all. It gave me the chance to know you, son of Peleus. I am glad of that."

\* \* \*

Death and bloodshed awaited them on the outskirts of Troy.

Upon arriving at the Greek camp, Odysseus watched Achilles search desperately for Patroclus, but their tent was empty. Before long, an exhausted Antilochus, son of Nestor, reached the tent, bearing terrible news.

"Hector has led his army past the River Scamander," Antilochus said, out of breath, "the sands are red with Greek blood."

They learned from him that Agamemnon himself went out to face Hector's forces. The King of Men had slain two dozen Trojans before the blood loss from an arm wound had slowed him down.

More distressingly for Achilles, Patroclus had also joined the fray. He had dressed in Achilles' armor to give the men courage, and his skills in warfare had been enough to fool the Trojans.

"Stay with Antilochus," Odysseus said to Iphigenia, "it's not safe for you out there. We will bring Agamemnon to you. You will save us all yet."

On the battlefield, Odysseus and Achilles found Agamemnon injured, being protected by two of his best generals, Diomedes and Ajax. "I have been taken out," Agamemnon said, "but he's unstoppable." Following Agamemnon's line of sight, Odysseus witnessed Patroclus, glorious in the midst of his aristeia, brandishing Achilles' ash-wood spear and killing the very best men in Hector's army: the Lycian King Sarpedon, son of Zeus and grandson of the hero Bellerophon; Sthenelaus, one of Hector's closest friends; and Cebriones, Hector's own driver. The Trojans came for him in waves, but Patroclus pushed them back, trapping them between the stockade and the sea.

Achilles couldn't take his eyes off Patroclus, but Odysseus focused on Agamemnon. Sneaking past the protection of Ajax and Diomedes, Odysseus related to Agamemnon their journey to rescue Iphigenia, the Challenge of the Twins, and how his favorite daughter was waiting for him back in Achilles' tent.

It took a while for Agamemnon, weak with blood loss as he was, to truly understand what Odysseus was saying. In the midst of all the chaos that surrounded them, Odysseus kept repeating to Agamemnon that his eldest daughter lived, until the King of Men finally believed it, until Odysseus could see the end of this war in Agamemnon's face. A sign that it was truly over.

At that precise moment, golden light split the heavens open, and from that divine light descended those who had watched over Odysseus and Achilles from Olympus: Athena and Hermes. The earthly manifestations of the gods put a pause on the bloodshed. Both Trojans and Greeks held their swords and spears suspended in the air, shocked by this heavenly sight. When the goddess of wisdom raised her hand, they let their weapons fall to the ground. They could not deny the gods' will. The war was over.

But not all gods wished for peace, and there was one who would not be placated. The golden god of archery and augury. Odysseus marveled at Apollo's hatred of Achilles. The god had built the walls of Troy himself, and yet he would rather the city fall than see Achilles succeed.

An arrow covered in the flames of the sun pierced Patroclus's shoulder. Hector stood with his bow raised, his eyes clouded by the powers of the archer god, and Achilles screamed.

But Apollo was not done. As Achilles charged forward, Apollo struck Patroclus again and again, shattering his ash spear and layered shield, wrenching off his breastplate and helmet, leaving him unprotected and pushing him towards his enemies. The men around him now realized the man in Achilles' armor was not Achilles.

A self-fulfilled prophecy, Odysseus thought. The danger Achilles had foreseen he had brought upon himself. His curse, and the curse of his mother.

The fury of the real Achilles could not be missed. He fought his way into the heart of the Trojan ranks, with Odysseus right behind him. Together they were a beast of war. All intentions of peace, all hope of resolution, their work to rescue Iphigenia – it was all forgotten. Pushed to the back of their minds by the demons that stirred within them. Violence was all that remained.

And they did great violence against the Trojans. They maimed, sliced, impaled. And somehow Hector still seemed so far away from their reach. Before Achilles and Odysseus could get close to him, Hector's men convinced him to fall back to the other side of the river.

Odysseus knew they were playing right into Apollo's hands by letting their rage govern them in this moment, but he could not bear Achilles' suffering. He could not remain passive while a vain god doled his petty revenge from the heavens.

Odysseus went down to his knees in front of Athena and Hermes and begged them to protect his friend. Athena assented. She had been slighted as well. She had blessed their peaceful resolution, now she would sponsor their rage. After sending the messenger of the gods on an errand to Hephaestus's workshop, Athena rose up to the heavens, as swift as lighting, the sound an echo of an owl's screech.

The next morning, when Odysseus stood with Achilles by Patroclus's grave, Hermes returned with a gift.

"What are the gods' gifts to me? What is honor, or treasure, now that I have lost the one most dear to me? Nothing has meaning without my beloved Patroclus," Achilles said, as he collapsed to the ground in grief. Odysseus kneeled next to him and hugged him.

"Perhaps this will give you the only purpose for which you can now live," Hermes said.

He presented Achilles with the most glorious armor Odysseus had ever seen. A four-plated helmet with a crest of gold, a bright breastplate and light, flexible greaves. The shining shield was layered thick with bronze, silver, and a central core of solid gold.

Odysseus helped Achilles get into the armor, and with Odysseus's full support, Achilles became the monster he was destined to be. Without a shred of tenderness or humanity left in him, Achilles rode against the Trojans, against the mighty Hector. When he had Hector at his mercy, Achilles would hear no request, listen to nothing but his own fury.

"Lions and men make no deals. Wolves show no sympathy to lambs."

For twelve days Achilles dragged Hector's corpse around the walls of Troy. An avenging demon standing on his golden chariot of death, his two white horses so massive no other man alive could control them. This was to be the greatest stain on his legacy: his dark aristeia.

Brave Achilles, who had been so fond of his mother, who had loved his childhood companion more than life itself, who had slowly carved for himself a place inside Odysseus's heart.

Until the day he dies, Odysseus will think about the undercurrent of darkness that ran through Achilles, and how similar it was to his own. Had he awakened that darkness within Achilles, back when he brought him into this war, back when he had enlisted his help to plot Palamides' terrible death? Had he nurtured this darkness within Achilles during their merciless raids? Or had this darkness always been there? Had they been two kindred souls joined together by war?

After Achilles' death, Odysseus too became a monster. Athena never left him, and neither did the memory of Achilles. Governed by his grief, Odysseus had no mercy left in him. He wore Achilles' divine armor as he orchestrated and executed the sacking of Troy. He saw the face of Iphigenia in the faces of every Trojan that fell under his sword. After everything, Iphigenia was not able to escape her destiny, either. She still remained a harbinger of death.

As Troy burned, Apollo whispered his regret into Odysseus's ear.

As Troy burned, Olympus watched, horrified.

This brutality was Odysseus's doing. Here, finally, was his dark aristeia.

With the fires still raging behind him, Odysseus thought about Achilles, and wondered if perhaps they had not lost their fight against Apollo, against destiny and prophecy. Although it was tempting to blame the gods, perhaps they had failed to see the true threat: how easy it was to listen to their own demons, born and bred by long years of war.

Perhaps, regardless of how their dark impulses had come to be, the tumultuous journey to conquer them was both their greatest tragedy and their lives' work.

As the first rays of the morning sun fell upon Achilles' tomb, the eyes painted on the bow of Odysseus's pentekonter looked on, warily, towards a new horizon.

# Tears in the Sea
## Patricia Scott

The storytellers love to speak of my son. His life is a tale they claim is full of glory and honor. They never think about the others involved. Even the act that leads to his greatness as a hero of legend is but a footnote to the battles he fought. Isn't that the way of them, though?

It's always mothers who are forced to pay the bitterest price for war. The petty games men play for power swallow up entire generations. Instead of learning, they get greedier. The next war always seems built on the foundation of who lost their families in the last one. When I found out I was having a child, I prayed for a girl. The gods laughed. I wept.

My father has always said, as long as I can remember, the seas are so large because they're full of all the tears grieving women send into the world. Their mourning pushed the land apart to hold it all. Still, the wars never stop.

The first time I held my son to my chest, I vowed I would not add to those waters. Others may shed tears, but not me. Not for my child. What good is divine blood if a mother can't protect her own son?

Of course I knew the path I chose was discouraged. When the Fates give you a mortal male child, you are meant to accept it along with the heaviness crushing your heart. My intended duty was raising him to be sturdy and capable. He was supposed to be a fleeting portrait of strength and beauty, the best warrior they could train, until his life ended much too soon on a battlefield somewhere with scores of other dying sons.

I decided I would cast away Fate. I prayed for an answer and came upon an ancient story, whispered by an old woman who sat by the side of the road selling spells. She told me if I could gain entry to the underworld I could dip my son in the River Styx and make him invincible. Both of us would have to survive the journey, of course, and it was not something to be done with an infant. Babies are easiest to take before their time. There are things lurking in the dark who would like nothing more than to steal a new child for their precious life.

I breathed not one word to anyone, not even my husband. Every day, I took Achilles out to the sea to practice with him. No one thought to question me. All of them knew I was of the water; after all, wasn't my father the Old Man of the Sea? It was only fitting Nereus should see his grandson. I was expected to teach my boy to swim. I did. I also got him used to being dipped into the water, held firmly by one heel. Achilles never fussed, my beautiful boy, he accepted the water easily. After a year of practice, he happily opened his eyes and reached for the fish who schooled to him. I hoped he would not be so welcoming to the souls trapped in the Styx's waters.

I also hoped old Charon hadn't raised his prices. Even though I wasn't asking for passage, he would still need payment. Failure to note one living person, much less two, would surely result in swift and severe punishment. He charges less to ferry the dead.

My daily rituals did not concern my husband. Our child, his heir, was fed, growing, and healthy. He was not yet big enough to be taken from me in the interest of raising him to war. This part of the inevitable I had accepted. He would take up weapons and carve up other sons to serve some cause that wasn't his. I would be left at home, the only mother to know her boy would eventually return. The world was never fair. I am unsure who would try to claim it is, except those skewing the system to their favor.

The day came for me to take Achilles to the Styx. My son was strong. He could hold his breath under water for enough time for their power to take hold. I believed he saw well enough that he would not try to touch any of the lost floating in those waters. I chose a day I knew my husband would be busy. On those days, he wished for nothing more than for us to be out of his way. He expected me to take Achilles elsewhere, lest his first explorations of speech disrupt the important things my husband was doing.

I swaddled my son in enough cloth to keep him warm against the chill of the Underworld. My own cloak would provide additional comfort if needed. There are many entrances to the Underworld. I decided to descend through a cave. Achilles was still small enough that I could carry him the entire way. He watched the stalactites until the light became too dim for him to see. I didn't think to bring him a light. A sea nymph's eyes are quite accustomed to gloom and dark. The comfort of my arms and the darkness around us lulled him to sleep. His tiny mouth fell open as he dozed.

Thoughts of him growing to manhood pulled at my heart, tying knots in my stomach. As much as I wished to rid the world of the cruelty of war, I recognized my own powerlessness in the effort. I can protect my child. I cannot change the very nature of man. They cling so fiercely to their ideas of the sanctity of violence. The only method to entirely prevent Achilles from becoming one of them was unacceptable. I could not remove him from the face of the Earth when I brought him to it. Even the fact I had the thought brought me to tears.

Taking him to Hades' Realm and putting him in the River of the Dead was my only recourse. He will be invulnerable to the weapons of man, I told myself. I am protecting him, I repeated. My child will not fall to the whims of men who believe themselves powerful. I will not become one of the women who replenish the sea. I kept telling myself all these things as I carried him on the journey.

As we continued, the air grew stale. The smell of minerals and dust lay heavy all around us. My son could breathe, but it was not the kind to keep him healthy, only alive. Still, it would not do for me to rush into the Underworld. There are things besides its guardians lying in wait. You never want to attract their attention. When the smell of the caves got stronger, Achilles turned his face to my chest and breathed in the scent of clean fabric.

I kept the careful tread of one unconcerned by one's surroundings. The dead who follow this path know their destination and are unafraid. Creatures who thrive in this place are not interested in them. The dead belong. My ancestry gave me the ability to see this path, am I not related to Hermes by blood? The trail fairly glowed white before me, though it cast no light beyond its guiding thread. My cousin provides his own light bodily; I am not so fortunate.

Our progress was sedate, but steady. One of the most disorienting features of the trip is how time ceases to exist. The markers of sunlight, weather, animals, all of these things disappear in the depths of the Earth. Even deep within the ocean, there are currents and changes of temperature. Animals are more rare, but still participating in all their natural rhythms. Caves to the Underworld forsake these cycles, as realms of the gods so often do.

The terrain looked so similar, it was nearly impossible to gauge our progress. There are no signposts in the Underworld. Eventually, from out of the gloom, I heard the faint rush of the River Styx. It must run fast and deep enough so those who do not bring the fare cannot wade across. It must not be so mighty the Lone Ferryman cannot steer his boat. The quiet so prevalent in the depths of the caverns makes even the slightest noises deafening.

Of course, the Styx is not the only challenge visitors to this realm face. When we got a few steps further, a giant shape loomed into view. Three pairs of glowing red eyes followed my movement. I could feel the warmth of the enormous, three-headed pet of Hades. Cerberus growled. The caverns shook.

"Hello, boy," I whispered.

The Fearsome Guardian of the Nether Realm whined softly in response.

"I mean no harm, friend, you are a very good boy. The best companion any god could have. You are doing your job very well."

I reached slowly to pat one velvety foreleg, thicker than the trunk of any tree. The caverns shook again with a thumping I realized was the wagging of a giant tail.

"What a sweet friend you are. I've brought you some treats. I only want to see the river and show it to my son. Will you let us?"

I offered six meat rolls to him, two for each of his heads. Each tongue lolled out to wrap around my hand, taking the food and leaving a prodigious amount of drool. The Mighty Three-Headed Dog of Hades stepped away. I proceeded on.

The rushing of the Styx grew louder, though I still could not see its banks. Achilles pressed closer to me, chasing my warmth against the cold. Yet another thing which never troubles the dead.

Finally, I reached the dark, glistening waters. Eddies of gray foam curled around each other, breaking as they struck rocks or the banks or each other. The waters carry gossamer images, almost pearly against the stark black of the river, of faces twisted in fear and pain as they tumble endlessly in the river as it descends ever deeper. Translucent hands break the surface, grasping for purchase on boats or bodies. They hope for the salvation of being pulled from the water. Though they are in the water, they are not of it.

I shifted Achilles to my hip and knelt in the sucking mud. Cold seeped through my robes. I ignored the wetness around my knees. I longed for the sun's warmth and brightness. It was enough to make me consider turning back with my goal incomplete. With a deep breath, I steeled myself.

I dipped my hand in the Styx and swirled it in a wide circle. The waters obeyed me, forming a wall that deflected the lost souls away from us. Achilles was fully awake by then, staring in the darkness. He did not understand. I hoped he would not remember.

"Just as we practiced, sweet boy. Momma is going to put you in the water for only a short time, and then I am going to pull you right back out. Are you ready?"

What a gift of the Gods it is, the trust children have for their mothers. He answered with a deep inhale of breath. I could not hesitate then. I gripped his heel firmly and dunked him into the aquatic circle I'd made. He held still, so blessedly still. I held him for the count of seven. Then I pulled him from the water in the smoothest motion I could, catching him in the dry part of my cloak. His tiny body shivered, then settled.

"And what brings a sea nymph so far from her home?"

The voice rasped from the darkness, grating against disuse. Old Charon appeared only moments later, using a long, ebony pole to steer his boat towards me. The lantern at the bow shone weakly silver. It offered no true comfort. Though, perhaps dead eyes see it brighter. The boat glided within inches of us, before Charon set the pole in the bottom with a sharp stab into the mud. The Styx and its lost souls churned around him.

"I am protecting my son."

The scrawny, ancient man choked out a strangled laugh.

"You risk angering the Fates. But when has love ever begat wisdom?"

"I am doing what I have to. He is my son."

Charon lifted one shoulder, closing his eyes and pulling back one corner of his mouth to thin his already minuscule lips.

"No matter. I do not answer to them. Or to anyone but Hades. So, then, what offering have you so I can keep away the need to tell him of this little scheme?"

I took out four gold coins and two moonstones. He snatched them out of my hand lightning fast and hid them away somewhere in the folds of his musty old chiton.

"Go then. You've finished what you came for, be gone to the surface with you."

I turned from him and held Achilles a little closer. My urge to hurry overwhelmed me. I fought it. Once again, I took up the litany not to make haste. At each step, I told myself not to bring attention to us. The shining thread stretched before me. I followed it steadily. Cerberus did not meet us again. We were not dead trying to leave, nor were we living trying to enter. We were no longer his concern.

I kept my boy securely wrapped in soft, warm fabric. Though he was dry, the chill clung to his skin. I hoped the sun would burn that away. Though, perhaps if the cold of the Styx stayed with him, they would not be able to make a warrior out of him. I did not think my husband would be so cruel as to discard a child who could not engage in battle. I dreamed of Achilles learning poetry and philosophy and art. He could find his own way in the world. The Fates would be angry at being thwarted, but what was one child not fighting in a war? They could anoint someone else to take his place. I let those thoughts keep me from running.

The way out of the Underworld did not feel as long as the journey to Styx. It may have been shorter, for all I know. The Gods are not fond of keeping time, especially not mortal time. My first hint the end of the journey was nearing was the sweet air flowing towards us. I took deep, grateful breaths to clear the dust from my nose and lungs. Achilles even turned his face away from me to take in the unsullied breeze. We emerged from the cavern and my eyes immediately began streaming tears. I let them wash away my fear along with the grime. My son yawned and babbled, reaching one fist towards the sea.

I waded out with him in my arms. The brilliant blue-green water washed my feet and the hem of my cloak. I thought about kneeling to wash away the mud, but when I looked down, I saw it had dried and fallen away from my knees. I stood in the sunlight at the edge of the surf until my legs began to tremble and I feared I might drop my child. The sun did, indeed, bake away the chill of the Styx. I kissed his brow and carried him home.

Of course, all of you know the rest of the tale. From the time he could walk steadily, Achilles trained in the disciplines of war. He was formidable with any weapon he used. They filled his days with endless training and drills and practices, honing his instincts and reflexes for the battlefield.

With such consistency, it was a matter of time before they saw that while blows would land, they would inflict only minor hurts which healed quickly. It soon became a vicious game among the boys who knew him. They loved to see if they could hurt Achilles. Once the men realized, they decided it was time to put him in his place. Soon the vicious game became endless trials. Could Achilles be killed? They decided he could not. Every method they tried, and they tried every one they could think of, failed. My boy absorbed their violence with easy grace. He was as confident they could not hurt him as they were. He did not take their attempts seriously. How could he? They didn't work.

Then came the damned siege of Troy. One of the most pointless battles to ever be immortalized by foolish men chasing glory for their own vanity. What was it really? A king throwing a temper tantrum over a woman who didn't love him anymore. He could have simply let her go, found another, there were other women just as beautiful. Certainly there were other women who would have stayed faithful. Instead of destroying his nation, he might have looked past his pride and exiled her, banishing her from the home she purportedly loved. That is, if she loved anything. Oh, yes, I have much to say about Helen and her selfishness, but equally do I blame her stupid, vengeful husband.

My son was called to war. He went. Honor dictates it so. He vowed to be a warrior and so he must follow where his Fate would lead. I wanted to tell him Fate had no hold over him. He would not listen. So, I kissed his brow and wished him well and waited for him to come home.

After weeks, each side chose champions, thinking they would save their armies from starving. The Greeks, naturally, selected their invincible soldier. Achilles had earned a reputation before then, but he solidified it during those battles. Nothing Troy might send against the Great Achilles could hope to succeed.

An archer named Paris stepped forward. He was the only one willing to take on my son. He hoped distance might spare him. Then the Fates and the Gods decided to have their way. Achilles' sandal broke. His foot slid. He lost his balance and fell backwards. Paris had already loosed an arrow. Had Achilles been on his feet, it would have struck between them. Instead, it pierced his heel. It struck the heel where I held him in the Styx. The arrow embedded in the single part of my son I had not protected. I had thought nothing of it, he would be standing. Who would strike a warrior in one of his heels? That traitorous archer.

Achilles cut the arrow from his body. He stood and strode forward. They say he never slowed. When he reached Paris, Achilles stabbed him squarely through the heart, ending his life. Achilles sank to his knees. He lived three more days, reveling with his fellow soldiers over their victory.

On the fourth day, he did not wake. His heel was black as the waters of the Styx. He fought no more. A boy on a horse brought me the message. I strode out to the shore where we had stood so many years before, letting the sun shine upon us. I added my tears to the sea.

# Achilles in the Underworld
## Susan Shwartz

Shades wandered through the underworld. Kings and princes, their bodies burnt, only dreamed. Their lives were gone. If they touched, they brushed through each other. The tall gray and lavender asphodel pierced through the illusion of their bodies. Nothing mattered now.

Borne by winds from the five rivers that warded Hell, the smell of fresh blood caught their attention.

Achilles raised his head. For the first time since his funeral games, when he had crossed the Styx, he came fully alert. Drifting near his back as always was the shade of Patroclus. He was the only warmth, the only awareness in this afterlife. His shade had met the warrior prince when he stepped out of Charon's skiff and drawn him into the place where they had to spend eternity.

Now, Achilles turned his head to look at the flickering ghost that had been friend, kinsman, physician, and lover. Shade that he was, he managed to smile. Patroclus's eyes grew distinct, bright. He too smelled the black blood that brought back memories of life.

"Someone has made an offering," Patroclus said. "A considerable sacrifice," he added.

Knowing that someone needed something, someone wanted something, someone was calling them pierced the monotonous twilight of Hell. Did the fact that some living man had made a sacrifice truly make a difference? The languor of this unlife returned, but Achilles fought it off. Of course it did!

Patroclus at his back, Achilles headed in the direction where the odor was strongest. His footsteps lengthened, grew more forceful, almost as if he once more strode the ringing plains of windy Troy before that perfumed coward Paris had shot from hiding, stealing Achilles' short and glorious life with one arrow. Patroclus, though, he had died in honorable battle with Hector, Troy's greatest champion. Now that was a death Achilles could respect, not like his own. He had forgiven Patroclus for claiming it.

If Patroclus had not borrowed Achilles' armor, he would still be alive. Achilles wished he were. He had forgiven him for that too.

Patroclus tilted his head slightly. *What? Live and leave you alone when I knew your span of life was short?*

Even in Hell, they understood each other so well. Even here, they spoke together without words. If they could not share life, at least they shared their death. Their bones intermingled in one urn. Here in hell, their shades met too.

Achilles nodded, strangely comforted. He led the way forward toward the scent and the heat of blood sacrifice lured them. The tall, pale asphodels brushed their thighs. Achilles brushed them aside with a return of his old impatience.

The feast of black blood steamed in a pit dug by a bronze sword: a cubit in length, width, and depth. Around the pit rose fainter fumes – wine, honey, and milk, sprinkled with barley meal. Sheepskins lay nearby, meat piled within them. The shades clustered around the pit, eager to drink. Achilles saw warriors in torn and bloody armor, women young and old, prophets, princes, even the occasional servant, braver than the rest. He recognized many. Except for Patroclus, they were nothing to him. Nothing mattered except for the rich heat of the black blood. Teiresias stood to one side, blood staining the ancient prophet's lips. He had already drunk, as had a few others Achilles did not recognize.

A man whose sharp bronze sword rested across his legs warded off the begging shades. A man of flesh, breath, and blood. A living man. Achilles could not quite identify him.

Achilles drew closer and inclined his head as if saluting a host. The man beckoned Achilles forward with that sword. When Patroclus would have followed Achilles in death as he had in life, it waved him away. Achilles would have left with him, but Patroclus gestured him to go on ahead and partake of the blood he longed for.

No longer able to resist the blood lure and welcomed by his host, Achilles complied. He approached and knelt beside the pit. Resisting the urge to plunge his face into the blood and gulp it down until he was sated, he sipped at the steaming sacrifice with the manners of the prince he had been born.

The blood offering warmed Achilles. It quickened his shade. Body and mind, he wakened. Now, he recognized the man who held the sword. It was as he should have expected if he had been fully aware. Odysseus, his hair and beard grizzled, his eyes wry, nodded at him and grinned. His teeth might be brownish and worn with age and use, but they were still almost as strong as the old man's wits.

In life, Achilles had thought poorly of the bandy-legged conniver's warrior skills, except as a bowman. But he had learned better than to underestimate his cunning. Ruler of a poor island, Odysseus relied on them the way Achilles had relied on helmet, armor, and shield.

Using his wits, Odysseus had always thwarted Achilles. When he had been hidden among weaving maids, the old man had tempted the girls away with jewels and fine cloth, but identified Achilles by setting out an array of fine weapons. Before the war, Odysseus had used the idea of a marriage to Achilles by advising the High King Agamemnon to bring his daughter to Aulis and sacrifice her to gain a favorable wind. Once at Troy, if Odysseus had not advised him, Agamemnon would never have demanded that Achilles yield his prize of honor, the lady Briseis, whom Patroclus had promised him as a bride. Achilles had seen Agamemnon wandering through the fields of Hell, but had not bothered to greet him.

Patroclus withdrew from the blood. Mannerly in death as in life, he waited among the heroes, prophets, princes and aged women for his turn at what was a feast to their shades. For the first time since the terrible last day when his body had been returned to the Argive tents, he and Achilles were parted. It was almost as unsettling as being dead.

Achilles drank again. The blood warmed him. His wits and feelings returned. Odysseus would never be his first choice of companion, but he was still a living man, a tie to the world that gleamed above. Achilles would have wept, but lacked the tears.

Alert as a shade would ever be, he wiped the dripping remains of his feast from his sharp-cut lips to greet Odysseus, son of Laertes, with proper respect. "If any man were rash enough to enter Hades," Achilles said, "it would be you. We are the outworn dead. This is no place for you."

Odysseus grinned. "I really came to speak with the prophet Teiresias." His face changed, showing anguish. "I need him to tell me how best I can reach rugged Ithaca. I want to go home. I have traveled for years, but Poseidon has blocked me. My ships are mostly broken, my men gone. I am all but alone, while you rule here as you did in life."

The blood coursed through Achilles' shade, rousing him to anger. "Don't dare to offer me false comfort," he told Odysseus. "Just to be alive again, I would walk the sunlit earth as a man of no birth or fortune, a servant, even a slave, rather than rule over all the dead that have perished since the first man died."

Achilles could not stop himself. Like a boor at a banquet, he lapped up even more of the blood while all about him, the shades whispered and crowded forward.

Again, Odysseus waved them off with his bronze sword. "You will receive your due," he told the disembodied spirits. They backed away. Odysseus smiled at the success of his words.

"Tell me of my son," Achilles begged. "Has he won honor in battle? Does my father live in health? He is old now, and I am not there to aid him."

## ACHILLES IN THE UNDERWORLD

He was dead, burnt, and in his urn, yet it was surprising how much this news still mattered to him.

Odysseus's bright eyes watched Achilles with what he realized now was compassion. "I have not heard how Peleus goes on," he admitted, focused on himself and his own plots as always. "But your son Neoptolemus traveled with me to Troy. He was wise in counsel, excelled only by Nestor and myself. He made sure to be in the forefront of battle. When you last saw him, he was a youth. He has become a strong and handsome man who knows no fear, a son in which any man – even you – could take pride."

For the first time since his death, Achilles' heart beat with pride. He nodded thanks at Odysseus and backed away. The wily man gestured again with his sword. Now he beckoned Patroclus and the other shades to take their turn at the blood he had provided. The clustering shades hid him from Achilles' sight.

The blood had made Achilles strong again, had brought body and spirit more closely aligned to the world up above. It heated his veins and restored him to a semblance of life, like a rash man at a feast.

Patroclus rose from his knees, wiping the blood from lips that seemed to release the breath of life. He resumed his place at Achilles' shoulder. As the shades dispersed, they could see their host again and nodded courtesy at him for his hospitality. Then, together, they walked across the field of asphodels. The gray and lavender blossoms rose from their spikes. Now, Achilles could feel them brush his legs. Stone and ground were hard beneath his feet. It was almost like being alive. By all the gods, he missed it!

Now, he did not need Odysseus. Let the rogue go about his plots, whatever they were. Achilles had contrived a plan of his own. He would no longer be trapped in Hades. If, as Odysseus said, Achilles ruled the warriors of the underworld, he would summon the princes and kings whom he had led at Troy. He would make peace with Agamemnon. He might even see Hector and ancient Priam, and swear peace now that they all were dead.

Heading that noble company, Achilles could storm Hades himself and escape back to the world above. He could bring his men with him, greet his father Peleus, and reassure his mother, the goddess Thetis. After all, she had grieved at his choice of a short but glorious life. She would be pleased to see him live again. And he could even see his son. Perhaps there would be grandchildren.

Rejoicing in the blood he had consumed, Achilles shouted out the war cry he had used after Patroclus's death, when he had chased Hector around Troy's high walls. Answering cries rang out from the shades who followed him, kindling the familiar excitement of battle. Here in Hell, Achilles had no horse, no chariot, no charioteer, but what of it? He and the shades he led would storm Hades on foot. They would throw Dis down from his high seat, and he would claim Persephone, Queen of Hell, as his prize. Would he establish himself on the throne of Hell? Or would he breach its walls to seek the outside air again? It was scarcely a choice.

First, though, the conquest. Achilles ran forward. But as he ran, the blood coursing through his veins grew weaker. The death wound in his heel opened and shed blood across the grass and flowers. He could ignore the pain only so long. He faltered and fell, measuring his length in the asphodels. When he put out a hand to push himself up, it looked almost transparent.

Familiar arms encircled him and bore him up. A beloved voice rang out over his head as Patroclus called for aid for Achilles, dearer than life. He heard a horse galloping and looked up, eager to see what animal ventured into Hades.

"Ho, get back, you shades!" came a shout. It was no horse, but a centaur; not any centaur, but Chiron himself, centaur, healer, and father figure to Achilles in his youth. The wisest of men yoked to the noblest of all horses. He was long dead, and Achilles still grieved for him. Even in his prime, Chiron had been healer, not warrior. Now, he galloped three times around Achilles and waved off the shades he had thought to lead into battle. They too were growing paler, weaker, losing enthusiasm along with the blood-borne strength.

"Rest!" ordered Chiron.

Light faded from their eyes, and the shades, no longer intoxicated by blood, lowered their heads and walked away. Their temporary unity dissipated. Once again, they wandered Hell's fields of asphodels.

Patroclus helped Achilles stagger over to the centaur. Their eyes met. Both were still a little mad from the blood they had drunk. How had Chiron evaded the blood fever?

Chiron's eyes were calm. "I drank no blood, my son," he said. "Patroclus drank very little."

Patroclus knew his arts. He had learned them from Achilles, who had studied with Chiron himself as a boy, yet forsaken medicine for arms. And now they were all dead, all in Hades, surrounded by rivers, wind, and that damnable, inescapable asphodel.

"Can you walk?" Chiron asked. "I could carry you, but..."

Chiron was too august to bear a foolish warrior on his back, and he knew it. But out of love for Achilles, he would bear him. Out of love for Achilles, Patroclus would help. Achilles shook his head. He could no longer feel his hair brush his shoulders.

"I will walk," he declared. He was a shade. He had no weight. Walking should be no trouble at all.

Chiron produced a flask from a strap around his neck: not the shapely, muscular arch of a horse's neck, but a human neck and throat, encased in a tunic of what looked like linen. He nodded at Patroclus, who took the flask, opened it, and passed it to Achilles.

"My turn to teach," Patroclus told his companion. "Yours to heal. Drink this."

Achilles tried to thrust the flask away. "I will not drink Lethe water. I do not wish to forget what Odysseus told me."

His memories. His history. His son. His fine, brave son.

"It is only herbs," Chiron told him. "You will sleep until the last of the blood, which gave you this hot-blooded false mortality, is out of you. The wound in your heel will heal again. Then, we can talk."

Patroclus pressed the flask against numbing lips. Achilles drank. Now, he would have all too short a time before he had to rest. "But…"

"But we have all the time in eternity to talk, to plan, to think. Perhaps to learn. Let us assume medicine is useless. Granted, I do not believe this. The shades here bear wounds in the heads and hearts as well as the ones in the bodies that sent them here. Or, if you prefer, we can speak of the philosophy you studied as a lad: the stars, the music, minerals, the very nature of the world."

Achilles fell back. The herbs were taking effect. He would fade into the dark for however long it took to cleanse himself of the blood, but he would at least be surrounded by those who loved him – not like Agamemnon, who had wished to use him and betrayed him. Or like Odysseus himself, who came for the knowledge he wanted and left chaos in his wake.

Shade though he might be, he yawned. Tears ran from the corners of his eyes down his face and over his lips. He was drifting, drifting off. He let his eyes roll open and stared up. Beyond Hades, above the circles of the living world glittered the stars.

Chiron and Patroclus would keep watch while he healed. When he woke again, his second schooldays would begin. This time, he would learn better. After all, he had eternity in which to grow wise and the best company in the underworld in which to do it.

# Immortality in Song
## Rose Strickman

It's on days like this that I think of him.

The sun beats hard and hot into the courtyard, and a breeze blows over the wall. The tide must be low, for that same breeze brings with it the smell of salt, algae and sea rot. That smell brings back memories. Memories of the camp, sprawled out alongside the sea. Memories of days gone formless with heat and grief. Memories of him.

I shake my head, trying to drive them away. I'm sitting in the shade, spindle dangling from its thread of twisted wool. On one side of me, sitting on the bench, is a basket of fluffy, freshly carded wool; on my other side are skeins of thread I've just spun. Around me, the garden lies languid and hazy in the sun, all my herbs and flowers. A lizard goes darting under a broad leaf. And my daughter's voice floats up to me as she drifts through my garden, like a dream of the heat-drugged day.

"Thalia!" I call, and she comes toddling over, half-stumbling over the pebbles and dry earth. She's only three, but already beautiful, hair as dark as my own, eyes a shining clear blue as unlike my own as could be imagined.

"Look, Mama!" she says, showing me the pretty pebble she found in the garden. Her little face is lit with an innocent smile.

"Very nice, dear. Here, come sit by me…" With some difficulty, I pull her up onto the bench, clearing aside the skeins. She sits by me, swinging her short legs, and pats my rounded belly.

"You're having a baby," she says solemnly.

I nod. "A new little brother or sister for you."

Thalia's face twists into an adorable frown. "Don't want a brother," she says decisively.

"Very well!" I laugh. "Perhaps it will be a sister."

The wind blows harder, bringing with it the faint sound of a man singing far away. This isn't so unusual – my husband is the lord of a great estate, with many workers – but his voice is unfamiliar. And the song he sings…

*"Brave Achilles, fleet-footed,*
*Threw himself upon the foe.*
*A lion ravaging the gazelles,*
*A lion, bloody-mouthed…"*

My whole being clenches. The spindle wobbles, the thread going uneven. My hands are shaking too much to control it.

"Mama?" Thalia stares at me, sucking her fingers. Those sea-blue eyes…

The door to my courtyard garden opens and my husband steps out. Thalia goes running to him, arms out. "Papa!"

"Thalia!" Demetrius bends down to scoop her into his arms. He embraces her, brown eyes bright with pride and affection. "How's the most beautiful girl in the world today?"

"Fine, Papa!" She kisses his cheek.

"Glad to hear it." He swoops her around, making her giggle, before depositing her on the ground. "And how's the most beautiful woman in the world today?" he asks, sitting down beside me.

I give a smile. "I thought Thalia was the most beautiful woman in the world."

"She's the most beautiful girl. You're the most beautiful woman." Demetrius rubs my wool between his big fingers, rough from cultivating the olive groves.

"Don't knot up my wool," I scold. "Anyway, if I'm the most beautiful woman, where does that leave Helen of Sparta?"

"I have never set eyes on the Spartan Queen, nor do I wish to," Demetrius says firmly. He stretches out, my big, dusty, utterly ordinary husband, and heaves a deep sigh. "The harvest should be fairly good this year."

"I'm glad to hear that." I start spinning again, smooth and even. The song has died away, leaving a silence broken only by the bleating of goats and the murmuring of waves.

Demetrius eyes me sidelong. "You could come out to see the groves, you know," he says. "After the baby's born. We might go down to the beach together too. Thalia would like that."

"I thought a good woman should stay in the house." I keep my eyes on my spinning.

"No one would object if you were with me. Your women could attend you." He looks around. Thalia is humming to herself, tearing up a lavender bush. "Where *are* they? And Thalia's nurse?"

"I sent them off. I wanted to be alone with Thalia for a bit." The spindle twirls in midair.

Demetrius is still giving me that odd look. "How long has it been since you've left this house?" he says at last, quietly. "Four years you've lived here, and you've never even gone to make sacrifice to the gods. Not even when Thalia was born."

I hunch my shoulders, turning away from him. "I'm fine." He's still frowning at me, so I say, "I heard a man singing earlier. A traveling bard?"

"Probably on his way to the village," Demetrius says. "I expect he'll sing for the villagers. It might be fun to go listen, you know."

"Not if he's singing the same song I heard earlier." I shake my head.

Demetrius stares at me a long moment. "You can't hide from him forever, you know." His tone has grown darker, harder, like his gaze. He looks like the battle-hardened warrior he once was, rather than the farmer and benevolent landlord I've grown to know. "Men will sing of Achilles and his deeds for all the generations to come."

"I know that!" I jump to my feet, too fast. I stagger, head spinning, before I regain my balance. "Thalia, stop tearing apart my plants…"

I head down the garden to my daughter, my husband shaking his head at my retreating back.

* * *

That night, after I settle Thalia down with her simple supper in the nursery with her nurse, I prepare for my own dinner. I may no longer be a queen, but I still have duties as the lady of an estate, albeit a reclusive one. Therefore, my women garb me in a fine linen gown, a veil over my head, bangles, earrings and a necklace. Thus prepared, we all go to the megaron.

It's a small place compared to the royal hall at Lyrnesses, but comfortable and cozy, the pillars freshly painted only a few years ago. A great fire burns in the central hearth, air wavering with heat above, and the benches are crowded with Demetrius' guests, tenants and dependents. By all rights, members of my own family should number among those present. But of course I have no family left.

In any case, the company is loud and convivial; Demetrius boasts that no one ever leaves his tables unsatisfied. It still seems strange to me to see women seated among men, but the Greeks are less strict about this than the people of my birth. They've only grown more lax in recent years, when the wars to the east reduced the countries of Greece to women, old men and boys.

I proceed to the high table, ignoring the glances and whispers that follow me. I am well-used to the tenants' curiosity about me, the strange, reclusive lady their lord brought back from the war. But one pair of eyes does not follow me. They belong to a young man seated near the fire, a staff leaning on the bench. A worn leather case, presumably containing his lyre, sits on the bench beside him. Thin and ragged, his eyes stare straight ahead. Even in the firelight, I can see that they are milky and occluded. He's blind, I realize. A blind young man I've never seen before.

I make it to the high table and sit down beside Demetrius. "Good evening, Eirene," he says, using the name we agreed upon before he took me from the ruined shore that had once been my home.

"Good evening, Demetrius. Who is that man?" I ask while my wine is poured. "The blind young man sitting by the fire."

Demetrius hesitates. "You're not to get angry," he says in a low voice.

"Demetrius." My fist clenches in my lap. "What have you done?"

"He's the singer who's passing through," Demetrius says, not meeting my eyes. "I had to at least give him dinner and a bed…"

"Demetrius!" I hiss through my veil, one hand on my pregnant belly. "I told you I didn't want—!"

"What was I supposed to do, turn him away at the door?" he snaps. "It's our duty to offer hospitality. It's only for one night." He pats my hand. "Call in the supper, would you?"

Fuming, I stand up and clap my hands, sending the slaves scurrying. A cheer rises as the doors open and the servers come in, carrying trays, bowls and amphorae, steam wafting off the piping-hot food. It's an ordinary night, not a sacred feast, nor a night with important guests, so the food is nothing special – just bread, cheese, olives and fish – but our guests cry out in approbation and tuck in with a will.

Shielded by my veil, I watch the blind bard. He eats with a hearty appetite, devouring everything on his plate and wiping it with a heel of bread afterward. I'm a little surprised at how dexterous and confident he is in this strange environment, blind as he is, but I suppose he's used to it. For the first time, I wonder what it's like, wandering the rough, dangerous roads of Greece completely in the dark. What kind of man is this, to have chosen such a life?

Dinner goes well and despite myself I relax, eating and drinking under my veil and talking to Demetrius. I've actually half-forgotten the bard by the time the final course is cleared away. I'm preparing to stand up to leave the megaron, taking all the women with me, when the head of Demetrius' men stands up, flushed and swaying with drink.

"Lord Demetrius! Tonight we have a bard among us, a singer who has passed through many lands." He waves a hand at the bard, still sitting on the bench. "Shall we hear his news, then hear his song?"

"Yes! Yes!" Both men and women bang their cups against the tables, shouting with enthusiasm.

I try to catch Demetrius' eye, but he avoids my gaze and I know I've lost this battle. "All right!" he shouts. "Bard! Tell us news of far-off lands. Sing us beautiful songs!"

A storm of cheering rocks the hall. I sit frozen as the bard gropes for his staff and lyre case and stands up, feeling his way to the center of the megaron. Bathed in flickering firelight, flames reflected in his unseeing eyes, he looks almost like some messenger of the gods. A hush falls.

The bard opens his leather case and takes out a beautiful lyre. The hall murmurs at the sight, firelight gleaming on the polished olive wood, carved with winged women, strings glistening. The bard takes a moment to tune his instrument, tightening or loosening strings and striking them to judge their music. Silvery notes ring out.

At last, the bard straightens and runs a hand across the strings, a trill of music to capture his audience. "Greetings, Lord Demetrius and Lady Eirene!" he says, and bows. His voice, even in speech, is beautiful, golden notes to the silver notes of his lyre. "Greetings, too, to all your followers here tonight." He gives a general bow to the audience. "May the gods bless you for the hospitality you have shown tonight. I have come from far-off lands, have roamed all corners of Greece. And I do bring grave news: Prince Orestes of Mycenae has killed his mother, Queen Clytemnestra, in vengeance for the death of his father, King Agamemnon."

A murmur of consternation runs through the megaron, cries of unease and astonishment. We'd heard rumors, of course, but it's something else to have them confirmed. A deep pang runs through me. I never met Queen Clytemnestra, but I always had a soft spot for her, ever since I learned she killed Agamemnon, a man I loathed with all my soul. "He killed his own mother?" I call out boldly. "Such blasphemy!"

"The gods agree with you, Lady Eirene." I wonder how the blind bard knows who it is who spoke. "The Furies have driven Prince Orestes mad, and he now wanders far from his home."

"Perhaps he can expiate his sin," Demetrius says, though he sounds troubled. "Perhaps he can win back his honor."

"With the help of the gods, any man can win back his honor." The bard strikes his lyre again, a glittering rain. "Great Achilles himself abandoned his honor and won it again, dying in glory before the walls of Troy. Shall I sing the song of Achilles, lord?"

I throw a glance of mute appeal at Demetrius, but he's not paying attention. The tale of Prince Orestes has shaken him, and he wants to think of heroism now, rather than villainy. He wants to think of his old friend. "Please do, singer," Demetrius says, and everyone but me bursts into cheers.

The bard's fingers fly across his lyre, and the music begins slowly, almost stealthily, rising from the lyre to fill the whole megaron, until the night is colored by music and our thoughts drift free. And through that gorgeous, befuddling mist of music, the bard's voice rings, pure as gold, lighting the way to his story.

> *"Sing to me, O muse, and tell me*
> *Of fleet-footed Achilles, golden as the dawn…"*

Oh, he was golden all right. Golden as a leopard, golden as a lion, as beautiful and savage as a great cat. Those eyes, blue as the sea. Sometimes I thought that was what I hated most: that someone so violent could be so gorgeous. That he could kill my brothers, destroy my city, enslave me and still put me under his spell when he sat golden in golden light, singing to his lyre, as now the bard is singing.

> *"Son of a goddess, sacker of cities,*
> *Who traded long life for immortality in song…"*

My breath comes harsh and ragged. I cradle my unborn child and stare at the tabletop with clenched teeth. The memories are coming hard and fast now, jagged flashes as sharp and abrupt as the Greeks' swords when they fought before Lyrnesses, before Troy itself. His hands on me, his mouth. Me moaning as waves of reluctant ecstasy ran through me. I didn't believe he was the son of a goddess before he took me to his bed, but oh, I believed it afterward. Maybe *that* was what I hated most: that he could not only make me his concubine, but he could also make me enjoy it.

*"Tell me how Achilles quarreled*
*With great Agamemnon*
*And nearly forsook the war with Troy*
*Over dark-eyed Briseis."*

That name.

I don't realize that I've jumped to my feet until I'm halfway out of the megaron. The world is spinning around me. Voices rise after me, surprised, alarmed, but they are blurred past all meaning. I can't breathe in there. I can't. I can't.

I reel into the small atrium behind the megaron. Many of the slaves sleep here at night, but right now it's empty and shadowed. Silent. I stagger to one of the benches along the wall and collapse. I claw off my veil and let my head fall into my shaking hands. Around me, the world spins, memories mixed with reality, until I cannot tell past from present.

All these years I've spent hiding from the past, only for it to lie in wait and ambush me.

"Lady Eirene?"

I jerk up at the unexpected voice. It's the blind bard, standing in the dim light of the atrium, his lyre back in its case, holding his staff in one hand. His unseeing eyes stare blankly.

I draw myself up, even though he cannot see me do it. "Why are you here?" I demand. "Where is my husband?"

"Back in the megaron." He steps forward, feeling the way with his staff. "I asked to apologize and make amends, and he allowed me back here. Men do not see me as a threat," he adds simply.

"And are you?"

"Not to women I have upset." He draws to a halt some distance away. "I have caused you pain, Lady Eirene, and I am sorry for it."

I wipe my eyes. "Not your fault, I suppose. Everyone sings songs about Achilles." I can't keep the bitterness from my voice. "The greatest of warriors. The best of heroes. Sacker of cities. And in our lifetime too."

"You are a Trojan," he says in tones of realization. "Lord Demetrius brought you back from the war."

"I'm hardly the only one," I snap. Then I sigh, exhaustion washing through me. "It's not your fault," I murmur. "Achilles' fate was to choose between a long life of obscurity and immortality in song. He made his choice. He told me once—" I break off, realizing my mistake.

But too late. Incredulous realization spreads across the bard's face like the rosy light of Eos, goddess of the dawn.

"You…" He staggers, nearly falling. "You are not Lady Eirene. You are the Lady Briseis!"

"No—!" I cry, but he's already thrown himself to his knees, bowing before me like I'm a goddess.

"My lady, I have sought you high and low, to hear your story from your own lips! But none knew what had become of you. To find you here… Truly, this is a gift of the gods! My lady, I have so many questions to ask, such a song to weave—"

"NO!" My shout echoes off the ceiling, so loud I can hear the flapping of wings as the birds sleeping on the roof take off in fright. "No, I will not answer your questions. You will sing no songs about me!"

"But why not?" Bewilderment cuts across his euphoria. "I am composing an epic, Lady Briseis, about the war and Achilles' part in it. Your role was so important and no one knows how it even ends—"

"And that is as it should be!" I'm on my feet again, heart constricted with emotion, barely able to get a breath as the words tumble out. "Demetrius married me at Achilles' command on the shores of Troy. He married me for love of Achilles, and for love of Achilles he swore to protect me. I took the name Eirene and together we have hidden my identity ever since. If the truth ever emerged…what do you think would happen? All of Greece would arrive at our doorstep, bringing war and violence with them – or worse things. Do you think I want to be caught in Achilles' fate? It is a miracle, a gift from the gods, that I have escaped it, that his daughter has escaped it—" I break off again.

"His daughter..." the bard whispers. "You – you bore Achilles' child?"

"My daughter, Thalia." I slump, all the anger and vehemence draining out of me. I think of Thalia's eyes, that clear sea-blue. The same eyes as her father. "She was conceived before the walls of Troy but born here in Greece, known to all as the daughter of Lord Demetrius. Just as this second child I carry is Demetrius'." I lay my hand on my swelling abdomen. "Please, bard: tell no one. Take this secret to your grave. Achilles chose immortality in song over long life. I have made the opposite choice. I choose a long life in obscurity for myself and my daughter."

Still on his knees, the bard is silent a long moment. "You are a part of Achilles' story, Lady Briseis," he says at last. "As long as men sing of Achilles, they will sing of Briseis too. And they will sing Achilles' song forever."

"They may sing of me," I say, "but they will not sing of my ending. I have left Achilles' story with my daughter, and our lives and our endings are our own. We will live our lives and go quietly to meet the gods. Or we will if you swear me your silence now."

A long moment passes. In the megaron, I can hear massed voices, Demetrius leading his guests in a raucous song. No doubt he's passing around the wine, hoping to get the guests drunk enough to forget what happened tonight. It does not touch me or the bard. We stand in suspended silence, me waiting, him thinking.

## IMMORTALITY IN SONG

"Very well," he says at last. He bows low again, forehead to the floor. "I swear by Father Zeus and by the Muses who have guided my life that I will never tell anyone of your ending, Lady Briseis. I will sing of you in Achilles' song and then let you leave that song and fly free. And never shall I mention your daughter or her name. She shall be free of Achilles' fate." He bows again. "If I break my word, let the Muses break my voice and leave me speechless."

Relief fills me, making my limbs go loose. "Thank you," I whisper. "Thank you, blind bard."

He climbs to his feet. "Far be it from me to gainsay the wishes of Achilles' beloved," he says, inclining his head.

I almost laugh at this. Whatever was between me and Achilles – and even now I cannot explain or describe it – it certainly wasn't love. "What's your name, bard?"

"Omiros," he says.

"And you intend to compose an epic about Achilles, Omiros?"

"Yes, Lady Briseis. I believe it will live on forever," he says simply.

I know it will. The fate that Achilles chose will see to that. "Just remember, blind Omiros," I say quietly, "that for every hero there is a victim. For every victory cry raised by men, there are a thousand wails from the women they defeated, enslaved, raped. And love and hatred are not so different as men believe."

"I will remember, Lady Briseis," Omiros says, and I believe him. "I will take my leave tomorrow, and never trouble you again. But before I go, is there any service I might do for you?"

"Yes," I say after a moment. I sit down on the bench again, straightening my skirt. "Sing me a song. Not a song of war or heroes. Sing me something gentle and sweet. Play a lullaby for my unborn child."

Omiros bows and takes out his lyre once more. The olive wood gleams in the dimness. With an ascending trill of notes, Omiros begins to sing, a sweet, simple song about olives ripening on the branches.

I sit and I listen to the music like a golden rain around me. One hand steals to my belly, to the child sleeping there. Tomorrow I will go make a sacrifice at the shrine of Eileithyia, I decide, and ask for a safe, easy childbirth. I blink at the sudden force of this resolution. Well, Demetrius should be pleased, anyway. Perhaps I will take Thalia too, and we can make sacrifice at the altar of Artemis, ask for her blessings for my daughter.

For too long have I hidden away. It's time to live again. And out of the ashes of Achilles, I feel my heart unfurl its first tender petals, like spring after a long winter.

# The Healing Mountain
### Adam B. Widmer

A great splash leapt up from a slow-moving pool in the river. Its final droplets landed very near the boy on the rocks. His friends were swimming. He was waiting.

Ajax returned to the surface with a shout, "The mighty Achilles! Defeated by a little water!"

The boy on the rocks didn't look at them, though he could feel the eyes of Patroclus watching him from just above the water. The boy never looks, and he never swims. They cannot see what he sees.

"I don't swim," Achilles said evenly.

"It's getting cold anyway," said Patroclus, swimming to the bank.

Ajax followed him grudgingly and they clambered out of the water and back into their tunics. "Seriously though, your mother is a sea-nymph," Ajax said, leaning against a tree to pull on his sandal, "and you can't swim?"

In a flash, Achilles' knife left its sheath and flew across the clearing, burying its point with a shiver inches from Ajax's head. Achilles met the other boy's eyes. "I said I *don't* swim, not that I can't."

"Alright," Ajax conceded, hands in the air. "Alright. Just making conversation."

He continued to make conversation all the long way back up to their camp, leading Patroclus by several paces with Achilles trailing at the rear. Ajax passed the time by complaining loudly about the days they spent huddled together in Chiron's cave, discussing philosophy or medicine. He boasted of his preference for things like hunting, or sparring, or actual combat. He hadn't seen any actual combat, but he never tired of pretending that he had. The other two simply let him get away with it. Things were easier that way. And besides, they knew the truth, so what gain was there in arguing? This was the manner of reasoning Achilles and Patroclus had learned from Chiron while Ajax was refusing to pay attention.

The three of them continued on that way, Ajax jabbering up ahead, Patroclus occasionally feeding him a reply, and Achilles wandering on in silent contemplation.

Achilles was thinking about the water.

He thought about the water for hours whenever he left it behind. He always tried not to look, but try as he might, he wasn't able to keep his eyes off it entirely. Every time, without fail, there would be a moment of complacency or forgetfulness or relaxed ease, and he would find himself scanning its surface. And every time, without fail, he saw the bodies.

Six of them. Swollen. Floating. Crowded around him.

When he was much younger, he would scream and cower and clutch at his mother or the nursemaids. Didn't they see? Didn't they realize? How could they possibly wade out into the water?

But they did not see. They did not realize. Achilles was far from a man now, though he would have pretended otherwise, but he had learned years ago that it was best not to acknowledge the bodies in the water. Or the way they were unknowingly nudged aside by bathers and boats. Or the striking resemblance they bore to Achilles himself.

He shook them from his mind just in time to hear Ajax lamenting the end of the days-long break they had been given by Chiron.

Time spent discussing philosophy or learning the healing arts certainly did not feel like time wasted to Achilles, but they could only spend so many hours shut in a cave talking before they began to lose their minds. Chiron knew this, hence the breaks.

They relished these days. The freedom to release their conscious thoughts and drift about the healing mountain as they pleased. He would never tell the others, but Achilles found it was in these unstructured days, with his mind wandering aimlessly from point to point, that the teachings they were given in the cave truly crystallized. It was out here, without guidance, where they took on real meaning.

He suspected their tutor knew this, too.

"Ah, well. Couldn't last forever," sighed Ajax. "But hey," he clapped his hands together loudly, the sound rippling through the trees. "We hunt tomorrow! Better bag something, or the horse will be displeased."

"He's a centaur," Patroclus muttered.

"What?"

"I said Chiron is a centaur, not a horse," replied Patroclus. "And he's one of the most learned beings in all of Greece. It wouldn't kill you to show him some respect."

"I know," moaned Ajax. "And I do respect him. Honestly, I really do. But he can be so...unpleasant when we come back empty-handed. So, tomorrow," he continued, glancing over his shoulder, "we stick together! With Achilles on our side, we can't lose. He is an absolute killing machine!" Ajax laughed.

"He is more," Patroclus said, with a meaningful glance toward Achilles.

This was true, and Patroclus knew it.

A year after he was born, Achilles' mother Thetis threw the customary name-day celebration for him. Many Olympians attended, out of respect for Thetis's immortal lineage. All had gone reasonably well until Thetis overheard a pair of her Nereid sisters. They had a bit too much wine, and talked a bit too loudly about her son. She swept over to confront the two.

They blushed and admitted that, yes, they had been discussing baby Achilles. That there had been a prophecy given by the Fates about her son. That it was well known around Mt. Olympus, but had been deliberately kept from her. Thetis demanded they explain this prophecy at once.

This is what they told her:

Her son Achilles had, in fact, two destinies. He could go off to war, where he would win great victories for his home, and fame and glory for himself; becoming the greatest, most acclaimed, and most beloved warrior in all of history. But he would also die extremely young.

Or he could live to a ripe old age, eighty years or more, knowing nothing but peace.

But he would have to choose. If ever Achilles went to war, he would usher in a life of glory, and condemn himself to an early grave. If he stayed away, he would die an old man.

Thetis had told him about the prophecy just before he was sent to study under Chiron. Achilles wasn't even sure if his father knew, but he had told Patroclus in a moment of vulnerability.

He knew, of course, what his mother wanted. Every mother wishes a life of peace and longevity for their children, Thetis had told him as much. And Achilles did see some appeal in this. He was an excellent healer for a boy his age, and he liked helping people. The looks on their faces when he successfully treated an animal in their herd, or quelled the fever of a sick child. It was fulfilling. It could lead him to a long and satisfying life.

But...glory.

What athletic young man didn't crave the intoxicating scent of glory? The adoration of his peers, and even his elders. Physical prowess had always been evident in Achilles, and word about some of his deeds had already begun to spread. He loved the looks he got when he entered a village. The whispers. The questions.

The prospect of such an early death, however... It did take some fun out of all the glory business.

Achilles felt these twin destinies pull at him, like physical forces, threatening to split him down the middle as the trio reentered their small camp.

Checking the snares further out, the boys were rewarded with two fat rabbits. It was a fine evening meal, and they lay down in their blankets under the darkened sky.

\* \* \*

Achilles was drowning.

Again.

Or...maybe not drowning? He was certainly underwater, far enough down he could not see the surface, but not so far down that there was no light. An eerie, directionless glow permeated the space around him. But he felt no water in his mouth. His lungs did not burn. His throat had not closed.

He'd had this dream so many times over the years, but it had never occurred to him that perhaps he *wasn't* actually drowning. He wasn't breathing, to be sure, but he also found that he had no need to breathe. He was still and floating as usual, but there was less panic with this new realization.

Less panic, but still some terror. There were, after all, the bodies.

Six of them. Again. Lifeless limbs floating in the vague teal light of the sea.

Their consistent appearance was disturbing, as was their resemblance to him. But neither felt as strange or distressing as the fact that they aged along with him. This dream had plagued Achilles since before he was old enough to speak, and the bodies of those six boys were always his age. Back then they were toddlers. Tonight they were nearing adulthood, just like him.

Recognition that he was not drowning came with an increased awareness of the dream itself, and Achilles wondered if there were other assumptions he'd made that would prove to be untrue. With a great effort, he reached out and found that he could indeed wiggle his fingers. This meant that he wasn't trapped, captive as he had always believed. Wiggling fingers led to clenching fists led to flexing elbows. Before long, he was swimming.

Gliding through this strange sea, Achilles got a good look at the faces of these figures for the first time in his life. And he knew immediately that the stories were true.

He had pretended not to hear them when the nursemaids thought he was asleep. Convinced himself that he had made them up in the nonsensical state between sleeping and waking. Pushed them so far from his mind that they were less than a forgotten memory. But the stories were true.

Achilles was not an only son, as he had been told. He was, in fact, one of seven. When Thetis gave birth to her first son, he was happy and healthy. Gods be praised! The midwife placed the child in its mother's arms, and left to fetch its father, Peleus. When the two returned to the birthing chamber, the baby was dead. No marks, no scars, no explanation from the weeping Thetis.

When Thetis gave birth to her second son, he was happy and healthy. The midwife placed the child in her arms, and went to fetch Peleus. When they entered the birthing chamber, the baby was dead. No marks, no scars, no explanation.

Over the years, six sons were born healthy, and dead within minutes. Peleus grew increasingly distraught. No healer or midwife could give him a reason why this might be happening. He began to fear he would never produce an heir. And so, Peleus decided he must witness the mysteries of birth in order to solve a mystery of death.

A viewing hole was made secretly in the wall of the birthing chamber, and on the day of the seventh birth, Peleus stood in the adjacent room and witnessed the birth of his seventh son. The baby was happy and healthy. The midwife placed the child in Thetis's arms, and left to fetch Peleus, closing the door behind her. Then, for reasons known only to her, Thetis lifted the boy over a bucket of salt water by the birthing chair, and held him under the surface to drown.

Peleus immediately launched himself through the door of the birthing chamber and pulled the baby from the water. The child wailed, coughed, and spluttered, but he was alive. He was breathing. On his name day, he would be called Achilles, and the mother who tried to drown him would be told of his twin destinies.

Everyone on his parents' estate had known the truth, and Achilles had absorbed that truth, too, despite all his efforts to push it away. It simply did not fit with the knowledge that his mother loved him. Thetis had shown Achilles nothing but the deepest affection in all his living memory.

And yet, the stories were true.

They were his brothers. The boys, drowned at birth, now floating through his dreams and haunting every body of water.

Achilles swam into the cluster of them. Floating. Passive. Unmoving.

He was struck by the similarities in their faces, their builds. So alike, and so different. That uncanny resemblance that only siblings seem to have.

Once closer, he noticed the eyes.

They were unblinking, but not lifeless. He moved toward one of his brothers, and saw that there was a spark behind the other boy's eyes. As Achilles approached, his brother's eyes followed him. They roamed, just as his always had, searching the approaching Achilles from head to foot.

He had drifted within inches of the other boy's face when the mouth opened. Just dropping wide, at first. Then moving back and forth slightly, the rest of the body still limply floating. There was no sound, but the fear on the boy's face was unmistakable. And the words... They came slow at first, but the words could be read on his lips.

*Where...are...we?*

The brother's hand suddenly shot out and grabbed the front of Achilles' tunic, pulling him even closer.

*Where...are...we?*

He tried to free himself from the grip.

*Where are we?!*

Achilles woke, gasping for breath and covered in sweat. Dawn had just broken.

\* \* \*

Silence followed the three boys as they stalked their way through the forest that morning. In some ways, this was the part of the hunt Achilles liked best. Those quiet moments searching for prey. He had the concentration born of focused movement and the freedom of his private thoughts. But he also had the comfort and security of his companions' presence, flanked out on either side of him, Ajax a handful of yards to the left, Patroclus to the right.

Of course, the dream still consumed much of Achilles' mind. In the darker reaches of his subconscious, he had suspected for some time that the other boys in the water might represent his brothers. Unwilling to accept what it meant – that they were dead, that their mother had killed them – Achilles had refused to acknowledge the mere existence of the idea. He felt he had no choice but to accept it now. The experience grabbed hold of him in ways he couldn't explain. It brought forth ideas that seemed impossible, but felt like solid fact.

What if they weren't really gone?

What if somewhere, in another life, in another existence, each of them was the seventh son? The one saved from the water on the day of their birth. That would explain why they all looked the same age. Why they continued to get older along with him. Why all seven brothers seemed conscious, if frozen, in the watery dream.

Perhaps, in their own realms, each one of them was alive. Each one facing the same twin destinies, their paths having not yet diverged. What if, for each of his brothers, Achilles was just another body floating in the water?

Maybe the dream is some kind of accidental conduit that ties their worlds together. Could it be possible the nightmare that has chased him throughout his life was actually offering him…a chance?

To be someone's brother?

To save another boy, in another world, from a terrible fate?

A momentary glint of bone-white broke Achilles from his reverie.

Another step, and the rest of the stag came into view. Its striking antlers shook gently in the dappled sunlight of the clearing as it grazed. Achilles put up a hand to alert his friends, and they slowed their pace, spreading out to surround the animal as they approached. They were within range and downwind. It hadn't spotted them yet, but no one had a clear shot. Too focused on the prey, Patroclus loudly snapped a twig beneath his foot.

They all froze as the stag lifted its head.

For a fraction of an instant, the animal made eye contact with Achilles. Then it tore off into the trees. Without a moment's thought or hesitation, he sprinted off in pursuit.

"What are you doing?" Ajax called after him. "You'll never catch it!"

But Achilles ran on.

The stag was definitely gaining distance, but he could still see it through the trees. Arms pumping, spear gripped tight, Achilles knew there was always a chance. Somehow, he picked up more speed. They were running downhill. Just as he realized what direction the animal was leading him, he heard the splash.

A moment later Achilles shot out of the trees, pulling up short at the pool in the river where his friends had been swimming the day before. The stag was clambering out on the other side, shaking off and snorting water from its nostrils.

It did not run.

The animal just stood there, waiting. Staring at Achilles. Boldly presenting its chest. As though it knew he was no longer a threat. As though it knew what he saw in the water, and that he wouldn't dare swim across.

Achilles reared back, and hurled his spear. He followed its arc, watching the tip glint in the sunlight. In that moment, he wanted to show the stag. To punish the animal for taking advantage of his greatest fears. For making him feel weak and small. The spear soared across the full breadth of the river, and sank squarely into the stag's chest.

A vengeful smile began to spread on Achilles' face as the animal fell.

It was wiped away when the noise began.

A horrible, soul-shattering scream filled the valley, expressing suffering the likes of which Achilles had never experienced. The kind of suffering his mother must have felt, driving her to drown her children on their first day of life. The kind his father surely experienced at the death of each of his sons.

Achilles knew he must end that suffering.

Without thinking, filled with remorse and sympathy for the animal, he prepared to dive. He was halted, as always, by the sight of the bodies in the water. His brothers stretched across the width of the pool, floating along the path between himself and the stag.

But they weren't actually there. Not really. He knew that now. They were each on their own shore in their own world. Standing exactly where he stood. Carrying the same name, the same history, and the same twin destinies he carried.

For them, Achilles was just another body in the water.

And so, he dove. The instant he broke the surface, the bodies disappeared, leaving Achilles to make his way across alone. Now that they were gone – now that he knew who they were – he wished they could be there with him. He climbed out onto the bank, sparing a glance over his shoulder, but his brothers weren't there. He did not think he would see them again.

At least, not while he was awake.

Dripping wet, Achilles knelt down before the stag, and saw precisely what he expected. In his anger and frustration, he had misjudged his aim, and missed the heart by inches. The screaming had stopped. The animal's breathing was shallow and labored.

His first thought was that he could heal it. He knew how. Pull out the spear, scrape the scaly green corrosion from its tip, apply that to the wound, and say the right incantation. The animal would recover. He had seen it done. Here on the shoulders of the healing mountain, it was certain to work.

Patroclus and Ajax appeared from the trees on the opposite bank, standing some ten yards apart from each other.

"Did you see that?" Ajax shouted to Patroclus. "Achilles ran down that stag *on foot!*"

Kneeling beside the animal, Achilles stared into its eyes. For an instant, his hand hovered halfway between the shaft of his spear and the knife on his belt. Destiny pulled that hand in both directions. Achilles thought of his brothers, and chose.

With one smooth motion, he unsheathed his knife and cut the stag's throat. The suffering was over in seconds.

As he rose to the cheering and adoration of his friends, Achilles felt whole. A gentle smile on his face.

Somewhere, in another life, in another existence, he hoped another boy had made a different choice.

# Last Stand
## Ernie Xu

I can see nothing before me.

Shadows nudge me forward. I let them. They swirl around me, weaving between my legs, butting up against my ankles, softly purring. I follow their beckoning, limping after them. Why let the shadows guide me? Well, why must I do anything anymore?

This is a time outside time. The shadows blur in and out of the trees. It's so dark the trees appear liquid, allowing the shadows to absorb and re-emerge as if tendrils of a mist, tugging me along as in a current. Everything is slightly wrong here. I can barely see the trees around me but I don't need to see to *feel* that nothing is right. If Hades hears my thoughts no doubt he'd rebuke me: pompous Achilles, what is *right*, exactly? Or what is *wrong*, for that matter? You think you know what's right, but you're still here, and you'll be here for eternity. Don't be afraid to be wrong, darling.

I used to feel such strong, broiling, boiling emotions. Love, lust, fear, rage, grief. Now, there is nothing. Not even emptiness. I've felt emptiness, absence, before. It hurts upon the realisation. Then the pain subsides slightly as your heart acclimatises, but the ache promises to stay. When I had found Patroclus lying in the dust, the whole *world* was dust! The sun hung heavy in the sky, a brilliantly bright day. Cheery. The air was thick with the scent of iron. His body was heavy like the sun. I remember not knowing heaviness until that very moment, when I strained to lift him while my entire body was enveloped in pain, wrapped tightly in pain each individual organ inside and out. I strained, trembling, then fell to my knees, continuing to tremble. I cradled his head in my weak, useless arms, feeling the warmth fade from his skin – how could warmth be dissipating when the sun beat down so relentlessly?

My heart was rage, flaring, crackling, spitting. Fierce sorrow, guilt, indignation, only served as kindling, igniting me, consuming me. But even as I fought, even as I did unspeakable cruelties in the name of love, I knew that I had love no longer. The light of my heart lay in the dust, having burnt brightly but now flickered and extinguished. Hollowness began to seep in, a darkness poisoning my veins. With every enemy I felled, I felt the absence keenly. A horrific revelation settled upon my shoulders: others' void did not, could not, null mine. Then the pain dulled. It didn't happen right away, nor did it happen gradually, but I remember waking up one day and the pain wasn't there. Instead, an ache nestled deep within my core.

I remember that ache, but I don't feel it anymore.

I know these things mattered to me so deeply, so thoroughly, before. I do remember. I just don't feel it anymore. The trees understand. They're apathetic to all hell.

The shadows have led me back into my cavern. Hades, the curmudgeon, has allowed me to reside, undisturbed, in a corner of his Underworld. But I suspect he's uneasy with my aimless roaming; perhaps the shadows have been sent by him to herd me back into my pen.

Seated upon my throne of bones, I make a lazy sweeping gesture and the shadows scatter. All but one. One shadow continues crouching by my feet. My left foot. Cowering, whimpering. I kick at it. A sharp pain shoots up my heel. A heel never to heal. The shadow shivers and whimpers some more, scurries a short distance away, then, appearing to notice my wince of pain, approaches me again. It settles itself down beside me, curling itself into a ball.

"Why are you still here?" I whisper. Its dark swirling form seems to flicker twice – blinking? It nudges closer, stretches out, brushes against my foot. A chill runs up my leg, then, like a balm, soothes the pain in my heel.

I close my eyes. It's only a matter of time before the shadow grows bored of my moping and quietly leaves in the night. A piece of the night returning to the night. Everyone leaves. Even Patroclus left.

We had reunited when I died. But time flows like water through me, extinguishing the flames that had once burnt so bright. Patroclus, his laughter like sunlight, broke through the gloom, but, as I've said, nothing is *right* here. His laughter echoed. I could see him, could feel him, but I felt as if I no longer *knew* him. Hell, I no longer knew myself. Who am I? Only yet another shade of a hero, a soul of the dead. The only reason I can see and feel Patroclus is because I am just as ghostly as he is. I continue to wear my armour, the bronze glinting faintly in the dim light of the Underworld, but I don't know why I do. I have no use for it anymore. It has no use for me, in the emptiness of eternity.

Patroclus wandered with me in those...years? Time means nothing here, except to wash away any traces of myself. Patroclus wandered with me for a while, disappointed in my despair. I wonder if he still wanders these shadowed halls, searching for me as I search for something beyond this weight. I hope to, I fear to bump into him. How is he now? Would we still recognise each other? Does he miss—? Would he still—?

I rise, shaking off the remnants of my reverie. The shadow quivers in response, as if sensing my shift in intention. I begin to walk, dragging my spectral feet across the cold earth, following a path I cannot see. The shadow, now emboldened, dances alongside me, weaving a tapestry of darkness as it flits between the skeletal trees.

* * *

My little shadow follows me wherever I go. It used to remind me of my solitude but now its presence comforts me – who says a great warrior can't have a little shadow for a companion? I smile bitterly. Although...it's less little than before. It used to be wispy as it darted around, occasionally nudging against me. Once, it nudged a little too hard, lost its balance, and passed straight through me. That seemed to give it quite the fright, and it wouldn't answer to my beckoning for a while. Finally, I tossed it a shard of mirror, which followed a gleaming curve in the dim light. The shadow re-emerged from its sulk, darting after the shard, swirling around it, casting smoky shapes upon the ground. It darted back towards me, leaving a trail of soft, lingering darkness. With a tinkle, the shadow dropped the shard by my feet.

Perhaps now it has learnt its lesson, and hasn't passed through me again. But I suspect that it couldn't even if it tried, for the shadow has grown significantly taller since it had first found me and refused to leave. Its wispiness appears to be more solid, more stolid. It often stands stoic beside me, standing to attention, guarding me. Guarding me from what? I'm not sure.

Now it pulses around me, urging me on. I laugh at the absurdity. "Little shadow, you don't even know where I'm going."

Hades lingers in the back of my thoughts, "What are you seeking, Achilles? Following a shadow now? Are you desperate? What are you desperate for?" And when I don't answer the Hades of my mind, he sniggers, "Why do you seek glory here, Achilles? You might not think it, but you're the one who chose this path, you know. And now, you are but one among many, adrift in an eternity of shadows."

I may be adrift. But maybe my drifting has its own purpose, for it has brought me to the banks of the River Styx, where the waters murmur secrets in a language long forgotten. The surface shimmers faintly, a thin, beautiful veneer masking the chaos beneath. As I approach, I sense a disturbance in the currents – an unfamiliar presence weaving through the darkness. The darkness that shrouds everything is, in turn, shrouded by something. A fog? It is difficult to see. But, like everything else, the fog doesn't behave as it should. "Achilles, the determiner of right and of wrong, of should, would and could," jeers the Hades-of-my-mind. The fog seems to only exist for me, for it came upon me suddenly, with a hint of dramatism, to blind me to my immediate surroundings. Yet I can see, faintly, that the path I had drifted along to reach here remains crisp, fogless.

"Achilles," a voice calls out and I almost dismiss it for the voice of false-Hades, but for its resonance and clarity, cutting through the thick fog of my mind. I turn towards the voice, coming along the riverbank. A figure emerges from the fog, cloaked and hooded, a light exuding from where the face should be, so bright that I'm unable to look directly into their eyes, wherever the eyes may be. "I have come seeking your counsel."

"Who are you?" I ask, my voice, thankfully, steady.

"I am a child of Ares, a demigod lost to time, cursed to wander this desolate realm for the violence I once embraced." The figure steps closer, revealing a glimpse of their features. But to stare too long means the light quickly blurs out anything identifiable. "I have discovered a prophecy that speaks of a way to challenge the eternal order of the Underworld. A hero of great renown, such as yourself, might possess the power to alter the fate of the dead."

My heart stirs, an ember igniting beneath layers of ash. "Tell me more."

"There exists an artefact – the Chthonic Codex – a map hidden deep within the Labyrinth of Lost Souls. It holds the power to reshape the boundaries between our world and the mortal realm. But retrieving it is no simple task; the Labyrinth was designed by Hades himself, a twisted maze of trials and illusions meant to ensnare the unwary."

I hesitate. This quest could lead me to what I'm seeking, to a sense of purpose in this forsaken afterlife. I'm not sure what I wanted out of my wandering – perhaps hoping for a chance encounter, a reuniting – but isn't this better than even what I had hoped?

The demigod produces a scroll, unfurling it with an elegant flick of their wrist. "With this map, you can navigate the Labyrinth. But know this: it will test you, exploiting your fears, your regrets. You must be ready to face the darkness within."

"Give it to me," I demand, my voice even firmer now. What could be darker than the shadows that undulate constantly in my periphery? My entire world is darkness now. Darkness is no longer something I should fear. I take the map, its surface oddly warm against my spectral fingers. I glance up. "Won't you be coming with me?"

"I am bound to this riverbank by an ancient pact forged with the spirits of the water. My essence is intertwined with these waters, and should I stray too far, I risk unleashing chaos upon the realm. But fear not, brave Achilles! When you uncover the map, follow my instructions to activate the summoning spell. Speak the words I've taught you, and I shall lend you my strength from afar. Together, we will face whatever challenges arise, even if I cannot be by your side."

As I prepare to depart, my shadow tugs at my feet. "Come, little one," I whisper. "Let us find our purpose." It seems to hang back a little – I don't feel its tugging for a while – but I concentrate my attention on the scroll in my hands. By the time I've boarded a raft, my shadow is beside me again, helping me steer, and I barely notice its reluctance.

* * *

We ride the current many moons down the river, round a bend where the water collects into a dip in the bank. The gentle rhythm of the water guides us back into the darkness. Stepping onto the riverbank, I scan the dense brush surrounding us. The map glows a soft pink, searing my fingertips. Something waits just beyond the foliage. Letting the map light the way, I push through the undergrowth, and stumble upon an entrance to the Labyrinth – an immense maw in the earth, its dark filaments spiralling inward like a snarl. The moment I step inside, my heart races; thousands of shadows swirl around me, wrapping me in an eerie embrace.

But my shadow steps forward – among the other shadows it appears even taller than before, a trick of the murk? It stretches itself ever taller, then a chasm yawns open in it, like a mouth opening wide, and lets out a silent scream – silent because I can't hear it, but there must be something menacing about it because all the other shadows release me and reel away.

"When did you learn to do that?" I look down, for my shadow has returned to its usual state, about half my height, stoic and demure. It seems to shrug its shoulders, should it have any shoulders, and continues to accompany me deeper

## LAST STAND

into the thickening air, which carries the distant cries of lost souls and the echoes of battles long forgotten.

It's hard to tell if the walls of the Labyrinth are made of stone. I assume they are, but the further I plod into the Labyrinth, the less they're visible, stretching further and further away from my two sides. I'm vaguely aware that the path before me twists and winds, but the darkness, like a buzzing magnetic force drawing me forth, clings to me so tightly that it's difficult to orient myself.

Suddenly, I stagger. My shadow shoots forward a tendril to steady me. The magnetic force let go of me so quickly and completely, I hadn't even realised how much I've been relying on it to pull me forward. But a buzzing sound remains. I nod towards my shadow. "Do you hear that?"

My shadow, of course, doesn't reply, but steps closer towards me, cocking its tendrils into a question. "You don't hear it? Like bees…. But, I suppose, maybe you've never met bees? Have you ever been—?" Before I can finish my thought, the buzzing pierces through my ears and penetrates my head, knocking around inside my skull. A torrent of bees crash over me, burrowing into my eyes, ears and, when I try to call out, my mouth. A million pinpricks of stinging pain spread from inside my face, down my neck, to my abdomen, and to the tips of my fingers and toes. The pain becomes searing, blinding, blindingly white.

A white flash. And I find myself standing on the windswept shores of Troy, the salty air burdened by the stench of blood, sweat…. The white sands glow under a golden light spilling across the horizon, casting elongated shadows that dance like spectres upon the sand.

The spectres twist and turn, shifting towards each other, away from each other. And I'm thrust back into a mess of sounds, a mess of pain. A deafening clash of metal reverberates through the air – the sharp, unmistakable ring of swords striking shields punctuates the frenzy. Guttural roars, faces scrunched up, distorted – in fury, fear or anguish? – charging into battle alongside me. I am one of the faces. My comrades, their armour glinting in the fading light, each man a beacon of courage in the maelstrom. Yet, even as they fight, I see a foreign glint etched on their faces.

I hear the sickening sound of wind being cut – arrows slicing through the air – and I feel a sting in the back of my knee, then my calf, then the back of my heel. *But this isn't how it happened*, I think before I fall, landing hard in the sand, no, the dust, a trickling into the dirt, a red glow seeping into the earth. I feel my heart constrict with every beat, as if trying to conserve my blood, which now flows steadily into the earth pressed up against my jaw, my shoulder, my side. The earth absorbs my lifeblood until it can absorb no more and still my blood flows steadily out of me. I'm limp and light, in a puddle of my own making. The puddle grows, capturing me in a crimson mirror. I'm buoyant upon the sound of a great sloshing, a red tidal wave. I'm buffeted along by sticky waves that drench me, fill me.

I'm suddenly light, scooped up by a pair of steady arms. I cough. "Is it…you?"

I've long suspected that my shadow is simply a dark figure born from the recesses of my mind. Any physical contact I make with it, then, is merely a simulation. How, then, am I actually being carried?

My shadow shifts and morphs, its form as fluid as my memories, the very embodiment of my guilt and my strength – the two one and the same for, without my strength, would I have the capability of acting so brashly, of causing such pain? My shadow deposits me upon soft ground – sand – then seems to shrink to the height of my hip. It reaches up a tendril to encircle my hand, holding my hand, urging me to confront what I wish to forget.

Some shadows swirl around us, coiling around us like serpents, whispering their regrets, each hissing a reminder of my failures. One of the shadows pauses in midair, sheds its skin, and a face opens up. I feel a grip on my heart as I recognise Antilochus, a comrade whose laughter used to fill the air like music before the storm. His smile opens up into a snarl as I recall the moment I couldn't save him. The pain of that memory claws at me, snagging at my skin, threatening to pull me under, but my shadow squeezes my hand, its presence grounding me.

With a deep, shaking breath, I step forward, embracing the vision. "I remember you," I say, my voice wavering. "You fought bravely, and your sacrifice was not in vain." The illusion wavers along with my voice, as if a mirage trembling under the faintest breath, and I feel the weight of his loss begin to lift, the sharp edges softening into a bittersweet remembrance.

The next vision unfurls before me, a battlefield drenched in twilight, where my brothers-in-arms lie scattered like fallen leaves. I move among them, despair swelling in my chest, the cries of the dying echoing in my ears. One man, his armour tarnished and his body broken, looks up at me, pleading for salvation. My heart aches as I reach for him, but my hands pass through the illusion, and I stumble.

My shadow companion, sensing my turmoil, grows larger, enveloping me in a shroud of dark energy. *You are not defined by your failures,* a tinkling voice resounds in my head, like a thousand tiny glass shards hitting against each other in the wind.

I nod. I kneel beside the spectre of my fallen friend. "You were a light in the darkness," I whisper, "and I will carry your memory with me always." As I speak, the image begins to dissolve, the shadows receding like a tide pulled back from the shore.

One by one, the memories come and go, each one demanding acknowledgment. But with each vision, my shadow companion stands steadfast, urging me to confront my past rather than flee from it. I face the faces of those I lost, no longer shying away from the pain, but allowing it to wash over me, and I lean into it, riding the waves of pain.

Finally, as the last memory fades into the twilight, I stand alone on the shore once more. The air is still, the echoes of battle replaced by the soothing whispers of the ocean. I glance at my shadow, the last remaining shadow, who shifts back into a gentle wisp of darkness and releases my hand to stand silently beside me as the shoreline fades about me.

I step forward and I'm back in the Labyrinth. But instead of an unfathomable darkness, a weathered pedestal stands erect before me. An otherworldly light radiates atop it. The Chthonic Codex. The air hums with energy. I'm immediately drawn towards it, but I feel a tug at my elbow. My shadow, now about the height of my chest, grabs me with a weak tendril. Another tendril is positioned before it, as if shielding it from the light...from the Codex?

"Hey, it's okay." I gently pull away from it and unfurl the scroll the demigod had given me. Before I could even announce the summoning spell, the demigod appears in a blast of light.

"With this," the demigod states, accepting the map, "we can challenge the boundaries of the Underworld and offer a new possibility to the souls trapped here."

Together, we ascend from the depths of the Labyrinth, the artefact in his hand. A profound sense of accomplishment surges within me. For the first time in ages, I feel a purpose, a potential to rewrite the fates of countless lost souls. The prospect of my name echoing through the ages – even in the Underworld...

"Achilles. Thank you for participating in my trial of judgement. Your despair shall be delicious."

A chill weaves through me, holding me back even before I can react. My shadow surges forward, snapping and snarling towards the demigod, who shakes within his cloak.

"What are you saying?" I whisper, even as my shadow whips out tendrils sharpened like spears.

"My name's Tartarus." Tartarus dodges my shadow's attacks, smoothly and swiftly. I realise his shaking is laughter, which he now lets loose into the night air. "It has been lovely to know you."

"So, has this all been for nothing? All these months I've spent—"

"Ah, but here, time is but a cruel illusion. You should know this already, pompous Achilles."

"Hades?"

"Hades?" Tartarus laughs. "Didn't you hear what I said? I'm Tartarus. That old geezer, he wouldn't be able to pull off a stunt like this! *I've* perfected this! This art form!" He sweeps his sleeves around. "The Labyrinth? The Codex? This map?" – he snatches the scroll from my bewildered hands – "None of it is real!" He cackles as the scroll crumbles to dust. "Isn't that clever?"

Fury ignites within me, propelling me towards Tartarus. Pain flares in my heel. Yet my shadow intercepts, an instinctive barrier of protection, pulsing with a tinkling energy. *Violence cannot heal you, Achilles. You've fought long enough.*

Tartarus seems to be irritated by my lack of response. His head darts back and forth between my shadow's sharpened tendrils, mouth opening and closing to recommence his speech, but my shadow slashes and stabs and, in a fit of rage, Tartarus seizes my shadow out of the air. With a swift motion, he casts aside his hood, unveiling a blinding radiance that drains my shadow. It kicks and shrinks.

A guttural scream releases from my throat, and I slam my body forward, trying to knock Tartarus over. But in that fleeting moment, my shadow reaches out, seizing the sword at my side. With a decisive plunge, it drives it into Tartarus, piercing a corner of itself along the way. Under the brilliance of the light that is Tartarus's face, I can finally see my shadow in a morphing, infinitesimal moment. My shadow, a shape I know, sheds its skin and reveals an ashen grey face, framed by long, wavy hair, richly dark. His eyes are deep-set, a mix of greens and browns, shimmering with intelligence and, now, determined tears. His lips are full and carry a slight, knowing smile.

Then, everything explodes.

Light and shadow entwine into each other, consuming both Tartarus and Patroclus, enveloping them in a blinding brilliance. Just before the world erupts, I reach out trying to grasp hold of Patroclus's radiant face, and then they are lost to the light.

* * *

Dawn is breaking. But in the Underworld, everything is wrong, and dawn is just a cluster of shadows on the horizon leading to nowhere. I know what I must do, where I must go, but I would give up this newfound purpose for the quiet boredom I had shared with Patroclus, all those moons ago, in all its many forms, which I pompously took for granted.

# A Glass Heart in an Unbreakable Ribcage

Lily Zimmerman

The night that Peleus and Thetis's child was to greet the world, the queen of Phthia vanished from her bed chambers. King Peleus was not enraged to hear the news, instead going alone to the shoreline of his kingdom to wait.

The ocean pushes and pulls under a full moon, Artemis well at work. It will be a few hours yet until her brother breaches the horizon. Peleus stands in the shallows to wait. From the ocean she came, to the ocean she went, but to him she will return.

A wave breaks further offshore, his wife emerging from the foam as it dissolves back into the water. The sea breeze tugs at her loose and silky hair, casting it to the side of her as she walks atop the waves toward him. Her shawl glitters and flashes against the rising sun, wrapped around a child. *Their* child.

Thetis's face remains neutral as she steps onto shore, her feet never sinking fully into the sand. Even her hair does not behave as a mortal's would, swaying gently in the breeze like the waves she came from. Peleus's eyes gravitate to the babe, to blond hair that shines golden in Apollo's light and a healthy flush to its face as it sleeps curled into its mother's bosom. He reaches out and Thetis hands the child over.

"Be gentle," Thetis tells him, as if Peleus would be anything but, "he is tired."

*He.* A son. A breathy laugh slips out of his chest to ghost across his son's face, making the babe's face twist in its sleep. "My son," he tells the child, cradling him close. "Your name shall be—"

\* \* \*

"—Achilles! Lord Achilles! Please, get down from there before you hurt yourself!"

Achilles spares a look down at the servants below him, each of them no bigger than a grape at this height. His hair, golden as the ornaments in his father's throne room, tickles the sides of his face, barely damp with sweat. The view ahead of him makes even the slightest effort worthy: Phthia, its sun-bleached roads and the colorful tapestries hanging from the mercantile pavilion like army banners. From this distance, the people wandering in the maze of streets are even smaller than the servants. Is this how the mortal world appears to Olympus?

He wanders from side to side of the rooftop, the servants scuttling under him like a school of fish, wringing their hands and begging Achilles to come down. He will…after he's had his fun.

His eyes catch the neighboring roof – the roof of the throne room, higher than the roof Achilles stands on with six feet of open air between. Achilles has made higher, longer jumps while hunting with his father. He crouches down, the servants wail in terror. He pushes off, putting one foot in front of the other. He reaches the edge and tenses his muscles, ready to jump—

The corner of the roof crumbles from under him, stealing his footing and his breath as he begins to fall. Rational thought abandons him. His eyes widen, his arms flail in some desperate imitation of Icarus as he approaches the stone ground at breakneck speed. He closes his eyes right as the back of his head hits the stone.

He stares up at the sky, dazed, but not hurt. The world above moves on, clouds with the texture of sheep's wool roll over the blue of the heavens, quickly blotted out by a harried servant shoving his face into Achilles'.

"My lord, are you alright? Did you—"

\* \* \*

"—hear? King Peleus's child is unkillable."

"How is such a thing possible?"

"His mother, our queen, is a goddess. Is this not to be expected?"

"It's unnatural. No one should be able to survive a fall from that height."

"Or have an arrow bounce off their chest."

"I heard a dagger broke against his back."

"Do you remember how he—?"

Achilles takes his ear off the door to the servants' quarters, his curiosity sated with poisonous rumor and hearsay, leaving his stomach queasy and his feet unsteady.

Why do they whisper of him in fear? Why are they afraid that he cannot die? Why does anyone want him dead at all? What has he done to have bows aimed at him and blades leveled his way? He's as close to understanding it as he is to Olympus itself.

The moonlight dances on the floor of the hall leading to his room – coming in from the windows facing the sea. Dread pulls at his ankles, heavier on one side, slowing his steps until he pauses at the window to stare.

His mother is of the sea, from the sea she came, to the sea she will go, once Achilles and his father are gone. Yet Achilles cannot bring himself to like the sea – he can barely stand the sight of it now. The wind sounds like a howling scream when it passes this hall. Combined with the steady rush of waves on the shore, it fills him with a fear deeper than anything he's ever known.

There's a memory – so ingrained in the fabric of his being he can't think of a time without it, so faded that he cannot recall. All he remembers is the rushing water, the howling screams, and someone speaking to him past both. He can't make out the words, the noise of everything else drowns it out, but he thinks they're apologizing.

Under his breath, with only the wind, the moon and the sea as his witness, he whispers, "What—"

* * *

"—did you do to me?"

His mother's hands stall against the back of his neck, nails digging into the flesh. Achilles remains unconcerned. They won't pierce him. They *can't*. She is a goddess, born to the Old Man of the Sea. Achilles is…something else. His skin refuses to be cut or scraped, his bones do not break. Even his mother, goddess that she is, bleeds. The liquid that flows from her is as gold as his hair, the prick to her sewing finger healing in moments. Achilles has never bled before. Should the day ever come, would it be red that spilled from him? Gold? Or something else entirely, something unknown to man or god?

Mother inspects her hand with an idleness that fills Achilles with impatience. Like the tides that will not be swayed, she will choose when to answer him. If she answers him at all. Achilles bites his tongue hard, his teeth will never cut it, but he still feels the pressure, the feel of bone digging into flesh, and it steadies him.

Her voice is crackling seafoam, airy and crumbling away. "I did what I had to."

"Why?"

She pauses, her needle touching the tip of her sewing. Her next words are more solid than the last, a fine seashell tumbling in the waves. He tries to imagine what this tone would sound like under a stream of water and wails. He doesn't care for how well it matches up. "Because I love you."

"I never asked for this."

"I know, but seldom does anyone get what they want, mortals and gods alike."

# A GLASS HEART IN AN UNBREAKABLE RIBCAGE

"Which one am I, mother? God, or mortal?"

She pushes the needle though the fabric and does not speak to him again. Achilles retreats to his room, taking the long way around to avoid the hallway of screaming sea breeze and rushing water. He slams the door behind him, curling his hands at his sides while his breath escapes him in quick bursts.

His mother did not say what she did, but her lack of denial damns her. What happened to him that night? Why was he underwater? What were those screams, of which even the memory sends a chill down his spine? Who did they belong to?

Mother is a goddess, surely she has reasons for not telling him. Divine reasons, reasons he cannot question without risk of slighting the gods. But the excuse rings hollow in his heart, and the reverberation is painful enough to bring tears to his eyes.

"What am I?" he whispers, craning his head upwards and begging the gods, for his mind can conjure no answer. "Please, tell me. What—"

*\* \* \**

"—would you like for your birthday, Achilles?"

Achilles suppresses a sigh, standing in the midst of his father's advisors and the servants that weave between them with plates of wine and food. His birthday hasn't been an object of joy for himself in quite some time – not since the people of the palace and Phthia beyond learned of his invulnerability. Gifts which had been bestowed with affectionate smiles and joyous laughter the previous year were given with averted eyes and awkward well-wishes ever since. Achilles mourned the change, but only for two years – after which he had resigned himself to the distance between him and his people.

King Peleus saw this and made efforts to alleviate the pain of it through a simple act: on Achilles' birthday, he's not just one year older, but one wish richer. Anything he wants this day – so long as it's within the king's power – will be granted without question. Were he a greedier person, Achilles could request the finest of finery, an entire pack of impeccably bred hunting dogs, or even a palace made in his name, but he has no taste for it now. What good is any of it when he has no one to share it with aside from his own parents?

He did end up asking for the dogs. He didn't demand they be of perfect pedigree, but King Peleus never did things by halves when it came to these wishes. The dogs had been pleasant company; they could play with him as roughly as they liked with no fear of hurting him. But one fateful, fatal day, he made the mistake of sharing some of his meal with them. He hadn't known anything was wrong until Ōkús, the leader of the pack and bearer of most of his affection, started to writhe on the floor, foam leaking from his mouth.

They executed the servant who gave Achilles the food, but it did not make the flame of the pyre he made for Ōkús burn any lower.

Achilles couldn't bear to look at the rest of the pack after the fact, eventually giving them to a respectable hunter on the outskirts of the city. Achilles made him promise to take care of them, but never tried to see if the hunter honored his oath. When faced with the potential pain of the truth, Achilles finds that he prefers this particular question unanswered.

Someone snickers behind him; he turns in place and watches how they stiffen and try to avoid his eyes. He turns to his father – addressing the king without looking at him is too great an offense, even for a curiously beloved son like him. "I apologize, Father, I cannot seem to think of anything this year." Achilles' voice slips out breezily, not particularly regretful, not particularly anything at all.

He had given it thought – though sparingly, usually while he was in bed waiting for the medicine his mother brewed to lull him into a dreamless sleep. Asking for something he truly didn't want seemed like an insult to the spirit of this little tradition between him and his father. Better that he asks for nothing at all so that next year, should he have something in mind, King Peleus can fulfill it with a happy heart and a conviction that through his actions, he brought Achilles happiness as well.

Happiness... Achilles thinks the last sliver of it burned up with Ōkús' pyre. There is no one who wants to keep his company, no one he can confide in or trust. He's not sure if poison can beat this seemingly perfect invulnerability of his, but he would have learned had he eaten some of his food before sharing it with his beloved pet.

A companion who likes him is impossible, a companion who doesn't fear him is ever more so. The fear in the people of Phthia is too great, and it would contaminate most anyone outside the city if Father ever brought one in. Their honesty digs into skin that refuses to bruise or break, but had they been more duplicitous, Achilles would be dead. By what means is unknown, but Achilles hears the water roar in his ears whenever he thinks of it and the certainty settles into his bones like a fine coat of ash from his would-be pyre.

This is one request King Peleus cannot fulfill. Phthian or not, whoever was brought in would be obliged to the king to hide their real feelings, regardless of what they were. So Achilles keeps it close, right next to his heart – where no dagger can pierce it and no sword can cut it out of him.

It's better this way. Achilles spares himself and this potential companion a waste of time and effort. He'd much rather work on training with his weapons than be forced to wonder if this 'companion' brought him poisoned food. Father is a good man, but this is one thing that would do more harm than good.

King Peleus's smile falters, but recovers quickly. His eyes, however, have unmistakably dimmed, in disappointment or pain, Achilles can't claim to know. "Very well, my son. But should you think of something before the day is through, speak it and it will be done."

"Of course, Father." This is enough, Achilles tells himself. This is enough. "This is—"

\* \* \*

"—Patroclus, he will be your companion from now on."

'Patroclus,' no other denomination or epithet attached. It could be that aside from his impressive size he's done nothing of importance himself, but a boy who can be taken in as a ward to the king of Phthia would have to be the son of someone who could give an epithet of their own. And yet 'Patroclus' remains just that, 'Patroclus'. Achilles finds himself growing curious – not of the other boy himself, but of the circumstances that brought about his arrival.

"I hope you two will grow to be good friends," King Peleus continues.

Friends? That's far more intimate than a companion, who can be anything from an acquaintance you only talk to now and then to a stranger you share a strip of road with. If a companion who likes him was impossible, a friend of any kind is beyond Achilles' imagination. His father, the hero-king who won favor and a wife from the gods with his virtues, dares to hope too much of this.

If anything happens to Achilles, Patroclus is likely to be held responsible, but that threat hangs over the servants, too, and it hasn't stopped a handful of them from trying to kill him over the years. Best to keep his distance while maintaining the appearance of closeness. He is nothing if not a filial son, and naive as Achilles thinks it is, King Peleus so badly wants something to come of this, and so Achilles will make a token effort.

He sighs through his nose and speaks. "I was about to go to the training fields. Come with me – I can see if you're a good sparring partner or not."

Patroclus's eyes light up with the idea of a fight. Maybe this 'companionship' won't be so dull after all. "Of course, my lord!" He closes the distance in four strides and keeps pace with Achilles when he departs – but not before bowing to his father.

"What weapon do you use?" Patroclus asks, swiveling his head to observe the walls that hang heavy with tapestries his mother has weaved over the years.

"Anything that fits in my hand," Achilles replies. Swords, spears, javelins, Achilles aims to become a master of them all, but he doesn't need them to make himself lethal. With his strength and speed, even a tree branch could be fatal if he brought it over someone's head. "And you? You've had longer to train, you must have a favorite weapon picked out already."

Patroclus grins. "I'm a spearman, my lord. Through and through. Though I still have a lot to learn."

"Then I will use a spear for our spar."

"You're very kind, my lord."

Achilles stops. Patroclus stops with him. Kind? No one would ever dare to call him *kind*. He's the unnatural prince, the boy who cannot be killed. He is not *kind*. "Then it seems you still have much to learn about your new lord," Achilles says, masking his shaken mind with an indifferent tone.

"I'm ten years old, my lord, and you are nine. I think we have quite a bit of time to learn about each other."

The smile Patroclus gives him is quite insolent. It's like he hasn't heard any of the rumors at all – and King

Peleus would have ensured he was well-informed so as to anticipate the treatment Achilles receives around the palace. Yet Achilles cannot find the words to chastise him, so he starts walking again, Patroclus in tow. "We will fight until one of us yields," Achilles tells his now 'companion'. He already knows the outcome, his strength, endurance, and speed are beyond comparison. It will be interesting to see how such a confident yet modest boy will react to being thoroughly trounced.

Patroclus's grin stretches even wider, like a sail catching in the wind. "Of course, my lord! I look forward to facing you!"

Such eagerness. Will any of it remain after the third or fourth defeat? Achilles doesn't typically bother himself with such ponderings, but he finds himself wondering now.

They spar a total of ten times. By the end of it, they are both covered in dirt, but only Patroclus has any scrapes to his knees and arms from when he either tumbled to the ground or was nicked by the tip of Achilles' weapon. Achilles would have similar wounds, but the metal spear simply glances off of his invulnerable skin. Patroclus was not sore over his loss, choosing instead to dust off what dirt he could from his clothes and send Achilles a wide grin.

"Your spear work is fantastic, my lord."

"As is yours," Achilles returns, surprised to find the words taste genuine. He looks at the small cuts on Patroclus's bicep and cheek, an uncomfortable sense of guilt settling on him. "Come. We have to go to the healer and tend to your injuries." He's heard tales of men dying of small cuts that disrupt the humors of the body. It would only look worse for Achilles to lose a companion so soon after gaining one.

"Of course, my lord, lead the way."

\* \* \*

Over time, Patroclus proves himself to be a worthy companion. He is quiet, yet capable of holding conversation – sometimes prompting it himself should he think the silence has gone on long enough. He was foreign to the ways of Phthia, but fixed this flaw early on, listening to the servants' chatter alongside Achilles to learn of the inner workings of the palace. His anger when they spoke of Achilles burned hot, but it burned quietly at Achilles' request. Yet there is no denying how the servants suffer mild misfortunes more often these days. Whenever it happens, Achilles always looks subtly to Patroclus, who avoids his gaze with a tiny, satisfied smile.

The hallway to his room does not haunt him the same way anymore, not when Patroclus is there, his voice muffling the rushing water and his frame next to Achilles' blocking the worst of the screaming wind.

Three more birthdays come and go, and Achilles finds it easier to make his wishes. Gifts, Achilles finds, are better when shared with a friend. A new pack of hunting dogs find a home in the palace. Whenever they're not training, Achilles and Patroclus play with and train the pack to hunt. On their first excursion, they bring back two sizable boars, giving most of it to the servants to cook for dinner, but setting aside a small portion to dry out and turn into treats for the pack.

Mother sees the change in him and comments on it one day. "You are happier, now that Patroclus is here."

Happy. Achilles considers the word and the weight behind it, finding that it's not as heavy on his tongue as it was before.

"It will break you," Mother tells him, with all the foreboding of a swelling storm tide. "Perhaps not now, perhaps it will be years down the line, but it will break you."

"Maybe," Achilles says. "But I already knew that."

His heart is the only way to hurt him; it's something he learned years ago as he built Ōkús' pyre. Letting people close cannot end in anything *but* pain, but Patroclus burns so bright and warm, Achilles can savor it before his hand draws too close, before the fire is nothing but ash. Surely he is allowed that much. Surely he need not harden his heart to be as unbreakable as his skin. If he had to do so after experiencing such joy as these last three years, he thinks he would perish before it was said and done.

Should he die, let him die as Patroclus sees him: brave, strong, and kind.

# Biographies

### Amber S. Benham
*The Second Fate*
(First Publication)
Amber S. Benham is a 22-year-old aspiring author who lives in London, where she previously studied Classical Studies at King's College London. Her education and passion for antiquity, queerness and feminist literature dominate her authorship as well as her personal reading habits. Amber has previously been published for a nonfiction piece in *ROAR News* and a fiction retelling of the Carthaginian Queen Dido in *Classics for All*.

### Jonathan S. Burgess
*Ancient & Modern: Introducing Achilles*
Jonathan S. Burgess has a BA in American Studies from Colby College, an MA in Classical Studies and Literature from the University of Kentucky, Lexington, and a PhD in Classical Studies from the University of Toronto. Since 1995 he has taught at the Department of Classics at the University of Toronto. His major publications are *The Tradition of the Trojan War in Homer and the Epic Cycle* (2001), *The Death and Afterlife of Achilles* (2009) and *Homer* (2015). A forthcoming publication is *The Travels of Odysseus*.

### Hammond Diehl
*The Achilles Wheel*
(First Publication)
Hammond Diehl has been to the Greek island described in this story and can confirm that at least half of what is written here is 100 percent true, including a fairly recent trend involving sexy, flat, ill-advised houses. If you go, tip your bus driver. Well. Hamm's work has appeared in *Lightspeed*, *Strange Horizons*, *Diabolical Plots* and more. Hamm lives in Los Angeles and writes under the comforting blankie of a pseudonym. Follow Hamm, if you like, via Bluesky at @hammonddiehl.bsky.social.

# BIOGRAPHIES

**Corey D. Evans**
*The Boldest of the Greeks*
(First Publication)
Corey D. Evans is a groundskeeper living in the United States, but writing is one of his passions. He previously published articles in fitness blogs, contributed to a column in the *Gringo Gazette*, and edited theological works for Dispensational Publishing House and Trust House Publishers. When not working or writing, Corey enjoys adventures with his wife and six children.

**Kenzie Lappin**
*How Achilles Grew Up*
(First Publication)
Kenzie Lappin has written for several publications, such as *Cosmic Horror Monthly*, Brigids Gate Press, *Apex Magazine*, WordFire Press, Air And Nothingness Press, and more. She loves science fiction, fantasy and mythology. Check her out on Twitter at @KenzieLappin. She loves science fiction, fantasy, and a mixture of both. She has always had a fascination with mythology. The tragedy and legend of the myth of Achilles is one of the most interesting facets of storytelling to explore!

**Prof. David D. Leitao**
*Foreword*
David Leitao earned his BA in History from Dartmouth, then his MA and PhD in Classics at the University of Michigan. He has published widely on Greek mythology and religion, including a book entitled *The Pregnant Male: Myth and Metaphor in Classical Greek Literature* (Cambridge University Press, 2012). He taught for many years at San Francisco State University, where he is now Professor Emeritus of Classics.

**Russell Hugh McConnell**
*The Last Angry Hero*
(First Publication)
Russell Hugh McConnell was born in Toronto, Canada, but over the years he has wandered through many strange lands. After being shipwrecked on the coast of Texas, he now ekes out a living in the wild prairie by teaching writing, literature and liberal arts to interested (and uninterested) passers-

by. He has published stories in the anthologies *Dragonesque* (2023), *Familiars* (2024) and *Last-Ditch* (2024), and has a story forthcoming in *Pulp Literature* (2025).

**Zenobia Neil**
*The Choice of Iphigenia*
(First Publication)
Zenobia Neil writes historical fantasy and mythic retellings about the ancient world. Her novels and short stories focus on the power of women, magic and love. Zenobia portrays a diverse, sexually fluid ancient world where gods have too much fun, and mortals find ways to cheat fate. Her last full-length novel, *Ariadne Unraveled*, is a Minoan version of the myth of Ariadne and Dionysus. Visit her at www.Zenobianeil.com.

**Mari Ness**
*Waiting for Clear Waters*
(First Publication)
Mari Ness lives in central Florida, among slowly growing live oak trees. She is the author of *Through Immortal Shadows Singing*, a poetry novella about Helen of Troy, and several other small books, as well as multiple stories and poems that can be found in Reactor.com, *Clarkesworld*, *Uncanny*, *Lightspeed*, *Nightmare*, *Apex*, *Nature Futures*, *Beneath Ceaseless Skies* and several other publications and anthologies. For more, visit her website at marikness.wordpress.com, which also usually lists where she can be found on social media these days.

**Parker M. O'Neill**
*Spindle, Rod, Shears*
(First Publication)
Parker M. O'Neill lives and writes in upstate New York, where he spent his childhood devouring all the information he could find about ancient Greece. He is a recent winner of the Elegant Literature Award for New Writers, and his fiction appears in *Apex Magazine*, Flame Tree Press and *Crepuscular Magazine*. Find his socials at linktr.ee/parkermoneill.

## BIOGRAPHIES

**Celeste Plowden**
*Achilles in City Island*
(First Publication)
Celeste Plowden has been a fabric designer, real estate title examiner, fine artist, showroom model, blues singer, dog lover and student of early modern history, writing romance tales with dark connections to supernatural beings in historical settings in places she has lived: New York and London. Her Amazon bestsellers include *Mirth*, short stories; *The Harpsichordist*, vampire novel; *Blue Jay's Nightclub, A Romance of Prohibition New York* and various short stories for speculative and horror ezines on the web. Celeste holds a BFA in the History of Art.

**Sultana Raza**
*Veiled Stratagems*
(First Publication)
Of Indian origin, Sultana Raza's poems have appeared in numerous journals/anthologies, including *Columbia Journal, New Verse News, Star*Line, Penumbric, Apex & Abyss, London Grip, Classical Poetry Society, Blaze Vox* and *Sparks of Calliope*. Anthologies include *Musing on Muses* and *Nephilim*. Her fiction received an Honorable Mention in *Glimmer Train Review*. Her CNF was published in *Literary Ladies Guide* and *Litro*. An independent scholar, she's presented papers on Romanticism (Keats) and Fantasy (Tolkien) in international conferences. https://www.facebook.com/sultana.raza.7

**Chey Rivera**
*The Eyes of the Pentekonter*
(First Publication)
Chey Rivera (she/her) is a bilingual writer from Puerto Rico. Her speculative fiction is inspired by ancient legends, her home island's history and, occasionally, by gothic tales. Her work is out now in Elegant Literature's 35th issue, *Paradise Plundered*; in *Other Worlds*, an anthology by A Coup of Owls Press; in the *Monstrous* issue of The Icarus Writing Collective and elsewhere. You can find Chey on Instagram @readbychey and on Bluesky and Twitter/X @criverawrites.

**Patricia Scott**
*Tears in the Sea*
(First Publication)
Patricia Scott grew up in the far wilds of western Nebraska, with two and half TV channels and parents who were almost adult supervision. She is a lifelong fan of fantasy, horror and sci-fi. An autobiographical piece, 'The Stars Were Stolen', was turned into the short film *First Stars I See Tonight* by the HitRECord community. She has also had stories published in *The Shattered Veil* and *Blood Crown*. She also collects dragons and books.

**Susan Shwartz**
*Achilles in the Underworld*
(First Publication)
Susan Shwartz has been nominated for the Nebula, the Hugo, the World Fantasy Award, the Philip K. Dick and the Edgar. She has published 30 books and over 100 pieces of short fiction, with articles in *The New York Times*, *The Wall Street Journal*, *Amazing* and *Analog*. Upcoming stories deal with the Soviet Space Program, Eleanor of Acquitaine, PTSD in the Revolutionary War and Grendel's dam. Susan holds a Ph.D. in English from Harvard University.

**Rose Strickman**
*Immortality in Song*
(First Publication)
Rose Strickman is a speculative fiction writer living in Seattle, Washington. Her work has appeared over 60 times, in anthologies and e-zines such as *Sword and Sorceress 32*, *The Last Girls Club* and *The Dragon's Hoard 3*. Her booklet *Island of the Drowned* appeared as a Tiny Terrors publication with Graveside Press, and she has self-published several novellas on Amazon. Please see her Amazon author's page at amazon.com/author/rosestrickman, or follow her on Bluesky @rosestrickman.bsky.social.

**Adam B. Widmer**
*The Healing Mountain*
(First Publication)
Adam B. Widmer is a writer based in Knoxville, Tennessee, with a flair for speculative fiction and a love for reimagining classic characters. After

a nearly ten-year hiatus, he has recently returned to writing with vigor. Adam spends his non-writing time running a small business, making music and searching for inspiration. Stories of myth and magic are stories of the human condition, and they call to him.

## Ernie Xu
*Last Stand*
(First Publication)
Ernie Xu is a Sydney-based emerging writer and artist, specialising in printmaking (etching and linocut) and painting (gouache). She writes mostly short stories and that one novel that has been in the works for nigh on seven years and has since run way out of control. Her work explores mythology and speculative fiction, seeking ways to use mythology as a device to describe our own futures through storytelling. You can find Ernie on Instagram @ernie.ink.

## Lily Zimmerman
*A Glass Heart in an Unbreakable Ribcage*
(First Publication)
Lily Zimmerman is a 24-year-old first-time published author who has been writing for over 10 years. With a passion for fantasy and mythology, she hopes to publish a novel one day. Lily's other interests are video games, embroidery and going to aquariums. A few favourite authors of hers are Christopher Paolini, V.E. Schwab and Pierce Brown. She has no previous publications, which makes this one all the more special.

# Authors and Core Sources of Achilles Mythology

Our knowledge of the Achilles myth derives primarily from the works of the ancient Greek poet **Homer** (born c. 800 BCE). The attributed author of both the *Iliad* and the *Odyssey*, Homer is a largely mysterious figure with little surviving information about him available. References to Achilles also existed in certain works within the Epic Cycle. One such work (now lost) was *Cypria*, attributed to **Stasinus** and later summarized in *Chrestomathy* by **Proclus** (born c. 500 CE). Another such work (also lost) was *Little Iliad* by **Lesches** (born c. 600 BCE). **Apollodorus** also wrote of Achilles and the Trojan War.

# Myths, Gods & Immortals

Discover the mythology of humankind through its heroes, characters, gods and immortal figures. **Myths, Gods and Immortals** brings together the new and the ancient, familiar stories with a fresh and imaginative twist. Each book brings back to life a legendary, mythological or folkloric figure, with completely new stories alongside the original tales and a comprehensive introduction which emphasizes ancient and modern connections, tracing history and stories across continents, cultures and peoples.

# Flame Tree Fiction

A wide range of new and classic fiction, from myth to modern stories, with tales from the distant past to the far future, including short story anthologies, **Beyond & Within, Collector's Editions, Collectable Classics, Gothic Fantasy collections** and **Epic Tales** of mythology and folklore.

Available at all good bookstores, and online at flametreepublishing.com